The Space Between Us

Anie Michaels

Edited by
Krysta Drechsler

The Space Between Us

© Copyright Anie Michaels 2014

Prologue

The familiarity of his arms was like a drug. No matter what I was feeling – happy, sad, panicked, flustered, agitated, angry – when his arms wrapped around me, so did peace. I moved my chin up to look at his face. Dark, thick, beautifully long lashes dusted across his cheekbones as he slept – lashes many women would kill for. And although the lashes were feminine to an extent, when his eyes were open there was no mistaking his masculinity. Eyes the color of slate gray hid behind those lashes, and when he used them to look me over, when he perused my body with them, I could feel the smoothness of the granite they resembled silking over my skin.

His face was beautiful. A strong square jaw left room for one dimple that sat on his left cheek. His unmarred skin was smooth and creamy besides just the few dark freckles that gave him a distinct look. We were both still young, just eighteen, but he was already so manly I shivered to think what he would look like in five or ten years.

I leaned up to press a gentle kiss just at the bottom of his chin and as he roused I pretended to look apologetic, but really I wanted him awake. I wanted him, period.

"Awake already?" His voice rasped, still groggy from sleep. "What time is it?"

"I don't know," I replied honestly as I trailed kisses along his jaw, following the line of his jaw down the slope of his neck. He pulled away to look at me.

"Charlie," he said softly to me. "Are you sure? I don't want to hurt you," he said all too sweetly as he placed his hand on the side of my face.

"I feel fine," I whispered, trying to convince him I was indeed okay.

"Aren't you, uh, sore?" He asked sheepishly. I grinned at him and shrugged my shoulders.

"Asher, I know I lost my virginity a few hours ago, but I was far from chaste before that. I'm not sore at all." He gave me a concerned look.

"You'd tell me if you were hurt, right?" I nodded at him. "You'll tell me to stop if it gets to be too much?" I nodded again and then leaned up to press my mouth to his.

"You're already too much," I said against his lips. "But I get what you mean." And with that he took me under him and made love to me for the second time in our lives. Loving him was easy and beautiful, and I wish I'd taken more time to cement the memories in my mind. There was no way to know that in such a short time everything would be taken from me. Everything.

Part I

Chapter One

I heard the thunk-thunk of something hitting the ground next to me, but I didn't look up. I just continued to draw in my notebook. It wasn't my choice to move to a new town and not having anyone to spend recess with wasn't making my first day at a new school any easier. The pencil in my hand trailed lead across the paper and I know eventually it will look like *something*, but right now it's just lines and scribbles. All my drawings start out that way. My hand just kind of goes where the pencil takes it, but it always turns into something.

More thunks. More rocks and pine cones landed near me and I finally turned my head to see where they are coming from.

"Hey. New girl." A boy with red hair and freckles covering his face stood at the bottom of the hill I was sitting on. His hand went up over his eyes trying to keep the sun out. "New girl," he said again.

"Yeah?" I answered.

"What grade are you in?" He shouted at me.

"Fifth," I yelled back.

"What's your name?"

"Charlie."

"Charlie?"

I paused and tried not to roll my eyes. I had to deal with this my whole life.

"Yes. My name is Charlie and I'm a girl."

"That's a pretty stupid name," he said through laughter. I turned back to my drawing, not willing to debate with him about it. I've been dealing with it since I started school. I never knew why my parents chose a boy's name, but it didn't matter. I was stuck with it. More gray lines appeared, circling around each other, some darker than others. Then something bounced painfully off of the back of my head. My hand reached up to the injury and my head snapped back to look behind me again. Another rock headed straight for me but I ducked to the side to avoid it.

"Hey!" I yelled at the red-headed boy who was now taking aim at me again. "That hurt!"

The boy dropped his arm a little, still grasping the rock in his fist.

"You've got a boy's name. Can't you take a little pain like a boy?"

Suddenly another boy came up behind the redhead and shoved him to the ground.

"What's your problem, Ryan?" The boy towered over him, fists clenched at his sides. "You can't go throwing rocks at girls, Dude. You're messed up." Ryan brushed his hands on his jeans, trying to free the dirt and pebbles stuck to his palms from landing on the ground.

"I didn't even throw them that hard and they were small."

"Doesn't matter. It's wrong." The dark haired boy looked over at me, and then back to Ryan. "I think you should apologize," he said.

"Give it up, Asher. You're just sticking up for her because she's got a weird name just like you." Ryan stood up, spared one look back at me saying nothing, but then turned away and walked towards the school building. I still rubbed the small knot that was forming on the back of my head.

"Are you ok?" Asher asked, walking up the hill towards me.

"Um, yeah, I think so," I said, still trying to rub the pain away.

"Is it your first day?"

"Yeah, I just moved here."

"Do you want me to take you to the nurse?"

"No, I'll be ok, but thanks." I gave him a small smile and turned back to put my notebook into my backpack.

"So, you've got a weird name too?" He asked.

"It's not really a weird name. It's just not supposed to be a girl's name."

"What is it? Bob? Max?"

I laughed. "My name is Charlie." He tilted his head to the side, seeming to contemplate what I'd told him.

"That's not a weird name. There's another girl who goes here whose name is Casey. That's a boy's name I guess. It's could be worse; you could be Frank or something."

I laughed again. "Asher isn't a weird name, either. I like it."

"Thanks," he said as he came up right next to me. "So, why'd you move to Willow Falls?"

I shrugged my shoulders, trying not to let on that I didn't really want to talk about it. "I just go where my dad tells me to."

"Oh. Are you sure you don't need to go see the nurse? I don't mind showing you."

"No, I'm good," I said with a small smile.

"Well, I guess I'll see you around." He gave a small wave and walked back down the small hill. I continued to put my things away and the longer I thought about Ryan and the rocks he threw at me, the more I thought about why I was here in the first place.

Thinking about my mom and how she died was never fun, but it was something I found myself doing often and usually at times when it was inconvenient - like now. The tear that fell down my cheek wasn't because Ryan had thrown rocks at me, but because my mom died. My dad didn't know what else to do, so he moved me away from my friends I'd had all my life to be closer to my grandparents. That was the reason for the tears, not Ryan. But I couldn't let anyone see. I'd never live it down if I was caught crying on the first day at a new school.

No one would know that every time I wiped away a tear it was because I pictured my mom laying in a hospital bed, tubes and wires coming seemingly from every available inch of skin, eyes closed, chest moving only slightly with each shallow breath. It was not because some idiot didn't like my name. My shoulders slumped, my backpack came to rest at my side, and I looked up to the sky trying to calm down enough to go back to class. Deep breaths - one after another.

I managed to get my emotions under control and headed back to my classroom. The rest of the day dragged on, time slowed down by the loneliness of not being around anyone I know. A girl sat in the desk next to me and I caught her looking in my direction more than once since lunch. My eyes drifted over to her and again, she looked at me. I pushed my black, stick-straight hair over my shoulder, turned my head towards her and gave a faint smile. She smiled back and just that one moment made the day not totally suck.

I gave my attention back to the teacher at the front of the room but a few minutes later I felt something poking my elbow. I looked over and the blonde girl next to me handed me a note. Taking it from her, I hid it under my desk to unfold it.

Hi! My name is Reeve. Did you just move here? What's your name?

I looked over at her as she stared straight ahead at the teacher, convincingly looking like she was interested in the geography of Africa at the moment. I took a pen out of my bag and replied to the note and then, when the teacher turned his back to the class for a moment, tossed it onto her desk.

My name is Charlie. I did just move here. First day.

I watched her read it and then she scribbled under my writing and handed it back to me.

How do you like it so far?

I read her question and shrugged my shoulders. Then I wondered how I was supposed to write that in the note.

It's ok, I guess.

When she read my response, she looked over at me and smiled. She folded the note up and put it in her backpack. She didn't pay much attention to me for the rest of the day.

When school was over, I walked out of the building and headed towards the field that sat on the side of the building.

"Charlie!" I heard my name and turned around to see Reeve running towards me. "Hey! Where are you going?" She came to a stop in front of me, her backpack swinging from side to side behind her with every step.

"Walking home." Home was such a weird word to use. Home was hours from here, back in my old neighborhood. I was really walking to the house we'd just moved into, but it didn't feel like my home.

"Cool. I walk home too, but I live that way," she said as she gestured in the opposite direction. "There's this place, The Range, it's just a few blocks over. Sometimes after school I go there to hang out. It's kind of like a coffee shop, but cooler. You can just be there and hang out with friends. They have some video games and comfy couches to read on. Anyway, maybe sometime you would want to go with me? It's better than just going home and doing nothing," she said with a smile. Before I could think about it I was smiling back at her.

"Ok, I'll have to ask my dad first, but I think it will be ok."

"Great!" Just as Reeve's smile grew wider, my eyes landed on the boy from earlier, Asher, walking past us. He saw me too and kind of nodded his head, giving me a very small smile. I smiled back at him weakly, embarrassed, remembering how we'd met and what he'd done for me. "Did Asher Carmichael just smile at you?" Reeve looked at his back as he walked away, but then looked back to me confused.

"Uh, I guess."

"Oh my gosh, he's so cute. How do you know him?" My mouth opened to answer, but I looked back at him, no words coming out yet. Cute? I hadn't noticed. A few of my friends from home had crushes on boys, but I never understood it. He wasn't ugly, but I wouldn't call him cute. Puppies were cute.

"I just met him at recess." I looked down at my hands that had started fiddling with the hem of my shirt. "He told another boy to leave me alone."

"He stuck up for you? Oh, em, gee. He's *so* cute. Who was bothering you?" Her words came out at a million miles per hour, and as she spoke she used her fingers to twirl her hair around and around. Eventually the hair got tangled and she had to yank her finger free, but then she'd just start all over.

"His name was Ryan. He had red hair."

"Ew. Ryan Miller? He's a jerk. Don't worry. If Asher told him to leave you alone, he will. Why was he bothering you?"

"He was making fun of my name," I said as I shrugged my shoulders. I didn't tell her about him throwing rocks at me, that was a little too humiliating.

"What's wrong with your name?" She asked, truly confused.

"It's a boy's name."

"Oh, well that's a dumb reason to make fun of someone. You don't even pick your own name. So he's really making fun of your parents. What a jerk."

It was hard to tell for sure when she was done talking. I waited a second or two before I spoke.

"It's ok. I'm used to it. Anyway, I'll ask my dad about The Range. Maybe I'll see you tomorrow?"

"Definitely. I sit right next to you, so it would be hard not to see me." She smiled, then blinked, staring at me.

"Ok, well, I'll see you tomorrow, then."

"Ok, bye!" Reeve turned around and bounced towards the other side of the school. I watched her for a few seconds still a little dizzy from her rapid talking. I finally turned and continued towards the break in the fence that went around the school that would let me out onto the street of my new house.

The field was probably meant to be used for sports like soccer or football, but there were no goals or bleachers on the sidelines, just grass. There was a trail that went around the field made of bark dust and looked like it might be used for running. There was only one cut-through in the fence along this side of the property. The fence backed up against a row of houses, some of which you could see into the backyards. Most of them had big bushes that made it hard to see anything besides the roofs. The cut-through was lined by trees and covered in gravel. It was only about fifty feet long, but it felt like a tunnel. Once you were inside you were secluded, shrouded by trees and bushes. Treetops canopied the walkway and tall shrubs on either side boxed you in.

Once you came out the other side, you were just plopped right into a neighborhood. You could either go left or right. My new house, if I remembered, was on the left. I took the turn and noticed that Asher was walking ahead of me, about a half block up the street. I watched him as he came to a stop in front of my house, looking up at the blue two-story house my dad had bought without even seeing it. My grandparents lived in Willow Brook, so they had been able to check it out for him, but still, it was a little crazy. Asher only stood there for a few seconds and then continued down the street, turning right at the end of the block continuing on the sidewalk. Maybe he had known the family who lived in the house before us and missed whoever had been there. That made me think about my friends back home, and I wondered if they were missing me. Maybe Dad would let me use his cell phone to call Lucy after dinner.

The house was empty when I opened the door - empty of everything. Hardly anything was unpacked so there were no pictures hanging on the wall, no dishes in the cupboards, but even more disturbing to me was how empty the house was of any feeling. I was so used to my old house; it held all my memories. So many memories. I remembered baking cookies with my mom, rolling out sugar cookie dough on the island that sat in the middle of the kitchen. I remembered her flattening the dough with the rolling pin, blowing her brown hair out of her face, smiling at me, pretending not to see me sneaking pieces of dough into my mouth. This new kitchen meant nothing to me, held no memories. I'll never hear my mother's laugh in this kitchen or play monopoly with Lucy.

I turned from the empty room and went up the stairs to my bedroom which, thankfully, was at least partly put together. My dad had been sure to get to my room first. I collapsed on my bed and must have fallen asleep because the next thing I heard was the doorbell ringing. At least, I assumed it was the doorbell. My old house's doorbell rang once, a single chime. This doorbell went on forever and sounded like a grandfather clock. It rang the entire time I walked to the front door. I was so irritated by the obnoxious bells that I swung the door open with more force than necessary. I was surprised to see Asher standing on the other side.

"Oh, hi," I said, caught off guard by the sight of him on the porch.

"Hi. My mom made these and asked me to bring them over. She wanted to welcome you to the neighborhood."

I looked down at the plate he handed me and tried really hard not to let it show on my faced how upsetting it was to get a plate of homemade cookies from his mother. I took them and thanked him, manners always won out.

"Did you know the family that lived here before me?" I asked him, trying to get my mind off the fact that he had a mother who made cookies and how unfair it suddenly seemed.

"Yeah, my best friend Trace lived here. His Dad's job transferred him all the way to Minnesota so they moved. My mom said that maybe someday I could go and visit him over summer vacation."

"That sucks that he moved, but it's cool that your mom would let you go see him," I offered.

"Yeah," he said but then paused. "Is your head ok? You know, from earlier?" My hand automatically moved to rub the small bump that had formed where the rock hit me.

"Yeah, it's no big deal. Thanks again for stopping him."

"I saw you made friends with Reeve." I shrugged.

"She seems nice. She talks a lot." He laughed at my comment.

"That she does. But you get use to her, I guess." He rocked back and forth on his heels a few times and I stood there, not really sure what else there was to say. "Well, I walk to school every morning so if you want, you can walk with me."

"Ok, maybe I'll see you in the morning."

"Ok, see ya later." He turned and walked down the porch and I closed the door.

The next morning I waited in the front family room, peeking out of the window, until I saw Asher pass my house. As he walked by, I saw him look over towards my door. I could tell he was contemplating waiting for me or just continuing on his way. I breathed a sigh of relief when I saw him continue walking. After the way he saved me yesterday, the cookies, and the way he seemed to be too nice, I just couldn't bring myself to walk to school with him. I didn't want him feeling like he was obligated to be nice to me. I didn't want anyone feeling like they were obligated to me in any way. At that moment, I mostly just wanted to blend into the background and forget everything that had happened to me.

I kept my head down at school, sat with my drawing pad during lunch and recess, trying to let my pencil occupy my thoughts instead of the fact that even though I was lonely, I didn't want to befriend anyone. I walked across the field on my way home when Reeve came running up behind me.

"Charlie!" I turned to see her and she had a big smile on her face. "Hey, do you want to go to The Range with me today?"

"Uh," I hesitated. "I didn't get a chance to ask my dad yesterday. He's expecting me home." I said as I gestured towards the alley.

"Ok, well, let's walk to your house and ask your dad then." She started walking with a determined gait. We walked to my house together and there was not even one moment for me to get a word in. She talked the entire time, filling me in on all the kids in our class, what had happened on the latest episode of the television show she was watching, and how she had gotten a great deal on a new pair of jeans at a trendy store in the next town over. Her rate of speech was baffling and also comforting because I didn't have to say anything.

We went into my house and I called my dad, who agreed I could go with Reeve as long as I was home for dinner. He sounded excited and relieved that I had made a friend, and he probably would have let me leave the country with her if he thought it would have made me happy. I put my book bag on the counter and we left, walking back the way we had came. Halfway across the field Reeve caught me off guard by asking me a question.

"So, what does your dad do?" The silence that came when she paused for my answer was strange. I appreciated her incessant talking.

"He works in construction."

"Like, building houses and stuff?"

"Yeah, mostly. Offices. Anything really."

"That's cool. What does your mom do?"

And there it was. The moment I dreaded with every person I encountered - having to talk about my mom.

"Nothing. She died." Reeve stopped walking and her mouth gaped open. I couldn't look her in the eye, so I stared at the ground, hoping she'd recover quickly and continue talking about unimportant, distracting things like she had the entire way up until now.

"She *died?*" I nodded my head, not saying a word. "How?"

"Cancer."

"I can't imagine not having a mom," Reeve said quietly as she started walking slowly.

"Me either."

The Range was actually a pretty cool place; there was nothing like it back home that I had ever seen. It was part coffee shop and cafe, part arcade, part pseudo-library where the no talking rules were lifted. There were board games, video games, books, a few computers to use the internet, couches, bean bag chairs, there was even a hammock in the corner of the reading area. There were mostly younger kids there, sixteen and under, it looked like. Obviously, once kids got their driver's license they found cooler places to hang out.

Reeve led me to where the counter was and we both ordered a soda. Reeve then headed towards a table where a few girls sat. I hesitated, nervous about sitting with a bunch of girls I didn't know. I missed Lucy immediately. Reeve sat down and motioned to the chair next to her. I sat down and tried to smile without looking like I was in pain.

"Guys, this is Charlie. She just moved here," Reeve said excitedly. I gave a small wave to match my small smile.

"Hey, Charlie. Where'd you move from?" A blonde girl across the table asked.

"A town about five hours from here. Bridgeport."

"Never heard of it. I'm Celia, by the way," the blonde girl responded.

"It's a small town," I said quietly. The girls continued to talk amongst themselves, and every once in a while Reeve would try to involve me in the conversation. I appreciated her attempt at making me feel comfortable, but I was still the new kid and it had always been hard for me to open up to new people. Especially now. The more I talked with these girls, the more they would want to know about me, and the more I would have to tell them. No thanks. I'd rather keep it all inside if I could.

"How long have you been growing your hair out?" Celia asked at one point. I absentmindedly reached for my hair which, if left down, hung well past my hips. It was thick, long, black, and very straight.

"Besides small trims, I've never cut it. My mom would never let me." I felt my own heart speed up at the mention of my mom, hoping the girls wouldn't ask me anything else that would make me talk about her any more. Reeve caught my eye and must have noticed my unease.

"Isn't it pretty? Rachel, weren't you going to ask your mom if you could dye yours blonde? Summer's coming and blonde would be a really good color on you. Is anyone doing anything fun for summer vacation?" And just like that, with words spilling out of her mouth, words meant to save me a little bit of discomfort, I thought maybe I had made a true friend. All the girls took turns talking about their plans for summer and I, for the first time in weeks, had a genuine smile on my face.

After we were there for a little over an hour I noticed a few boys walk in, Asher being one of them. Reeve immediately looked over to the group of four boys and turned to whisper to the girls at the table.

"Asher saved Charlie from Ryan yesterday at recess. He was bullying her and Asher made him stop."

"Shut. Up." Celia looked at me with interest. I shrugged.

"He didn't *save* me. It wasn't that big of a deal."

"She keeps saying that," Reeve said with a confused look on her face. "Charlie, if Asher made Ryan leave you alone, it's a big deal. He's so cute."

I laughed - a true laugh.

"And you keep saying *that*. What does that mean anyway? How is he cute?" I looked over at him and he looked like any other boy.

"I don't know. It's his eyes I think. And those cute dark freckles he has. Who has freckles like that? No one."

I took a closer look at him. Ok, Reeve was right about the freckles. They were unique anyway. Not the usual light brown color of freckles, but a dark brown. And they looked bigger than normal freckles, too. Instead of a lot of small ones, he had fewer larger ones. It was distinctive.

"Reeve, you're boy crazy," Celia said. Reeve just smiled. Asher walked past us and nodded at the girls at the table. Then his eyes turned to me.

"Hey Charlie."

"Hey Asher," I responded, desperately wanting him to walk away.

"I didn't see you on the way to school today. Should I wait for you tomorrow?"

"Yes!" Reeve practically shouted. Asher looked at her briefly, then back to me.

"Should I wait?" My earlier appreciation for Reeve having saved me from talking about my mom quickly dissolved and was replaced with irritation for putting me in this, almost worse, situation. How could I say no now?

"Uh, yeah, sorry about this morning. I was running late." He smiled widely, a dimple appearing on his left cheek.

"No problem. I'll see you in the morning." He walked back to where his friends waited.

"He wants to walk to school with you?" Reeve asked, eyes almost bugging out of her head.

"I'm sure his mom is making him; she made him bring over cookies yesterday afternoon."

"Oh my gosh. He's so cute," Reeve repeated. Luckily the conversation moved on to something else.

The next morning, like I knew he would, Asher waited for me at the bottom of my driveway.

"Hey Charlie," he said with a smile as I approached.

"Hey," I said, looking at the ground for a moment to gain some courage. "Listen, you don't have to walk to school with me. I know your mom is probably making you walk with me. It's fine." I paused, waiting for him to respond. The seconds it took for him to speak were very heavy and filled with my rapid heartbeat.

"My mom isn't making me walk to school with you, Charlie. Can't I just *want* to walk to school with you?"

I shrugged.

"Hey," he said as he crouched down to get me to look at him. "What does this mean?" He shrugged his shoulders at me in an exaggerated way. I exhaled loudly and turned to start walking towards the school.

"I guess I just don't understand why you would want to walk with me."

"My best friend just moved away and I use to walk to school with him every day. I guess I just thought maybe you were looking for a new friend as much as I was. I'm sorry."

Regret and shame washed over me. It hadn't occurred to me that he might have needed someone to be there for him. I was too wrapped up in my own unhappiness to even consider that perhaps, the boy who lost his friend as well, might have needed me to be his friend.

"No, I'm sorry, Asher. I'm not good at meeting new people and making friends. I've never had to. I lived in my old house since the day I was born. My friends back home have been my friends since I was born. I've never had to make new ones. I'd really like it if we could walk to school together." I looked over at him, hoping the sad look was gone from his face. I was rewarded with a dimpled smile.

"Great. I hate walking alone."

Asher and I walked to school nearly every day until, finally, we were old enough to drive.

Chapter Two

It was the Saturday before the first day of high school, and even though I had spent a wonderful summer with Reeve, I was anxious for the summer to end because that meant that Asher was coming home. A month before school let out, we walked to school and he dropped the biggest bomb my 13-year-old self had ever experienced – well, besides my mom's cancer.

"So," Asher said as we slowly made our way towards the middle school. "I have something to tell you."

"Ok," I said, drawing the word out to emphasize my apprehension. "You're being very cryptic right now."

"My grandfather called my parents last night and told them that he needed help on his farm back in Oklahoma. He asked my parents if I could come and help him for the summer."

I stopped in my tracks and turned to face him.

"You're going to Oklahoma?" He winced a little and nodded his head. "For the *whole* summer?" He nodded again. "You're kidding. Asher, this isn't funny at all."

"I'm serious. I guess one of his farmhands quit and my parents think it will build character or something if I go and do farm stuff all summer."

"But we had plans this summer! You were supposed to teach me how to skateboard! We were going to ambush Reeve with water balloons every day! We were going to fish in the creek under the bridge in the park. Asher, this ruins everything."

"I'm sorry, Charlie. There isn't anything I can do about it. My parents bought a plane ticket last night. I leave the Monday after school gets out."

"We've got to cram a whole summer's worth of plans into one weekend?"

He laughed. "I suppose."

"So not funny, Asher. I love Reeve, but I can't imagine spending all summer with her. Her idea of summer vacation is laying on her front lawn in a bathing suit and flirting with boys," I said as I kicked a rock that was in my way. The rock skittered across the pavement farther than I planned and I winced as it came dangerously close to a parked car.

"You're not going to do that, are you?"

"What?"

"Lay in her front yard in a bathing suit."

"Oh, um, I don't know. Probably not." Then, suddenly, it was tense. This had only happened a few times before with us. We would be talking or hanging out, and suddenly out of nowhere one of us would say something or do something that was new to our usual friendship dynamic. A few weeks ago we were sitting in his garage and we decided to walk to the store to get smoothies. He reached both of his hands out to me and helped me up. He pulled a little too hard and I rocketed into his chest. Not only was I closer to him than usual, but he didn't let my hands go for a few moments. We stood there, chest to chest, holding hands, and it felt – different. My heart sped up and my lungs hurt because I was breathing so fast. I didn't understand it, but I didn't hate it either. After a few moments he dropped my hands and stepped away.

"We should get going," he said, trying to sound nonchalant, but I knew he had felt the weirdness too.

"Yeah, the smoothies might run out if we don't hurry." I tried to be cool and calm as I briskly walked out of his garage towards the street. It was awkward for a few blocks but then something made us laugh, I can't remember what, but then everything was back to normal.

Asher asking about me in a bathing suit was weird. But weird in a good way almost. I couldn't explain why I liked it, but I did.

The weekend before he left was epic. I didn't master the skateboard, even though I tried, but we drenched Reeve every day until the morning he left for the airport. She was so mad at us, but we didn't care. Her recovery time was minimal and it was worth it to watch her scream as water was splashing all around her. We laughed until our bellies hurt every time. We spent one whole day under the bridge at the park trying to catch the tiny little fish that swam through the creek there. We caught tadpoles too, but we never kept any of them, always throwing them back just happy to have actually caught them at all.

Today was the day Asher was coming back and excitement raced through me. I missed him over the summer. We only spoke on the phone a few times while he was away. My heartbeat did its explosive beating thing again when Asher remembered to call me on my birthday. I wasn't expecting him to call at all, it never occurred to me that he would.

"Happy birthday, Charlie," he said, and I couldn't help the giant smile that broke out over my face.

"Thank you, Asher. That is really sweet of you to remember my birthday."

"Of course I remembered your birthday; you're my best friend, Charlie." I couldn't explain why my stomach dropped when he said the word friend, but it did. I was so confused by my body's reaction to all of this. I was excited when he called, but sad when he referred to me as a friend. I *was* his friend and he was mine. There was no need for any of this silliness, so I shook it off.

"Are you doing really cool farm things over there in Oklahoma?"

"Uh, I guess. It's just really hot and I am outside most of the day. Lots of lifting heavy things and wrangling animals. But, I'm not bored, so there's that."

"Sounds fun," I said sarcastically.

"What have you been doing?" He asked.

"Not a lot," I sighed into the phone. "Reeve is dragging me to the mall a lot. We sit in the food court while she checks out guys. We sit on her lawn in the front of her house listening to her stereo. Honestly, we don't do much. She listens to the radio and reads, and I draw. We talk. That about sums up my summer. Oh, and sometimes we go to The Range."

"Are you in your bathing suit?" He asked quietly.

"Right now?" I asked, confused by the question.

"No. When you're sitting on her lawn."

"Uh, not usually. She is most of the time. I don't know." I didn't know how to answer his question. I didn't want to lie to him, but I felt like if I told him that I had been in my swim suit on her lawn it would make him angry for some reason. I didn't want to make him angry, especially not when he's so far away. I just wanted him to smile. "This summer would be much better if you were here," I said quietly. There was a long and silent pause. I'm not sure why I said what I did, or why it felt like it was really important but it was. And for another reason unknown to me, whatever he said in response was really important too.

"I miss you too, Charlie," was his answer and a smile immediately spread across my face. "I'll be back in just a few weeks. We'll start high school and I will save you from Reeve."

"Meh, she's not that bad. She's just not you." Another sentence that seemed to come from nowhere. "Anyway, thanks again for calling for my birthday. Have a good rest of your summer over there in Oklahoma."

He didn't call me for the rest of the summer, and even though I would always want to talk to him, I was ok with it. Our last conversation was confusing enough, I didn't want to feel weird talking to him. I knew when he came back home and everything went back to normal, all the weirdness would melt away.

I sat by the phone, trying not to look like I was waiting for him to call. My dad walked by every once in a while and gave me a small smile.

"Charlie, his flight might have been delayed. Or maybe, his parents want to spend an evening with him. After all, they haven't seen him all summer either."

"Dad, I'm just drawing. If he calls, he calls," I said as I shrugged my shoulders. It was the least convincing thing I'd ever said, but my dad did a great job of nodding and walking to the other room. The phone suddenly rang and I jumped.

"Hello?"

"Hey, Charlie. Wanna go to the mall?" I rolled my eyes so hard I was sure I was going to lose one in the back of my skull.

"No, Reeve. I don't want to go to the mall. Go ahead without me."

"What are you doing?"

"Nothing, just drawing."

"Well then, come with me. I need someone to talk to while I guy-watch in the food court."

"No thanks. I'm in the middle of this drawing and I really want to finish."

"Oh fine. If you change your mind, I'll be at the food court."

"Ok," I said, knowing I wasn't going to change my mind. "Have fun." I hung up the phone and returned to my pad of paper that had the worst drawing I had done since grade school. I was distracted and nothing was flowing from me. It was just a big jumbled mess of lines. The phone rang again and I rolled my eyes.

"I haven't changed my mind. I don't want to go anywhere," I said, exasperated.

"Oh, that's too bad," I heard a voice say on the other side that definitely wasn't Reeve. "I was hoping I could see you for a little while tonight." My darned heart was doing that beat-so-fast-it-might-pop-out thing again.

"Asher?"

"Yeah, it's me. Were you expecting your other best friend to return from a summer away today?"

"No," I said. His voice sounded different - deeper. Maybe it's just the phone. He'll probably sound the same in person. "I just wasn't sure if you were going to spend the evening with your parents or not. I'm sure they've missed you."

"Yeah, but I can squeeze you in," he said, making me smile. "Meet me outside?"

"Now?"

"Do you want to wait any longer?"

I shook my head.

"Charlie?"

"No!" I almost shouted once I realized he couldn't hear me shaking my head. He laughed.

"Ok, I'll meet you out there."

I tried not to run to the door to put on my shoes, but I was definitely walking fast. My dad saw me dashing down the hallway.

"Did he call?" He shouted from his office.

"Yup!" I shouted back.

"Be home for dinner!"

"Ok!"

I reached the door and stopped at the mirror hanging in the entry way. I studied my face, making sure, for a reason new to me, that I looked ok. What did 'ok' look like? Was my hair crazy? No. Did I have anything on my face? No. I guess this was as good as it was going to get. I shook my head at myself; I never cared before what I looked like when I saw Asher.

I opened the door to the warm summer air. The sun was beginning to set, but still pretty high. Orange and red streaks were ribbons in the sky. I had another hour or so before dinner. I turned right at the sidewalk and absolutely could not help the enormous smile that spread across my face as I saw him walking towards me. I also couldn't help it when my feet started moving faster and faster until I was running towards him. He was running towards me as well and when we finally made it to each other, I jumped up into his arms and he swung me around. We spun for what seemed like hours. His nose was pressed into my hair and my face was snuggled into the crook of his neck. I didn't remember him ever smelling good, but he did. He smelled different.

When he finally put me down, we each spent a few moments unabashedly looking each other over. I saw him eyeing me, but didn't care because I was eyeing him. He was huge. He was big. He was perfect.

"You grew," were the first words out of my mouth.

"You didn't," he responded. He was right. I hadn't grown one smidge over the summer – in height anyway.

"No, seriously. You must be at least a foot taller than you were when you left." I went to stand next to him to gauge how much taller he'd gotten. I remembered before he left when we walked side-by-side if I looked over at him I was looking at his shoulder. Now I turned my head and I was looking at his chest. Even his chest looked bigger. "What did they feed you on that farm?" He laughed.

"You look different too, but you're still so small," he said. I shrugged.

"It's a curse."

"No, it's ok. I like you small. You're like those cartoons we use to watch back in fifth grade. What was it called?"

"We watched a lot of cartoons, Asher."

"It was on Nickelodeon and it was about those little people who lived in the forest." I scrunched up my eyebrows, thinking hard.

"You mean The Littl' Bits?"

"Yeah! That's them. They were tiny too, just like you. You're my little bit."

I felt the blood immediately rush to my face as I started blushing. I looked down at the ground to try and hide the crimson shade of my cheeks and the ridiculous smile I wore.

"Do you have some time? Can we go for a walk?"

"Yeah, I have to be back for dinner, so I've got about an hour." We started walking, with no real destination, and ended up back at our elementary school. We both took seats on a swing and just sat and talked. He told me about his summer on the farm and how his grandpa taught him how to drive on his old truck. He told me about how they took some cows "out to pasture", whatever that meant, and that they had to sleep in a tent for a few nights. He heard coyotes howling close to this tent and was really scared, but too afraid to say anything to his grandpa because he wanted to seem like a grown up. I told him I would have peed my pants if I heard a coyote outside my tent. He laughed.

"So, Bit," he said with a smile. I shook my head at his new nickname for me, pretending to be annoyed by it. "Did you and Reeve meet any cute boys at the mall?" I looked up at him when he asked the question, but his gaze was on the ground, his feet digging small holes in the bark dust. I shrugged my shoulders.

"Not really. Whenever Reeve would engage any of them in conversation I would just nod at them and smile. It was really boring."

"Good." He said. I couldn't look him in the eye.

"Did you meet any cute girls on the farm?"

"Well," he started. "There was this one girl. She was just there for the summer too. I spent a lot of time with her and we became really good friends."

"Oh," was all I could say as my heart fell all the way into my shoes.

"She had really pretty brown hair and a big black spot over her left eye." I looked up at him curiously. "Her name was Cupcake," he said, smiling again. I smacked him, an involuntary movement that I had no idea was occurring until it was over. "She was my horse," he said through the laughter that trilled out of him. I was too angry at him for his joke to notice how beautiful his laugh was, almost.

"Your horse?"

"Yup, she was pretty great. Best friend a guy could have on a farm."

"So you didn't meet any cute *human* girls?" This time he shrugged.

"There were a few girls who came around, mostly the daughters of the other farmhands. They weren't anything special. Besides, any time they tried to talk to me, somehow the conversation always came back to my best friend who was back home." I didn't try to hide my smile that time. I wore it proudly.

"Come on, Asher. It's time to go home."

Chapter Three

It was the first day of high school. Reeve and I stood at our very first locker which we were sharing. Something about having a locker was so cool. I was nervous about my first day, but I felt a little better because Reeve was so excited and confident.

At this point in our development, Reeve and I were pretty opposite. Her boobs came in during eighth grade and she was very proud of them. Her boobs got bigger, her waist got smaller, legs longer, and skin tanner. It was hard not to notice her or notice all the boys noticing her. Sometimes it was a little intimidating being next to her walking down the halls, but most of the time I didn't mind because it meant no one was looking at me. She wore clothes that accentuated her newly formed body and she liked that other people admired what she worked so hard to show off.

"Hey, Bit," I heard Asher's voice behind me. I turned around and rolled my eyes at him.

"Is this nickname going to stick?" I asked, trying to sound exasperated.

"He gave you a nickname? That's cute," Reeve commented, turning back to the mirror that was magnetically stuck to the inside of our locker as she finished putting on some lipstick.

I began to blush, trying to think of something to say when Asher saved me.

"Name the last time you didn't think something was 'cute'," he said, using his fingers to make air quotation marks.

"What? It's sweet the way you treat Charlie. People who don't know you probably think you have a massive crush on her, but I know better. She just totally has a big brother idolization of you and you have some weird need to be her bodyguard. You're going to have to get over that, Asher," Reeve said, pointing at him. "This year boys are going to start wanting to ask Charlie out, and they won't have the chance if you're always giving them those death stares and maintaining a three-foot bubble around her."

"He doesn't do that," I scoffed.

"Uh, yes he does. He has ever since seventh grade when Brady Collins told Asher he had a crush on you."

"Brady Collins had a crush on me?"

"No," Asher answered quickly.

"No?" Reeve challenged.

"No. He said he thought you were cute, not that he had a crush on you."

"And what is the difference?" Reeve asked with a smirk.

"Wait, he thought I was cute?"

"If he thought you were cute in seventh grade, he's gonna go crazy for you this year, Charlie." Asher groaned and ran his hand through his hair. That was something new I'd never seen him do before.

"What did you say to him, Asher?" I asked.

"Nothing. I just told him that you didn't date, that your dad probably wouldn't let you."

The idea that Asher had chased Brady off made me feel weirdly happy, but I knew I didn't want him to know that.

"You were probably right," I admitted. I wasn't even sure my dad would let me date now in ninth grade. Reeve put her bag in the locker and grabbed a notebook then slammed the locker door.

"All I'm saying is that Asher's got his work cut out for him this year if he thinks he's going to continue this whole Protecting Charlie's Innocence thing he's been doing for so long."

"I'm not protecting her innocence," he grumbled.

"Wow, look who filled out this summer! Charlie, my backseat's got your name all over it." The offensive words came from a guy we'd gone to school with before, but hadn't seen in a few years because he was older than us. The words hadn't even made it all the way out of his mouth before Asher pushed him up against the wall of lockers. His forearm pressed into the boy's neck, and I heard Asher growling some words at him, but I couldn't make them out. The boy against the lockers held his hand up as if surrendering, and after a few moments Asher let him go. I saw his shoulders moving up and down rapidly, and heard his breaths whooshing in and out of his lungs quickly.

I was frozen where I stood. I had *never* seen Asher be even remotely violent. I had no idea what I should do. Asher finally turned around to look at me, but I didn't recognize the look in his eyes; it was nothing I had ever seen from him. He held my gaze for a moment, then turned and walked the opposite direction. It was all I could do to watch him walk away. I wanted to go after him, but I didn't know what to say, and I, honestly, was a little bit scared of him at the moment.

"What was that?" I whispered, more to myself than anyone else.

"That, my friend, was Asher claiming his territory," Reeve replied.

"What territory?"

"You."

"He doesn't think of me as territory."

"Well, that guy's throat begs to differ," she said motioning towards the guy still trying to recover from Asher's outburst. Something in my gut tried to tell me that this was huge. Something changed in the last five minutes, something that was going to alter our friendship. I could feel it.

"Come on. Let's find our classes."

I didn't see Asher for the rest of the school day. I looked for him every time I turned a corner, every time I walked down the hallway. During lunch I thought for sure I would see him walk through the doors to the cafeteria, but he never showed up. This was not how our first day of high school was supposed to go. I was sad he wasn't around for me to talk to, to see how his day was going, but even more than that, I was worried about him.

By the end of the day I was frazzled and anxious. Reeve stayed after for an orientation, so I went to leave and started the walk home. Very few times in the last four years had I walked home from school alone. Unless he was sick, Asher always walked with me. His absence from the walk felt deeper than it should have. Him not being there to walk me home felt like I had lost him in another way completely. I pushed open the heavy metal door that led to the side of the building that pointed towards my house.

My heart skipped a beat when I saw Asher standing at the edge of the school property, waiting for me. I tried to keep my pace steady and not rush to him, but I couldn't help it. When I finally made it to him my arms moved without my permission and wrapped around his waist and I pressed my cheek against his chest. We never really hugged all that much, and when we did it was simple, friendly, and over quickly. This was different.

When his arms came around my shoulders and pulled me into him, I breathed a sigh of relief. A peace and a calm that I had been seeking all day in his absence flooded my system. I took a few steadying breaths and couldn't help but notice that he smelled amazing. I might have taken a few extra breaths just to make sure I got my fill of his new and enticing scent.

"I was worried about you," I mumbled into his chest. I felt him pull away, but not far enough that he had to let go of me. I looked up at him.

"You're not mad at me?" I didn't understand why he thought I would be angry and I took a step back in confusion.

"Why would I be mad at you?"

"Cause I totally lost my cool on that guy." He sounded so angry with himself and I just wanted to make him feel better.

"He was a jerk." He looked down at his feet now, hands in his pockets. "What he said wasn't cool and I'm glad someone was there to stick up for me."

"I saw your face. When I turned around, I saw it. You were scared of me."

What was I supposed to say to that? Was I scared? Yes, a little. But not really of him. I was afraid of the situation, that it was going to get out of hand, that perhaps Asher was going to get hurt.

"I wasn't afraid of you. I was caught off guard is all." His eyes snapped up to mine, the grey in them was darker, alluding to his distress.

"I'd never hurt you, Charlie. Not ever. Not physically, not emotionally, not in any way."

"Asher, stop. I know that."

"I never want to see you look at me like that again."

"What happened, anyway?"

"What do you mean?"

"I mean, he said something stupid and you kind of just lost your mind. What happened?" He shook his head slightly then shrugged his shoulders.

"I heard what he said and, I don't know, something inside of me snapped. The idea that he was thinking about you like that. The image of what he said made a picture in my head. I just couldn't take it. Before I knew what was happening, I had him up against the wall."

"What did you say to him?" He looked at me and I saw a moment of panic in his eyes, but it was gone in an instant.

"I didn't say anything to him." I cocked my head to the side and gave him a glare.

"I heard you say something to him, Asher. What did you say?"

"Honestly, if I said something, I don't remember. Maybe you just heard the sound of my arms crushing his throat." He sounded disgusted with himself. I felt terrible for him, but I also felt a tiny bit responsible. Obviously I can't control what some random guy says about me, but I couldn't help the feeling it gave me when I thought about the fact that all this happened because Asher was trying to protect me.

"Well, I can guarantee you he won't be talking to me for the foreseeable future."

"Good." He said harshly.

"Where were you all day?"

"I left and went home. I was too angry at first to be there, then I just decided to scrap the whole day and start over tomorrow."

"You didn't have to come back for me," I said, trying to hide the fact that I secretly loved that he was here to walk me home. He gave me one of the most beautiful smiles I'd ever seen.

"I'll always come back for you, Bit."

Chapter Four

It had been a few months since school started and things between Asher and I were back to normal – almost. There weren't many more uncomfortable situations between us. No more instances of touching longer than usual or breathing him in just to keep his scent within me. Guys at school were keeping their distance, although it was hard to tell if it was just because of Asher's outburst the first day of school, there still being some residual fear that if any of them spoke to me he might go all caveman on them again, or if they had just gone back to not noticing me like any other day. Either way, I didn't mind. It didn't seem like my dad did either.

"Charlie Bear, how are the boys treating you at school?" He asked me one night over dinner. I finished chewing the bite I had just taken while shrugging my shoulders.

"They don't really pay me any attention," I said while still looking down at my plate. I didn't want to talk to my dad about boys.

He raised his eyebrows at me. "I don't believe that for a moment," he scoffed.

"It's true. One boy said something terrible to me the very first day and Asher nearly killed him." The fork that had been on its way to my father's mouth was stopped mid-air, and his jaw hung open. After a second or two he closed his mouth and put his fork back down.

"Is that so? What did this boy say to you?"

I rolled my eyes while poking the food on my plate, supremely uncomfortable with the direction of this conversation. "You don't want to know, Dad."

"Yes, I do. Answer the question."

I let out an exasperated sigh, still not brave enough to look him in the eye.

"He might have mentioned how I filled out over the summer and then added something about the back seat of his car," I mumbled as quickly as I could. I peeked my eyes up at him only to see the red flush spread from his neck all the way up to his hairline. His hands gripped in solid white fists on the table and I could hear loud breaths whistling through his nose. "Dad, it's not a big deal. Like I said, Asher made it known that it was not ok." It took a little while but my dad finally calmed down a little and managed a drink of his water. It looked like he was trying to formulate his next statement. I felt it was going to be important.

"Charlie, what would you have done if Asher hadn't been there?"

"What do you mean?"

"Exactly what I asked you. That boy says something profoundly inappropriate and uncalled for to you in the hallway and Asher is nowhere to be found to defend your honor. What would you do?"

"Uh, ignore him and keep walking?" That's probably what I would do, but I wasn't really going for honesty. I was just trying to give my dad the answer he was looking for so that we could move past this horrid discussion.

"Any boy who disrespects you in public will only do worse in private. At this age, Charlie Bear, boys are too focused on the, uh, physical aspects of a relationship with a girl. It's important that you realize that just because a boy says things to you that you might find, uh, flattering, you need to have respect for yourself and your body. Any boy who says things like that to you isn't worthy of your time or attention."

"Dad, please, let's not do this," I said as I started to stand up to take my plate into the kitchen.

"Charlie, sit." I instinctually sat back down quickly. Dad used his 'I mean business' voice, which he only reserved for times when I knew it was best to obey him. "You're in high school now and it's important that you understand how the male mind works at this age. Now," he paused, again trying to put something together in his mind. "When boys your age are interested in girls, there is a chance that they are thinking about a physical relationship with her more than she might be.

Boys are more curious, more driven by hormones, and sometimes more, well, uninhibited in a sexual nature."

"Have you met Reeve?" I joked, trying to lighten the mood. My dad's eyes grew wide and I immediately regretted my joke. "I'm kidding! Jeez, Dad. Reeve isn't like that. I mean, she's flirty and boy crazy, but she's not – you know," I tried to insinuate what I meant because, Lord knows, I didn't want to say it. He let out a loud breath.

"Ok, good. Don't scare me like that." He reached up to try and loosen the neck of his shirt. He looked a little warm. "All I am trying to say is that even though I am glad that Asher was there and did the right thing, he won't always be. Boys are going to try to date you, Charlie Bear. They're going to ask you out, and they're going to want to kiss you and possibly more." He wiped the palm of his hand over his forehead which was now beaded with sweat.

"Dad," I said softly. "I am not ready to date boys. I'm not even really interested in being someone's girlfriend. The boys at my school are pretty immature and dumb. You've got nothing to worry about. Plus, Asher seems to do a good job of keeping them away anyhow."

"So long as we're on the same page that you're not allowed to have a boyfriend until you're sixteen and you understand what I'm saying about boys, I think we can end this conversation."

"Oh, thank God," I said quickly and jumped up from the table. After putting my dishes in the sink, I headed towards my bedroom but was stopped by the sound of the phone ringing.

"Hello?" I said as I answered.

"Hey, Bit. What are you doing?"

"Just finished dinner."

"Wanna go shoot some hoops with me?"

"You mean watch you shoot hoops while I try to throw a round thing into an impossibly small hole?" I had never been very athletic, so playing a sport with Asher was usually pretty pointless.

He laughed. "Yeah, that."

"Let me ask my dad." I held my hand over the mouthpiece of the phone and yelled through the house. "DAD! Is it ok if I go to the elementary school and play basketball with Asher?" My dad came around the corner and I smiled at him sheepishly.

"You've got school tomorrow, so be home by nine. And tell Asher I want to talk to him before you leave." I felt my eyes darting all around the room, trying to figure out what my dad wanted to say to Asher. My dad turned and walked away, leaving me nervous.

"Uh, yeah, I can go but my dad wants to talk to you before we leave."

"That's cryptic."

"Just get over here." I heard the line go dead and knew he'd knock on the door soon so I went and changed into some hoop-shooting clothes. When the damn doorbell rang, and rang, and rang, I headed downstairs to find Asher already inside and my dad closing the door behind him.

"You ring that doorbell every time only because you know how much I hate it."

He smiled a big toothy grin. "Not gonna lie, Bit. It's the highlight of my day."

"Asher, come with me into my study," my dad said.

"Ok," he replied and started to follow my father. I started following too, but made it only a few steps before my dad stopped me without even looking back.

"Charlie, wait in the living room." I stopped in my tracks and watched Asher disappear into the study with my father. I had no idea what he was going to say to him, but I knew it made me nervous. I wandered into the living room and sat on the couch bouncing my knee up and down, trying to distract myself. Ten minutes later I heard the door open and walked towards it. I saw Asher come out first and my dad's hand was on his shoulder. They were both smiling, although Asher's smile looked a little forced.

"Can we go?" I asked, desperately.

"Yup. Nine o'clock, Charlie," my dad said as he raised one eyebrow at me.

"Got it." Asher and I walked out of the house and started the mindless walk to our elementary school. A walk I could take blindfolded I'd done it so many times. We were silent for half the walk and finally I couldn't take it anymore.

"What did my dad say to you?"

"Not much."

"Asher Carmichael, don't you lie to me."

He laughed at me. "You sound like my mom," he said through his laughter.

"Asher, tell me right now what he said to you!"

"Ok, jeez, Bit. Take it down a notch." He took a breath in and let it out loudly. "First he asked me what happened on the first day of school and made me tell him *exactly* what that guy in the hallway had said to you."

"Oh my gosh. How embarrassing." I dropped my head into my hands.

"Then he thanked me for sticking up for you and defending you. He followed that up with an anti-violence campaign," Asher said, laughing again.

"Then what?"

"That was it."

"No. You were in there with him for ten minutes. What else did you talk about?"

"Just drop it, Bit."

"No! Tell me," I begged.

"He just wanted to make sure I knew that you couldn't date until you were sixteen," he said quickly. My eyebrows scrunched up in confusion.

"Why would he tell you that?" He didn't answer me. "Asher? Why did he say that to you?"

"I don't know, Charlie." He sounded a little angry. "I think he just wants me to remember that you aren't allowed to date anyone." I shook my head, still not really grasping what was going on.

"Wait, does my dad think that *you* want to date me?"

"I'm not sure," he said as he bounced his basketball on the pavement as we made our way to the hoops hanging under a large covered area. "It's not a big deal. Let's drop it."

"Ok," I said quietly. "I'm sorry, I didn't mean to make you upset." He stopped bouncing the ball and looked over at me.

"I'm not upset, promise. Now, let's play Horse."

"Ok," I tried to smile, but still felt the tension coming off of him. It wasn't until I had lost the first game that I felt like we'd moved passed the awkward moment of the evening. I watched him dribble down the court and then execute a perfect lay-up. He was gifted when it came to sports. I was cursed. But I enjoyed trying to keep up with him, sometimes. I breathed a sigh of relief. I didn't want there to be weirdness between us. Something told me, however, that the weirdness was something I was going to have to get used to. Things were slowly changing between us. I could feel it. And I knew he felt it too. I just didn't know what we were going to do about it.

Freshman year continued without much incident. Asher and I still walked to and from school together, until basketball season when Asher made it on the Varsity team. It was quite a big deal to be put on the varsity team as a freshman and he was doing amazingly well. He didn't always get to start, but he always played, and I was so proud of him. Reeve and I went to most of his games and cheered him on. I even had my dad help me make a special jersey that had seventeen on it, his lucky number.

At one of his games, a girl who looked like she could have been a junior or senior sat next to Reeve and me. She saw me cheering Asher on and kept sending glances my way. Finally she said something to me half-way through the game.

"Your boyfriend is really good." I turned toward her, finally able to look at her without it being weird. She had long blonde hair and it was split in to two braids that hung down past her shoulders. Just as I started to answer her, Asher made a three-point shot and the crowd erupted into intense screaming. After a few seconds the noise died down enough that I was able to answer. I leaned towards her but only turned my head far enough to make sure she heard me, but not far enough to take my eyes off the court. I didn't want to miss anything.

"He is really good, but he's not my boyfriend."

"He's not?" The blatant surprise in her voice had me turning to look at her again. "That's interesting."

I did not like the way she said that. It was as if I had just told her that there was one piece of chocolate fudge cake left just for her.

"I just always see you guys together, and you're always at his games, wearing his jersey." She said, looking at me with a perfectly pleasant expression on her face that for some reason I wanted to smack off of her.

"Well," I said, trying not to sound too irritated by her, "Asher is my best friend and I am just supporting him."

"So, he's single?" Single? He wasn't dating. You couldn't be "single" unless you were on the market, right? Asher wasn't on the market, was he? I tried to keep the panic from my eyes.

"He's not dating anyone, no." I murmured.

"Interesting." There was that damn word again. I exhaled loudly. Reeve, sitting next to me, heard everything. She leaned over to me.

"Just tell her he's taken," she whispered. My head snapped back to look at her.

"But he's not," I whispered back. She rolled her eyes at me.

"Yes, he is. You guys just won't admit it." I felt the blood rushing to my face. I hated how easily I blushed anymore.

"We're just friends, Reeve, for like, the thousandth time." I said with exasperation. Reeve winked at me, and then leaned forward and half-shouted to Pippi Longstocking next to me.

"Hi, I'm Reeve, Asher's friend. You know, number seventeen? Anyway, I heard you asking about his status and he is definitely single. And he loves blondes. You should ask him out." I was sure the heat with which my stare pinned Reeve down was going to melt her face right off. Making sure my face was hidden from the blonde beauty I mouthed at Reeve, "What are you doing?!" Reeve shrugged, rolling her eyes, then leaned into me.

"Maybe you guys just need a push." She grinned wickedly at me. I scowled back at her.

"How do you know he likes blondes?" I asked, not sure where the question came from.

"I don't know if he likes blondes, but I'm betting on brunettes," Reeve answered with a wink.

I was thoroughly confused, but too distraught to do anything about it. I knew Asher and I were just friends, but I never considered that he might date someone. And I wasn't prepared to deal with the idea of Asher going out with someone. As much as I liked to spout to people about how we're best friends, I couldn't ignore the fact that I became territorial and jealous thinking about the blonde girl asking him out on a date.

After the game, Reeve and I waited in the hallway outside of the locker room like we always did. We stayed a ways away because there were always a ton of people milling around and we would just get in the way. Eventually, I saw Asher come out of the locker room. He looked up to find us in our usual spot and my favorite smile graced his face when our eyes locked. I couldn't help but smile back at him. My smile fell from my face when I saw the blonde beauty intercept him as he was halfway to us. She stopped him by placing her hand on his arm. He was caught off guard and looked down at her hand, which she left on his arm for a ridiculous amount of time. When she finally removed her hand, it was only to push back some stray hairs that had come loose from her braids and tuck them behind her ear. I watched as Asher's eyes followed her movements and my stomach turned when I saw a smile cross his face.

She was obviously doing most of the talking, and he nodded and spoke a few words here and there. At one point I saw him get a little confused, then he looked down at his feet. When his eyes came back up to hers, he said something I couldn't make out. They exchanged a few more words, but then she walked away and he continued towards us.

"Let's see what Mr. Carmichael has to say about that," Reeve whispered to me before he made it close enough to us to hear.

"Hey, Asher. Good game. Who was that you were talking to?" Reeve asked eagerly.

"Uh, Samantha? I think that's what she said her name was." He turned to me and smiled. "Hey. Like the game?"

"Parts," I said with a shrug. He gave me a questioning look. "Your three-pointers were amazing."

"Thanks, Bit," he said with a dazzling smile.

"What did Samantha want?" Reeve asked, queen of subtlety.

"Uh," he said, suddenly uncomfortable. "She asked me to the Spring Fling." The Spring Fling was the semi-formal dance that the high school put on for all the students. It was coming up in about a month.

"No way! She's really pretty. What did you say?" Reeve was being really pushy and it irritated me. Asher shifted uncomfortably and I saw his eyes dart to me before he answered.

"I said no."

"Interesting," Reeve said. I began to really hate that word. "Why would you say no? She's an upperclassman and really pretty."

"Because I don't want to go with her." He said sharply, shooting hard stares her way. My eyes batted back and forth between them, trying not to get caught in the crossfire.

"Is there someone else you want to go with?" She asked him.

"Reeve, drop it," he said.

"I just don't understand why you would turn down a perfectly good date. It makes me think there's someone else you'd rather go with." I saw her eyes turn on me.

"Reeve, that's enough," I said quietly. I didn't like the feeling I was getting from their conversation. Part of me wished Asher wanted to go to the dance with me, but more of me wanted everything to remain the same.

"You guys are hopeless," she sighed. "Ok, well, my dad is probably waiting to pick me up. I will see you guys tomorrow," she said, sounding way too cheery. She walked away and left Asher and I staring at each other uncomfortably.

"Are you ready to go?" Asher asked, breaking the silence.

"Yeah," I responded quietly. I turned to walk down the hallway with him. Once we got outside, I felt a little more relaxed. It was dark so I couldn't see Asher all that well and welcomed the idea that he couldn't see my face as clearly anymore either. Reeve stirred up all kinds of thoughts and emotions in me that I didn't know if I was ready to deal with. It was spring and even though it wasn't raining, there was still a chill in the air. I wrapped my arms around my waist.

"Here," Asher said as he slipped off his jacket and wrapped it around my shoulders.

"Thanks," I said and offered him a small smile. I pulled it tighter around my body. It was huge on me and could probably wrap around me twice. All the extra fabric caused it to bunch up in front of my jaw and I couldn't help but inhale the scent that permeated from the collar of the coat. It smelled like him. The intoxicating smell of Asher, mixed with the scent of the wet pavement was almost too much for my body to handle. I felt my heartbeat speed up, and I tried to keep the expression on my face even and unaffected.

"So, about the Spring Fling," Asher said, breaking the silence of the unusually quiet walk we were sharing.

"What about it?" I tried so hard to sound normal, but all I could hear was my heartbeat pulsing in my ears.

"Well, I was thinking, maybe we could all go in a group. I mean, I know your dad won't let you go with a date, but maybe he'd let you go with a big group of people."

"I guess there's no harm in asking."

"Do you want to go to the dance? You know," he said quickly, "with a group of people?"

"Sure," I said just as quickly.

"Cool. So, I won't go with anyone in particular, and neither will you. We'll go together, you know, with everyone else. But we'll all be there together, as a group."

"That sounds good," I said, trying not to smile. Even though the conversation was making me nervous, his excited rambling was making me laugh. I couldn't really remember a time when Asher was nervous. Before I could stop to think about the words that came out of my mouth, I asked, "Why didn't you just say you'd go with Samantha?" In the darkness I saw the corners of his mouth creep up into a smile, but his voice came out cool and controlled.

"She isn't who I want to go with." I looked away before he could catch me watching him or see my smile. This was good. We would go to the dance, but not together. Not with anyone else, mind you, but not as a date. I took a deep breath. This was ok.

That night when I returned from Asher's basketball game, my dad sat at the kitchen table reading a book, waiting for me.

"Hi, Charlie Bear. How was Asher's game?"

"Good," I said as I took off his jacket, frowning that I had forgotten to give it back to him.

"They win?"

"Yeah. Asher scored some awesome three-pointers too. He's so good."

"If he works hard, he might be able to play college ball. He's got a lot of potential," Dad said, still looking at me. I gave him a small smile.

"So, Papa Bear," I said sweetly. He knew something was coming by my term of endearment. I grew out of calling him Papa Bear when I was about seven, even though his nickname for me would never die. I was ok with that. I liked that my dad still called me Charlie Bear. "Asher, Reeve and I were talking, and we all want to go to the Spring Fling together with a group of people. Do you think it would be ok if I went?"

"What is the Spring Fling?"

"It's a dance at school. It's semi-formal, so I would probably need to get a dress."

"A dance, huh?"

"Yeah, but none of us are taking dates. We're just all going to go as a group, like, a big group of friends." I'm not even sure I believed what I was saying, so I was sure my dad was going to see straight through me and bring up what was really going on. I wiped my sweaty palms on the back pockets of my jeans. I tried to remain cool; I really wanted to go to this dance. I could admit that to myself even if I wouldn't admit it to Asher or Reeve. But if my dad knew *why* I wanted to go so badly, there was a chance he wouldn't let me. His no dating rule was still in play.

"Who all is going in this 'big group of friends'," he said, using his fingers to make air quotes. I smiled at him a little.

"Well, it would be Reeve, Asher and me. Then probably some guys from the basketball team, and Lizzy. You know, just a group of kids, going to a dance," I said nonchalantly. I tried to get him to smile. I was trying to hide the fact that I wanted to go to this dance more than anything in the world. My dad looked at me for a few moments, unblinking. Then I heard him take a deep breath in and saw him shift in his seat.

"Ok, Charlie. I'll let you go to the dance." As excitement flowed through me, I closed the distance between us and threw my arms around his neck in a tight hug.

"Thank you, Daddy!"

"Don't thank me yet. I have some restrictions." I pulled away from him and frowned a little.

"Ok... what are they?"

"I have to have dress approval, I will drive you and Reeve to and from the dance, and you will have to come home right after. No after parties of any kind." I would not reveal to him that I was so thankful he was going to let me go at all that these stipulations were completely fine with me.

"Ok," I said with mocked sullenness. Suddenly I thought about dress shopping with my father. Nothing sounded more mortifying. I winced as I asked my next question. "Do you think it would be ok if I went dress shopping with Reeve and her mother?" I saw him mulling the question around in his mind.

"I think that would be ok, so long as you understand that if I don't approve of the dress we will just take it back and buy something potatoe-sackey." I giggled at his joke, but he didn't look like he was joking.

"One more question," I said with the sweetest smile I could muster.

"Yes?"

"Do you think, since I won't be going to any parties afterward, that I could invite Reeve to spend the night here?"

"Of course, that's fine."

"Thank you, Daddy!" I flung my arms around his neck again, giving him a tight squeeze.

"Anything for you, Charlie Bear."

Chapter Five

The night of the dance came upon us quicker than I could have imagined. Reeve and I were in my bathroom putting the final touches on our outfits and I couldn't believe how different I looked and felt when I saw my reflection in the mirror. I felt like Pinocchio when he turned into a real, live boy. The transformation was unreal. I went shopping with Reeve and her mom for a dress and luckily my dad approved of my choice.

I wore a peach-colored, halter-style dress with ruching along the midsection. It had a tiered skirt with different fabrics making up each layer. I thought the visual of the different fabrics flowing down the length of the skirt was so beautiful that I knew I wanted that dress immediately. The skirt also cut at an angle, making it even more appealing in my eyes. The long side of the skirt came down to just above my knees, with the high side reaching to mid-thigh. It was different and pretty. I loved it. My dad was a little chagrined by the skirt. I knew he thought the high side was a little high, but honestly, most of my legs were covered and once he saw Reeve's dress he couldn't complain.

Reeve's dress was absolutely stunning. I would never wear anything like it, but she was braver than I was, more daring. Her dress was a bubblegum pink color, strapless, with a sweetheart neckline. It also had this amazing piece of black lace that wrapped around half of it, covering one breast and half of her skirt. It was also short, very short. Reeve was much taller than I was, so she had way more leg than I could ever hope for. I was sure my dad was going to throw a blanket over her when he saw her come down the stairs in her dress. His eyes bulged out of his head almost making me laugh. Reeve's mom stood at the bottom of the stairs snapping pictures of us, telling us how beautiful we looked.

"Reeve, that dress is gorgeous on you. And Charlie, you look stunning."

"Thank you, Mrs. Anderson," I squeaked, not use to taking compliments. After a million pictures were taken, my dad sullenly herded us out to his car. He didn't say much on the drive over but when he pulled up to the school he turned around and gave us a stern look.

"I will be waiting to pick you both up right here at ten thirty, sharp. Do not be late and, uh, have a good time."

"Dad, don't worry, everything will be fine. It's just a dance." I tried my best to make him feel better, but I knew he was uncomfortable. I was his only daughter heading off to my first dance and my mom wasn't around to give me all the normal 'talks' girls my age were supposed to be having with their mothers. I knew my dad was feeling my mother's absence tonight and I understood how hard it was for him; it was hard for me too. I rubbed his forearm gently and then leaned forward and kissed his cheek. "See you in a few hours, Daddy." I gave him a bright smile and we climbed out of the car.

"Asher is going to freak when he sees you in this dress," Reeve said as we walked through the metal doors into the school.

"Shut up. Everyone is going to freak when they see you. You look amazing in that dress, Reeve, like, hot." She smiled brilliantly at me and I smiled back at her. We walked into the gymnasium which was transformed for the dance.

White curtains draped everywhere with different colored lights shading areas in bright flashes of prismatic hues. There were big, round, white lanterns hanging from the ceiling, spaced evenly around the white flower streamers that also hung from the ceiling as well. It didn't look like the gym we ran laps around, instead I felt like I'd wandered into a cloud – a cloud currently hosting a rave, but a cloud nonetheless.

Reeve grabbed my hand and took me through the crowds of people on the dance floor. Everyone looked amazing. So many girls wore beautiful dresses, their hair perfectly styled, laughing and dancing with boys wearing sharp suits and shiny shoes. Everyone smiled and bounced to the music. The happiness was contagious and I found myself smiling while admiring all the gorgeous people surrounding me. My eyes flitted from person to person, taking in their dresses, their smiles, their dance moves. I was enthralled by it all and completely enamored by the whole experience.

My breath caught in my lungs and my body hit an invisible wall when I spotted him across the cloud. He stood with some of his friends, talking and laughing. I could only see his profile, but I could already tell he looked incredible in his dark suit. When I stopped walking, Reeve was tugged backwards. She shot me a confused look, but then followed my gaze and caught me staring at Asher. She yelled into my ear, "He looks good, Charlie." All I could do was nod. He looked amazing. My tummy was doing all kinds of weird swirls, and it felt incredibly empty and hollow.

I turned into Reeve and pulled her arm so that she brought her ear down to my lips.

"I don't think I can go over there, Reeve."

"Why?"

"I don't know. All of a sudden I'm not feeling well."

"Charlie, everything is going to be ok. You're just nervous. Hey," she said, trying to get my attention. I looked up at her. "It's just Asher." Just Asher. Only Asher.

I thought about what she was saying and even though it was *just* Asher, I didn't feel like I was just me. I felt like someone else, or like I was becoming someone else. Asher was my best friend, the first person who cared about me here. The only person who cared enough to push me to come out of my shell. He'd been my best friend for years and if anything took that friendship from me, I didn't know what I would do.

"I'm scared," I confessed to Reeve in a moment of mouth-filter malfunction.

"Of what?"

"That something will happen to ruin our friendship."

Her face softened and she placed a warm hand on my shoulder. "Asher would never do anything to hurt you, Charlie. Do you like him? You know, like, more than the boy who is your friend?"

"What does that even mean?" I laughed nervously, trying to avoid answering the question.

"You know what it means. Do you have feelings for him?"

"I have lots of feelings for him," I answered, hoping the obviousness of my answer would be overlooked.

"No, I mean, do you have romantic feelings for him." Reeve looked annoyed at my dodging of her questions.

"I don't know, Reeve. He's Asher." I lied, to Reeve and myself.

"Well, I think you should go over there and just see what happens. I know he's looking forward to seeing you." I took in a deep breath and let it out loudly, knowing the thumping of the bass from the music would hide my nervousness.

"Ok, let's go." I'm not sure there would be anything I could do to prepare myself to talk to him right now, so I might as well just go over there. It was only Asher, after all. Reeve grabbed my hand and resumed pulling me through the crowd again. As we inched closer to him, I saw the moment when he realized I was near. His shoulders moved back, he stood up straighter and turned his head in our direction. I could no longer hear the loud beat of the music or the laughter ringing through the gym; all I could hear was my own heartbeat and it was racing. His eyes locked on mine and I saw the corners of them wrinkle a little, knowing he was smiling but too lost in his eyes to look away. When his eyes moved from mine it was to look slowly down my body, taking in my dress. The thump-thump of my heart sped up knowing that he was looking at me – really looking. My mouth was dry, my palms were sweaty, and my stomach was somewhere in the parking lot.

Then, all of a sudden, I was right in front of him. I could not remember walking up to him, but here I was, staring at him.

"Hi," I squeaked out at him.

"Hey, Bit." I couldn't help but smile at his nickname for me. It calmed me a little. I tried to remind myself that no matter what, Asher was my best friend. "Uh," he stammered, running his hand through his short hair. "You look amazing." He looked at my body again. My dress, he was looking at my dress.

"Thanks. You look really good in your suit too." I replied, proud of myself for getting out an entire sentence. Then I noticed the color of his tie: peach. I looked at him quizzically. "Your tie," I said pointing to his chest. He looked down and touched it lightly. Then he nearly killed me by touching my arm and leaning into me to speak into my ear. My eyes closed involuntarily. His nearness and his breath on my skin sent chill bumps spreading like wildfire.

"Reeve told me what color your dress was. I hope you don't mind." I shook my head and I'm sure my expression was that of shock. "I know you couldn't have an official date," he said into my ear again, making everything turn to jello again. "But I didn't want anyone thinking that you were available."

"Available?" I stammered.

He smiled at me and then walked towards a large round table, pulling me with him. He picked up a box from the table and pulled out from it a beautiful corsage made with one peach colored rose surrounded with baby's breath.

"Here," he said as he slipped it over my wrist. "Every girl needs a corsage at a dance." I looked from him, down to the flower, and back up to him numerous times. My mouth was broken and I couldn't even find the words appropriate at that moment. Eventually I was able to shake off my surprise as his thoughtfulness, but still not able to form words. I mouthed 'thank you' to him. He winked at me and I nearly fainted.

We turned back around and joined our group of friends closer to the dance floor. Reeve shot me a smile and I glared at her playfully, knowing she was in on the surprises that Asher had planned for me. For the next hour or so we all stood in a group, talking loudly over the music, dancing in place, taking breaks for punch and generally having an awesome time.

I tried not to focus too hard on the fact that Asher seemed to always find a way to touch me. Sometimes his arm was around my shoulders in a friendly way. Sometimes he wrapped it around my waist in a more personal way which made my heart jack-hammer in my chest. At one point, he took his hand and slid it into mine, gripping it gently. I looked up at him and he gave me a shy smile. We never held hands before. I never held hands with anyone. I was instantly concerned with how hand-holding worked. Should I link my fingers with his? Was he holding my hand because we were friends? Did other people think we were holding hands because we were dating? Were we dating? If I had to let go for some reason, was I allowed to wrap my hand around his again? Did I have to let go?

I felt him give my hand a squeeze, pulling me from my hand-holding freak out. I looked up at him and he was smiling.

"You ok?"

I nodded my head, trying to smile, but I'm sure I looked like I was going to be sick.

"Are you ok with this?" He asked as he squeezed my hand again, indicating he was asking about us holding hands.

I nodded my head again.

"Can you say something? It would make me feel better about all of this." I swallowed hard, trying to push down my nerves.

"I'm ok with this," was all I could manage, but it satisfied him enough that he gave me another wink. This time I really smiled.

I think because it was a school dance, the DJ played fast songs we could all dance to, but eventually the DJ turned on a slow song. The atmosphere in the room changed from fun and happy to nervous and sweaty. Some kids immediately paired off. Couples that were established took no time and wrapped around each other. The rest of us stood in a moment of uncomfortable edginess. I noticed many people looking around either looking for someone to ask to dance, or trying to make themselves look bored perhaps hoping someone would ask them. All I was doing was trying to avoid Asher's gaze. Our hands were still linked, palm-to-palm, and I was nervous that he was going to ask me to dance with him.

I felt him lean in closer to me, then I felt the small breeze of his whisper move past my skin.

"Will you dance with me, Bit?"

Every nerve in my body screamed no. No way. If I didn't step all over his feet, surely I would throw up on his shoes. My mind wasn't ready for all of this to be happening. Just hours ago we were just friends, and now we were floating around on this confusing cloud of *something more* and all I felt was confused. Yet, even though my mind screamed no, my body said yes. A small nod was all Asher needed to lead me onto the dance floor, still holding my hand.

We walked into the middle of the crowd of teenagers swaying to the music and Asher stopped and turned towards me, a small smile playing across his face. He unclasped my hand and brought his palms to my waist, resting them on the bell curve just above my hips. I tried to stifle the sharp breath I sucked in when I felt his hands on me, but I wasn't sure he didn't hear.

I wore high heels, so I was taller than usual, and my head came just up to his chin. I reached up and, with butterflies the size of swallows fluttering around my stomach, I clasped my hands around his neck, trying desperately to avoid his gaze. I was afraid of what I would see in his eyes or what he would see in mine. I felt him touch me just below my chin and brought my face around to look at him.

"Charlie, relax. This is just you and me. It's us, Bit. Don't be nervous." A shaky breath escaped me as his finger trailed up from my chin and moved over my cheek to my ear where he tucked away a lock that had gone astray. His fingers moved down and sifted through my long tresses, fingering the strands until he'd touched the entirety of their length. I couldn't take his gaze anymore so I moved my cheek to rest it against his chest, sighing into him, trying to let my nerves leave my body with my breath.

We swayed back and forth, moving to the slow melodic tune of a song sung by a woman with a low alto voice. I tried to focus on the lyrics, but I was too distracted by keeping meticulous track of every point of contact between our bodies. My front was pressed to his chest, and the longer we danced the closer I pressed in, eliminating the space between us. His hands eventually moved to wrap around my waist, resting on the small of my back, his fingers splayed out, claiming so much of me. I never imagined what it would be like to have Asher's hands on me, but I knew at this moment I would never want anyone else's.

"You're so small, Charlie," he whispered to me. I pulled back slightly to look up at him, puzzled by his comment. "All these years, I've seen you, I've hugged you even. But right now, as I'm holding onto you, I am amazed that something so important to me and so vital to my life can be wrapped up in such a small package." His arms tightened around me and I heard a small gasp leave my lungs. He lifted me up so my feet left the ground and our faces were level. I held on around his neck and he had me firmly around my middle. He rested his forehead against mine and I felt my eyes drift closed.

"You mean everything to me, Charlie. I'm not sure I even understand what that means fully right now, but every day it becomes clearer to me. You are my everything."

His words zipped through me, electrifying my pulse and racing through my veins. We were two friends, standing on a dance floor, still nearly children, dressed up as adults, and we were at a crossroads. Our foreheads still touching, our ragged breaths intermingling, our paths intertwining at this very moment.

It was all too much for me.

I twisted away from him and slowly slid down from his grasp. My hand was still on his chest when I looked up at his face, twisted in concern and confusion. My fingers gripped his shirt, not wanting to let go, but I knew I had to. This was more than

I had bargained for. I took a deep breath and broke our contact, heading towards the doors that would lead me outside.

Once I was out the doors, I took in deep breaths like I'd been underwater for hours. I couldn't seem to get enough air. I found a wall to lean against and tried my best to calm my lungs. After a few minutes Reeve came out and found me trying to breathe normally again.

"Charlie, what happened? Asher told me you were upset and to come find you." Of course Asher sent her.

"I just want to go home," I said, sounding small.

"First tell me what happened." She sounded concerned, but also demanding. I looked down at my hands, trying to find a way to relieve the anxiety that was building within me.

"I think," I started, but lost my nerve, bringing my hands to my face. My head was starting to pound and I just wanted to lie down.

"Charlie, just tell me. You'll feel better."

I let out a large breath, again just trying to regulate a normal breathing pattern. I felt like if I could master breathing at the moment, I could master anything. Finally, I felt like I could finish a sentence.

"I think things between Asher and me are changing." I cringed with the words coming from my mouth. Admitting it was giving it life. Saying it was making it true. At least, that's what it felt like to me. My eyes shot open in surprise with the sound of Reeve's laughter ringing through the air. She held her stomach, laughing big belly laughs, and after a few moments a few tears started to make their way down her cheeks.

"Why are you laughing?" I asked, horrified.

She took a few minutes to compose herself, but could only stop laughing long enough to sputter a sentence at me.

"Things have been changing since school started, Charlie." Her statement shocked me, but made sense at the same time. All year, even as early as the very first day when Asher defended me against the foul-mouthed boy, things were slowly morphing. But what happened tonight seemed like a warped-speed metamorphosis. Everything had been magnified. Illuminated.

"What am I going to do, Reeve?" I sounded just as panicked as I felt.

"What do you mean?"

"I don't know. What's supposed to happen now?" Reeve looked at me like I was crazy.

"Do you like Asher?" She asked that question so effortlessly, so callously, I was almost angry at her for asking such an important question with such little concern.

"Of course I like Asher." I stated, dumbfounded, confused and a little angry.

"No, I mean, like, do you *want* him?"

"Want him?" I felt permanent frown lines forming on my forehead and I could feel my pulse pounding in my temple.

"You know, do you want him to kiss you? Hold your hand? Be your boyfriend?"

"Be my boyfriend?" Too much. This was all too much. "I just want to go home." I heard her exhale, then I heard her heels click on the pavement as she made her way towards me.

"Ok, Charlie. Let's go wait for your dad. But be aware that just because you're running away from this right now doesn't mean it won't be waiting for you in the morning. I don't think Asher is going to let up any time soon. And honestly, he was really upset when you ran out on him." That tidbit of information piqued my interest.

"He was upset?"

"Well, yeah. He was worried about you." That tugged at my heart. I didn't want him to worry about me.

"Could you just go back in there and tell him that I am fine, that I am just going to go home. Tell him I will talk to him later." Reeve gave me a long and lingering stare.

"Ok, I will go and tell him, but you are going to have to talk to him about all this at some point."

"Not tonight." I was exhausted. I watched Reeve walk back towards the building and I stumbled around the corner to head towards where my dad would pick us up. The heels I wore turned out to be a big mistake and my feet were rebelling against them. I leaned up against the wall, waiting for my dad to show up, trying to forget, for just a moment, that things between Asher and I would likely never be the same.

The next afternoon I was in my room doing what I always did when I was upset – I drew. My mother always encouraged my art and it was something we shared up until her death. My mother was a painter, but I enjoyed drawing. At the moment I used charcoal and was fiddling around when I realized I had drawn two hands holding each other. I tried hard not to think about why my mind had gone there, but I knew why. I knew I would have to talk to Asher eventually. I just wasn't sure what I would say.

I didn't have long to think about it though. I heard a soft knock on my door and turned to see him leaning against the door frame. He looked worried and that, in turn, worried me.

"Is everything ok?" I asked immediately concerned.

"I don't know. You tell me." He said quietly as he walked into my room and sat on my unmade bed. I took a moment to look at him, trying to sort out my thoughts.

"I am sorry I ran out on you last night, Asher. I shouldn't have left like that."

He looked down at his hands fidgeting with the hem of his shirt.

"Did I do something wrong?"

"No." The word was out of my mouth in a nanosecond and I hadn't even contemplated his question. Did he do something wrong? No, not wrong. Thinking back to the night before and how Asher had treated me – holding my hand, dancing with me, matching his suit to my dress in a gentle nod towards possession – and I knew I wouldn't have changed any of it for the world. What I would change, however, is the way it made me feel. "Asher," I began as I moved to sit next to him. "Last night was so wonderful and I appreciate everything you did for me. But I never expected any of it and it just sort of caught me off guard."

"How I feel about you caught you off guard?"

"I guess," I answered. Now I was the one looking down to avoid his gaze.

"Listen, Bit. I'm sorry if I overwhelmed you last night, but the way I feel about you isn't just something that happened yesterday. I thought I was pretty obvious about it for a while now." He sounded frustrated and the last thing I wanted was for him to get angry. Had his feelings been obvious? Reeve always pointed out whenever Asher did things that seemed more than friendly, and even though I knew deep down that things were changing between us, I always tried to push it aside. I knew other boys didn't ask me out or flirt with me because they would have to answer to Asher.

"I don't know what you want from me, Asher. And I'm afraid that what you want I won't be able to give to you. I'm just scared," I uttered in a moment of unfiltered honesty.

"Charlie," Asher said with compassion in his voice. I looked up at him and for a moment just saw the same old Asher I'd known since I was eleven. We were interrupted by my father clearing his voice from the hallway, looking into my room with mild concern. Asher immediately stood up from the bed and stuck his hands in his pockets.

"Good afternoon, Asher."

"Hi, Sir."

"Charlie Bear, I am going to head out and get some paperwork done at the office." His eyes darted back and forth between me and Asher. "You guys gonna be ok here?"

"Yes, Dad," I said, fighting the urge to roll my eyes, something I knew would get me in more trouble than it was worth.

"Ok. I'll be back for dinner."

"Bye, Dad."

"Goodbye, Sir," Asher said, sounding nervous. I watched as my dad walked away from the door and after a few moments we heard the front door close.

"Since when do you call my dad 'Sir'?"

"Since he started looking at me like a threat," he said, sounding grumpy again. "Listen, Charlie, can we just have a real conversation? I'm tired of avoiding everything that's going on and I just want it all out in the open." The idea of being truly honest with him in this moment terrified me.

"Aren't you even a little bit afraid?" I whispered.

"Afraid of what, Charlie?" He asked quietly.

"That everything will change and never be like it used to be? That our friendship will be ruined?"

"By what? Caring for each other? I already care about you and we're still friends."

"That's all you want? To be friends who *care* about each other?"

"What I want and what I'll get are two very different things, and I am at least smart enough to know that much. So, no, I don't just want to be friends. But ignoring the things that are happening between us isn't cutting it for me anymore. I just want to talk about it."

"Ok," I said, finding my bravery. "So talk."

"I know I haven't been very subtle in regards to the feelings I have about you, but I haven't ever just talked to you about them either." He took in a deep breath and I felt my chest expand as I unknowingly did the same. Everything was going to change for us after this, I could tell. "When I first saw you, that very first day in fifth grade, I immediately felt a pull towards you. I'd seen boys pick on girls before, but never had I felt compelled to protect someone as much as I did you." He ran his hand through his short hair, something I was beginning to associate with his frustration.

"Even though I didn't know your name, I had never met you, and I couldn't fully understand my feelings, I knew you were mine."

Every synapse in my mind fired all at once. My lungs seized up, my stomach dropped, my fingernails dug into my thighs. I stared at him, watching him work through his feelings as he laid it all out for me. He sat on the bed with a loud sigh.

"I was eleven, Bit, and I had just lost my best friend. It felt natural for us to become close, to hang out all the time and goof off. And I did just think of you as a friend. But even back then I knew that if another boy had tried to befriend you it would have made me angry. Slowly, as time passed, I began to see you as more than just my friend, just the girl down the street. I couldn't help the way my body responded to you. I couldn't control the thoughts I was having. I tried to. I really did. Then we spent the summer apart and for me, everything was different."

He looked up at me then, and I saw a mixture of happiness and apprehension in his eyes. I wanted him to continue, wanted him to know that I wanted to hear the rest. I scooted over on the bed and took his hand in mine; a move I never thought I would have the courage to execute.

He looked down at our hands and moved his fingers to slide down and fit perfectly in between mine. My hand looked ridiculously small against his, but it also looked wonderful.

"Before I left, the idea of you being here without me drove me crazy. I fought with my parents, trying to get them to let me stay. I used really lame excuses, like wanting to get a summer job or even taking summer classes, when really I just didn't want to leave you. If I wasn't here to fend them off, I knew the boys would start coming around." I had to laugh because it was ridiculous. Luckily, Asher smiled at my laughter. "Then I left and I swear I thought about you every day, Charlie. I missed you. I missed my best friend, but I also missed the girl who I wanted to spend all my time with. We've always been inseparable and that time away from you was hard."

"I missed you too," I said softly. He gave me a small smile.

"Then I came home to a completely different Bit than I left," he said as he stood up, letting go of my hand. "Something happened to you over the summer. I'm sure if I had been here every day the difference wouldn't have seemed so drastic, but it was like you had changed overnight. And all of a sudden every guy was noticing you." He paced around my room and all I could do was watch him nervously walk from one end to the other. I had no idea what to say or do.

"When I pushed that guy against the locker, that first day of school, I knew I was in over my head. I am not proud of what I did to him, but in that moment I couldn't control myself. I instantly knew every thought he was having about you in his mind because I was having the same thoughts. I knew how much he wanted you, because I wanted you just as much, if not more. So I decided to just step back a bit. I couldn't go around pounding every guy who looked at you, even though I desperately wanted to. As far as I could tell you weren't interested in any of them, so I tried to stay out of it, tried to reign in my feelings.

"But I'm not sure I can do it anymore, Charlie. I can't keep the way I feel about you locked up inside of me anymore." He stopped pacing and looked at me, a question in his eyes. I tried to take in everything he was telling me. I wasn't really surprised. On some level I had known that our relationship was slowly changing. It was just time to come to terms with the fact that we would probably no longer be the same friends that we started out as when we were eleven.

"What do you want from me?" I asked honestly. I didn't know where to go from here.

"For starters, I just want to know how you feel. You know, about me. About us."

In this moment, I felt like I stood on a cliff. I was on the edge of the rest of my life and everything after this conversation depended on what I was about to say. Everything felt wildly important and that stressed me out.

"How can you promise me that after this, after we spill out everything we feel for each other, we won't ruin our friendship? Because I will take your friendship over anything, Asher. You're the best friend I've ever had and I won't do anything to jeopardize that." I felt panic rising in my voice even as I spoke about us losing what we had. My hands started to shake and regular breaths were stolen from me, replaced with shaky and shallow inhalations posing as breathing.

I felt him wrap his arms around me. My cheek pressed into his chest as he held me, his chin resting on the top of my head. I took a few breaths, very aware of the clean yet spicy scent coming from him.

"There's nothing that could happen that would take away our friendship, Bit. I wouldn't let anything take you away from me." His lips moved against my hair and I felt myself calm with his words. "If you don't feel the same way about me, if you aren't having the same trouble I am keeping everything on the friend level, I will get over it. I will accept whatever it is you have to say and I will try to move on, and we can go back to being just friends."

"And you want honesty, right?"

He chuckled and I felt it vibrate through his shirt. I pulled back to look up at him and saw him smiling.

"I was hoping I could insist on it," he answered. I pulled farther away from him so that there was a little space between us.

"Last night was so wonderful, Asher. You have to know that, if anything, I ran away from you because I was feeling too much." I looked up at him through my eyelashes, trying to gauge his reaction. All I saw was a smile and a dimple. That alone made me feel a little better about baring my soul. "I haven't had any of these problems you've been having. I haven't really ever given it much thought. I've always been yours. There's never been a question for me. If anyone had me, it was you." I watched his smile grow bigger, the dimple becoming even more pronounced in his cheek. "But," I said loudly, trying to make sure he knew I wasn't finished. "I'm not sure where to go from here. My Dad won't let me date and if last night is any indication, I need things to go slowly. So, it seems to me like this might all be a little premature to even be talking about." I saw his shoulders slump and, to be honest, mine did too.

"I'm not saying things need to change, Bit. I am fine being your friend, for now. Even now, as friends, I still get to be near you, hug you, and maybe even hold your hand sometimes," he said as he slid his hand into mine and linked our fingers. I felt a shy smile come over my face. "But," he stopped mid-sentence and let out a frustrated groan.

"What is it?" I asked, his sudden mood swing concerned me.

"Honesty, right?"

I nodded at him, eagerly waiting to hear what was upsetting him.

"I just want to see if you wouldn't mind waiting for me too."

"Waiting for you?" I couldn't understand what he was asking.

"Be my friend. Be the same Bit you always are. But I need to know that when you can, and when you're ready, you'll be with me."

I tilted my head to the side slightly.

"You want me to promise you that we'll be together eventually?"

"Ok, that might have come out wrong," he said sighing and shaking his head, sounding frustrated. "What I want is to be sure that I'm not in this alone. The last thing I would want is to be feeling all of this for you, waiting – patiently – and for you to be on a completely different page. I guess I just want to be sure that you feel the same way about me as I feel about you."

"Asher, I've never had a boyfriend. I've never held hands with anyone. And I've never examined my feelings for anyone like I have with you. Whatever this is between us, I'm sure I want it and I want it to be with you."

The smile that spread across his face was priceless and it made me smile as well.

Chapter Six

The next few weeks passed with ease and each day brought new and exciting things for Asher and me. He respected my need to not advertise our feelings for each other in public, but I couldn't help but smile when he would hold a door open for me, or place his hand on my back as we walked down the hall at school. All of these things could very well have happened before the dance, but with our newfound semi-relationship status, everything that used to be normal was now amplified.

It wasn't until the week before school was out that things were brought to an abrupt halt.

I heard the doorbell ring and couldn't help the rolling of my eyes. Either there was a delivery person on my doorstep or Asher rang it just to irritate me. I listened to its never-ending dinging as I walked to the front door. When I pulled the door open and saw Asher standing on the other side, I knew something was wrong.

"Hi. What's wrong? You look really upset." I pulled the door open all the way and stepped back, silently inviting him to come in.

"Can we go for a walk? Maybe go to the school for a little while?"

I grabbed my keys and closed the door. We made it half way to the school and he hadn't said a word. I was really beginning to worry.

"Asher, please tell me what's going on," I asked softly. He looked over at me and I could see the sadness in his eyes.

"Let's wait until we get to the school." I nodded, but reached over and took his hand in mine, giving it a small squeeze. We walked hand in hand the rest of the way and even though I was concerned about whatever was upsetting Asher, I was also fighting butterflies in my stomach knowing this was the first time we held hands since the dance. We were out in public, holding hands, and the idea of what it meant made me feel like I was floating.

We made it to the playground of our elementary school and we sat on swings next to one another. We swayed to and fro in silence. I tried to sit and wait patiently, letting him tell me on his own. Eventually he let out a loud breath so I turned to look at him.

"My parents are sending me away again this summer."

"What?" All the butterflies which previously had been swarming around my stomach were now replaced with an immediate emptiness that hallowed out my entire being. He dropped my hand, only exaggerating the feeling of loneliness, and stood up to pace in front of the swing set.

"My grandfather needs help again this summer and my parents are making me go. We fought about it all night. There's nothing I can do." He looked over at me, his sadness now mirroring my own. "I'm sorry, Bit."

"Wow. That really sucks." It wasn't the best response I could give, but it was honest.

"I know," he replied. We were both silent for a little while. "What are we going to do?" He finally said.

"What is there *to* do?" I held my hands up to indicate surrender. "We'll do what we did last year. Ride it out and have a happy reunion at the end of summer." He stood in front of me and I put my feet in the bark to stop my swaying motion. His gray eyes were striking as he looked down at me.

"I don't want to be away from you for that long." Welcome back, butterflies.

"Asher, everything will be ok. It's only a couple months. We'd be bored here anyway. How many times can we sit under the bridge or play basketball?"

"I don't care what we do, Bit. You know that. I just want to spend time with you." He was really sullen now, and even though I was upset that he was leaving hearing how much he was going to miss me made the situation a little more bearable.

"There's nothing you or I can do about it. Being angry won't fix anything. Last year we hardly spoke while you were gone. Maybe this year we can, I don't know, write letters or something. We don't have to be totally separated."

"Just because we didn't talk doesn't mean I wasn't thinking about you all the time," he said, flatly, making me laugh.

"When did you get so open with your emotions?" I said between giggles. "You've never been this mushy about anything. Ever." In the last few weeks he'd said more romantic things to me than I'd ever heard him say. I regretted my comment before it was completely out of my mouth, but could do nothing to stop it from being uttered. I saw his face still and his eyes glaze over with what seemed to be a mixture of sadness and frustration. He crossed his arms over his chest. He stared at me for a few minutes and I could see the sadness creep across the features of his face.

"Asher-"

"I think I need to go home," he said curtly and turned to walk back towards the alley.

"Asher." I stood up from my swing and followed him. "I'm sorry, I didn't mean to hurt your feelings. Will you please stop and talk to me?" I talked to his back as he kept walking, not giving me any indication that he was going to let me apologize to his face. "Asher, stop. Let me apologize." He turned around so quickly that I almost ran into his chest.

"You don't need to apologize, Charlie." I cringed at the use of my given name. It felt wrong coming from his mouth. For almost a year I had been almost exclusively Bit. "If you don't want me to talk about how I feel about you, I won't. It's that simple. I thought we were on the same page. I thought that my going away for an entire summer would bother you in some way, but I'm glad we've straightened this out."

"Calm down, please. I'm sorry," I said, honestly. "This is all new to me too. I've never heard you talk like this before. It just caught me off guard. Please don't be mad." I very cautiously reached down to where his hand lay at his side. I took just the tips of his fingers in mine, hoping he wouldn't pull away. When he let me take it, I moved my hand to fully embrace his palm, squeezing it once our hands were fully linked. "We are on the same page, Asher. It does bother me that we'll be apart for the summer. I'm not going to miss my best friend this summer, I'm going to miss the first boy who ever held my hand, the first boy who ever danced with me. I'm going to miss you."

I saw him breathe out a sign of relief. He pulled me into him and I welcomed the comfort of his chest pressed against my cheek. His arms around my shoulder felt heavy and perfect.

"Are we ok?"

"Yeah, Bit. We're ok."

And we were. He went away for the summer and we both got acquainted with emails. We shared a few phone calls throughout the summer and I was beyond ecstatic when one of the phone calls came on my birthday. I never doubted that he would remember, but it meant a lot more this year than it had in the past. We never lacked for anything to talk about, there were never any awkward pauses, and we never stopped missing each other.

Chapter Seven

"Can I tell you something that might be really embarrassing?" He asked me one night while we were having a rare conversation over the phone. When he was on the farm we didn't get a lot of time to talk to each other.

"Sure..." I answered skeptically. I was laying on my bed, on my back, with my head hanging over the edge.

"Do you remember the last day I was home? When we were both going back to our houses and it was the last time we were going to see each other before I left the next morning?"

"Yeah." I remember that goodbye. It was the most painful and beautiful moment of my life. I didn't cry, but only because I kept pushing my fingernails into the skin of my palm to distract me from the need to release the sadness that was taking over me. I was torn apart that he was leaving, but behind all that, past all the hurt and longing and aching, I was so happy we'd made it to that point. I would miss him *differently* this year, and I would treasure that fact all the months he was gone. I heard him push out a nervous breath and it made me nervous.

"I wanted to kiss you so badly that night." And now my breath was gone all together. I remembered the moment he was talking about. We stood on my front porch after he'd walked me home from sitting under the bridge by the creek for the evening, trying to distract ourselves from our sadness. He picked me up in a giant hug and had held on forever, but not long enough for either of us. He loosened his grip and I slid down his chest, the friction of our bodies and clothing rubbing together causing all kinds of strong yet confusing things to happen to me. He rested his forehead against mine and I could feel the air from his mouth brush against mine. I couldn't see his mouth, but I knew exactly where it was and how far I'd have to move to make my lips press against his. I was scared. I'd never kissed anyone before and I wasn't sure I knew how. I wanted to kiss him so badly, but I couldn't get past the idea that I would mess it up somehow. And just when

I thought I'd gathered up enough nerve to move the inch and half it would take to change my life forever, he pulled away. He placed a tiny kiss on the crown of my head and I sighed, partly in relief and partly in regret.

"I wanted to kiss you too," I whispered. Now I heard him sigh.

"Good. That's good."

"Good?"

"Well, I'm glad that you wanted to kiss me too. But honestly, I'm glad we didn't."

"Why?"

"I didn't want our first kiss to be a goodbye."

Our first kiss took place the day he came back that summer. We planned to meet under the bridge, in our usual spot, after dinner. He had flown in that afternoon, but had to spend some obligatory time with his parents before he thought he could sneak away. I spent the entire day watching the clock. I knew when his plane landed. I knew when he had probably arrived home, and I was filled with nerves knowing he was just a block away, in his house, so close to me.

As I walked to the bridge in the park where we had spent so much time as little kids, I tried hard to determine if I was going to be sick or not. My stomach was in knots, the anticipation of seeing him again was more than I thought I could handle. I placed my hands over my belly and rubbed along the white eyelet fabric of the new dress I had purchased, telling myself it wasn't exclusively for Asher, even though it totally was. I mumbled comforting words to myself that did nothing to comfort me. "Everything is going to be ok. It's just Asher. You've known Asher all your life. He's the same boy you grew up with." But he wasn't. I talked to myself until I looked up and suddenly saw him.

His back was to me as he looked out over the pitiful stream the flowed under the bridge. The sun was setting and it cast an orange hue over everything, making everything glow in a way that only happens in the summer. As if he could sense I was there, he turned and his eyes met mine. My belly continued to flip and flop everywhere and I could feel my hands begin to tremble, but I couldn't stop walking towards him.

I made it to him, stopping when there was very little distance between us, and pushed my hair back behind my ear. I still fiddled with the fabric of my dress, and went to open my mouth to greet him when I felt his finger under my chin. He lifted my face until I was looking up into his slate gray eyes. I watched those eyes as they grew closer and closer, and I saw him close his eyes right before I felt his lips touch mine.

We stood there, Charlie and Asher, best friends since fifth grade, sharing our first kiss.

He was right when he decided our first kiss shouldn't be a goodbye. This hello kiss was perfect. A greeting. A beginning. Something new.

I was so nervous, all my insecurities threatening to take the kiss over. I made myself remember this was Asher and the moment was already perfect. His lips moved against mine slowly and gently. He pressed in harder and I felt my lips slide partially into his mouth as his captured mine. He moved again, his mouth opening slightly, then closing his lips around mine, the contact sending waves of a new kind of pleasure straight to my belly. His hand came up to cradle the back of my head, pressing our mouths together even more. I heard myself let out a small moan against his mouth and I was instantly embarrassed and felt my face flush. I pulled away and put my hand to my mouth, turning away from him.

"I'm sorry," I mumbled through my fingers. I can't believe I just *moaned*, like, right into his mouth.

"Hey," I heard him say as he turned me around by my arm to face him. "Hey, Bit," he said as he ducked down to look at me. "Don't be embarrassed. I'm not embarrassed. That was good. I'm glad you were enjoying yourself." I rubbed my hands over my face and I could feel it was flaming red and hot. "Hey, look at me. Charlie, look at me." I growled in frustration but tilted my head up to look at him. "Hi," he said softly. I couldn't help but smile. "I missed you." I melted a little inside.

"I missed you too, Asher. I'm sorry again. I'm not sure why I did that." He took his hand and ran it through my loose, black hair, causing tingles that made me shiver.

"You were enjoying yourself. There's nothing wrong with that. People like kissing. That's why they do it all the time, I assume. And I'll admit," he said tugging on my hair just a little so that I looked up into his eyes again, "I liked that you were enjoying it so much."

"I'm so glad you're home," I said as I moved into his arms.

"Did you have a good summer?" He asked, his words a little mummbly from his cheek pressed to the top of my head. I shrugged my shoulders and loved the sound of his laughter echoing through his chest. I pulled back from him and saw his eyes glide down my body. It might have been the first time I didn't feel self-conscious about his eyes running over me; I wanted him to look, to see me, to like what he saw.

"Do you like my dress?" I held out the hem of my skirt and gave a little twirl. I heard him swallow and saw his head bob up and down in a nod, his eyes not leaving the flesh of my bare legs. "Good."

He caught himself staring and returned his attention to my face. "Do you want to walk around the park?"

"Sure." He took my hand without hesitation and I was elated. From under the bridge we walked toward the path that led around the park, circling the small pond that was in the center. We strolled along the path talking about our summer apart, filling in the blanks of what we'd already covered in phone conversations and emails. We came up to the gazebo that sat along the shore of the pond and Asher headed in, pulling me along with him.

We went to the far railing, looking out over the water. There were tall cattails sticking up from the water and a few smaller ducks navigating through the tall reeds. I pressed into the railing, hoping to see the swans that sometimes congregated near the shoreline. I felt Asher's chest press against my back and every sense was magnified. The low hum of the crickets turned into an orchestra of chirping, the gentle breeze was now a gust swirling the fragrance of the surrounding flowers around us. But the touch – his body pressed into mine – was my favorite.

"Bit," he said quietly.

"Yes?" I breathed rapidly and hoped he didn't notice, his nearness making it hard to draw air into my lungs normally. I felt like I was starving for oxygen.

"Will you be my girlfriend?"

Of all the words that he could have uttered at that moment, those were some I wasn't expecting.

"You want me to be your girlfriend?"

"Um, yes?" Now he sounded unsure of himself. "Don't you want to be my girlfriend?"

"Um, yes?" I offered, hoping to make him smile by using his words. He did smile, but not as brightly as I would have liked. "But, I don't think I *can* be your girlfriend. Not yet anyhow."

"Let me worry about your dad," he said confidently. I turned to look at him, but his hands remained on the railing, caging me in.

"You think you can convince my dad to let me date you an entire year early?"

"Like I said, let me worry about it." His confidence and demanding words made me fill with warmth.

"I'd love to be your girlfriend," I managed to whisper, still holding his gaze.

"I'd really love to kiss my girlfriend." His mouth came down to meet mine and the last thing I saw before I closed my eyes were his gorgeous eyelashes and dark freckles across his nose. I felt his lips press into mine again and wondered instantly if every kiss for the rest of my life would be better than the last. This kiss felt effortless and perfect. His hands moved from the railing to my waist making the muscles in my abdomen jolt alive with his new touch.

We were exploring each other, but also exploring the idea of kisses. I learned that when I pressed my lips firmly onto his I could make him lose his breath. I heard him inhale so quickly that it seemed as though he was caught off guard by how he felt. I learned that Asher liked to run his fingers through my hair while we kissed and in turn, I enjoyed the feeling of his fingers raking through my long hair just as much.

When I felt his tongue press against the seam of my lips, I hesitated for a moment, but opened for him. At first I was stunned into paralysis. I feared I had no idea what I was doing, but then I felt Asher run the back of his hand along my cheek and knew I could trust him to lead me. I concentrated on matching him and trying not to embarrass myself, but felt all the anxiety was worth it when I felt him slow down. When his mouth came to almost a complete stop and our lips were simply connected, as if he were savoring and cherishing that moment, *that* was when I let my guard down and gave in to the kiss.

Eventually, long after the sun had set, we reluctantly parted, forced from our gazebo by the chill of the summer night. We walked home and Asher kept his arm around my shoulders, which I appreciated because I hadn't thought to bring a sweater.

"So, when we get back to your house I'm going to talk to your dad." Asher sounded determined but also a little scared.

"Tonight?"

"Yeah. I don't want him to think we're sneaking around behind his back. I want to be up front and honest with him. Is that ok with you? Do you mind if I talk to him tonight?"

I shook my head. "No. I don't mind. I'm just not sure how all of this is going to go over with him. You know how he can be, especially when it comes to me."

"It'll be ok."

And it was. That night we went into my house and after Asher asked to speak to my father alone I retreated to my room. I sat there for forty-five minutes in nervous agony. Finally, my bedroom door opened and I saw my father's face as he poked his head around the door.

"Can I come in?"

"Yeah." I sat down on my bed and left enough room for him on the corner.

"So, you and Asher, huh?" He sighed heavily, almost like he had been waiting to exhale for years.

"I guess that's up to you, Daddy."

"So here's the deal, and this deal only pertains to Asher. If you guys decide to break up, you still aren't allowed to date anyone else until you're sixteen, understood?"

"You're going to let me date?" I exclaimed, a little confused but more excited than anything.

"Yes, but there are stipulations." I rolled my eyes at him. Of course there were. "First, you will not be going out alone on dates. If you want to go out with a group of friends, that's fine. But no solo dates. Second, he is no longer allowed in your room, under any circumstance, whatsoever. When he is here, the two of you are in the living room or the kitchen. Third, if you miss curfew even once then you will not be allowed to see him until I say so. I'm serious about this Charlie. There will be no warnings or second chances. Miss curfew once and it might all be over. Lastly, if your grades begin to drop or your attitude changes, I will end it and push dating out even farther than sixteen. Do you understand all of this Charlie?"

"You're going to let me date?" I asked with an excited smile. He groaned and rubbed his hands over his face.

"You're a good kid, Charlie. And I trust you. I trust you to be the daughter that your mother and I raised. I trust you to make good decisions and to come to me if you have any problems or questions." I nodded enthusiastically, knowing that realistically the chances of going to my father about dating problems were slim, but I knew what he meant. I knew I could be with Asher and stay true to who I was. "I also trust Asher. He's proven to me that he understands how important you are to me, and I know he will treat you with the respect that you deserve." I flung myself into his arms and wrapped mine around his neck.

"Thank you, Papa Bear," I whispered in his ear. He groaned again.

"You don't get to call me Papa Bear when I've just agreed to let you have your first boyfriend." I pulled away from him.

"You'll always be my Papa Bear," I said with a scowl. "What did he say to you anyway?"

"That's between him and me. All you need to know is that he came to me in a very grown up and mature way and stated his case. I couldn't argue with him, and he withstood my questioning. I was satisfied with his answers and we came to an agreement." I frowned at him.

"That doesn't sound very romantic. It sounds more like a business arrangement."

"Well, hopefully he's saving all his romance for you," he said while playfully batting his eyelashes at me. I laughed and blushed at the same time. After such a serious conversation it was good to see my dad making jokes. My dad kissed my forehead. "Goodnight, Charlie Bear." He left the room and I sat on my bed trying to wrap my mind around what had just happened.

Asher had done it. He'd convinced my father to let me date. To be his girlfriend. What in the world had Asher said to him? I would have to get him to tell me the next day. I walked over to my vanity and grabbed a hair tie, pulling my long hair back into a pony tail. Once it was secured back, I took a moment to look myself over. I had my first real kiss that evening and also made out with Asher for the first time, and yet I couldn't really see a difference. I guess that was good. No one else would be able to tell that I felt so tremendously changed.

I shrugged my shoulders, switched off the lights, and climbed into bed. My mind was racing and I knew I wasn't going to fall asleep any time soon, but I was content to lay in my bed and let my mind wander over what it meant to be with Asher.

We started our sophomore year as boyfriend and girlfriend, holding hands as we walked down the hallway. And although I felt like everything had changed, apparently no one else in the school felt the same way. I kept waiting for people to mention our new status, or notice us holding hands, but people treated us the same way they always had. At lunch the first day, I asked Reeve about it.

"Don't you think it's weird that no one has noticed that Asher and I are holding hands?"

"What do you mean?"

"I mean, no one seems to notice or care that we're together."

Reeve chuckled and turned to me. "Charlie, you and Asher have been together since fifth grade. Your relationship is only news to you. Everyone else has just been waiting for you guys to figure it out."

So that's what we did. Asher and I figured *us* out. We went to football games, school dances, movies; all the places teenagers should go. We spent most of our time out with groups, but my dad still allowed us to go to the park and the school alone, figuring out in public was safe territory. He was mostly right.

We found private places to kiss. The gazebo, the swings, the tree-covered arch through the alley on the way to the school. There was nothing as exciting as kissing Asher. It was exciting because it was new, at first. Then it became a new kind of exciting. Asher was always, without fail, respectful of me and my body. He never pushed my boundaries and always waited for me to move us forward.

At first, our kisses were sweet. We were so happy to just be kissing each other; that offered enough excitement. But eventually we both realized that a kiss on the neck, or a kiss on the shoulder or the ear, brought on a different kind of excitement. Mouths began to wander, both of ours, and I began to acquaint myself with desire. Slowly, over the year, we explored each other.

One night, about a year into our relationship, an hour before I had to be home, it was dark and we were on a bench far into the park. We hadn't seen anyone in the park for about an hour as it was getting chilly. Asher had his coat unzipped and I had my arms threaded around him, at first to keep warm, but now body heat wasn't an issue. Now I was using my arms to hold him close to me as we made out in the darkness. Without thinking much about it, I moved my hand underneath his shirt and felt everything inside me clench as my fingers came into contact with his bare stomach. He gasped at my touch, seemingly just as surprised as I was that I had made the move. Our lips separated, but only enough to breathe, our faces still touching as my hands remained on his body.

"Is this ok?" I asked him. He nodded.

"Don't stop," he said quickly, then pressed his lips to mine again. There was a new level of passion moving between us and the high it gave me made me brave. I began to move my hands up his torso, feeling the strong muscles of his abdomen. Every ridge bumped between my fingers and it was a new way to see him. I used my hands to paint a picture in my mind of what his chest looked like, memorized his body with my mind as if to draw it later.

I felt his hands gripping my shirt, tugging on it, and I let my bravery make me bolder and I drew his hands up my stomach, trying to give him the go ahead to do a little exploration of his own. His hands moved hesitantly over my ribcage and I felt his fingertips graze the very edge of my bra. The sheer excitement of knowing his hands were so close to my breasts caused all kinds of things to malfunction and go haywire in my body. My arms and legs began to tremble as if I were cold. My heart seemed to be pumping blood quicker than it ever had before, and my mind kept thinking thoughts like, "His hand is near my boob," and "He's going to touch my boob."

When his hand finally made it over the rim of my bra and that first contact happened, I felt him stop breathing. He stopped kissing. He stopped everything. His hand gently rubbed on the underside of my left breast and the rest of our bodies froze. His hand moved up and over the mound and the vibrations his hand made on the cotton fabric brought new zings of arousal to my body. My mouth opened without permission and I made a noise against his lips that sounded like a whimper.

Our faces were just centimeters from each other and I saw his eyes searching for mine. Our eyes connected, our bodies rigid with the new sensations of excitement coursing through us, Asher moved his hand to fully cup me. Gently squeezing, softly gripping, he seemed to be taking great care in familiarizing himself with my breast. His other hand slipped beneath the fabric of my shirt and slid up along my back, the tips of his fingers sneaking beneath my bra strap.

His thumb brushed over my nipple and the jolts of sensation zipped through my whole body, causing me to gasp.

"Is this ok? Are you ok?" Asher asked, his hands stilling.

"Yes," I said as I pressed a kiss against his lips. "It just feels, uh, really good." I instantly felt the heat of my blush creep over my face. His face, however, was overcome with a smug look of satisfaction.

He kissed me again, a little harder than our previous kisses, more insistent. His hands roamed a little more freely, his confidence bolstered by my admission. I felt his hand on my back rubbing against the strap of my bra and I knew he was silently asking for permission to unclasp it. My mind ran at hyper-speed. I loved the way he made my body feel and I wanted him to continue, but I just kept thinking about how I was straddling him on a park bench. Then his thumb did that brush-over-my-nipple thing again and any self-control I thought I had went out the window.

I reached behind my back and unclasped my bra for him, assuming he'd have a hard time with it on his own. My bra hung loosely from my shoulders, only being kept on by the shirt I was still wearing, but he had enough room to sneak his hand beneath the fabric and touch me, skin on skin.

"Are you sure, Bit?"

If my eyes had been open he would have seen me roll them. What kind of girl unclasps her bra and then tells the boy whose lap she's sitting on not to touch? But my arousal and need at the moment prevented my snarky comment from verbalizing. I just nodded and said, "Please." My voice sounded strained and deep. I don't recall ever hearing my voice like that before. He didn't waste any time and I felt him move his hand beneath the underwire, his soft fingertips slowly moving over the bare skin of my breast. His other hand came from behind my back and moved to tend to the neglected one.

He stopped kissing me and it seemed he couldn't actually do two things at once at the moment. He pressed his forehead against mine, his hands holding me, and I tried to ignore the hardness I felt building beneath me. I felt his erections before, but never once had I been brave enough to talk about them, let alone try to touch him.

It was my turn to wear a smug grin. He seemed to be lost in me, really enjoying the moment. His hands moved slowly, but covered a lot of ground. Suddenly, I felt him firmly pinch both of my nipples and give them a gentle tug.

"Ah!" I yelped, half in surprise and half in a state of why-the-hell-does-that-feel-so-good? He instantly stopped at my gasp and rubbed his thumbs over them. I was thrown into a new level of sensation overload and bit my lip to try and not cry out again. An "Mmmmm" did manage to slip past my lips which seemed to catch his attention and his mouth found mine again. He began kissing me while lazily thumbing my nipple with one hand. His other hand slid down my back and found its way just inside the waistband of my jeans. He must have felt me tense at the thought of his hand inside my jeans because he stopped there and concentrated on the hand inside my shirt.

He kneaded and cupped my breast all while kissing me passionately. I felt a familiar pinching feeling between my legs; I experienced it more and more frequently with Asher. It felt as though a rubber band was being stretched tightly inside of me, right at the juncture of my thighs, and that at any moment it could snap from all the pressure. This time, the delicious tight and pinching feeling was accompanied by a new warmth, a hot wetness. Part of me was embarrassed by these new things my body seemed to be doing all on its own, but most of me didn't care at the moment and could only concentrate on Asher and his hands and mouth.

When I finally pulled away from him, not really wanting to go home, but knowing it was getting late, Asher pulled me to his chest and held me for a moment. This gave my body a chance to calm down and my mind a chance to sabotage me. I started wondering how he felt about me and my body, now that he'd had a chance to feel me. As he often did, he noticed the change in my body, my muscles tensing as my mind ran away with itself.

"What are you thinking, Bit?"

I shook my head slightly, still resting in the crook of his neck.

"Talk to me. Please." He sounded concerned.

I shrugged my shoulders and I heard him exhale loudly. He grabbed my shoulders and pushed me back and away from him, trying to see my face.

"What is going on up there?" He asked, now a little irritated.

"I don't know. I'm just a little worried." That was the best I could give him.

"Worried about what, exactly?" It took me a few moments to build up enough courage to answer him, but I knew he wouldn't accept my dodging any more of his questions.

"I'm just worried that I'm not, that my body's not, what you like."

"You think I don't like your body?"

"No," I said exasperated. "Yes." I sighed. "I don't know." I breathed in and out a few times and then looked him in the eyes. "I *think* you enjoyed that, I mean, I could, uh, *feel* you enjoying it. But I'm not stupid enough to think that any sixteen-year-old guy wouldn't enjoy feeling a girl up. I guess I am just worried that I'm not what you want."

"What do you think I want? I'm here with you, Bit. Why would I want to be anywhere else?"

I shrugged.

"I don't know. Maybe you like girls with bigger boobs or girls who have bigger butts. How will I ever know if every time you put your hand up my shirt that you're not wishing I had a little more, uh, boobage?"

"Boobage?" He asked, chuckling.

"Don't laugh, Asher! This is serious. You didn't say one word while your hand was up there. That left a lot of room for interpretation."

"I didn't say anything because my brain was malfunctioning. I was living the dream I'd been having for months, maybe years, when my girlfriend let me get to second base."

"Well, a little positive reinforcement would have been appreciated. I was practically moaning and *grinding* on your lap and you gave no indication that you enjoyed my boobage." I had to admit, I was being a little bit of a brat, but sometimes insecurities brought out the ugliness in me. I was glad he smiled at my new word. I didn't want him angry; I really just wanted reassurance.

"Babe, you're perfect. I couldn't imagine a girl more perfect for me. And as for your boobage and granting me the supreme privilege of rounding the next base in our relationship, well, I really *really* enjoyed it. Really," he said, bumping his forehead lightly against mine. I reached behind me to clasp my bra and then laid my hands on his chest.

"Could you just do me a favor and remember, for future occasions, that sometimes a girl needs a little reassurance?" He tilted his head a little and had a confused look on his face.

"I will do my best to give you whatever you need, but I think you're missing something here, Bit." He pushed my hair off my forehead, sliding his fingers behind my ears, securing my windblown hair. "I never look at you, at your body, and wish for something else. You're all I've ever wished for, all I could ever hope for. When I'm touching you, when you let me put my hands on your skin, the only thought running through my head is how lucky I am that I get to be the one, how lucky I am that you've let me close to you in this way. I'll be forever grateful for the privilege of *you*."

My heart fluttered and my insides melted. I was the lucky one.

"Come on," I said as I pressed a kiss to his lips quickly. "We better get going." I stood up from his lap and started walking down the path towards the bridge we spent so many days under throughout our lives. He was a few steps behind me as I was trying to give him a little room to calm down from our new base rounding. I heard footsteps rushing up next to me and I felt him take my hand, but he didn't slow down and started pulling me towards the bridge. I had no choice but to keep up with him, a smile growing across my face at his playfulness. We ran down the embankment and ducked under the clearance of the bridge.

Suddenly, Asher pushed me up against the wooden support, our bodies hidden from view. It was dark under the bridge, most of the light blocked, but I could just make out his silhouette. His face was close to mine and I could feel his breath puffing out against my lips. I felt his hands come to cradle my face and he pressed a tiny, gentle kiss to the very corner of my mouth.

"When you run from me it makes me crazy," he whispered. I tried to swallow the lump that appeared in my throat.

"I wasn't running from you," I answered.

"Yes, you were. The conversation got deep and you took off. What are you afraid of?"

I thought about his question. What was I afraid of? Nothing. Everything. My hands came to rest upon his forearms and I felt his thumb start to slide back and forth across my cheek, silently comforting me, giving me courage to answer his question.

"I'm afraid that I'll let you in, you'll see me, and you'll realize that you don't want me anymore."

He pressed his mouth against mine again, slowly and softly. He stopped kissing me, but didn't pull away, leaving his mouth resting against mine.

"I love you," he promised against me.

My heart hammered in my chest and my hands gripped his arms. His mouth pressed into mine again, kissing me until my mind could wrap around what he'd said.

He loved me.

We never said those words to each other before, never verbalized what I felt so deep in my body and soul. It was never necessary. I knew how I felt about him and hoped that he felt the same way. Hearing him say he loved me brought me a lightness and euphoria I didn't know I was missing. His mouth pulled away from mine again, this time far enough away that I could catch my breath.

"I love you Bit. I love everything about you: your mind, your mouth, your body, your sense of humor, your hair." He slid his hands back through my long hair as he rattled of his list. My eyes closed at the sensations of his hands sliding down my hair, but also because I wanted to hear him; I was listening with everything I was. "I love you, in every sense of the word, in every capacity imaginable."

"I love you too" I whispered. It was so quiet, I wasn't sure he heard me, but he pressed his lips to my mouth and I felt him smiling.

Part II

Chapter One

"Charlie, it's time to go soon. Are you ready?" I heard my father yelling up the stairs to me. I looked around my room. Even though all my furniture remained, along with most of the decorations hanging on the wall, the room seemed empty. I tried to push away the sadness that was trying to force its way in, but found it difficult to focus on the exciting parts of leaving for college. I just kept thinking about my father here all alone. He didn't deserve to be alone. I gave my room one last look and headed down the stairs with my overly-stuffed duffel bag.

"Dad, I think I should stay here and just go to the community college," I said as I met his eyes. He cocked his head at me and smiled.

"Charlie Bear, I will be fine. You've worked too hard to go to the community college. Besides, Reeve and Asher will be with you too. This is going to be the most exciting thing you've ever done. Don't think you have to stay here to keep me company."

"I just don't want you to be alone." The thought of my dad spending every evening by himself was devastating. I looked over at his recliner, which he already spent too much time in already, and had images of him sulking in it every night. It made something inside my chest squeeze my heart. My dad deserved to be happy, not lonely.

"Just because you won't be around all the time doesn't mean I'll be a sad, pathetic lump on the recliner. I promise. Besides, who's to say I'm not just waiting for you to be out of the house before I turn into an eligible bachelor." He raised an eyebrow at me, obviously trying to make me smile. I smiled for him, but not because what he said was funny, but because what he said was true. My dad was an eligible bachelor. In his mid-forties, he was devastatingly handsome. He still maintained his built physique simply by working at his construction job, his dark salt-and-pepper hair made him look distinguished and dapper. I only ever saw him wearing blue jeans and tee shirts but once, for my senior banquet a few months ago, I saw him in a suit and I almost didn't recognize him. Even all of my friends at the event commented on how handsome he was. I always knew he was good-looking, but just recently I accepted that he was truly beautiful.

"Are you going to start dating?" I asked curiously. He hadn't been on a date in all of my eighteen years except, of course, with my mother. He shrugged his shoulders, a trait I picked up from him, and looked away from me, perhaps a little embarrassed.

"I don't know. Maybe. I was thinking about it." His head dropped low as he tried his best to keep his eyes from mine. "Would that bother you?" My heart hurt for him.

"No, Daddy. I won't mind. You deserve to be happy. Mom wouldn't want you to be alone." Silence fell over both of us at the mention of my mother. It was still hard to think about her being gone, but the truth was, it had been eight years since she passed. My dad put his sadness aside and had done an admirable job raising me alone ever since. I couldn't fully grasp what it had taken for him to pull himself up and be both parents. I knew that some days were harder than others for him, but he was the best dad I could have ever asked for, and that made it difficult to leave him, even though I knew I needed to. "I'll be back to visit soon, Dad. Corbett is only a few hours from here," I said trying to move us out of the painful memories of my mother.

"You better," he said with his wonderful smile, and I knew he would be ok. We both heard the honking from the driveway and I knew Reeve arrived to drive us away from the town we had done most of our growing up in. "I can't believe I let you and Reeve talk me into letting you take yourselves to college. I'm supposed to go with you, move you in to your dorm, say goodbye."

"We don't need a sappy goodbye, Dad. I don't want that. Just give me a hug and tell me you'll miss me." I smiled at him, trying to ease the situation that was turning out to be more painful than I anticipated. He came up to me and wrapped his giant, warm, papa-bear arms around me. I snuggled into his broad chest and breathed in his scent.

"I'm going to miss you," he whispered into my hair. I felt the familiar pinch in my throat as I tried to keep from crying. "Don't be too crazy, but have fun. Make sure you don't walk home alone after dark and remember that you can always call me." I smiled at his sentiment, worried about me always.

"I love you, Daddy," I said into his chest.

"I love you too, Charlie Bear." I felt him kiss the top of my head then pull away and quickly turn from me to pick up my bags. I suspected he was also trying to hide his face from me, afraid to show me how much it hurt saying goodbye. I didn't need to see his face to know his pain, because I was feeling it too. I turned to the door and pulled it open to see Reeve sitting in her open driver's side window, half hanging out of her car.

"Are you ready to party, Charlie?!" She yelled from where her car sat on the street. My dad stepped out behind me and a panicked look crossed her face. "I mean, uh, are you ready to study so hard we have no energy to even think about parties?" She said with a smile, halfway trying to cover what she said, but understood that it was a lost cause.

"Reeve, I'm going to pretend I didn't hear that, and then I'm going to tell you what I told Charlie. Be careful. College is going to be exciting and fun, but you have to be smart too. And you can always call me if you need something."

"Thanks, Papa Bear," she said sweetly, sliding back down into her seat. Reeve was the only other person on the planet that called my dad Papa Bear and she's the only one I would allow it from. Reeve had both of her parents, but that didn't stop my dad from treating her like one of his own, and I loved him even more for it.

He loaded all my bags into the trunk of Reeve's SUV and then pulled me into another hug, though this one was shorter and more playful.

"When is Asher getting there again?"

"He left yesterday. He'll be there to help us move in."

"Good. Make sure he watches out for you."

"Like I have to even ask him," I said rolling my eyes.

"I know. I know," he said and then paused. "I'm proud of you, Charlie. Have fun. And call your father."

"I will, Dad. I love you."

"I love you too."

The three-hour drive flew by, as any road trip with Reeve tended to do. She either talked a million miles per hour, or sang along to some pop song, and I was usually observing. It was dangerous to try and interrupt her long rambling monologues. I've been steamrolled many times in the past. So I usually just listened and nodded, giving her the occasional "uh huh," when the time called for it. She was in her element when she had someone who had no choice but to give her their undivided attention. I didn't mind. She was my best friend. As much as she spoke, she listened when I needed her to. And she understood me more than I was willing to think about or examine.

When we finally pulled up to the university, I couldn't believe the amount of cars that were all trying to fit down the exact same street that we were headed. My first instinct was to regret not having my dad come with us. This was stressful and I wished he was there to lead the way so that I could just follow behind. I took a deep breath and readied myself. This was life now. I was an adult. It was time to start taking charge. I missed my dad.

All the apprehension I felt seemed to float away at the sight of Asher on the side of the road. He was up the street a bit, standing on the side of the road, between two orange construction cones. I watched from our car, crawling along at a snail's pace, as a few cars tried to park between the cones. He waved them away with a smile that clearly said, "Move along". He even used his hand to wave one or two away. When he spotted Reeve's SUV, he stepped a little farther into the street and started waving at us. My smile grew even bigger.

"Wipe the grin off your face Charlie; it's making me gag."

"Come on, that's totally sweet," I said as I motioned towards him with my hands.

"Barf," she responded. I knew she was kidding. She loved Asher almost just as much as I did. And even though she wouldn't admit it, his devotion to me, at the moment, was benefiting her just as much as it was me.

Once we finally made it to the reserved parking spot, Reeve expertly slid her SUV into the space, executing a perfect parallel parking job. I swung my door open and was met by Asher and his heart-stopping grin.

"Hey, Bit," he said. I beamed at his nickname for me. He came up to me and I wrapped my arms around his neck as his hands slid around my waist. "Like your personal parking spot?"

"Hmmm. How did you manage to pull it off? Why didn't anyone from the university make you leave?"

"I can be persuasive when I need to be," he said, smiling even bigger. I knew then that whoever had tried to get him to leave was female and he'd been able to charm them into looking past his irritatingly cute behavior.

"Lucky me," I said and tipped up to kiss his lips. He came down to me, because even if I stood on the very tip of my toes I would never be able to reach his mouth, the height difference between us was at least a foot. I thought back to a day when we were the same height, fond memories of our childhood. Memories that were brushed away by the sweetness of his kiss.

When he pulled away, he pointed towards a table set up with official people sitting behind it.

"You get your keys at that table over there. I will grab your bags."

Reeve and I headed towards the table and stood in line with other students who were flanked by their parents. Did I rob my dad of some rite of passage by coming alone? I felt a twinge of guilt looking at all the parents helping their children get their keys. I also saw the tears forming in their mother's eyes, and their dads patting their sons on the back, trying to avoid an over-emotional goodbye. I asked my dad not to come, in part, because I didn't want a sad goodbye. But I also didn't want him here to witness all the men who still had their wives. Times like these only served as reminders that my mother was no longer alive. He didn't need that - not today.

"Perfect!" Reeve exclaimed as we made our way to the dorm room we'd been assigned. "Our room is right next to the bathroom!"

"Ugh," I remarked. "Our room is right next to the bathroom."

"What's wrong with that? It's great. We won't have to walk down a long hall dripping wet and hiding in a towel. We can just run into our room." As if he had been summoned by her words, a guy came out of the bathroom wearing only a towel with beaded water still hanging on his chest. He gave us a brief look and then threw a wink our way.

"Uh, why is there a half-naked guy on your floor?" I shrugged my shoulders at Asher as he moved past me to put my bags on my bed.

"I'm sure he lives on this floor. He went into one of those rooms down there," I said as I motioned down the hallway. I saw his shoulders stiffen and watched as he slowly turned towards me.

"This is a co-ed *floor*?" I shrugged again, not wanting to say anything that would make him upset. "No shrugging, Bit. Words."

"I thought I mentioned the dorm was co-ed."

"Right. You said the *dorm* was co-ed, not the floor." He ran his hands through his dark hair. He took in a deep breath and then let it out slowly. I saw some of the tension leave his body, but he was still wound tightly. I crossed the room to him and noticed Reeve slipping out of the room to give us a moment.

"Ash, I'm sorry. I guess I didn't think to distinguish between the two. I wasn't trying to keep anything from you." I stood right next to him and I put my hand out to touch his arm. At our contact he turned towards me and I felt his hands come up to cradle my face.

"Why will you let total strangers live with you, but not me?"

My breath came out quickly, letting on that I was annoyed by his question. It was a discussion we'd had all summer long. Asher desperately wanted to share a dorm room, to live together our freshman year of college. I desperately wanted to have a normal college experience and share a dorm room with my best friend. Somehow, for some reason, he took this as rejection and it made him upset. Every time he brought it up, we argued. He eventually dropped the subject, but I always felt it was more because he was tired of talking about it rather than him being secure in our separation.

"You've got to stop this. Just because I don't want to live with you doesn't mean I don't love you or want to be with you." He looked into my eyes like I hid the secret meaning of life in them. He searched for something. I wasn't sure I had the answer he was looking for. "What can I do to make you understand that I need this year? I need to live with my best friend. I need to have this experience. We're only going to be college freshmen once, Ash. We have this one chance. Don't ruin it by being jealous. You've got no reason to be. Tell me, what can I do?" He exhaled loudly again and rested his forehead against mine.

"Promise me you won't walk down the hall in a towel?" I could hear the smile in his voice.

"Will you buy me a bathrobe?" I asked, only half joking.

"I'll buy you a damn muumuu," he said, a full laugh escaping his lips. I relaxed, knowing the argument was past us. He pressed his lips to my forehead. "I'm sorry," he said seriously.

"Everything's changing and I just don't want us to drift apart. I am afraid you'll feel like I'm holding you back. I'm trying to hold on to you because I'm afraid you'll slip away." I looked up into his eyes wondering how he could doubt anything about our relationship.

"Everything is changing, Asher. We are changing. But that doesn't mean we can't change together. I want us to experience everything together. And we will get our chance to live together, just not this year." I paused, hoping that finally he was taking in what I was saying to him.

He kissed the tip of my nose and then quickly moved away again.

"Let's get your stuff unpacked and then I'll take you to the frat." And just like that, he seemed fine again. I shook my head at him slightly, marveling at his ability to go from angry to fine from one moment to the next. When Reeve finally came back to the room, she had an iced coffee in one hand and was furiously texting with the other.

"There is a coffee shop just three blocks over. And there were so many cute boys along the way! I got three phone numbers just on the way there." Reeve was, for lack of a better word, boy-crazy. She was constantly dating, most of the time more than one boy at a time, and she had no shame about it at all.

"Pace yourself, Reeve. We've been here a total of one hour. There will be plenty of time to meet guys."

"We're headed over to the house in a few minutes. Do you want to come with us?" Asher asked her. I rolled my eyes at both of them. The last place Reeve needed to be was a frat house.

"I have been waiting all summer to go to a frat house," she said wistfully. This time Asher rolled his eyes too.

"Well," I said, trying to sound excited. "Let's get this over with."

Asher was what you'd call a "Legacy". His father and uncle were both members of Gamma Beta Phi, and his cousin was a current member. Therefore, even though freshman weren't usually allowed to move into the house until after rush, Asher was given special privileges and given a room without question. He would eventually share it with whichever freshman was assigned as his roommate, but for the next two weeks he got it all to himself. Both his father and uncle made very generous annual donations to the house, so none of the brothers batted an eyelash at us as we walked in; he was as much a brother as any of the rest of them.

We drove by the house before, when we'd come to visit the campus during our senior year, but I'd never been inside before. We stood in a room that looked like it was used as a dining room. There were tables similar to those found in our high school's cafeteria with attached benches. The house smelled like beer. There was no other way to describe it – well, beer and boy. It was a distinct smell, not bad or good, but *there*.

Asher led us through the rest of the house pointing out different rooms, but they all looked similar. Pretty much empty, sparse furniture, and pretty gross. It was as if for the last ten years they hadn't really given the place a good cleaning. There was no garbage or clutter, but no one had taken a mop to the floors in ages, cleaned the windows, or even thought about plugging in an air freshener. Our shoes made crackling noises as they were ripped from the sticky floors as we walked.

"Do all the frat houses look like this?" I asked, wrinkling my nose.

"Like what?" He asked, completely unaware of the state of his new living area.

"Like a bunch of college boys live here." I answered, rolling my eyes. "Babe, this place is gross." Asher looked completely shocked and a little hurt.

"You don't like it? It's huge. And fratty." I could tell he was a little upset that I wasn't in love with the house, and I felt a little bad that I'd let my first impressions slip out to him. He didn't need me telling him I didn't like his frat house. He looked forward to being in this frat for as long as I had known him. I slipped my hand into his and gave him a gentle squeeze.

"It's definitely fratty," I said with a smile. "It could just use a cleaning," I said as sweetly as I could.

"Well, I'm sure once all the rushes are picked, they will have us scrubbing the whole house from top to bottom. That's what rush week is all about – being their bitches." I nodded in understanding, trying not to let my face show how disgusting I thought it would be to have to clean the house. Just then a guy and a girl walked down the wide staircase that led into the foyer. They stopped on the bottom step and the blonde girl turned to kiss the guy on the cheek.

"I'll see you later?" She asked, her hand lingering on his chest.

"Yeah. Sure. I'll call you." He smiled at her, but even I could see his smile was forced and fake. She smiled at him, lingering on the bottom step, but eventually turned towards us, heading for the door. Her eyes stopped on Asher and her smile grew even wider.

"Hello, Asher," she crooned at him.

"Hey, Tracy," he said politely. Her eyes wandered down his body as she took him in and I found my hand sliding into his, gripping it tightly. She winked at him and then pushed past us, leaving through the sliding door.

"Hey, Asher. Giving the grand tour?" The guy on the stairs asked with a smile. He was obviously older, an upperclassman. He had blonde hair that swooped over to one side and striking blue eyes. I saw Reeve perk up at his entrance and she adjusted her posture, pulling her shoulders back, pushing her chest out even further. Shameless.

"Hey, Caleb. I was just showing the girls around. This is Charlie, my girlfriend, and our friend Reeve," he said gesturing towards us. Caleb smiled at me but his eyes moved over to Reeve with interest.

"Reeve, huh? That's an interesting name. Is it short for something?" Her eyes lit up with his attention.

"Nope. My parents were just trying to make sure I didn't have the same name as anyone else."

"Gotcha. Do you go to CU?" He leaned up against the wall and crossed his arms over his chest.

"Charlie and I are freshman this year," she said.

"Will you be rushing a house?" The side of Caleb's mouth turned up with his question. Reeve absentmindedly started twirling a piece of hair around her finger.

"Charlie and I are both going to rush, and just pray we get into the same house."

"Ah, I'm sure you'll be fine," he said.

I felt Asher's face come in close to mine and his breath on my ear sent shivers down my spine.

"Come on," he whispered. "I'll show you my room." He tugged on my hand as he pulled me towards the stairs. As we walked past Caleb he gave Asher a nod and I heard him ask Reeve if he could give her the rest of the tour. I smirked because I couldn't decide which of them was in for more trouble. I followed Asher up two flights of winding stairs and then we walked down a long and narrow hallway lined with closed doors. It looked very much like our dorm. He stopped at a room and used a key to open the door. He swung the door open and let me enter first.

I was surprised, and relieved, that his room seemed much cleaner than the rest of the house. It was pretty simple – two beds, two dressers, one window. I could tell which side was his because I recognized the familiar comforter on his twin-sized bed. I sat down and ran my hand over the bedding, not expecting to feel so homesick all of a sudden. I'd only been gone a matter of hours. Asher knelt down in front of me and pushed my knees open so he was wedged in between my legs, his hands spread on top of my thighs.

"You ok?" He asked, always ridiculously in tune to how I was feeling. I put a smile on my face.

"Yes, I just didn't expect to see your bedding here. Made me sad for a minute." He looked a little confused and started rubbing his hands up and down the tops of my legs.

"Why sad?"

I shrugged.

"I guess it just caught me off guard. Seeing something from home mixed in with your new room – it just makes it really obvious that we're not at home anymore."

"Bit," he said sweetly as he tucked a piece of my long hair behind my ear, "It will be ok. We will go home and visit all the time. You'll see. In a few days you won't even notice that you're not at home." I smiled at him, not willing to tell him that it would take more than a couple of days to convince myself that my dad would be ok by himself. "Besides," he said as he leaned in closer to me. "There are advantages to being here." My eyes closed by their own will when his lips connected to my neck.

"Hmmm, and what would those advantages be?" I asked, my own voice sounded breathy and far away. He didn't answer with words but with his mouth trailed kisses up and down my neck. Like every other time he had his mouth on me, my heart beat wildly in my chest and my breathing came in rapid short pants. He pressed my shoulders back until I was laying on the bed and he pulled my shirt up so that it bunched up underneath the edge of my bra. I felt his big hands glide over my stomach and then his lips were on the sensitive skin around my belly button.

"Ash?" I groaned.

"Hmm?"

"Ash, Reeve could come up here any minute." I don't know why I even tried to stop him, especially when I knew I really didn't want him to. I wanted his hands on me, his mouth. I always felt the connection between us, even in the mundane. Sitting on the couch watching a movie, I felt it. Holding his hand as he drove us to dinner, I felt it. Fighting with him about stupid shit, yeah, I felt it then too. I always felt it. There were invisible cords that tied us together and I loved feeling the pulling and tugging on them as we navigated through life together. But when we physically connected, everything was in Technicolor. His breath on my skin was a thousand feathers. His hand running along my thigh was a thousand hot and knowing hands, overwhelming and welcomed. He was the first person I ever let touch me, the only one to ever touch me. I knew I'd do anything to make sure that stayed true for the rest of my life.

"Caleb is with her and she'll never be able to find this room anyway," he said between kisses on the soft tissue of my waist, his mouth skirted too close to the top of my shorts to allow my body to do anything but writhe underneath him. "Please," he whispered against me asking permission, his nose inhaling me as it swept across my skin. I reached down and took his face in my hands and pulled him up to my mouth. Once our lips crashed together everything intensified and was frantic. His hands were no longer enough; his lips not giving me the relief I was searching for; the weight of him on top of me not heavy enough to keep me from floating away.

I tugged on the hem of his tee shirt, pulling it up over his head, and allowing him to do the same to me. At the sight of me in my bra I heard a groan escape from him before he came back down to kiss me senseless once again. This is how it was between us. There was always a line, and once we crossed it, there was no going back. There was inevitably some floodgate and once opened, everything came crashing through. Then, most of the time, it was a competition. Who could kiss the deepest? Who could make the other moan the loudest? Who could last the longest before they gave in to the pleasure? It wasn't a bad game to play, but it had gotten us into some tricky situations in the past. And I was well aware that I usually lost these battles. Asher and I had spent the last year exploring our sexuality with each other, and there was nothing about my body he wasn't absolutely and acutely tuned in to.

His hands moved down to the button of my jean shorts and he expertly pulled them open and slipped them off of me, not even leaving my panties behind. He was obviously in a hurry and who was I to slow him down? He leaned back onto his knees with his trademark smirk on his face. He knew he'd won the first silent contest; he'd gotten me to give in. He slowly unbuttoned his jeans and pushed them down to his knees, then fell forward again onto his hands so he was hovering above me and I used my feet to push them the rest of the way off. He began his slow trail of kisses again, down my belly, choosing one leg to follow all the way to the knee, then made his way back up. All the while I reached behind my back, unclasped my bra and threw it to the floor wanting to be rid of it. As soon as my breasts were free from the lace, they were covered again by his hands.

Looking down at him, all I could see were his brown locks of hair and strong shoulders. His mouth was still working on my stomach and thighs, and now his hands were kneading my breasts feeling heavier by the minute. This was all very lovely, but it wasn't nearly enough.

"Asher." That was all I needed to say. He knew what I was asking for. He also wasn't going to give it to me so easily. I saw him tilt his head up just enough so that I could see the smile in his eyes. I tried to maneuver myself to find something that would help me relieve the pressure. My knees spread wider and I could feel his hardness between us. My hips thrust upwards, searching for him, and I swear I heard him chuckle as he moved his body farther down mine, making the friction I was looking for impossible.

I won a small victory when I felt his breath on my core – hot gusts of air. He was contemplating, weighing his options, trying to decide if he'd rather taste me or continue his torture. I smiled because I knew what his decision would be and I was happy to wait the few seconds until he came to the same conclusion he always did. I felt his hands on the insides of my thighs, holding me open. A low and guttural moan escaped me as his tongue took its first glide along my opening. My back arched and my hips tilted as if to eliminate the space between us. The swirling of his tongue only intensified as he used his thumbs to spread me open further. There was nothing left between us, just him and me. And then I watched as his dam broke, his floodgate opened, he crossed his line.

He sucked at me with unmatched fervor. The rhythm he created, switching between teeth and tongue, licking and sucking, was enough to make my legs quake and eyes roll back in my head. All I could do was thread my fingers through his hair, tug on it to hold his mouth to my core, and try not to scream and shout loud enough for anyone else in the house to hear.

"Oh, God. Asher..." This was my mantra. I wasn't religious, but everything became holy when I was with him.

"You taste so fucking good," he murmured against me, then went back to his ministrations. It could have been seconds or hours or minutes, but eventually I came. I crashed. I fell.

I breathed heavily as he made his way back up to me with his eager smile because he knew what was waiting for him. I tried not to smile back at him, but it was impossible.

"Hi," I said softly as I swept my hand through his hair damp from sweat.

"Hey," he replied with an equally soft voice. His forehead came to my cheek and he rubbed along me until his face came to rest in the crook of my neck. I felt the tiniest kisses along my skin as I wrapped my ankles around his thighs, tilted my hips to just the right angle, and guided him into me. Once he was all the way in, once I could feel him stretching and filling me, he paused. I felt his breath, hilted and uneven, against my neck.

"Why does it feel this way?" He whispered against my skin. His voice sounded strange - strained and emotional.

"Feel what way?"

"So perfect," he answered. My arms came around his back and I tried to pull him closer to me, but I couldn't. We were already pressed together fully - nothing between us.

"It's perfect because it's right," I replied, running my fingers through the hair at the nape of his neck. My breath was stolen from me as he started to draw out and slowly pump back in. He started a torturously slow rhythm that my body both loved and hated. I met every thrust and was still needing more.

"Asher, please, faster or harder. I need something." He took my request and quickened his pace and strengthened his stride. He pushed me higher and higher. His strong thrusts coupled with his loving touches never ceased to create a frenzy within me. I was gripping his back, tilting my hips up as if to offer him every part of me, and he was always willing to take. His hands were never still, always searching for the touches that set me off, the caresses that made me tremble. Our bodies fit each other, sliding against one another, coated in a sheen of sweat. When his thrusting hips found the spot within me that made me cry out, he honed in on it and drove into me with fiercely sharp blows. He groaned as he drove into me and I couldn't hang on any longer. I felt my muscles clamp down on him, my legs quaking as my orgasm ripped through my body.

He grunted at my release, still thrusting into me, giving me every opportunity to feel him as I came. On the tail end of my release I heard him groan again and then he stilled, his breaths panting out over me, prickling my skin. After he emptied himself into me he collapsed, his face finding the crook of my neck, making me smile lazily.

I knew he needed a minute to come back to me. He always did. I took the opportunity to trail my fingers down his back, trying to soothe him and also calm myself. I felt him exhale heavily and smiled as he kissed my neck sweetly.

"Hold on, Bit." He pulled up and jumped off the bed. I watched as he started digging through a box near the door, pulling out a box of tissues. He came back to me and used a tissue to clean me up, a gesture that I found heart shattering and intensely intimate. He threw the tissue in the trash can and then laid back down next to me. I curled into his side, resting my head on his chest and throwing my leg over his. I felt him begin to run his fingers through my impossibly long hair. The tingles rushing down my spine from the sensations of him not only touching my hair, but my hair brushing against my naked skin as it fell from his hand. "This is what our life will be like now, Bit. We have complete freedom." I looked up at him and saw a wide smile on his face. "We can be together whenever we want. No more sneaking around, or sex in the backseat of a car, trying to hurry before you hit curfew," he said with a laugh.

"Hey, some of our best times have been hurried and in the backseat," I said, pretending to be offended. He kissed my forehead.

"I know. But I'm excited to just be with you. Whenever I want. And I'm not just talking about sex. We can sleep in the same bed. We can walk to school together. We can shower together if we want. We can just be." My heart warmed with his words. I had been thinking the same things all summer. We had been together for so many years already, but now we were starting a new reality. Everything would be different. Better.

"It's going to be great," I whispered. Just then we both heard Reeve calling our names from somewhere in the hallway. I laughed. "But Reeve will always be around to interrupt, so that's not changing." I heard him groan in annoyance, but he got up anyway and started putting his clothes back on. She knocked on the door just as I was putting my shirt on and pulling my hair free from the neck of it.

Chapter Two

We had survived our first few weeks at college and Homecoming was this weekend. Reeve and I got ready for the big football game in our room. The actual football game wasn't the big attraction, our team actually sucked. It was a big game because the Greek system held a parade during halftime and the student body voted on the best float. Delta Phi Beta, the sorority Reeve and I both ended up rushing, won the last five years in a row so the pressure was on to deliver again this year. Reeve, myself, and all the other freshman pledges worked countless hours on the float and I was confident that we had it in the bag.

So far I wasn't finding it difficult to balance classes, Reeve, new friends, the sorority, and time with Asher. Although, if you asked him, he would complain that we didn't see each other enough. I loved that he wanted to see me as much as possible, but sometimes it just didn't work. I was, however, sad that I hadn't been back home to visit my dad yet. When I called and spoke to him, I always told him I would come home soon, and he always told me not to rush and that he was doing fine. He told me during one of our talks that he went out to coffee with a woman he'd met on some online dating site. I cheerily said, "That's great!" and then changed the topic so quickly I almost gave myself whiplash. I knew it was good for Dad to date, but I guess I wasn't ready to hear him talk about it. I knew he wanted me to make him feel like it was ok, but it just wasn't something I could do in the moment and I felt bad about that.

A knock on the door drew me out of my thoughts. I pulled the door open and smiled as Asher stood on the other side. He looked amazing with his dark jeans and black tee shirt that hugged his chest and biceps in just the right way. I loved it when he wore black. It added to the darkness of his eyes and hair.

"Hi," I said as I kissed him quickly on the cheek. When I pulled away, he grabbed my arm and hauled me back to him, my hair swinging around behind me. One of his hands ended up around my waist and the other hand gently came up to the side of my face. The smile on his face melted me a little, and the intense way he looked in my eyes made my belly flip in way I had grown use to when it came to him.

"I need more than a simple kiss on the cheek," he said and brought his lips to mine. The kiss started out simple and innocent, but the longer his lips moved against mine, the longer his tongue teased mine, the deeper and more intense the kiss became. His hand left my waist and I felt him grip my hair at the base of my neck and slide it to the end near the curve at the small of my back. A slight moan escaped me and I felt him smile against me.

"Guys, seriously, we don't have time for this." As quickly as his smile spread across his face, it left. I felt his irritation grow. He put his forehead against mine and he exhaled loudly.

"Do you always have to ruin everything?" He asked of her. I pulled back and gave him an annoyed look. Reeve definitely had a tendency to interrupt us, but she didn't do it on purpose and in this instance she had a point.

"Hey," I said a little more angrily than I had anticipated. "Don't talk to her like that. This is her room too and she has every right to be here." He rolled his eyes and dropped his hands to his sides.

"Sorry, Reeve. That was rude of me." Reeve eyed him suspiciously.

"You've been touchy lately, Asher." Her eyes moved back over to me. "You would think he wasn't getting any." Then she laughed. She called over her shoulder as she left the room, "I'll see you at the house, Charlie. Maybe you guys should finish what you started." I heard her laughing all the way down the hallway and into the stairwell.

"What's your problem?" I asked him as I moved across the room to grab my purse and jacket. "Reeve is right. You've been particularly grouchy the last couple of days." I saw something flash across his eyes and immediately knew he was keeping something from me. I moved back across the room to stand in front of him. "Ash, if there is something wrong you need to tell me." He exhaled and when his breath left his body, I saw his shoulders slouch.

"Things are just a little crazy right now." His hands came up and rubbed over his face, as if he were trying to wipe away his frustration. I closed the space between us and wrapped my arms around his waist.

"What can I do to help?"

"Just be you, Bit. And keep calling me out on my shit. I don't want to be an asshole. There's just a lot going on right now."

"You'd tell me if it was something more than that, right?"

"Of course," he said as he bent down to kiss me. He pulled away too soon for my liking, but we had places to be. "Let's go." He swatted my butt as I slid past him through the door. Once outside he laced his fingers with mine and gave my hand a squeeze. I smiled up at him but noticed his smile didn't make the lines around his eyes form. His eyes weren't sparkling like they usually were. My mind immediately began to search for things that could be wrong. Had something happened with his parents? Were classes getting him down? Pre-law was a lot to take on and his father had really high expectations for him. Had I been doing enough to make him feel like a priority? Of all the possible problems I could come up with, that was the only one I could directly affect. Sometimes it was very easy to take our relationship for granted. There was a finality and sense of being settled when it came to Asher. I knew he was it for me, that we were it for each other. The real deal. The forever kind of love.

We crossed over the pedestrian bridge that led through a small wooded area. I stopped walking and Asher noticed when my hand tugged on his. He turned around and gave me a concerned look.

"Something wrong?" He asked, his eyebrows furrowing in the middle. I grabbed his other hand and pulled them both behind my back, forcing his chest to come into mine. My neck strained as I looked up at him towering over me.

"Do you remember the first time you told me you loved me?" I asked him. He gave me a sexy half smile, but still looked confused.

"Yeah. It was under our bridge at the park. Why?"

"I've loved you, in one way or another, since the day you stopped Ryan from throwing rocks at me in fifth grade. There's never been anyone else for me, Asher. And there never will be." I saw as his smile grow and I saw the light come back into his eyes. "Who we are right now – college students, boyfriend and girlfriend – this isn't who we are meant to be; this is simply one of the bridges we have to cross to get to the rest of our lives together." I saw his head begin to dip towards me and I raised up on my toes to kiss him. Our hands were still linked behind my back but he pressed them against me, pulling me further into him. I sensed people walking past us, a few people grumbled that we were blocking the path, but none of it mattered. He matters. We do. His mouth moved against mine and my mind went hazy as his tongue slid against the seam of my lips. Slowly, we used our mouths to affirm our love to one another. Nothing was as perfect as the way Asher kissed me. His teeth pulled gently on my bottom lip as he ended the kiss, sending shockwaves down to my belly.

"I love you, Bit."

"I love you, Ash. One hundred percent." He chuckled and then turned to ease back into the stream of people heading towards the stadium.

Not only did we win the game, but our house won the float competition. Who knew that getting cute co-eds to recreate scenes from *Magic Mike* would garner such an enthusiastic response from the crowd? Luck was in our favor that so many women came to the game and they screamed louder than their male counterparts when the time for voting came. No one out screamed college girls when faced with shirtless male strippers – no one.

Reeve and I were at the frat that night for the after party and things, as I was growing accustomed to, were getting a little crazy. The frat had what they called an "Around the World" party. All the doors in the house were shut and locked aside from a few sprinkled throughout. Each unlocked room was assigned a different country and liquor accordingly. The idea was to visit each room and get a drink from each country, completing your trip around the world. Each room had a brother assigned to it who gladly took part in getting girls drunk.

I attended a few parties at the house since school started, but this one seemed to be a little wilder than the rest. Every once in a while I caught a glimpse of Reeve bouncing around the dance floor or getting a drink from one of the guys. I caught sight of Tracy, the girl who'd not-so-subtly checked out my boyfriend as I stood right next to him. She was at the frat a lot and seemed to be making her way through a lot of the brothers. I rolled my eyes as her long blonde hair swished around at her animated flirting. She irritated me more than I liked to admit.

Asher did his duties as a brother and made sure everyone was having a good time. Periodically he stopped as he passed by me and asked if I was enjoying myself, kissed my temple, and then left me to tend to all the partygoers. I walked through one of the main rooms of the bottom floor when one of the brothers came up to me with a bottle of peppermint schnapps in one hand and a bottle of Hershey's syrup in the other.

"Open wide," he said to me with a slimy smirk on his face. I rolled my eyes in disgust and turned away.

"Charlie, I'm kidding. Really, here," he held up both bottles like they were a prize. I looked at him trying to put a name to his face. I recognized him because he was a part of Asher's frat, but I couldn't remember ever really talking with him. The fact that he knew my name told me he knew I was with Asher, so he was more than likely not trying to use a smarmy pick-up line on me. I relented and moved closer to him, pointed my face up, and opened my mouth like a baby bird, much like I'd seen many girls do in front of him tonight. He smiled. I closed my eyes. I felt the sting of the schnapps as it hit the sensitive skin under my tongue, then I smelled the sugary sweetness of the syrup as it mixed with the cool peppermint liquid.

"Close your mouth and shake." I heard him say loudly into my ear to combat the noise of the music. I followed his instructions and shook my head back and forth, mixing up the contents inside. My mouth tasted like a peppermint patty. It was delicious. I swallowed and then blushed slightly when I opened my eyes to find him still staring at me.

"Which country is that from?" I asked, partly trying to be a smartass and partly trying to hide the fact that I was uncomfortable. He hadn't moved back from me, even though there is no need for him to be standing so close anymore. I stepped back to try and put some distance between us but I bumped into someone. My stomach dropped because I knew exactly who I'd backed into. I felt the hardness of his abs and chest up against my shoulders. His hands came up to my arms and gripped me sturdily, helping me keep my balance.

"Blake." That was all he said. I figured that was the name of the guy I was standing too close to. Blake nodded at Asher and walked away. I felt Asher's hands spinning me and I turned my head up to look at him.

"I was just taking a shot from him," I yelled over the music. His finger came to my chin and tipped my face up towards his. I thought he was coming towards me to kiss my lips and I involuntarily licked them, tasting the chocolate and peppermint still lingering on them. His mouth bypassed mine and moved to my ear instead.

"I know, Bit. But that doesn't mean I have to like finding you staring up at him with your body so close to his." My heart dropped hearing his words. I never wanted to give him a reason to feel like I was not completely his. I was nothing if not his. I pressed my cheek into his, putting my lips right next to his ear.

"Take me to your room."

He pulled back and looked in my eyes for a few moments, then his hand slid down to lace his fingers between mine. He turned and led me to the staircase. Once we were to his room, he pulled out his keys, unlocked, and opened the door. I walked in first and breathed a small sigh of relief to see his roommate was not there. I sat on the edge of Asher's bed and watched him as he placed the "Do Not Disturb" sign on the outside doorknob. That sign usually bothered me. I didn't like the idea of the guys in his house walking by his door knowing or assuming anything was happening inside. It was none of their business. But in this case, I was glad he pulled it out and announced to the world that we needed some privacy.

I watched as he walked to his dresser and as he faced away from me, he reached behind his neck and pulled his tee shirt over his shoulders. His bare back was strong and muscular. I could see each individual, defined muscle move as his arms free themselves of his shirt. He was beautiful.

"I'm sorry." The whisper was out of my mouth before I even had a chance to realize I said anything. He stilled, but eventually turned his head over his shoulder to look at me.

"You have nothing to be sorry for, Charlie. I know nothing happened. You just took a shot from him; that's the whole point of this party."

"I'm not sorry for taking a shot. I'm sorry for giving you a reason to feel, even for one second, that I would lend myself to anyone else. That anything I give to you so freely or happily, is ever given to anyone else."

"I don't like the idea of lending you in any capacity."

"You'll never have to," I replied.

"I'm sorry I make you feel this way. You have every right to have fun at a party. You weren't doing anything wrong."

"If it made you feel anything besides happy or loved, even for one moment, then I am sorry." I stood up and walked over to him, placing my hands on his ribcage. His skin was warm and tight over his muscles. I reached up on my tiptoes and placed a kiss right between his shoulder blades, then rested my cheek against his back. "I love you."

"I know, Charlie." I felt him turn and his hands were on my face. "You don't have to prove anything to me." I felt the sting of tears in my eyes. The painful lump started to form in my throat. "Bit, what's wrong?"

I got a little relief that he called me Bit. He never used my nickname when he was upset with me, so to hear him say it eased my worries a little. I shrugged my shoulders and immediately saw him roll his eyes with a smile.

"Tell me," he pleaded.

"I have spent so much time trying to encourage us to be independent of each other that it never occurred to me that we could grow apart." I took a deep breath. "Back home, no one would have ever flirted with me the way he did. No one. Everyone knew that we were together and no one ever tried to mess with that. And I'm a little disappointed in myself that I let him stand that close to me. That I let him flirt with me."

"Would you have kissed him? Would you have let him touch you?" Asher asked with a gentleness in his voice.

"Never," I said with absolute conviction.

"Then you're getting all worked up over nothing." He rubbed his thumb over my cheek and I could see him thinking hard about something, figuring out a way to put it into words. "We're going to be tested, Bit. There are going to be a million different scenarios in which we'll be given an option to choose us, or ruin us. I *know* we're going to be ok. Everything I do is for us. There will never be a day or a time when you aren't my first priority, and I know you feel the same way." He placed the smallest and most chaste kiss against my lips then rested his forehead against mine. "The hardest part will be having faith in each other's ability to keep choosing *us*. You will have to trust me and I will have to trust you."

"I trust you. I trust us. And you can trust me. I promise."

"What else can I do with you?" He asked, his voice suddenly darker and deeper. Bolts of excitement shot through my entire body and I shuddered when they ended at the core between my legs. Asher saw my reaction to his words and laughed softly. "I haven't even touched you yet, Bit."

"I'm pretty sure you could make me come with just your words," I whispered against his mouth, wanting him to take mine so badly.

"Hmm..." he groaned as he rubbed his mouth across mine. Not kissing me, but teasing me. "That sounds like a challenge. I accept the challenge, however, we'll have to test your theory some other night. Tonight I want you. All over me."

And there was a challenge I would accept. He gripped my hips and picked me up so I was level with his eyes. I always felt like a feather when he picked me up and I'm pretty sure it made him feel big and strong. No denying his size, he started growing one summer and never really stopped. When he stopped growing tall, he started growing muscle. I loved all his muscle. He wasn't bulky or beefy, he was hard and powerful. His arms were just big enough to hold me and make me feel protected and safe.

His lips crushed mine and my hands found the back of his head, hanging on to his hair. He walked me over to his bed and laid me down. He stood over me, undoing his belt, looking at me like he hasn't eaten in days. He was hungry. His pants fell to the floor and he crawled over me, trailing kisses all along my body where his mouth could reach my skin. Up my forearms, the sliver of skin between my jeans and my shirt that rode up my stomach, along my collar bone. Everywhere he kissed I felt warmth bubbling to the surface of my skin. His mouth traveled along my jaw, over my chin, and when he finally made it to my lips, there was a knock at the door.

"No *fucking* way," Asher nearly growled. "Go away!" His face came back down to mine and he tried to start his seduction over.

"Asher?" I heard the voice and immediately I was off the bed and ran to the door. I yanked it open and saw Reeve on the other side, tears streamed down her face.

"Reeve, what's the matter?" I asked as she walked past me into Asher's room. She hadn't noticed that he wasn't wearing any pants, and he hadn't tried to cover up the fact that he was only wearing a pair of boxer briefs. Luckily for him the interruption was enough to calm him down a bit so that even though he wasn't necessarily covered, he wasn't indecent.

"I was hoping," she said between hiccups and tight breaths holding back sobs, "that you would be ready to go back to the dorm."

"What happened, Reeve?" I brought her in and sat her down on Asher's bed. Asher exhaled loudly and started putting his clothes back on. Reeve wiped at the skin below her eyes, trying to erase the wetness from the tears streaming down her face.

"I was downstairs dancing with Caleb. We were having a good time and he told me he had a drink in his room he wanted me to try. At first I didn't want to go, but I guess I figured there were drinks all over the house, and that was the whole point of this stupid party." She shook her head and I could tell she was starting to blame herself for whatever had happened next.

"So, I went with him to his room, but once I saw that his room was locked and no one else was in there, I stalled. I told him I forgot my purse downstairs, I tried to leave."

My stomach began to turn as she was telling me the story. I didn't know exactly where the story was headed, but I could guess and my blood was starting to boil through my veins.

"What happened?" I heard Asher ask, his voice sounded just as on edge as I was feeling.

"He told me my purse was safe, grabbed my hand and convinced me to go in." She started crying harder, but still silently. "When he shut and locked the door behind me I started to panic. I told him that I needed to go, but..." She couldn't continue. She cried uncontrollably now. I brought her head to my shoulder and ran my hand along her smooth hair. I looked over her head at Asher and recognized the rage in his eyes. He tried to control himself and I wasn't entirely sure that I wanted him to exercise control in that moment. But I knew we needed to hear the whole story before he went off to confront Caleb.

After a few minutes of holding her and trying to soothe her, I softly asked, "Reeve, can you tell us what happened?" She pulled back from me eventually and tried to dry her eyes and nose on the back of her hand. Asher produced a box of tissues for her and she gave him a small smile, but it was only on the corners of her mouth, it didn't light up her face like it usually did.

"I asked him to let me out and he said that I didn't want to leave and that he knew what I really wanted." I could actually feel the tense waves and rage flowing off of Asher from hearing that one sentence. "I kept saying no, but he cornered me and then he pushed me up against his closet door and kissed me." Her face dropped into her hands and she let out a few more sobs. "It shouldn't be a big deal, I've kissed him before, but this felt different." She looked up at me, her eyes bloodshot and her face red and puffy. "I was scared," she whispered.

We both jumped when we heard Asher punch the wall. He moved over to his desk chair and picked it up off the floor and slammed it back down so hard one of the wheels went flying across the floor, broken off from the force of his blow.

"Can you tell me what happened next?" I asked gently.

"He had me by my arms and he forced me over to his bed and tried to make me lie down. I was telling him no, and I couldn't understand why he wouldn't stop. He was supposed to stop!" She became panicked. I knew I was going to lose her in a moment, but I needed to get the information out of her.

"Reeve, take some deep breaths. He can't get to you in here. Right, Asher?" I looked over at him, hoping he could help me.

"I'll fucking kill him, Reeve. Don't worry about it. I've got you."

I don't think I had ever loved him more than I did in that moment. I helped her take some deep breaths and when she had regained some of her composure she continued.

"I was on the bed, and he was over me, holding my arms down by my wrists over my head. He tried to get my shirt off. I kept telling him no and to get off of me." She sniffled again but kept going. "He kept calling me a whore and a cock-tease. I tried so hard to get him off of me. He leaned up a little, I think to try and undo the button on my jeans, and there was just enough room between us for me to knee him right in the junk."

My eyes went wide because, honestly, that is not what I expected to hear.

"You got him in the balls?" Asher asked from across the room. She nodded.

"Yeah, I got him good too because he immediately rolled off of me, holding himself and groaning. I jumped off the bed and he rolled right off it onto the floor. So then I kicked him in the stomach. I left right after that, but I heard him throwing up as I was running down the hall." She looked back up at me. "I figured this is where you were, so I ran straight here." She looked over at Asher.

"I'm sorry. I saw the sign on your door. I wouldn't have bothered you otherwise; I just didn't have anywhere else to go," she started crying again. Asher walked over and knelt down in front of her and tipped her face up to look at him.

"Hey, Reeve," he said in a voice so soft, even I was calming down. "You're one of my best friends. If you need me, I'm here. All the time. No matter what."

Nope. I had never loved him any more than right now.

She nodded at him. "Thank you," she whispered. His hand came to her cheek for just a moment and then he stood again and headed towards the door.

"Where are you going?" I asked. All of a sudden, panic was coursing through me.

"Well, Charlie, I'm going to go and kick Caleb's ass."

"Well, *Asher*," I emphasized his name, making it evident that I didn't appreciate his tone, or the fact that he used my full name. "It kind of sounds like she already did that."

"No, she defended herself. I'm going to beat his ass so hard that tomorrow he won't even remember his name." I stood up and went after him.

"Asher, no, don't. Please." I made it to him and grabbed him by the hand. He stopped and turned towards me but I saw his eyes rolling.

"Bit, I don't have time for this. Someone has to kill him." I took his face in my hands.

"Not you, Ash, please. Let's just call the police."

"We can't call the police! This whole frat house is full of underage college kids drinking! If I call the police so many people will get in trouble. He's the only one that needs to be punished."

"Ok, so, we take Reeve home – both of us – and tomorrow we go to the campus police. We'll report it. Let the school deal with him, Asher. Please don't go to his room. I need you with me right now." I knew I was playing dirty. I knew I used his inability to walk away from me when I needed him against him, but I didn't care. I cared that if he went down to Caleb's room he could possibly get hurt. "Please," I begged softly. I saw the moment he made the right decision. His eyes softened and his shoulders lost some of their tension. He bent down so that his forehead leaned against mine.

"Fine," was all he said.

We gathered up Reeve and all three of us walked back to our dorm. I took her into the bathroom and helped her get ready for bed. She had grown quiet on the walk home and now she seemed very distant and far away. Her eyes were glazed over and she wasn't responding to me normally.

"Reeve? Are you ok?" She nodded her head, but didn't say anything. "Hey, Reeve, everything is going to be ok. We'll go to campus police tomorrow and tell them everything. He'll never mess with you again." She nodded a second time and I couldn't help but worry. I didn't want to push her. I had no idea what was going through her head, but I would give anything for her to just look me in the eye or say one word. She was breaking my heart.

I walked with her back to our room and watched as she slid into her bed and hid under the covers. Asher sat on the edge of my bed looking at me expectantly. I quickly changed into my pajamas and walked over to where Asher sat and leaned down to kiss his forehead. The care and gentleness he showed Reeve in the last hour had blown me away. I knew he was constantly irritated by her interruptions and her boy-crazy ways, but she was also his friend. We'd grown up together. Granted they were probably only friends because of me, but they were friends, nonetheless. As I leaned up from the kiss he wrapped his arms around my waist and pressed his cheek into my stomach. I slowly moved my hands through his soft hair, letting him take the comfort from me he was obviously seeking. When he finally pulled away and looked up at me, I saw a new worry in his eyes and I knew what he was thinking.

He was glad it wasn't me who was assaulted at the party and felt guilty for thinking it at all. I wrapped my hands around the back of his neck and sat on his lap straddling him, bringing my face close to his.

"Hey," I whispered quietly, hoping to not let Reeve hear me. "I'm ok. Everything is ok."

"Everything is not ok, Charlie." I could feel his hands on my back, pulling me into him as if he needed to crawl inside of me. "I never thought anything like that would really happen. At least not to someone I know. What if Caleb had tried that on you? There's nothing you could have said to keep me from killing him, Bit. You're lucky I didn't kick the shit out of him as it is."

"Asher, nothing like that is going to happen to me. Does this suck? Yes. Did Reeve deserve this? No. We are going to tell the authorities and they'll take care of him."

"I don't know what I'd do if anything ever happened to you," he said, looking into my eyes.

"You won't ever have to find out."

He brushed his lips against mine and the kiss was tender, controlled, and loving. Passion was always under the surface of our kissing. I could always tell how he felt about me in his kiss, but this one almost felt like he appreciated the fact I was even there; I was his and I was ok. I felt the same way and tried to convey that to him. His hands still roamed over the skin of my back under my nightshirt and when I felt his loving kiss turn into something more carnal I pulled away. Bringing my hands up to his face I whispered to him, "I think I'm going to sleep with Reeve. I don't want her to be alone."

He nodded his head in understanding.

"Will you stay? I would feel safer knowing you were here."

"Of course. Always."

Chapter Three

The following weeks were hellish. The campus police partnered with the local police and charges were filed against Caleb. He was arrested by the police and the Greek Council at the university banned him from the Greek system. We all had to attend a hearing at the school for the university to decide if he was guilty and to sentence him. Reeve, Asher, some of the brothers from the fraternity, and I all had to testify.

The school found him guilty of attempted rape, which was a violation of the student code of conduct, and he was expelled. We were all so glad when the trial was over and done with, hoping once we could move past everything Reeve's mood would improve. The whole ordeal, from that terrible night at the frat house until the day of the sentencing, took about two months. The entire time Reeve was a shell of her former self. It was terrible watching her live as a hermit, only going to class, just scraping by with her studies, sleeping all day long sometimes. She didn't want to go anywhere or do anything. She never said more than a few words to me, even though I tried daily to break her out of her trance.

Two weeks after Caleb was expelled, I was beginning to worry she was never going to come back to me. It angered me to think that one very stupid guy took my best friend away from me. He had impacted her in such a way that she wasn't even the same person anymore. It wasn't fair – not to me and, most importantly, not to her. This was college and she should be having the time of her life. As I was walked to class with Asher, I tried to explain my frustration.

"I just want my best friend back. I feel like if she doesn't get better soon, there's really nothing stopping her from dropping out and going home at semester break. I know she's unhappy." Asher squeezed my hand and smiled sweetly at me.

"Everything will work out. Just give her time. I'm sure it's hard for her to just go back to the way things were before."

"I know. I'm not expecting her to just forget what she went through, or to flip some sort of switch and snap out of it, but something needs to give. I'm afraid I'll lose her if this goes on much longer."

"I think I have an idea," he said excitedly, out of nowhere.

"You do?"

"Yeah. Be in your dorm room at seven tonight and make sure she's there with you."

"Ok... I'm a little confused. What are you going to do?"

"It's a surprise. I don't know if it will work, but it's worth a shot, right?" He kissed me quickly on the forehead, let go of my hand, and started walking quickly in the opposite direction.

"What about class?" I yelled at his retreating back. He turned back towards me, but continued walking backwards.

"This is more important," he said with a smile. I couldn't argue with him, so I just waved. He winked and turned back around, continuing on his way.

Later that night I sat nervously in my dorm room, pretending to study, but really just staring at my psychology textbook. At seven on the dot, the dorm phone rang. I didn't know if I was supposed to answer it or not, so I pretended to be so wrapped up in my homework that it forced her to get out of bed and answer it.

"Hello?" Her voice sounded strained. I knew it was because she didn't use the phone very much anymore. I watched her face as she listened to the person on the other line who I assumed was Asher. I saw her eyes dart at me and I quickly looked back down at my book. I had no idea what was going on, but I didn't want to ruin it. She was out of bed and had said a word – vast improvements over yesterday already.

"I don't think so," she said quietly. She opened her mouth to say something else but was obviously cut off by the person on the other line. She rolled her eyes slightly and even seeing her do that made me smile. "Fine," she answered and hung up. She turned towards me with apprehension.

"What's up?" I asked, trying really hard not to look like I knew something was up.

"Uh, that was one of Asher's frat brothers. He said that something happened to Asher and that we should get over there ASAP."

"What?" I shrieked. This was not discussed as part of the plan. Had something really happened to him? Or was this just the ploy to get her to his house? I was up and off of my bed instantly, grabbing my shoes and jacket. Reeve took a seat on her bed and began to pull her covers up over her lap. "What are you doing? You've got to come with me!"

"Charlie, I don't feel like leaving. Text me when you find out what happened." That was it. The straw that broke the proverbial camel's back.

"Are you *kidding* me? After everything Asher has done for you through this whole mess, after all the years of friendship, after *everything*, you're just going to wait for a text to see if he's ok? Who are you?" I breathed quickly, my harsh breaths making my chest heave up and down. "Get your fucking shoes on and come to the frat with me. Now."

"Holy shit, Charlie. Calm down." She got up and I let out a loud breath when I saw her start to get ready to go. We walked to the frat but I was a good ten feet in front of her the whole time, too pissed to be next to her. The anger helped to ease the fear that something was really wrong with Asher. I tried telling myself that it was all part of the set-up, but I needed to see him just to make sure.

When we came to the frat house it looked dark and abandoned. It was rare to see a house forty college guys lived in with all the lights off, with no one on the lawn playing football, or passed out on the couch on the front porch. Something was off. We entered through the two sliding doors on the side of the house that led directly into the dining room.

"Asher?" I called out, hoping to hear his voice answer me. I didn't hear anything. "Reeve, who called you?"

"I don't know, just some guy."

I tried to make my way into what I thought was the TV room, but with no lights it was hard to tell if I was going to walk into a wall or not. As soon as we came around the corner and through the doorway, lights flashed on and I heard a large group of people shout "Surprise!" Once my eyes adjusted to the unexpected light I was completely shocked at what I saw.

The room looked like someone had shaken a bottle of Pepto all over it. There were pink streamers hanging from the ceiling, pink pillows and blankets were all over the floor. An abundance of pink cotton candy was everywhere, big jugs of pink lemonade, and a big pink banner hanging above the large fireplace that read "We Love You, Reeve". There must have been forty girls in the room, all dressed in pink. Some were from our sorority and surprisingly some were girls Reeve and I were friends with from high school. The swarm of girl came towards Reeve and started enveloping her in hugs. I felt the tears building in my eyes as I saw her smile. She was actually smiling. The grip that had been squeezing my heart for the last six weeks eased at seeing her enjoying the company of all of her friends.

"Hey you," I heard from behind me. I knew instantly it was Asher, but turned around just needing to see his face. I ran right into his arms.

"You're ok," I breathed into his ear.

"Yeah, sorry. I had to come up with something that would make her come too. I was hoping if you had an emergency she'd come out of her funk enough to at least come over here with you." He nodded towards her. "Looks like it worked."

"You did all of this?"

"Well, it was my idea, but all the brothers helped out. One of them even drove back home to pick up a few girls who couldn't get rides down here. We all feel really bad about what happened, and the house owes her this. We need to make it right for her." In that moment, I was so honored to even know Asher, let alone be his girlfriend. What eighteen-year-old guy says something like that? Or even comprehends the complexity of this situation like he did? And how was I so lucky that he wanted to be with me? I shook my head as all those thoughts raced around my brain.

"What is it?" He asked, looking in my eyes with his slate gray ones blinking back at me.

"Who are you, Asher? What kind of heart is beating in your chest that makes you the most compassionate and thoughtful man I've ever met?" I don't think I've ever referred to Asher as a man before. He had always been a boy, or a guy. But never a man. This was exactly what it was to be manly – to stand up for someone you cared about, to recognize a need they had, and do everything in your power to make a situation right. I never considered myself a woman either. I was a girl. But standing here in Asher's arms, knowing what he had done for our friend, made the woman in me want to be enough for this man. His answer was simply to lean down and kiss me. He pulled away and reached down to a table behind the couch. He turned back to me and handed me a bullhorn. I looked down at it with confusion.

"So, the brothers are all strictly ordered to stay upstairs. There are enough blankets and pillows and stuff so all you girls can enjoy your sleepover. Pizza is on the way. A sappy chick flick is in the DVD player. If you should need anything, use the alarm on the bullhorn and a brother will be right down."

"Are you serious right now?"

"Yeah, we don't play, Bit. Anything you girls need, let us know."

I looked down at the bullhorn and thought of all the possibilities that were held in my hand. I looked up at him through my lashes, trying to hide my smile.

"So, no boys allowed downstairs, but can the girls go upstairs?" He pulled me to him swiftly and tugged on the tail end of my hair angling my head up towards him.

"Anything you need, Bit, I've got it for you."

"Good to know," I managed to squeak out, causing him to smile and laugh.

"There are some pink pjs in the bathroom next to the kitchen for you and Reeve."

"You've thought of everything haven't you?"

"Pretty damn close."

Asher kissed me then, long and deep enough to hold me over for a while, but I wasn't sure I'd be able to stay away from him all night. After we changed into our pink pajamas, Reeve and I went back into the party. I smiled watching her talk with all of her friends, people she hadn't seen or spoken with in weeks. I thought about how it might have been hard for her to be back in the frat house, but all the girls were providing enough of a distraction that she didn't seem to be bothered by being back at the scene of her assault. I was glad for that. It would be hard to avoid Asher's frat, and I didn't want anything to come between her and I.

Throughout the night we found silly reasons to blow the bullhorn: asking for more pillows, asking the boys to turn down the thermostat, wanting our pizza to be warmed up in the microwave. After about five errands, one of the girls got the bright idea to mandate the boys do our bidding in their underwear. One of the upperclassmen, Miles, got on the bullhorn and made the announcement.

"Alright Beta men, hear this! When it's your turn to service the ladies downstairs," he waggled his eyebrows at us as he said this, "You must do so in your underwear. Boxers or briefs boys, no commando – none of them want to see that." A few girls groaned at the last part of the statement, and I was sure he was wrong about that. I looked over at Reeve and her face was bright with laughter. The boys were doing a great job of cheering her up. For the next few hours we did everything we could to get every Beta downstairs in his underwear.

Eventually the boys got creative and started fashioning underwear out of weird things you'd find around the house. One guy came downstairs with just a box a cheerios in front of his crotch. It was worth it to see the tears streaming down Reeve's face from laughing so hard. He hadn't really thought his idea through all the way and when he turned to leave, after bringing Reeve the ridiculous Q-tips she had requested, he forgot we could all see his naked ass. Hoots and hollers flooded through the room at the sight of his bare backside.

I tried to wait anxiously for Asher's appearance. Finally, Reeve got on the bullhorn and shouted towards the stairs, smiling through it all.

"Asher Carmichael, you get your ass downstairs and give my best friend a kiss!" All the girls in the room started clapping and yelling. It was pandemonium. I had seen Asher in his underwear, or less, many times, but it was a little nerve-wracking knowing that all the girls in the room would see him in the same state. He had an amazing body and I usually liked that I was the only one who got to see it. Right now, however, I would look past my feelings on the matter and just enjoy whatever he had planned. There was no way for me to prepare myself for what I saw when he came around the corner.

He strutted into the room, confidence at an all-time high, found my eyes, and walked right towards me – in a pair of *my* underwear. As if it were the most natural thing on the planet, he waltzed across the room sporting a pair of black lace, boyshort panties. My jaw dropped and my ears rang with all the screaming that was coming from the group of girls.

He found me sitting on the couch and without hesitation he straddled me, placed his hands on the sides of my face, and kissed me hard. In any other circumstance it would have been a hot kiss, but I just couldn't get past the fact that he was wearing my panties. I pulled away and looked in his eyes.

"You're crazy," I said, quiet enough so only he could hear me, but loud enough to combat the whooping girls.

"You're smiling; that's all that matters." He kissed me again quickly and then got up to walk back towards the stairs, stopping at the doorway to give a graceful bow. I just shook my head at him. He looked ridiculous.

"You're man has a fantastic ass," Lizzy, one of my sorority sisters said. I shrugged.

"I wish he would have worn the purple thong. It accentuates his backside better." I tried to pull it off without laughing, but it was impossible. Lizzy and I spent a good five minutes cracking up on the couch.

"You'd better be careful, Charlie. If you don't keep an eye on him, some other girl is going to swoop in and steal him away." My head snapped to the left to see who the voice belonged to and I wasn't surprised to see Tracy standing next to the couch. She had a slimy smile on her face and I narrowed my eyes at her.

"And I assume you think you're going to be able to steal him from me?" I asked, my irritation growing.

She shrugged her shoulders at me. "I just think he hasn't realized that there's a whole campus filled with girls who'd like to show him what he's missing."

"Hey, back off Tracy," I heard Reeve's voice strong and firm. "Asher isn't missing anything. But you're gonna miss the way your face looks with a straight nose if you don't back off of Charlie and leave, like, now." Tracy looked at Reeve and I like we were insignificant, but she did wander towards the door. She gave us a wicked smile and a little finger wave before she left. I huffed out an irritated breath.

"I'm gonna get something to drink. Do you guys want anything?" Lizzy asked us, obviously wanting to give us some time alone. I shook my head and Reeve said a quiet "No, thank you." After Lizzy walked away, Reeve turned so that she was facing me directly.

"Thank you for helping me with Tracy." I exhaled loudly. "She's becoming a huge pain in my ass."

"No problem," Reeve said quietly. She fiddled with her fingers in her lap for a moment, seemingly trying to get up enough nerve to say something else.

"I don't really know what to say to you right now, Charlie." She started playing with the hem of her pajama shirt. "I know I haven't been the best friend lately," she heaved out a loud breath. "I am just having a hard time moving on from everything." I put my hand on her knee and lowered my head so I could look in her eyes.

"Reeve, you *are* my best friend and I just want to make sure you're going to be ok. You don't have to put on an act for me. I understand if you're still hurt, or sad, or upset. I probably would be too. I'm just worried about you and I don't want to see you hurt yourself by going into isolation." I paused and looked down at my hands, not wanting to say too much. "I can see you drifting farther and farther away, and it scares me. I don't ever want to lose you, Reeve. I don't know what I would do if we weren't friends anymore." I felt a tear slide down my face, but this one wasn't from laughter. Letting myself think about how my life would be without Reeve tore a piece of my heart open. She was the sister I never had and I loved her tremendously. If she wasn't in my life, all the laughter and fun I shared with her would leave and so would a piece of my soul. I peeked up at her, trying to gauge her reaction. She wiped tears from her face as well.

"I'm so sorry, Charlie. I don't want you to feel that way. I love you and I'm going to try to snap out of this. I just need a little time and understanding. But never question our friendship. You mean everything to me." She wrapped her arms around me and pulled me into an embrace. I never needed a hug like I needed this one from her. I could actually feel some of the anxiety ooze out of me. "And thank you for planning this party. I didn't realize how much I needed this." I pulled away wiping my face and smiling.

"I didn't plan this. Asher did." Reeve looked sincerely surprised by this information.

"Why?" She asked, sounding mystified.

"He loves you just as much as I do, Reeve. He has been really torn apart by all of this. He just wants you to be happy again." She looked pensive as she took in all the news I had given her.

"I guess I just always figured he put up with me because he loved you."

I smiled at her.

"Well, sometimes he puts up with you because he loves me," I giggled. "But truly, you are one of his best friends. He would do anything for you." I waved my hand out to display the pink slumber party. "Hence this display of affection for you." I patted her on the knee again. "All the brothers here are really trying to make it up to you, Reeve. They all want you to be ok and to be comfortable here. You're important to Asher, so you're important to them. Let them make it up to you."

She smiled at me again. "I really am lucky to have you guys."

I shrugged my shoulders. "I know."

After the perfectly pink slumber party, we all tried very hard to get things back to normal. I saw Reeve try, every day, to get herself out there a little more. I was so proud of her and I tried to tell her every chance I got. When winter break came around, all three of us went home and I was happy Reeve only packed a suitcase to take with her, and not everything she owned. It thrilled me to know that she would be returning for the next semester. It felt like things were getting back to normal.

I rode home with Reeve, silently smiling to myself as she jabbered the entire way home. I hadn't heard her say so many words in weeks and I was more than happy to sit and listen to whatever she wanted to say to me.

When we pulled up to the street Asher and I both lived on, she looked over at me.

"So, what are you and Asher going to do now that you're home?"

I gave her a puzzled look. "What do you mean?"

"Well, there's barely a night when you guys have been apart since school started. Are you going to have a hard time sleeping apart from him?" Odd. I hadn't even thought of that.

I spent nearly every night with him and we alternated between his house and my dorm. Most of the time, ok half of the time, there wasn't even anything sexual about it. We just knew that we would sleep together. Wherever he was, I was. We never even really spoke about it. It was just the way things were. Reeve was right; I did think I would have a hard time sleeping without him. Impossible? No. Undesirable? Definitely.

"I don't know. I guess we'll just see what happens."

"Meaning that you'll have Asher sneak into your house after your dad has gone to sleep?"

I grinned at her.

"If that's what it takes," I said through laughter. She pulled up to my house and parked on the street. Asher slowly pulled up next to her car and rolled down his window. I got my bags out of Reeve's trunk and she waved as she drove towards her house. I walked over to Asher's window and set my bags down next to my feet, leaning into his window. "Hey. How was your drive?"

"Slow. Reeve needs to put the pedal to the metal a little bit." I rolled my eyes.

"You could have just passed her."

"No. You know I just want to make sure you get home ok." I gave him a small peck and then pulled back.

"That might be the most action you get for two whole weeks."

"Uh, what are you talking about?"

I laughed as I watched panic rush over his face.

"Have you thought about how coming back home for break has basically put us back into high school? I mean, there's no way my dad is going to let you sleep over. And I'm sure your parents won't appreciate me spending the night at your house." I saw the realization come over him.

"I'm not worried about it," he said confidently.

Mildly offended, I scoffed at him.

"Not worried about it? Well, fine then. Me either." I leaned down to grab my bags and felt him put his hand out and grab my arm.

"Babe, I only meant that there is no way I'm letting anything keep me from holding you at night. Our parents will understand. We're adults now." I narrowed my eyes at him.

"I think you are overestimating our parent's ability to see us anything other than their children. But if you're willing to give it a try, let me know what your parents say about me sleeping over at your house." I smiled at him snidely, knowing if anything it would be his mom who would be opposed to our hopeful sleeping arrangement. I was just like a daughter to her and she would definitely have a problem with me sleeping over at a guy's house, even if it was her own son.

"I'll figure it out, Bit. Don't worry."

"Ok, whatever you say. Tell your parents I say hi. And call me." I leaned into his window again to give him a kiss and felt his hand wrap around the back of my neck, holding me to him. He took the kiss deeper than I had intended, but I was enjoying it too much to complain. His mouth captured mine, my bottom lip being tugged on by his teeth. I was immediately angry at the metal door between us and needed more contact. I moaned in frustration and he immediately pulled away.

"That should hold you over until later," he said with a wink. I snarled at him and grabbed my bags. I walked around the front of his car and heard him yell out his window, "Love you, Babe." I turned towards him and stuck my tongue out at him. That'll teach him.

When I walked in the house I was greeted not only by the smell of cookies baking, but also by the sight of a woman in my dad's kitchen. I dropped my bags on the floor and watched as the woman jumped at the loud noise they made as they clattered against the travertine floor. She spun around, her hand clenched to her chest. She looked absolutely petrified and I'm sure I looked pretty pissed.

"Who are you?" I asked, and not too politely. I watched her remove the surprise from her face and plaster a smile on. She moved around the kitchen island, wiping her hands on the apron around her waist. The same apron I use to watch my mother wipe her hands on.

"Hi, you must be Charlie. My name is Angie." She held her hand out to me, waiting for me to shake it. I didn't even look down at it.

"What are you doing in my kitchen?" I said harshly, not even pretending to move to shake her outstretched hand. She took the hint and moved her fingers through her shoulder-length brown hair.

"I needed some parmesan cheese for dinner and your father was out. He ran to the store real quick. We thought we had enough time before you got home." She paused and let out a deep breath. "This must be surprising for you to come home and see a strange woman in your kitchen. I apologize. We didn't want it to happen this way, your father and I."

"That's my mom's apron." That's all I said to her before I turned and walked to my bedroom. I slammed the door when I got inside and immediately started pacing the floor. My heart pumped, adrenaline flowing through my veins. It took all of forty-five seconds before my anger turned into an aching hurt. I'd never felt anything like the pressure that was building in my chest. Something inside of me was expanding at such a rapid pace, surely I would explode any moment. And I did.

I collapsed on my bed, not even trying to control the sobs that were breaking free from my mouth. My legs involuntarily curled up to my chest and my arms wrapped around my knees. I was as small as I could be, trying to disintegrate all together. I didn't want to be in a place where my mother's things were being used by another woman. I wasn't ready for any of this. I don't know how long I cried, but eventually I heard my door creak open.

"Charlie Bear," I heard my dad's voice at roughly the same time I feel his big, warm hand on my back.

"I'm so sorry, Charlie. I'm so sorry."

"Who is she?" I asked, even though I already know the answer.

"That's Angie," he said quietly. He paused and then continued with, "she's my girlfriend." Knowing the words he was going to say before he said them didn't make them hurt any less. His admission was like throwing lighter fluid on a bonfire. My cries were just exacerbated. He didn't tell me to stop. He didn't try to reason with me. He just kept rubbing my back in slow and steady circles. Every once in a while his hand would travel up to my shoulder and he would give it a gentle squeeze. I knew he would sit next to me until I calmed down, so I didn't hurry myself along. I wanted to feel all of it, for my mom.

Eventually, though, the tears stopped and my breathing returned to normal. I turned my head to look at my father and was surprised and ashamed to see tears on his face as well. I didn't even notice he was crying. I sat up and wrapped my arms around his neck.

"Don't cry, Dad. I'm sorry. I'm not trying to upset you. I just wasn't prepared for any of this."

"Trust me, I didn't want you to find out this way." He paused and squeezed me a little tighter. "I thought you'd come home and I could introduce you properly. I thought we'd all sit around and eat dinner and you'd see how wonderful Angie is." I felt his hand smooth over my hair. "Please don't let this get in the way of getting to know her, Charlie. She's a wonderful woman."

I pulled away from him and wiped my tears from my face. The longer we sat here and talked about the woman who I assumed was in the other room, the sillier I began to feel about the whole scenario.

"Dad, stop. I am sure she's amazing. I can't imagine you spending time with anyone who wasn't. Honestly," I said through a sniffle, still trying to hold back the cries that are trying to take over. "I'm not upset that you're dating. I knew that would happen. I just didn't expect..." Another sob broke free and I let it come, crying into my hands. "I didn't expect to see a woman standing in our house wearing mom's apron."

"Oh, Baby," he said as he pulled me into him. I snuggled into his chest, trying to keep the crying at bay. "No one is ever going to take your mother's place. Not in your life and not in my heart. I love your mother and I always will. I am sorry that what you saw upset you and I can totally understand why. So will Angie when we explain it to her. Everything you're feeling is valid, Charlie Bear. It's ok." I took a few deep breaths and they sounded shaky even to me.

"How do you always know the right thing to say, Dad?"

"I generally just try to speak the truth."

"Well, it worked. Thank you. I am sorry I got so upset." He opened his mouth to argue with me but I put my hand up to stop him. "I know what you're going to say, Dad. I'm not apologizing for how I feel, I'm apologizing for how I acted. She didn't deserve that." He looked down at me and I saw the corners of his mouth turn up just a little.

"Charlie, I am so proud to be your dad." At that, we both smiled at each other.

"Good. Now give me five minutes to get myself under control and I would love to come and meet your girlfriend." He leaned down and kissed my temple.

"We will be in the kitchen when you're ready." I watched him stand up and walk out of my bedroom. I took a few more breaths, just making sure I really was in control of myself. I went to the bathroom, splashed some cool water on my face, and fixed the makeup that had been ruined by the epic breakdown I'd just endured. When I felt put back together and not on the verge of another emotional upheaval, I started towards the kitchen. My dad and Angie sat at the dining table, both had mugs in front of them, and Dad's arm rested on the back of her chair. With my head held high and a genuine smile on my face, I walked over to the table.

"Hi, Angie." I held my hand out to her, hoping she would take it. She reached out tentatively, but returned my smile. "I am sorry about the way I behaved earlier. I was just taken by surprise. I promise that I don't always act like that and I hope I didn't ruin my only chance at making a good impression." Her smile grew wider and she shook my hand gently.

"I'm so happy to meet you, Charlie. Your dad has told me such wonderful things about you."

I laugh a little because I knew it was true. "He's biased. You can only trust him about half of the stuff he must have told you. Unfortunately, Dad hasn't told me anything about you, besides your name and that you're dating." I shot my Dad a playful glare.

"I didn't want to tell you over the phone, Charlie. Maybe if you'd come home at all in the last three months we could have done this the right way."

"I, for one, say we all just forget that the last hour even happened and just have a nice dinner getting to know each other." I tried to be a real and true grown up, tried to put my feelings aside and be strong for my dad. I didn't want him to be unhappy and Angie really did seem like a nice woman.

"Deal," Angie said with a smile.

The three of us spent the next two hours eating a delicious meal Angie made, talking, laughing, and generally moving on from an awkward first meeting. I really liked her and I could tell my dad liked her too. It didn't go unnoticed by me that my dad's hand was on her thigh under the table, but it didn't bother me either. I've never wanted my dad to be lonely, and I hoped he was single all those years because he wasn't ready to date, not because he felt I would be bothered by it. It's been almost eight years since we lost mom. It was time for dad to find someone to be happy with again.

"How long have you guys been seeing each other?" I asked Angie.

"Well, we met in the middle of October, but didn't start seeing each other really until November. So, almost two months."

"What you are saying, then, is that you're still in the honeymoon stage of your relationship? So that means Dad is still on his very best behavior and hasn't given you the real insight into some of his more irritating habits."

"Charlie," my dad warned. I shot him my most mischievous smile.

"Dad, let Angie and me bond!" I said to him, turning to Angie I rest my elbow on the tabletop and place my chin on my fist.

"Have you witnessed his obsessive dishwashing tendencies?" I asked, thoroughly interested.

"Oh, you mean how he has to *wash* the dishes before he puts them in the dish*washer*? Yes, we've had this discussion. And what about his thing with towels?"

"You mean how he can only use a towel once? I don't know where that came from. His parents think it's weird too, so he didn't get it from them. Have you met Grammy and Pappy yet?"

"No, not yet. Your dad was hoping I would get to meet them on Christmas. You know, if it was ok with you that I tagged along for Christmas." I could tell she was nervous about asking me that, and it made me feel better about the whole situation that she was sensitive to the fact.

"If Dad wants you at Christmas, I want you at Christmas," I said simply. I saw Angie let out a small sigh of relief and my dad smiled. Just then I heard my phone ping. Pulling it out of my pocket I saw a text from Asher.

Hey Bit. Can I come over?

"Dad?"

"Yeah?"

"I'm so glad we've all grown since I've been away at college."

"Uh, me too, Charlie," he said, obviously confused.

"We're all adults, right?" I asked, keeping a straight face and a level voice.

"Yes. I suppose so. Why?"

"Well, Asher is going to come over here in a few minutes and he's going to sleep over. Since we're all adults, I thought I would let you know instead of trying to sneak him in after you've gone to sleep." I was like stone, keeping my facial expressions even and expectant.

"Charlie, I'm not comfortable with that."

"Dad, I'm not going to lie to you. Asher and I spend most nights together at school. You know I love him and you also know that he loves me. Keeping us apart is pointless. Neither one of us is a child anymore and I guess I would appreciate it if you treated me like the responsible adult you raised me to be." Dad looked absolutely flabbergasted. And to my ultimate surprise and delight, Angie leaned over to speak into Dad's ear. I heard her speak softly to him.

"She's a good girl. He'll be over after you go to sleep anyway if you refuse." I smiled at her because it was true. Dad let out the biggest and loudest sigh I'd ever heard. He was not use to being outnumbered by women.

"Fine, but your door stays open." I laughed out loud because it was ridiculous that he would request that, but I agreed.

Come on over and bring your sleeping clothes. Dad said you could stay the night.

I knew your dad was a reasonable man.

"Thanks, Papa Bear." I got up from the table and gave him a kiss on the cheek.

"You do not get to call me Papa Bear after you invite your boyfriend to stay the night."

I used both my hands to cup his stubble-shadowed face. "You'll always be my Papa Bear, Daddy."

Christmas break passed without much excitement. My dad begrudgingly allowed Asher to stay over at our house, but we made sure Asher never left my room until after Dad had left for work. No need to have awkward run-ins in the bathroom. We both pretended like nothing out of the ordinary was going on, even though it was like there was a giant pink elephant in the room no one wanted to address.

Asher and I attempted, at first, to be quiet and still enjoy our time together, but I quickly realized sex in the same house my father was sleeping in was a huge turn off. I developed a new appreciation for late-night snuggling and sleepy, morning sex. Asher, Reeve, and I spent our days together, catching up with other friends who had come home for break. We went to a few parties and it was good to see some people from high school, but I found myself feeling like I was over the whole scene. Parties with people I went to high school with felt, well, like high school.

Towards the end of our two weeks at home, Asher and I opted to spend evenings on the couch watching movies or playing board games with Reeve. It was relaxing and turned out to be the best way to spend our break from school.

My Dad gave me a shiny new laptop for Christmas, which I loved. Angie was really sweet and gave me a very cool pair of knee-high boots and a few blouses that were very cute. I was touched by her thoughtfulness and impressed with her taste in fashion. She joined us for a dinner a few times over break. I really enjoyed getting to know her and watching as my dad grew more and more comfortable being affectionate with her as the weeks went on. It was as if he was inching into a cold pool, trying to acclimate to the water, trying not to offend or upset me by their PDA. I appreciated the concern, but also found that I wasn't bothered by their being together as much as I would have guessed. I liked Angie and I liked how happy my dad was with her.

On Christmas Eve, Asher took me out on a date and made sure that it was a surprise as to where we were going.

"If you don't stop asking me where we're going I might have to gag you," he said as he navigated the snow-filled streets in his truck.

"You know I don't really like surprises much," I complained.

"Well, I think you're going to like this one," he said with a smile. How could I resist his handsome face when he smiled? I couldn't. I smiled too. We drove for another forty-five minutes, driving us farther and farther from civilization and out into the country. I was sure there was nothing out here that I would be excited about. Finally, he pulled onto a road that seemed relatively unused and we bumped around in his truck as it plowed over snow that had freshly fallen. The road disappeared under the snow and we were now just driving into oblivion.

"Where are we going?" I asked him nervously.

"Don't worry, Bit. I got you," he said as he shot me a smirk. His truck came to a stop and I narrowed my eyes trying to see where we had ended up. All I saw was snow directly in front of us, but a little farther up I could see someone standing next to something I couldn't quite make out. Asher turned towards me. "You ready for your surprise?" I smiled because he was so excited.

"Yes?" I giggled, this all seemed a little silly, but I loved it. He hopped out of his side of the truck and came around to open my door for me. The thrill that ran through me when he put his hands on my waist to help me down never went away and would never get old. He had magical hands and they did magical things to me. He took my hand and led me towards the man standing in the middle of what I could only imagine was a field covered by snow. The closer we got the easier it was to figure out what was going on. "Asher?"

"Yes?" I heard his answer but also felt it as he leaned down and whispered it in my ear.

"Did you drive me out into the middle of nowhere to take me on a horse-drawn carriage ride?"

"I did, indeed."

"Really?" He nodded at me. I never expressed a need or a want to take a ride on a carriage pulled by a horse, mainly because I guess I assumed these types of things only happened in movies. Surely not in real life would you happen upon a carriage waiting to take you on a romantic ride through the snow. "*Really* really?"

"Yes, Babe." He took my hand and led me closer. The man standing near the back of the carriage gave me a smile as we approached. "Charlie, this is Stan. He owns this horse and carriage."

"Hi Charlie, nice to meet you."

"Hi," I smiled back at him, suddenly shy. It seemed a little weird this stranger would be sharing in our date, but I tried to look past it.

"This is Utopia. She'll be our mode of transportation today." Stan walked towards the front of the carriage and I followed. He reached up and stroked the mane of the most beautiful animal I had ever seen. Utopia was all white, perfectly white, with deep blue eyes. She was gorgeous.

"Shall we?" Stan said to Asher.

"Babe?" Asher said as he held a hand out to me motioning for me to climb into the carriage. I managed to make it up and sat down on the comfy bench seat. Asher climbed up and grabbed a large plush blanket off the opposite bench and pulled it over us as he sat down next to me. He tucked us in, then wrapped his arm around my shoulders, pulling me in close to his side. I heard Stan make a loud sound that sounded like "Yah!" and the carriage lurched forward. After the initial takeoff, the ride was relatively smooth. We were very far out in the middle of nowhere so the only light around was from the moon. I couldn't see anything around us and wondered how Stan was even able to navigate, but decided not to worry about it and enjoy the experience with Asher's arm folded around me.

Even though all I could see was thick, black darkness around me, I could see plenty of stars. My eyes were drawn to the sky where the number of twinkling spots in the sky were immeasurable. We didn't live in a huge city, but you definitely couldn't see this many stars anywhere but out in the country, far away from any kind of city lights.

"It's such a beautiful night," I sighed. "I guess we're lucky it stopped snowing so that we could see the stars."

"I made a few calls," Asher said and I could hear the smile in his voice.

"You'd do that for me?" I asked, jokingly.

"Get rid of a few clouds? That's simple, Bit. I'd move mountains for you. Slay dragons. Build you the house of your dreams, going crazy in the process, waiting for you to come back to me, not sure if you ever will."

"Wait. *The Notebook*? You focus on the part of the book where they're apart? What about the end where they die together in each other's arms?"

"That part's sad."

"You'd rather be apart from me then end up with me for all eternity?"

"No. I'd rather dedicate my life to hoping you'll return then to be at the end of our time together," he said. "I'd rather be remembering all the time we had together than face the idea of not having any more time with you at all."

"Oh," was all I could respond with, and barely that. He pressed a kiss to my temple ending the discussion and we continued riding in silence, heading God knows where. The vibrations of the carriage plowing through the snow and the gentle swaying were nearly putting me to sleep. That coupled with the warmth of the blanket and Asher's body against mine were enough to make it difficult to keep my eyes open.

"Bit, we're here." I heard his voice as I felt him gently shaking me awake. I fluttered my eyes open and felt my lung expand, filling with the frigid air around me as I sucked in a surprised breath.

We were in a small clearing, surrounded by trees with white twinkle lights dangling from the limbs above. In the center of the clearing, was a swing set. Just a small one with two swings that you could buy at almost any store, but a swing set none the less. A few feet from the swings was a tall propane warmer and I could see the heat radiating off of it. The last thing I noticed was a cooler.

"Let's go play," Asher said, climbing down from the carriage, holding a hand out for me to join him.

"How did you get a swing set out here?" I asked, baffled at how much effort must have gone into this surprise. I stepped off the wooden step and he held me tight until I was safely on the ground, our chests pressed together.

"Mountains, Bit. Mountains." He took my hand and tugged me towards the swing set and I heard the carriage begin to move.

"Where are Stan and Utopia going?"

"They'll be back. I wanted you alone for a little while." His words sent shivers all over my body.

"Ok," I stammered. I wondered to myself how long he would be able to affect me this way. Would his suggestive voice and words ever lose their effect? I hoped not. He led me to the swings and turned me around letting me sit down. The chains were cold and I immediately wished I had brought gloves. I pulled the sleeves of my coat down over my hands and used the fabric to shield my hands from the freezing metal of the chain links. I watched as he walked over to the cooler and brought out a giant metal thermos. He poured steaming liquid into two small mugs that also appeared out of the cooler, brought one over to me, and I was enveloped by the sweet scent of chocolate.

"You brought cocoa?" I asked, smiling and excitedly taking the cup, willing it to warm up my hands.

"Well, I orchestrated the cocoa to be here for us. Long story," he answered, dismissively. I didn't care where it came from. I was just glad it was there. I took a tentative sip, not wanting to scald my tongue, but found it to be the perfect sipping temperature. Asher brought a cup with him over to the swings and sat down on the empty seat next to me. I used one hand to pull on the chain of his swing, bringing him close to me, and placed a kiss on his cheek. "This is so wonderful, Asher. I'm not sure how you pulled it all off, but it is amazing." I brought him closer still and kissed his lips gently, tasting the hint of chocolate left there by both of us.

"You didn't think I'd let Christmas go by without getting you a gift, did you?"

I shrugged. "You don't need to get me anything; you know that. But this is perfect. Thank you."

"What? This?" He motioned around with a hand to our surroundings. "This isn't your gift. This is simply the setting for the gift,' he said matter-of-factly. "Bit, how long have we been together?" He asked me, surprising me with the change of direction.

"Uh, officially, I guess we've been together for about four years now."

"No, I mean, how long have we been together?" He asked again, as if the distinction was clear.

"Since we were fifteen," I answered, still unclear how the two answers were any different.

"Charlie," he said with a little more gruffness to his voice. He grabbed the chain of my swing and pulled me closer to him so that our faces were just inches apart. I could see our breaths condensing as we both exhaled, the fog we created mingling together. "How long have you belonged to me?" I felt my stomach hollow out and I tried to swallow the lump that had formed in my throat.

"Forever," I whispered, my eyes darting down to his lips.

"Exactly," he whispered back. "And that's also how long I've belonged to you, Bit." That was something that was undeniable to either of us. The possession we felt towards one another was limitless and all-encompassing. Not only did we belong to each other but, in the end, we were one. Sure, in years to come there would be plenty of time to tie ourselves to one another in more traditional ways, but as far as we were concerned, there was not one part of me that was not tethered to him. Where I ended, he began. I never felt truly alone because I always had him.

"So," he continued, letting go of my swing, sending me swaying back and forth. "Although there's nothing in the universe that could keep me from making you my wife eventually," he said as he started reaching into his pants pocket. My heart rate skyrocketed and my mouth was immediately dry. "I know we're not ready for that step quite yet. But I don't want there to be any confusion." He pulled out a little black velvet box and held his hand out, palm up, presenting it to me.

"Asher..." I squeaked out, unsure of what I should say next.

"Don't worry. It's not an engagement ring," he said with a smile. I let out a small breath, the relief coursing through my veins. I was not, at nearly nineteen years old, ready to be engaged. "But it is a promise ring." My eyes darted back and forth between the ring box and his eyes, which were lit up with the most charming smile.

"A promise ring?"

"Yeah." He pulled his hand back and opened up the box. I focused on his eyes, trying to figure out what he was doing giving me a ring. I felt him pick up my left hand and slide the ring on my finger, but I still couldn't look down. When his eyes met mine I found a little comfort in the familiar gray pools. "Do you have any doubts about us?" His question caught me off guard.

"No," I answered, a little defensively.

"Good, neither do I. I was just checking. See, the thing is, there is a lot of stuff about my life right now that I am unsure about. I have no idea if I'm going to make a good lawyer. I can't even think about what I'll be doing next year this time. Where will I be living after college? What kind of law do I want to practice? Will I stay in the fraternity? Fuck, I'm not even sure what kind of cereal I will eat for breakfast next week." He ran his hand through his hair and I noticed that the air was puffing out of his mouth at a quicker pace. "But there's one thing that I am one hundred percent sure about and that's you."

I felt him squeeze my hand that he was still holding so gently in his own. I finally looked down and saw the ring he'd placed upon my finger. It was dainty, delicate, and perfect. A simple, slim, silver band with an infinity symbol glittered with small, sparkling diamonds.

"Asher, it's perfect," I managed. "I'm still a little unclear about what it means though."

"Don't get hung up on the meaning. It means everything. It means nothing. It means that five years ago when I got home from that first summer at my grandpa's farm, I saw a girl who'd turned into a woman and I knew she was mine. It means that every time I fell asleep, I closed my eyes and couldn't wait for it to be morning so I could see her again. It means that I've spent the last five years learning what it means to be *with* someone, not just be her boyfriend. It means that one summer day, under an old bridge, next to a shallow stream, I told the girl I was going to marry one day that I loved her. I loved her then. I love her now. And I'll love her forever until infinity." He bent his head down and kissed my finger right where the ring lay. "But the ring means nothing. It's my commitment to you, to us, and your commitment to me too; that's where the meaning lies. Don't get hung up on the jewelry, Bit. It's just a representation of what's already happening."

"Ok." That was all I could muster. My heart still pounded in my chest and I felt weepy little tears collecting in the corner of my eyes, but I had no words. No words I could weave together to create such magic as he gave to me. "Asher, I don't know what to say." My eyes were glued to the ring.

"Just say you'll wear it and that we'll always be together."

"I will always be yours," I said with as much conviction as I have ever felt. I know the words I said to him in this moment were the truest words I've ever spoken. If I lived, if I breathed, if I walked this earth, I was his. And maybe even beyond that.

He pulled me up from the swing and instantly I was in his arms. My hands, like they were finding home again, folded around his neck and my fingers threaded through his hair. His hands glided along my waist, just under the plush of my coat, and wrapped all the way around me, pinning me to him. He felt me shudder against him and pulled away just far enough to whisper in my ear.

"You cold, Bit?"

I just shook my head. The trembling wasn't from the cold, it was from the longing I felt running amok throughout my body. I felt it everywhere and as it swept through my system it stole my breath away with it. He moved me closer to the propane warmer anyway, and I felt the warmth waft over me. I pressed my cheek harder against his chest, my hands still able to reach his neck, if only for the high-heeled boots I was wearing.

His hands came to rest on the curve of my waist and I noticed that we were slowly swaying back and forth, dancing to no music, but dancing nonetheless. "Asher?" I looked up towards his eyes.

"Yeah?" He answered softly.

"I feel like the jacket I got you for Christmas is really lame now." He laughed, which is exactly what I was going for.

"I love the jacket. And I also love knowing that I can totally outdo you in the gift department."

"Should I even try to compete?"

"No. Just let me spoil you."

And I did. I enjoyed everything he did for me. He swept my hair out of my eyes and tucked it behind my ear. He placed small, teasing kisses on my bare skin where he could. I felt his lips along my neck, on my ear, then softly on my mouth. His hands gripped me firmly and pulled my feet from the ground, bringing my face level to his. Taking advantage, I wrapped my arms fully around his neck and used my hands to feel the muscle beneath his coat. His strong shoulders flexed with use as he held me to him. He held me like this for a few minutes, longer than anyone should be able to hold up another person, but he eventually put me down and like clockwork I heard the trotting of Utopia coming back to collect us.

Stan pulled the carriage right up to us and Asher held a hand out to help me up. I climbed in and took a seat, looking back at the beautiful setting Asher created for us. I frantically stood up and shouted, "Wait!" I pulled out my cell phone and tried to capture what I could of the most romantic night of my life on the tiny screen. I got a few shots and admitted to myself that it would never look as good in a picture as it did at that moment and gave up. I moved to put my phone away and he grabbed it from me and spun us around, holding his arm out, and took a picture of us. Right before I heard the 'click' created by the phone snapping the picture, I felt his lips press against my cheek. Instinctually, my eyes closed and I turned my head slightly into his touch. I saw the flash through my eyelids, but couldn't be bothered to open my eyes.

Chapter Four

Summer came quickly, ending what could only be described as a tumultuous first year of college. Reeve was almost back to her normal self and although she wasn't as outgoing as she used to be, she wasn't a recluse anymore. I felt like I had my best friend again. Reeve and I decided to head home for summer vacation, but true to tradition, Asher traveled to his grandfather's farm. We would have a few weeks at the beginning and end of break together, but he would be gone for the majority of the summer. His grandfather was getting older and needed a lot more help than he had in the years past, so Asher had a responsibility to go. I didn't mind as much as I had before. Summers together just weren't a part of our relationship. And I'd be lying if I didn't admit the excitement that fueled our reunions wasn't a big reason why I wasn't totally crushed to see him go. I knew when he got back we would be crazy with need for each other. Plus one long summer of working hard in the sun always returned a bronzed and buff Asher. No, I didn't complain. I just tried to return the favor and make sure I looked just as good for him. I was ok with him being gone, but goodbyes were never fun.

The day he left I tried to hold back my sad tears because I knew it didn't help him, but I couldn't stop the few tears that slid down my cheek. He kissed them away, whispering to me that he would miss me, that we would call each other every day. We would email, send letters, but I could hear in his voice he was just as upset as I was.

I looked up at him, his face blurred through the tears I refused to let go and watched as he leaned in to kiss me goodbye. I hated goodbye kisses. They were so sad and empty.

"I love you," he said against my lips.

"I love you too." I cried quietly.

"I'll miss you." I answered by kissing him again. Eventually he pulled away, kissed my forehead and walked away.

One month later I woke up to Reeve crashing through my bedroom door.

"Wake up!" She yelled as she jumped on my bed. I was startled enough to sit straight up in my bed and I felt my heavy ponytail whip around to the front of my face. I heard her laugh as I pushed my hair out of my face. "Time to get up. We've got stuff to do."

"What the hell could we have to do at," I looked over at my alarm clock, "eight am?"

"We're going to get you pampered, all courtesy of your lovesick boyfriend." My heart skipped a few beats at the mention of Asher.

"What?" I asked as a smile grew on my face.

"Yes. He is sad he can't be here for your birthday, so he's instructed me to take you out and make you feel wonderful."

I cocked my head to the side and frowned a little. "Aww...." I said, feeling that warm gooeyness take over my insides. He was so sweet. "My birthday is tomorrow though," I said, a little bit confused.

Reeve held up her hands. "Hey, I'm just following instructions." She stood up and pulled the covers off of me. "Get up. You've got ten minutes to get downstairs and don't wash your hair."

"Ok," I laughed.

Forty-five minutes later we were at a spa so exquisitely beautiful I couldn't help but look around and gawk.

"Hi, we've got appointments for nine am. Charlie and Reeve," she said to the receptionist behind her ornately beautiful hand-carved wooden desk. From that moment on it was one wonderful experience after the next. We had massages, manicures, pedicures, facials and the last stop was the hair salon.

"Uh, I'm not sure I want a haircut," I nervously said to Reeve. She turned to the stylist attending to me and gave her a serious look.

"We're on very strict orders from our benefactor for the hair. A *slight* trim, no more than a half inch, an extravagant wash complete with scalp massage, and a deep conditioning treatment. He wants her hair soft, shiny, and *long*. So seriously, don't cut it much." Reeve turned back to me and rolled her eyes. "He nearly made me sign a contract to make sure you wouldn't come out of here with your hair any shorter."

I didn't bother telling her all the times he pulled it while we made love or how he used it to manipulate my body to position me. I just shrugged. "He likes it long." And I liked keeping it long to make him happy. He's always loved my hair. Changing the subject, I casually mentioned how all this must have cost him a small fortune. I saw Reeve try to hide a smile.

"He's been saving the money he made from his grandfather to pay for your present. Don't worry Charlie; he loves you and wanted to do this for you. Well," she paused and the sneaky smile was back. "For us. I made him pay for me too, seeing as how I was forced to spend the entire day here with you." I giggled along with her because I could totally see her weaseling to get her way.

When the entire process was complete, we both looked and felt amazing. My hair had never been softer and my skin was glowing. I was relaxed and happy. All I needed was Asher's arms around me and everything would be perfect.

We got back into Reeve's car and I listened to her endless rattling until I realized we were not headed towards our part of town.

"Reeve, where are we going? Home is the other direction." She waved a hand at me like it didn't matter.

"I just have one more errand to run. It will only take a minute, promise." I sat back in my seat resigned to listening to her for as long as I was stuck in the car. Heaven forbid you reach to turn up the stereo or try to engage in conversation. When Reeve drove she wanted an audience, not a participant. I was so zoned out I never even noticed when the car stopped until Reeve opened her door and popped out. She walked around to my side of the car and opened my door too. I looked up at her, puzzled.

"Come on, Charlie. You've got a plane to catch."

"Excuse me?"

"You're flight leaves in an hour and a half, so you better hurry up."

"What flight?" Reeve rolled her eyes at me.

"The flight your boyfriend booked you so he could spend your birthday with him tomorrow. So, hurry up." She grabbed my arm and hauled me out of the car.

"I don't have any luggage. I didn't pack anything," I said, nearly panicked. I began to remember how much I hated surprises. Reeve walked to her trunk and popped it open, pulling out a rolling suitcase.

"Everything you need should be in here. If I forgot something I'm sure you can manage to pick it up when you get there."

"Is this really happening?" I was in shock. How had all of this been planned right under my nose? "Does my dad know where I'm going?"

"Yeah, he's in on it. All three of us were. Asher hounded us to make sure it all got planned while we still kept it a secret. You better have a freaking fantastic time, or he's gonna hear about it from me. This was such a pain in my ass." She moved in and pulled me into a hug. "But you're worth it. So have a great time, have some great sex, and tell me all about it when you get back."

"Reeve?" I mumbled into her shoulder.

"Yeah?"

"I've never been on a plane before. I'm scared."

"In the front zipper pocket of your suitcase there is a tiny bottle of vodka. Before you go through security stop somewhere and get an orange juice. Pour it in and chug it down. You'll be fine." She pulled away and winked at me.

"You really did think of everything."

"That was your dad's idea." I laughed and covered my mouth. The idea of my father giving the ok for his underage daughter to consume alcohol was completely ridiculous to me. It had me giggling all the way to the tiny store inside the airport where I bought my overpriced orange juice.

Chapter Five

Exiting the plane and walking through the unfamiliar airport was thrilling. I looked to every face I saw, every man I encountered was studied to make sure it wasn't him. I didn't want to miss him and I wanted to find him as soon as possible. The flight wasn't very long and the vodka helped ease my fears, but the anticipation of seeing him, knowing we would be together soon, was enough to make a girl sprint through an airport terminal.

I caught a glimpse of his face as I darted around other passengers reuniting with their families. My heart clenched in my chest and I pushed back the tears that threatened to spill from my eyes. My purse dropped from my shoulder and I ran as fast as I could to leap onto him. Luckily for us, he caught me and I sighed heavily as his arms wrapped around my waist. They were thicker and sturdier. Harder, even. I loved what summers on the farm did to his body. I could feel his stomach was rock hard as well.

"Asher," I breathed into his neck.

"Bit," he countered as he ran his hand down the length of my hair. "God, I missed you."

"I missed you too." We held each other there, in the middle of the airport, for a long while, neither of us willing to let the other go so easily. Eventually I released my arms from around his neck and pulled back to look at him. His hair was a little longer, his freckles were deliciously darker, and his eyes were a deep, dark gray, darker than usual. "Hi," I said shyly.

"Hey, Babe. You ready to get out of here?" His words held promises of time alone, time to feel each other, to reconnect.

"Yes." He pressed his lips to mine and all the promises his words held were vowed again in his kiss. His lips slid over mine and I was reminded how well my body responded to him. Pleasure rippled through my body, concentrating in my core at the juncture between my thighs. I only wore a pair of yoga pants and I knew he could feel the heat that began to radiate from my center.

"Ok, time to go," he said as he pulled away. "A few more minutes of this and we'll both get in a lot of trouble with the TSA. They frown on people having loud and rough sex in front of baggage claim."

"Loud and rough?" I gulped.

"Or sweet and quiet," he shrugged, "whichever you prefer. All I know is that I need to be inside of you, like yesterday."

We walked hand-in-hand to his car and shared kisses at almost every single stop light we caught. The first few were innocent and sweet, but slowly they transformed into passionate kisses that were beginning to feel like poor and unsatisfying replacements for other bodily contact. His hand found my thigh as we drove through the streets and I willed it to slide farther up, closer to my core where I desperately needed something – *anything*.

I expected us to drive to a farm, but was surprised again when he turned into the parking lot of a hotel. "We aren't going to your grandfather's farm?"

"Nope," he said as he turned off the car and got out. There was some serious lack of information going on here. I climbed out of the car and met him at the trunk where he was lifting my bag out.

"How long are we staying here?"

"Just two nights."

"Then what?"

"We'll go back to my grandpa's farm after that. I took a few days off, but then I'll have to get back to the farm to help out."

"How long am I staying?"

"Your plane home leaves in four days," he said with a smile. "So, two days here and two days on the farm. Is that ok?"

"Yeah." It was the best birthday present ever.

"Great. Let's go inside," he said while his eyes glimmered with excitement. He nearly dragged me all the way to the elevator once we were inside the lobby.

"Don't we have to check in?" I asked as he pressed the call button no less than forty times, as he eagerly watched the doors, waiting for them to open.

"I checked in before I picked you up. Don't worry about anything. I've got it all covered." The doors to the elevator slid open and I was hauled in. I assumed the elevator was empty but had no way to be completely sure because Asher had my back pressed up against the far wall before the doors even shut completely.

His hands roamed down my waist, over my hips, and slid back over my ass. His mouth was on my neck and I couldn't help but grip the hair at the nape of his neck.

"I've missed you so much, Bit. I think this has been the worst summer yet," he said through garbled words mumbled against the sensitive skin of my collarbone. His hands swiftly came around to my front and slid between my flesh and the fabric of my shirt. He cupped my breasts over my bra and I gasped as his thumbs teased my nipples aching for more attention.

"I missed you too. But I don't, oh…" His fingers applied more pressure to my breasts and sent spikes of pleasure throughout my body. "But, oh god, I don't think I realized how much until right now." Our lips found each other and the kiss devoured us. Suddenly Asher was pulling away and I was abandoned in my state of acute arousal, left cold. My eyes opened just as the doors to the elevator were opening. A couple, about mid-fifties, stood on the other side of the threshold and by the looks on their faces Asher hadn't pulled away quick enough to conceal what we were doing.

The four of us stood staring at each other for what seemed like a millennia, but eventually the woman cleared her throat and mustered a quiet, "We'll just wait for the next elevator." Asher stealthily moved forward to hit the button to close the doors and I watched with complete embarrassment as their faces disappeared behind the mirrored plates of the elevator doors.

"I can't even believe that just happened," I said as I rubbed my hand up and down my face, feeling the burn of my red face against my hand. Then I heard the distinct sounds of Asher laughing. "What is so funny?" I didn't find it amusing. It was embarrassing. "Asher!" He was gasping for air, he was laughing so hard. His finally bent down to rest his hands on his knees, trying to regulate his breathing.

"Babe, their faces. I'll never forget the look on that woman's face!" He started laughing all over again.

"She's probably never walked in on anyone mid-coitus in an elevator before," I said, exasperated.

"Bit, we were fully clothed. If anything, she saw you getting felt up. No nudity involved. Coitus interruptus. He's probably gonna get lucky tonight thanks to us." I studied his face, as red as mine but not from humiliation, from laughter. He looked young and happy. And he was mostly right. We were young and in love. So what if someone caught us making out? It might have been a hard-core make out session, but whatever. The doors opened again and Asher took my hand. "This is us."

The room he led us to was beautiful. I hadn't stayed in many hotels before, but I liked what I saw in this one. There was an enormous king-sized bed in the middle of the room, draped with a deep, royal purple comforter that looked like it swallowed a fluffy cloud. There were pillows to the point of excess and one very comfortable-looking chaise lounge near a balcony plush with greenery. I nearly raced to the bathroom to see the bathtub.

"Oh my goodness, Asher. There is a tub in here that would fit five very large, grown men. I might spend all two days in this very tub."

"Not all two days I hope," I felt his words as he came up behind me and rested his jaw on my shoulder.

I spun around and looked him in the eye. "Well, what else would I do with my time?" His answer was to lift my shirt over my head. I tried to hide my smile but it was hopeless.

The smile, however, went away on its own when I saw the look in his eyes. His gray eyes were even darker than normal and my belly flopped at the thought of what that meant. He wanted me. It had been over a month since we'd been together and I felt the familiar ache take up residence between my legs.

He ran the back of his hand down the skin of my shoulder, continuing own my arm. He leaned forward and pressed a kiss to the skin of the top of my shoulder.

"Your skin is so soft." He moved open-mouthed kisses up the slope of my neck, making me shudder.

"You spent a lot of money for me to get pampered at a spa. They paid a lot of attention to my skin." I tried to remain calm as his mouth moved behind my ear, as his hands roamed my back, unclasping my bra.

"You thought I was doing it all for you, to surprise you for your birthday." He pulled away, letting my bra fall to the ground at our feet. His mouth resumed its work on my collarbone, kissing in between words. "It partly was for you, to make you feel good. But it was mostly for me. Thinking about how you'd feel under my hands, how you'd smell after I got your clothes off, how relaxed you'd be for me. That's really why I sent you there." I closed my eyes as I felt his lips envelop the tip of my breast, covering my nipple, sucking it into his mouth. As he worked one nipple with his lips and teeth, his hand covered my other breast. He palmed its fullness and gently tugged my nipple until it puckered and pebbled. His mouth left my breast and I moaned when the cool air hit the nipple he left wet and painfully hard. He continued kissing down my stomach and I felt my knees shake, the sensations flooding through my body coupled with the anticipation of everything yet to come, making me unstable.

He abandoned my breasts completely and his hands came to the waistband of my yoga pants, pulling them down with him as he bent to his knees in front of me. My hands found his hair and I looked down at him as he lifted one foot after the other, freeing me from the rest of my clothes.

"God, I missed you," he said as he pressed his cheek into my belly, hugging me around my waist. He breathed deeply and I could feel the swishing of his breath against my skin every time he exhaled. I reached down the back of his neck and grabbed his shirt, urging him to lean away so I could tug it off of him. From where I stood above him, I could see all of his shoulder muscles flexing as he pulled the shirt from his arms. His biceps came into view and then his forearms.

"What have you been doing on the farm, Asher? You're even bigger than you were before you left, which is impressive."

"A lot of throwing hay bales and working off all my sexual frustration," he groaned. His hands wandered around the sides of my body, kneading my soft skin as he went along. "This has been the first time we've been away from each other since the first time we had sex, Bit. I wasn't prepared to deal with how much I would miss you, how much my body would miss you. I've been doing a lot of push-ups and crunches, just trying to exhaust myself into not wanting you anymore." He gently kissed my belly-button. "It never really works; I always still want you. I just fall asleep a little easier when I can't move a muscle." His hands were on my backside for a moment and he gave both cheeks a squeeze with an audible groan. He pulled his hands back to my waist and gently urged me back to lean against the counter.

I felt the cold countertop against my ass and his warm hands moving along my body still. His right hand moved down my leg and cupped my calf. He looked up into my eyes as he pulled my leg up so that the back of my knee rested on his shoulder, the bottom half of my leg folding over onto his back. I bit my lip as I saw his eyes wander to my center and I felt slightly insecure knowing how exposed I was at the moment. There was nothing to hide from him in this position. No way for him not to see all of me.

"You're so beautiful," he said as he ran his hands along the juncture where my legs met my hips, his touch teasing me.

In a moment of pure bravery I asked, "What do I look like?" I wondered what he saw when he looked at me, how he saw me.

I saw him seriously considering my question, taking time to think about his answer. "You look pink, different shades of pink. Some darker and some lighter." I felt his thumbs touch me, spread me wider and I gasped. Just the contact had me reeling. "You look warm, Babe. Snug. Dark. Beautiful." I tried to breathe steadily, but each breath got lost in the next and all I knew is the burning in my lungs matched the heat of my center. "You look wet, Bit." My head rolled back and I was glad for the counter to lean on because I'm sure I would have crumpled to the floor without it. "You look like you're mine," he rasped just before his tongue caressed me from bottom to top.

My entire body shook from the immense pleasure. One touch from him was all it took to send me away into a state of bliss. He kissed me tenderly, using his fingers to tease me and spread me. His tongue found my clit and took quick and furious swipes over it, causing me to cry out.

"Oh yes," I sputtered. Spurred on by my outcry, he pushed two fingers inside of me, softly moving in and out. The combinations of the quick flicks of his tongue and the slow torture of his fingers pushed me higher and higher. I felt my core tighten and my body began to tremble. My hands gripped the edge of the countertop, keeping me upright while my hips rocked back and forth hoping to find the release my body craved. "Asher, I need more, something..." I couldn't finish my thought. He moved his fingers inside me, coming forward and stroking the small area that hid deep within me that always made me breathless.

"Oh, God!" I screamed as my legs came to wrap around his head. He never wavered, just kept working me while my orgasm rolled through me, wreaking havoc on my body. My legs compressed around his head, my hands gripped his hair, and I lost all sense of self as I used his body to bring pleasure to mine.

Eventually my body calmed and yet he still kissed and nuzzled my sex. "I've been waiting for a month to watch you come apart, Bit." He said, placing one last tender kiss again my core. "That was a fucking awesome front row seat." He moved up my body, trailing kisses up between my breasts. He leaned in to place a kiss on my mouth and I turned, offering him my cheek instead. "What's the matter?" He asked, pulling away to see my face.

"Nothing," I said as I ran my hands through his hair, trying to distract him.

"You don't want me to kiss you?" He sounded hurt.

"No! I do. You're just all..." I motioned with my hand and waved it in front of his face. "Covered in me."

"You don't want to taste yourself?" He asked, curiously. I tried very hard to keep my face from wrinkling up.

"No, thank you."

"You taste amazing," he said with a smile. I appreciated what he said, but I didn't necessarily believe him. And I didn't want to find out if he was telling the truth.

"I'm sorry. I can't."

"I get it," he said, shrugging. "But honestly, one day, I would really like to see you try it. For me." I gave an awkward smile, slightly uncomfortable with the whole idea.

"You think it would do something for you to watch me taste myself?" I said as I tried not to let my feelings show through my face. He pushed a lock of my hair that came loose behind my ear and gave me a lopsided grin. He shrugged his shoulders. "Why?" I was honestly curious at this point. Thinking about the roles being reverse, having him taste himself, did nothing for me, besides gross me out a little.

"I don't know, Babe. It just would. I don't want to think about it if it's not gonna happen."

"Ok," I said.

"Tell you what," he said as he cupped my face. I could see him resisting the urge to lean forward and kiss me. "Why don't you go fill that tub up, pour in something girly, and I will brush my teeth and then come join you." I didn't feel right to walk away from him at that moment. Something was off between us. After the spectacularly intimate moment we had just shared, an invisible wall had just as quickly been built between us. He wanted something that I couldn't give him, or rather, wouldn't.

I moved forward to wrap my arms around his neck and kissed him behind his ear. "I'm sorry," I whispered. He groaned and pulled away.

"Don't. Don't apologize. You've got nothing to be sorry for."

"I'm not sorry for not kissing you. I'm sorry for the way we feel right now. How it feels in this room. I've never said no to you before. I don't like the way it's making me feel."

"How do you feel?" He stepped away from me fully. The two feet between us felt like twenty to me.

"I feel like I want to make you happy. I want to please you," I said, ending on a whisper.

"You do make me happy. You do please me."

"I want to *do* things for you," I said, trying to imply meaning.

"Stop dancing around your feelings, Bit. Tell me."

"If there's something you want, *sexually*, I want to give it to you. I want to be enough for you."

"Babe, you're more than enough for me. I don't need anything else from you. Forget I said anything. I had never even thought about it until just now. Kissing you after going down on you is not a deal breaker, it's just something that crossed my mind as sexy. Don't let it bother you. Besides, we're both going to have boundaries. You can't give me something you're not comfortable with because you're afraid of disappointing me. I don't want it then. I want whatever you're comfortable giving me."

"I don't like this," I said, looking down at my feet.

"What?"

"This!" I motioned between us, at the distance. "I don't like feeling like there's this *thing* between us. I've never felt this before. I don't want anything to come between us." I watched as he stripped his pants and boxer briefs off, now naked in front of me. He walked towards me and pulled me into his arms, wrapping himself so fully and so completely around me, I found it a little difficult to take a full breath.

"There," he said quietly. "Now there's nothing between us except for a little bit of residual sweat from our earlier exploits," he whispered in my ear, trying to make me smile. I let myself feel him pressed against me and I tried to let the tension go. I tried to *feel* him, remind myself who we were together, tried to convince myself that this wasn't a big deal. And really, it wasn't. I was not totally concerned that he didn't get to kiss me. I was really hung up on the idea of something coming between us. The idea of anything coming between us, that scared me. "I love you." I knew he loved me. I could always feel his love.

"I love you too," I responded honestly.

"Can we take a bath now?"

"Yes," I said with a small laugh. And we did. We bathed for hours, refilling the tub when the water got cold. We ordered room service and talked, covering all the details emails and phone calls forced us to leave out. We made love and I tried so hard to be everything he needed.

Chapter Six

"Happy birthday, Bit." I heard the words in my ear and felt his hands roaming my naked body as I lay in bed next to him. Asher. I was with Asher on my birthday. This never happened before. We were always separated and I've had to accept just hearing his voice over the phone wishing me a happy birthday. I opened my eyes and saw his face laying on my pillow, facing me, just inches away.

"Hi," I squeaked, still sleepy.

"How does it feel to be nineteen?"

"It feels early," I said as I stretched.

"We've got a lot to do today. So, you take a shower and I'll order breakfast."

"We have to get up?"

"Busy day," he said and swatted my naked butt.

He wasn't kidding either. We ran from one activity to another and he made sure to include my favorites along the way: I got my coffee, he took me to an art supply store and let me browse as long as I wanted, and he even took me to a book store. Towards the end of the day we walked down the street hand-in-hand when he stopped in front of a door and motioned for me to go in. I looked up and saw the word TATTOO painted on the window.

"Tattoos?" I asked, panicked.

"Well, you don't have to get one, but I'm going to."

"Really?"

"Yeah, I've been thinking about it ever since I turned eighteen."

"I don't get it. This is supposed to be my birthday, why are we getting you a tattoo?"

He kissed me quickly and pulled away smiling. "Because my tattoo is going to be your name." My eyebrows shot up and I shook my head.

"Asher, no. No, no no, no, no, no. You can't. No." My head shook quickly back and forth, my hair flailing around behind me and I unconsciously took a few steps backwards.

"Yes. Listen, I've given this a lot of thought and I want to do it. You can either come in here and keep me company or you can take a cab back to the hotel, but I really want you with me." I looked back and forth between Asher and the door to the tattoo parlor.

"Can you get something else besides my name?"

"No."

"Is there anything I can say to change your mind? This is a little crazy."

"What's crazy about it?"

"It's permanent, Asher."

"So are we."

There was nothing else to say. Even if I didn't think it was a good idea, I couldn't argue with that. Didn't want to. I was impressed, however, with how prepared he was. It did seem like he'd spent a lot of time thinking about the decision. He had a drawing with him that outlined exactly what he wanted, he knew where he wanted it, and there was no talking him out of it.

I watched as they prepped his arm, the spot right below his elbow on the backside. I watched as they placed the stencil and he stood up to look in the mirror, approving its placement. He showed it to me and asked, "How's it look?" He was so excited. All I could do was smile. I watched as he flinched when the needle dug into his skin, moving so quickly in and out you couldn't see it move, just heard the incessant buzzing. He put on a brave face, but I could tell at some points it really hurt him. It took about an hour and a half, but when all was said and done "Bit" was scrawled down his arm in a masculine yet flowery script.

"I love it," he said, moving in front of the mirror to examine it from all angles. I stood behind him and when he lowered his arm naturally, I could see my name, clear as day, etched permanently on his skin.

"You're crazy," I said under my breath. He heard me, of course, and we smiled at each other.

"You don't think you'd ever get my name tattooed on you?"

I shook my head. "No, probably not."

"Why?"

"I don't think I need a reason for *not* getting a tattoo. I still think you need a reason for the tattoo you just got."

"Why is it so hard for you to understand? This tattoo? It will last for as long as I live. When I die, this tattoo will still be on my skin, still be a part of me. But eventually, I will be gone, the tattoo will be gone, and you will be gone too. But, us? *We* will never be gone. We're forever. Infinite. So whether I get your name tattooed on me or not, it makes no difference. This ink, it's permanent, but it's nothing compared to how I feel about you."

I pulled him to me so that our lips were almost touching. "I think you're crazy for doing this, but I love you."

"That's all I need, Bit. I love you too."

The next two days went by too quickly. I met Asher's grandparents when we went to the farm and, although they were nice, they weren't much company. While Asher was out working the fields, or whatever he did the entire day he was gone, I spent a lot of time trying to draw the landscape around me. Thank goodness Reeve had thought to pack my drawing supplies. I wasn't a city girl, but I wasn't used to being in such a rural setting either. I tried perfecting my trees, worked on getting the shading of the wheat fields just right.

The last night of my visit Asher found me in the hay loft of the barn, where I had befriended the barn cat. This beastly cat must have made many meals of mice because he was massive. I couldn't even fathom how he'd made it up to the second story of the barn. He rubbed vigorously against my ankle, his pink, wet nose seeking out any part of me that he could accost.

"Bit, you up there?"

"Yeah. I'm hanging out with the cat."

I saw Asher's face appear as he climbed up the ladder to sit next to me. "Ah ha, you've met Sir Mouse-A-Lot." I giggled loudly.

"That's not really his name."

"Indeed. He is the best mouser in these parts. That's why he's so fat."

"How was your day?" I asked, looking over at him. His cheeks were pink as if he'd been in the sun too long. I looked over the rest of him and it seemed like his cheeks took the brunt of the sunlight.

"Long. I just kept thinking about how you're leaving tomorrow."

I scooted closer to him and rested my head on his shoulder. "Thank you for flying me out here. I had a really good time. Best birthday ever."

"I wish you could stay."

I sighed. "Honestly, I'd love to spend the summer with you, Asher. But there's nothing for me to do here."

"You could draw."

I looked over at him and took a moment to think about what he was saying. Asher had his moments of insecurity, just like any guy, and sometimes he just wanted me near him, especially when it felt like it wasn't an option. "I could draw, but eventually I would get tired of drawing. My dad would miss me and I feel like Reeve still needs someone around to keep her spirits up." I reached over and wrapped my hand around the back of his neck, urging him to look at me. "We've spent every summer apart, and even though I miss you like crazy, the best part of the summer is always the day you come back." I started playing with the hair on the back of his neck, liking the way it was still damp from sweat.

"I guess you're right," he said, wiping his hands over his face. He stopped and looked over at me, his gray eyes dim and a little bit sad. "But I'm still going to miss you."

"I'm going to miss you too, Asher. But I'm here right now." In that moment I think we both realized that we had only hours left together and that there were ways to show each other how much the other would be missed. I pulled his mouth to mine and climbed over his lap to straddle him. His hands came to rest on my backside and I trailed my hands up and down his chest, pouring everything into our kiss. I used my teeth to gently tug his bottom lip and won a low and rumbling groan from him, making my heart beat faster.

"I want you, Bit. Right here."

"I'm all yours, Babe." He wrapped one arm around my waist and rolled so I was under him. His mouth nibbled on my neck as his hands moved to unbutton my jean shorts. I pulled up on the back of his shirt, yanking it over his head. His mouth returned to my neck, but made its way down my body swiftly. He pulled down my shorts and panties and I lifted my hips to allow him to remove them completely. I quickly sat up and took my shirt and bra off, watching as he removed his pants.

Once we were both naked he dove back to me, laying me down on the hay. Any other time of my life I would have complained about the scratchy hay underneath my bare skin, but in this moment I simply did not care. All that mattered was the connection we were trying to make with one another.

He covered my body with his own, blanketing me with his skin still warm from all the hard work he'd done that day. His made trails of kisses along my skin, moving from my mouth, to my neck, to my shoulder and back again. His hand moved to cup my sex, his fingers parting me and slipping inside. My back arched off the floor and I whimpered into his mouth as his fingers worked me.

"I love the way you respond to me, Bit." He lowered his mouth to my breast and the combination of his mouth teasing my nipple and his fingers stroking me from the inside did nothing to calm the storm raging inside me. He was adding fuel to the fire. I heard his voice, but he sounded far away; I was lost in a new reality where all that mattered were our bodies and how we made each other feel. "I know every button to push and how to push it. I've mastered your body and there's not another person on the planet who could play you like I can."

I reached between us and felt him, hot and throbbing, between us. I ran my hand up and down along his shaft and watched as he lost his concentration. His mouth fell from my breast and his fingers eased their ministrations. He wasn't the only one who could bring pleasure. I loved watching him give in to the sensations, dropping all pretense and just *feeling*. His face fell to rest in the crook of my neck and I kissed along his shoulder while I worked him between my legs.

"I love you, Asher. And I love how turned on you get when I touch you." He groaned as I used my thumb to swirl the tip of his head, spreading around the drop of pre-cum that had accumulated.

"Please," he rasped. "I want to be inside you." I tilted my hips up and guided his tip into me. Then I felt his instincts kick in and he took control. At first he took long and slow drags through me, tilting his hips, fully burying himself into me with every stroke. I matched his rhythm and opened up for him, giving him access to the deepest parts of me. His thrusts matched his kisses and our bodies fell into a kind of synchronicity that made every fiber of my soul fall even deeper into love with him. This was so much more than just a physical connection. Every touch he gifted me with was one of love.

Eventually, he manipulated my body so that my legs were both folded to the side, and the new angle of penetration left me gasping for air, and grasping his arms, praying for the release that was hiding just out of reach. "Oh god, Asher," I moaned. This position brought his body closer to mine, and the way I was twisted at my stomach intensified every thrust and I feared I might explode. I'd never been this high before, never felt this kind of pressure. "Please." I didn't know what I was asking for. Relief? More? An End? I was at the mercy of my body and him.

"Tell me," he said. I was confused. Tell him what? "Tell me that you'll always be mine. Say it. I need to hear it." He moved faster and I felt my impending orgasm inching closer. I was afraid of what would happen when I finally reached that point, afraid I couldn't handle the kind of pleasure I was building towards.

"We belong to each other, Asher. I'll never be anyone's but yours. And you'll always be mine."

He moved me again so that my knees were bent and my feet were resting on his chest. He surged forward and I cried out as my release pounded through me. He continued to thrust as I came around him, my core clenching deliciously around his cock, everything inside of me liquefying. I'd never felt this kind of physical release. His movements just prolonged my orgasm and I struggled to breathe through it. My hands were in my hair, my back arched, every other part of me trembling.

"I can feel you, Bit. I can feel you coming. It's amazing. It's so... oh my God..." He thrust a few more times and I heard him finally give into his pleasure. I was still reeling and I feared I might never return to normal. I was altered. Moved. Split apart and put back together differently.

He finally collapsed on top of me, our sweaty bodies sticking to each other, our breathing rapid and intense. It took a few minutes before I was ready to come back to my senses. I realized I was lightly grazing my fingers along his spine, content to just be in the moment with him. I felt him pull away from me and saw his eyes come to rest right in front of mine, his face just inches away.

"That was amazing," he whispered. I bit down on my bottom lip and nodded in agreement. "You're amazing." He pressed his lips against mine and we melted together. There was no urgency or lust in this kiss. It was simply loving. "I'm going to miss you."

"I'll miss you too. But thinking about missing each other is what got us naked in a hay loft. Come to think of it, as much as I enjoyed that, I'd really like to take a shower now. I'm starting to itch."

That last night we spent together on the farm was quiet and a little bit sad. I never had to leave Asher before and I dreaded having our usual roles reversed in the morning when he took me to the airport. But, as sad as goodbye kisses are, hello kisses were ten times better. And that's what I kept telling myself on the plane ride home. I could wait to get my hello kisses.

Chapter Seven

Sophomore year of college started pretty much just like the previous. Asher tried to convince me to get an apartment with him and, again, I opted to live with Reeve in the sorority house. Reeve's emotional well-being improved over the summer, but I still didn't feel like abandoning her to live with my boyfriend. Asher's frat was just down the street and I knew we'd see each other all the time.

The homecoming game approached again, and even though Reeve seemed fine, I was on best friend high-alert just in case the anniversary of her attack were to bring back any bad feelings or memories. I wouldn't be any use to her today though, I was sick and in bed.

"Are you sure you don't want me to bring you anything?" Reeve asked me as she stood at the door, getting ready to leave for her morning class. I was curled up on my bed, trying not to move. I woke up with a stomach bug and was trying to fend off the nausea.

"No, I'm fine. I just need to lie really still so I don't puke anymore."

"Ok. Does Asher know you're sick?"

"Um, no. I don't need to tell my boyfriend that I've been throwing up. That's a surefire way to kill the romance. We've been together forever, but that doesn't mean he needs to know those sorts of things." Reeve laughed as she pulled her backpack up onto her shoulder.

"Ok, but you know if he finds out you're sick and you didn't tell him, he's going to be upset about it."

I groaned. "Fine. Text him and tell him I'm sick, but I'm fine, and that I'll be missing classes today." Reeve left grinning, probably because she knew what I was in for. Asher wouldn't leave me alone if he knew I was sick. He was kind of irritatingly adorable that way. I began to breathe deeply, in through my nose and out through my mouth, trying desperately to make the terrible feeling go away. It wasn't working and I could feel the urge getting stronger and stronger. Eventually, when I knew I couldn't avoid it any longer, I got up from the bed and ran to the bathroom.

About an hour later, after I had showered, I came back to my bedroom and found my phone blinking with several messages, all from Asher. I rolled my eyes and started to scroll through them when my door swung open to reveal him rushing through with a somewhat panicked look on his face.

"Bit, are you ok? Reeve said you were sick."

I laughed at his antics, a little disappointed that it took him a full hour to get to me. "Asher, you know guys aren't allowed upstairs," I admonished him. It was strictly forbidden for any men to be anywhere in the sorority house besides the foyer. If it were any other guy I would be worried about getting in trouble with the sisters for him being there, but I knew Asher could charm his way out of anything, so I tried not to let it get to me.

"Are you ok?"

"I'm fine. Really. I was sick earlier but I'm better now. I'm even going to go to my afternoon classes." He walked towards me and pressed his hands to my face.

"You don't feel warm. Are you sure you're alright?"

"Yes," I said as I placed my hands over his. "I think I must have eaten something bad because I was just sick for a little bit. Something didn't agree with me. But I'm better now, promise." He kissed my forehead.

"Want me to wait downstairs and walk you to class?" I melted a little at how sweet he was to me.

"Sure. But try not to let any of my sisters see you walking around up here. Be sneaky."

"Like Bond?" His eyebrows waggled up and down. "You could be my Bond Girl."

"After my morning, I'm nobody's Bond Girl. Today is not my sexiest day. Go downstairs and wait for me before someone catches you up here." I shoved him playfully towards the door. He did his best spy impression by flattening himself against the wall before he darted out of the room and I tried to hold my laughter in until I knew he couldn't hear me.

The rest of the day went without incident, but I still tried to lay low just in case I was really trying to fight off a bug. Asher and I spent a quiet evening in his room watching a movie and snuggling.

The next morning I had to get up early for class so when my alarm went off I tried not to wake Asher up. He looked adorable with his face smashed into his pillow, but I took a moment to admire the strong muscles on his naked back too. He really was the best of both worlds. Sweet and goofy one minute, then scorchingly sexy the next.

Our houses were only three blocks apart and the walk was nice early in the morning, and it gave me an opportunity to think about my day ahead of me. I was about half way to my house when I started feeling the saliva pool in my mouth and the familiar feeling of my stomach roiling about. I tried my breathing technique but knew it wasn't going to work. I was unprepared for the moment and was also completely mortified when I threw up in the bushes outside of the Phi Beta Pi house.

When it was over I hurried away from the house as quickly as I could, hoping no one saw me spewing all over their landscaping. I was nearly in tears when I made it back to the sorority, ashamed and embarrassed of what had happened. Obviously, I wasn't as well as I thought I was. I made it through the door before I felt another wave of nausea come over me and I raced to my room. I crashed through the bedroom door and just made it into the bathroom before I was sick again. The commotion must have woken up Reeve because as I was dry heaving into the toilet I felt her come up behind me and pull my hair back with one hand and rub my back with the other.

Eventually my stomach calmed and I sat, sweaty and disgusting, on the bathroom floor.

"Well, that was the grossest alarm clock I've ever woken up to," Reeve said, obviously trying to lighten the mood. She sat on the edge of the tub with a worried look on her face. "I thought you had some 24 hour bug or something."

I shook my head. "I think it was something I ate," I managed to say, all the while regretting opening my mouth. I could still taste the sick and distinct tang of vomit. I stood up to try to brush my teeth.

"Well, did you eat the same thing two nights in a row?" I turned to look at her and shook my head no as I brushed my teeth. "Hmm. That's really strange." I turned back to the sink and studied Reeve's face in the mirror. She was working something out in her mind and I could almost see the little gears in her mind working overtime. "Don't you think it's a little strange that you're only getting sick in the mornings?"

As soon as the words were out of her mouth I felt my world drop away from me. Reeve and I were still looking at each other in the mirror and I watched as her face moved from confused to shocked and I felt my face go from thoughtful to scared and entirely terrified.

"No." I said as I mouthed the word around my toothbrush. "No, no, no, no. Not possible," I said and then spit out the toothpaste mucking up my words. "Reeve, get that look off your face. It's not possible. I can't believe you would even say that out loud." I wiped my mouth on a towel and walked back into our bedroom.

"Charlie, I'm sorry. But, aren't you even a little bit curious about this? You've gotten sick two mornings in the row, but felt fine in the afternoons. When was your last period?"

"Three weeks ago! I'm on the pill, Reeve! I'm not pregnant."

"And you haven't missed any pills lately?"

"No! I've never missed a pill. It's practically my religion. I take them every day at the same time. I'm very responsible!"

"Ok, ok. I'm sorry. You're right. You're probably not pregnant." I shot a glare at her.

"I'm not."

"Well, if you're so sure you're not, then what's the harm in taking a test?"

"I can't just go and buy a pregnancy test," I half whispered, half yelled at her. "What if I see someone at the store? Or what if I know the cashier?" I was admittedly starting to panic.

"I'll go and buy it for you. No big deal. Charlie, people buy pregnancy tests all the time hoping they're positive. The cashier doesn't have to know you're just a sophomore in college without a job, or a marriage, or really anything at all."

"You are so not helping right now, Reeve." I walked over to my bed and put my head in my hands.

"I'm gonna go buy a test and then you'll know for sure." I heard her moving around the room and knew she was putting clothes on to go to the store for me. My brain nearly poured steam out of my ear trying to comprehend what was happening. Had I forgotten a pill? No, I was sure of it. Had I taken any antibiotics? I had heard from my doctor that antibiotics make the birth control pill ineffective. No, I hadn't taken any medication *except* the fucking pill. There was no way I was pregnant. It was an impossibility. I took some more deep breaths and watch Reeve continue to ready herself.

When she was all dressed she stood in front of me clutching her purse to her side. "There's no use getting yourself all worked up over nothing. Don't start to worry or panic until you're sure what you're dealing with." Those were her parting words to me as she left to buy me a freaking pregnancy test. Yeah right. Don't panic. Sure.

It might have been the longest thirty minutes of my life that passed until Reeve returned with a small brown paper sack hidden underneath her jacket.

"I didn't want to risk any of the sisters seeing it," she explained. I wanted to point out that no one would be able to see through the paper sack, but knew she was just trying to help me, so I kept my mouth shut. She pulled three boxes out of the sack and held them out to me.

"Three kinds?"

"Yeah. I figured you wouldn't be satisfied with just one." She shrugged her shoulders. "I wouldn't be," she added. I took the three boxes in my hand and took a minute to study the back of each one.

"Conveniently enough, the directions are all pretty much the same," I muttered.

"You've always been really good at taking tests," she said quickly. I gave her a puzzled look. "I'm sorry. I don't know why I said that. This is really intense and I just spouted whatever came out of my mouth. I know this isn't helping. Do you want me to get you some water? Do you think you even have enough pee to take all those tests at the same time? Maybe I should take one too just so that we have a control test, you know, like, one that will obviously be negative since I haven't had sex in a millennia?" I stood up and wrapped Reeve in a tight hug.

"Thank you for rambling. I know it's dumb, but watching you lose your mind a little made me feel better about the fact that I'm about to lose mine." I looked down at the tests again. "What if they're positive, Reeve? What am I going to do?"

"I don't know, Charlie. You'll have to make that decision with Asher, I suppose."

"Oh my god, Asher. I totally hadn't thought about him. Shit." I dropped my head into my hands. "This is all kinds of fucked up."

"You don't know anything yet. Go pee on some sticks. We won't know anything until you've done it."

I looked at the tests in my hands and then at the bathroom door. Was I ready to do this? Even though I was sure there was no way for me to be pregnant, I was so careful, it kind of seemed like none of it mattered at that moment. I had no control over the outcome of the tests and was totally and completely left in the hands of fate. I felt powerless and it was an unnerving feeling. I took a deep breath and convinced myself they would be negative. They had to be.

I took the tests into the bathroom and peed on all three sticks, which isn't as easy as all the commercials make it seem. I left all three tests sitting on the counter, walked back into the bedroom and sat down at my desk. I stared at the clock, waiting for the obligatory three minutes to pass. Both Reeve and I were stuck in some sort of purgatory for those three minutes. I stared at a clock and she stared at me. Frozen. I possibly had three more minutes of life the way I was used to it. Three more minutes of being a carefree, nineteen-year-old college student. Three more minutes to do everything in life I wanted to accomplish before I had kids. If you think three minutes goes by quickly, try waiting three minutes to see if your life was going to change completely. It's agonizingly slow.

When the time had passed, I looked at Reeve from my chair. "I can't look." She nodded at me and walked into the bathroom. She was in there forever, it felt. When she finally came out I couldn't read anything on her face. She could have just learned the secret of life and I wouldn't have ever known. She walked right up to me and placed the tests on the surface of the desk and placed a hand on my shoulder.

Two pink lines. A blue plus symbol. The word pregnant.

I was fucked. In all senses of the word: literally, figuratively, emotionally – fucked.

My hand came to my mouth and covered the silent sob that leaked out. In my head, I heard myself scream so loud that windows shattered. People came running. The cops came to investigate. In reality, I was silently dying inside. Mouth open, eyes watering, crying but not. I turned and found Reeve right there, wrapping her arms around me, softly running her hand along my hair, comforting me as everything I knew about my life was changed. We stayed like that, her arms wrapped around me as I cried, until I felt like I could breathe normally again. I pulled away a looked up at her.

"What am I going to do?"

"I think you should call Asher. He needs to be here for you right now."

Suddenly, telling Asher that I was pregnant seemed like the hardest thing I could ever possibly have to do. How would I explain this to him? How did this even happen? I wasn't ready to talk to him about it. I turned back to my desk and started searching the internet for a clinic I could get another test done at. I had seen them around before and I needed someone else to confirm this for me.

"Charlie, what are you doing?"

"I need another test. A blood test. These could be wrong," I said as I swept the three tests into the top drawer of my desk, landing right next to a calculator and a few pens. I slammed the drawer shut.

"You think all three of those pregnancy tests are wrong?" I turned to look at her.

"I need something else, Reeve. A doctor or a nurse to tell me the results. Please, just let me do this." She sighed loudly but didn't argue with me any more about it.

I found a pregnancy resource center not too far from campus that opened an hour ago. "Will you come with me?" I asked Reeve hopefully.

"Of course." I breathed a little easier knowing I wouldn't be going alone.

When we got to the clinic, nothing was going as planned.

"What do you mean you don't do blood tests?!"

"Just exactly that. We only do urine tests. They are just as accurate as blood tests." The woman sitting behind the desk at the clinic looked aggravated by my outburst, but also looked like she'd dealt with crazy college students freaking out over a pregnancy before. She was calm, but obviously wasn't going to take any crap from anyone.

"I already took three pee tests and they came back positive," I said, quieter now. Her face softened and she leaned a little closer.

"What's your name, dear?"

"Charlie," I nearly whispered.

"Charlie, it is very uncommon to get a false positive result on a pregnancy test. It happens, but it is rare. It is more likely to get a false negative. The tests you took at home, they are very reliable. But I would be happy to have our staff administer another urine test for you, just in case you need that to feel more secure about the result."

"I really wanted a blood test."

"Sweetie, even if you were at a hospital, or an OBGYN's office, they would still only give you a urine test. It's how we do it. I'm sorry you're upset. Would you like us to give you a urine test?"

I looked at Reeve and she just rubbed her hand along my back, trying to offer her support. I looked back to the receptionist and nodded. She gave me a slight smile and then took Reeve and I back to an exam room. She gave me a little cup that was sealed shut and gave me the instructions. I went into the private bathroom and peed in the cup, again, cursing modern technology for not making this whole process easier on emotionally ravaged women just trying to learn their fate. I washed my hands at least three times and took the cup back to the exam room.

A few minutes later a nurse came in and greeted me with a friendly smile. I tried to smile back, but I probably looked like I was grimacing. She was talking about the weather, how it was getting chillier. She took a little, tiny slip of paper and dipped it in the cup then laid it on a paper towel. She continued to chatter about how she'd spent her weekend. After a minute she looked back down at the paper and then smiled at me.

"Positive."

"Are you sure?"

"Yes. It's positive. You're expecting." I was not in the least *expecting* this. What a shitty way to tell someone they're pregnant.

I bit my lip, trying to keep the tears at bay again. I don't know why I expected a different outcome, but I had hoped.

"But I'm on the pill. I had my period just three weeks ago. This just can't be happening."

"I can't speak about your birth control, but I can tell you it is common for women to still menstruate even while pregnant, especially in the early stages."

"Why don't I know this? Why doesn't anyone talk about this?" I was about to lose it. I could feel myself breathing faster and my heart was beating quickly.

"You're free to remain in the room as long as you need, dear. Let me leave you with some information. Know that we are here five days a week and you can always come talk to one of our counselors if you need to." She handed me a few pamphlets. I sifted through them and gathered that they were information on the choices I was faced with. Abortion? Adoption? Parenting? There was no pamphlet for Crawling Under A Rock And Praying This Is A Dream.

Reeve and I walked home. For someone whose life had been so drastically altered in the last two hours, I didn't feel any different. I was tired, but figured that was from all the crying and the vomiting. Other than that, I couldn't tell I was currently creating a human being in my body. That was a real crime. Mother Nature should make it painfully obvious the instant you become pregnant. Your skin should change color or your belly should light up. Something. Anything to give us a clear indication. Something to help along the people, like me, who just couldn't believe this was happening to them.

When we made it back to the house I found Asher sitting in the foyer. He looked up when we came in and smiled. But his smile immediately turned into a frown when he saw me.

"Are you ok? What's wrong?" I obviously wore my current mental state on my sleeve. He held me immediately and I couldn't stop the tears that fell against his shirt as I rested my head against his chest. Our bodies could do amazing things: trick you into believing your birth control is working, grow a fucking person, produce enough tears to fill a lake and still have more left to cry.

"Why don't you guys go up to our room? I will keep everyone out of your hair," Reeve said to Asher.

"Thanks," he said and led me up the stairs to my room.

Chapter Eight

I felt his chest moving up and down. That is what woke me up. The sound of his breath leaving and entering his lungs, the rhythmic movement of my head bobbing up and down as he breathed, the warmth of his hands on my back. I don't remember coming to my room with Asher and I don't remember lying down with him, but I was curled up on his chest, our legs intertwined with each other, his arms wrapped around my body. My eyes fluttered open and I looked right into the slate-gray pools of metal looking back at me.

"Hey," he whispered.

"Hi," I responded, just as quiet. We looked at each other for a while. I was sure he was wondering what happened to me and all I could think about was what I was about to do to him. To us. Right now he was in his purgatory. His life was still the same as it was yesterday. He was still a nineteen-year-old guy with no real worries or responsibilities. And I was about to ruin it.

"Wanna tell me what's going on?" He said, running one of his hands through my hair. I took just thirty more indulgent seconds to remember us as we are in this moment, holding each other, loving each other. I didn't know how he was going to respond to my pregnancy, but I knew nothing would ever be the same.

"I got sick again on the way home from your house this morning." My voice was so quiet. I didn't have the energy to speak any louder. Perhaps I felt like saying it loud enough for someone else to hear it would make it more true. "Reeve and I were trying to figure out why I was sick again. If it was something I ate or a bug. Then we both kind of realized that both times I got sick it was in the morning." I turned my head slightly to look at him, waiting for the realization to strike him. Some sadistic part of me must have wanted to watch the look on his face as his world came crashing down around him. "Reeve thought I should take a pregnancy test."

I watched as the color slowly drained from his face. His chest stopped moving up and down because he stopped breathing. His hands did not brush through my hair. He understood what I said and what I hadn't said. I felt one solitary and lonely tear trek down my cheek and I did nothing to wipe it away. It was what it was. A symbol of how alone I felt in that moment, still wrapped in his arms, yet so far away from him.

"Did you take one?" He finally managed.

"I took four."

"And?"

"They all came back positive."

He sat up, forcing me to move from where I was laying on him. I watched as he slid to the edge of the bed, running one hand through his hair, the other resting on his knee. "You're pregnant?"

"That's what everyone keeps telling me." I reached out to press my fingers to his back, to make a connection, to feel something besides the fear that is coursing through my veins. He stood up the moment my fingers reach him and the contact was lost. I felt him moving away from me.

"You've been on the pill since forever," he pointed out, as if that would change everything I had just told him. I took a deep breath. He hadn't had hours to take this all in as I had. He was processing everything now and I tried to remain patient, giving him the same opportunity I had to freak the fuck out.

"I know, Babe. It didn't work."

"Didn't work? It always works. That's its *one* job. To keep you from getting pregnant. Did you miss a pill or something?"

I tried really hard to keep my voice even and not let anger take over my emotions. "No. I didn't forget to take a pill. I took them every day, like clockwork. Every. Day."

"Then tell me how this happened?" He paced now, back and forth from my door to my window. Back and forth.

"Sometimes things just happen."

"What are you going to do about it?" He stopped pacing and was looking at me. He was still across the room.

"It? What do you mean? We haven't even spoken about what our choices are."

"You have to get rid of it."

"Stop calling it an *it*! It's not an it. It's a baby!" He was instantly just an inch from my face. And even though just seconds earlier I wanted him to be close to me, I didn't want this Asher anywhere near me. He was angry and I could see the rage in his eyes.

"It's not a baby, Charlie. It's just a mass of cells right now. It's not a person, or a baby, it's a thing. It's a parasite. We *can't* have a baby. We're too young. We're both in school. We can't take care of a baby. Think about it. There's only one choice."

"There are *three* choices," I said, matching his tone. He'd never been this mad at me before, and I wasn't about to cower down in front of him. This was not the Asher I had been with for five years. "We can keep the baby and choose to be parents, or we choose adoption and give the baby to a couple who wants to have a baby. Abortion is also an option, but I'm going to be honest Asher, I'm not comfortable with abortion. I don't think I could do it."

"So, you're just going to have a baby? You're not even going to consider having it taken care of?"

"TAKEN CARE OF? Listen to yourself, Asher." I moved towards him, placing my hands on his face, trying to talk some sense into him. "This is a baby, *our* baby. You want me to just throw it away, like garbage? I can't do that. It's a part of us. No matter how you look at it, it's a piece of you and a piece of me, together. I can't get rid of that. I won't."

"Why did you ask for my input if it doesn't matter?" His voice was softer, but still angry.

"I want to make the decision together. It doesn't have to be today, or tomorrow, but I won't choose abortion."

"You'd rather drop out and become a teenage mother?"

He was right. I was now a statistic. I sat back down on the bed and gave in to the exhaustion, folding in on myself, curling around my knees. "I never thought I'd be having this conversation, ever. And even if I had considered the idea that you and I would be faced with having to make this decision, I never would have imagined..." my voice broke and the tears started again. Yesterday, even an hour ago, if I had broken down in tears in front of him there would have been nothing anyone could do to keep him from comforting me. "I never would have imagined you'd be so cold."

"I'm sorry, Charlie. I'm not trying to be cold. I'm trying to be realistic. How would we raise a baby? How could either of us get through school? How would I ever manage to make it through law school with a baby? I'm not dumb. I understand that you have all the power here to make whatever decision you're going to make. I just pray you make the right one."

"I wanted us to make the decision together. I wanted you to hold me and tell me that everything was going to be ok."

"Yeah, well, it seems like nothing is ever going to be ok again." We were frozen in place, me lying on the bed, tears still fresh on my face, and him across the room looking at me with disinterest, his gray eyes empty. "I'm gonna go. I need to think. Alone."

"You're leaving?"

"I can't stay here."

"Can I come with you?" I was desperate in that moment for the old Asher to come back to me. I searched for the warmth I knew he had the capacity for, but was holding back from me.

"I can't stay with you."

There was never, ever, a time when I thought I would hear Asher say those words to me.

"Ok."

Then he left.

When Reeve made it back to our room I'm sure she was paralyzed by what she saw. I was on my way to a complete mental breakdown. Everything that had been on my desk was now on the floor. My bedding was torn off and crumpled by the bathroom. The mattress sprawled on the floor. I sat on the overturned desk, leaning my back up against the wall, sobbing. She ran over to me and pulled me off the desk.

"Charlie, what's going on? Where'd Asher go?"

"He left me."

"He left you? What do you mean?"

"He doesn't want me anymore."

"You must have misunderstood him," she said, shaking her head, just as surprised about it as I was. "What did he say?"

I sniffled and wiped my nose on my shirt sleeve, stalling, not wanting to relive what had happened. "He wants me to have an abortion. I told him I didn't think I could. He said he couldn't stay with me." Her eyebrows furrowed and she looked confused.

"Couldn't stay with you right now, or couldn't stay with you any more at all?"

"Is there a difference? Right now is when it's most important that he stay with me. So, if he's gone now, he's gone."

Chapter Nine

A week went by and nothing changed. Reeve put the room back together, but I barely got out of bed. If I wasn't sick from the pregnancy, I was sick from the hurt. Reeve called, pretending to be me, and made an appointment for me to see a doctor. She was on a mission to keep me focused on the baby and I knew she was right.

By the time a second week passed, I was out of bed and going to class, although my mind was distracted and my grades were slipping rapidly. I tried to focus but my mind constantly wandered to Asher, wondering what he was thinking, wondering if he missed me, wondering if I would ever hear from him again. I had to, right? No one would just walk out on their pregnant girlfriend and never speak to her again. He wasn't that guy. My mind wandered to Asher often and my hand started wandering to my belly.

I'd never really known anyone who had gone through a pregnancy before. I was full of questions and no one had answers for me. But each day that passed I started to feel more and more connected to the baby growing inside of me. I wasn't sure how far along I was. I was hoping to learn that at the doctor appointment the next week.

I might have been crazy or paranoid, but I started to see my belly poke out just a little bit. I would lay in my bed at night and pull up my shirt, gazing down at my stomach. I was a little in awe of everything. I was scared shitless, no doubt, but I was also mesmerized by the tiny hill of a bump that I could see beginning to grow. I was creating a person. A baby. My baby. Asher's baby.

It was times like these, quiet moments in the evening when I was alone with my baby bump, that I started to feel really close to my mom. I could imagine how she felt about me as I grew in her belly. I could feel the love I was already developing for my child and I knew she had felt the same way. It wasn't short of magical the way I loved this baby.

It was my love for the baby that made me hold on to hope for Asher. I hoped, every day, that he would show up and hold me and tell me everything was going to be ok. I wanted nothing more than for him to want me, to want our baby, and for us to all be together. I knew we could figure everything else out as long as we were together. But I knew there was no choice left for me if I had to choose. I would always choose my baby. Always. I knew that if Asher came around and was suddenly ok with choosing adoption, I wouldn't be. That first day, when I was still in shock from being blindsided by an unexpected pregnancy, I thought I might have been capable of letting someone else raise my baby. But two weeks later, now that I bonded with the baby in my belly, I knew I could never choose adoption. I'd move home with my dad if I had to. I'd make any changes necessary to keep my baby.

I was still getting sick in the mornings, but the nausea seeped into the evenings as well. I was losing weight because I couldn't keep anything down. Reeve was obviously worried about me and her patience was wearing thin with Asher.

"He should be here taking care of you," she said to me the morning of my doctor appointment. "He should be the one going with you today, not me."

"You don't have to go with me," I said, feeling guilty about everything she had done for me in the last three weeks. She was right though. She shouldn't be the one going with me.

"Hey," she said as she came to stand in front of me. "There's nothing in the world that would keep me out of that exam room. I'm here for you, one hundred percent. I just wish Asher would get his head out of his ass."

"Have you spoken to him?" I asked hopefully.

"No. He won't answer my texts. I will text him today and tell him when and where the appointment is, and hopefully he'll surprise us both and show up." I didn't expect a different answer, but knowing that he wasn't talking to either one of us somehow hurt more than I had anticipated. I just wanted to know how he was feeling. I'd given him the space he asked for, but being apart from each other didn't make me any less pregnant.

I sat in my first class of the day when I felt a tight pinch very low in my belly. It made me wince, but was gone quickly enough. I took a few deep breaths and tried to concentrate on the lecture. In my next class, I felt the pinch again and it was more painful. I clutched my stomach and gave a small gasp. The girl sitting next to me leaned over and asked me if I was ok. I tried to keep a small smile on my face and nodded at her. She didn't look like she believed me, but turned back to the professor at the front of the class. A few minutes later the pain was back and I had to leave the class.

The pain was unreal, and it was coming and going in waves. I was in the bathroom, bent over in pain, trying to call Reeve. When I finally got ahold of her, I begged her to pick me up to take me to the hospital.

"Something is wrong," I cried.

"I'll be right there."

I made it to the front of the building and only had to wait a few minutes for Reeve's car to come screeching around the corner. When I got in, I was trying to keep the pain from my face.

"What's going on?"

"I'm just having some pains in my stomach. Can we stop at Asher's house first please?"

"Charlie, if something's wrong you need to go to the hospital."

"I need Asher." She looked at me hard for a few seconds and then pulled away from the curb. My stomach cramped the whole drive to his house and when Reeve parked, I had to take some deep breaths before I could get out.

"Do you want me to come with you?"

I shook my head. "I will be right back. I just need him to come with me." It hadn't occurred to me that he might not even be home. I hoped he was in the house; I needed him more at that moment than I ever had before.

I walked through the door that lead into the dining area. I gasped and grabbed onto a table to keep myself upright as pain shot through my abdomen. I cried out, but tried to muffle the sound, not wanting anyone to find me crying in the middle of their house. Once the pain subsided a bit, I walked gingerly towards the stairs. I started to climb the stairs slowly, one step at a time, afraid that some sudden movement would cause more pain. I made it halfway up when another bolt of pain rocketed through me. This time though, along with the pain, came a warm wetness between my legs. I was bleeding and the realization made me silently cry out. I slowly continued up the stairs and eventually made it to Asher's door.

Hot tears ran down my face, but I was still silent, wanting just to get Asher and get out of the house. I didn't need anyone finding me like this. Bleeding and crying in a frat house. I needed to get out of there unnoticed. I turned his doorknob and pushed the door open slowly.

I bled.

I cried.

I lost my baby, of that I was sure.

I stared at the only boy I'd ever loved, the boy who had promised me the world and then disappeared, laying underneath a blonde who was straddling him. Naked.

My hand flew up to cover my mouth. One hand silenced the pain I felt watching Asher fuck someone else, the other hand covered my belly, trying to hold on to the last moments I had with my child.

My mind was in shock, not wanting to believe that Asher would really be having sex with someone else. And I might not have believed it if I couldn't see my name, the name he'd given me out of love, in bold black ink, covering the arm that was wrapped around whoever was atop him. I left the door open and ran as quickly as I could out to Reeve's car. When I made it in the car, all the cries I held in came pouring out.

"Please Reeve, get me to the hospital." She peeled out of her parking spot and drove down the street.

"What happened up there?" Reeve looked panicked as she sped down the street. "Charlie, talk to me. What's going on?"

"I'm losing the baby, Reeve. I can feel it. I'm bleeding and I'm losing the baby." More sobs came from me, but I couldn't stifle them back, couldn't hold them in. My hands were occupied, cradling my stomach, the pain overwhelming. "Asher was in his room with some girl."

"What do you mean?"

"I mean, he was fucking someone else while I sat there bleeding in his doorway." Reeve was silent. I didn't really expect her to have anything to say. What was there to say? "I don't want to talk about it. Just get me to the hospital."

Once we got to the ER it was a complete whirlwind. The nurse at the admin desk saw me, saw the blood between my legs, and ushered me back to a triage room immediately. She tried to argue with Reeve that she couldn't come and Reeve promptly put her in her place. I managed to convince the nurse to let her stay with me, confiding in her that I had no one else.

I was given a gown and when I changed, I cringed at the amount of blood that I had actually lost.

"Oh my god, Charlie," Reeve said from her chair. I tried not to look, but it was impossible. Most of my pants were soaked with blood. After getting the gown on and climbing on the exam table, I could still feel more blood emptying out of me. The cramping was getting worse and it was all I could do to hold my stomach until the doctor came in.

A woman with dark hair entered the room pushing a machine. She looked me over, her face not showing any emotion, and introduced herself.

"I'm Dr. Lance. You're Charlie?"

"Yes. That's me," I squeaked.

"How many weeks pregnant are you?" She asked while she started fiddling with the machine she'd brought in with her.

"I don't know exactly. I haven't had my first pre-natal visit yet. My last period was five weeks ago." The doctor nodded and moved closer to me and the exam table.

"Ok, Charlie, I am going to do an ultrasound on your stomach to try and see what we're dealing with, ok?"

I nodded my head, unable to use my voice in that moment. I was already positive about what was happening. Dr. Lance squirted some gel on my stomach and then took something from the machine that looked like a remote control, placed it on the gel, and moved it around. I looked up at the screen and it looked like a TV without a signal – black, with little, white snow. Finally, there seemed to be a bigger black area on the screen and the doctor stopped moving the wand around.

"Ok, here's your uterus, Charlie." Time stood still. I silently prayed to hear good news. I begged someone, somewhere, to hear me and to save my baby.

"Do you see these two circular looking areas?" She said as she pointed to two small round objects on the screen.

"Yes," I managed.

"Those are the babies. You look to be about ten weeks along. But, I'm sorry, Charlie. Neither one has a heartbeat."

"Babies?" I cried.

"Twins."

"And they're gone?"

"I'm afraid so."

"Oh my god," I cried. I rolled over onto my side, caring nothing about the doctor or her examination, and gave in to the wave of grief that washed over me. I felt arms wrap around me and I heard Reeve's voice in my ear, whispering apologies and comforting words I didn't understand.

Even though I knew what was happening before we entered the exam room, hearing the words, being told that I lost not one but two babies, broke me. For just a moment I wanted to die with them. I wasn't sure I had anything left to continue on for in this life. I pictured Asher's hand on the small of that girl's back, him enjoying another woman, while I was losing my babies. I couldn't possibly imagine walking out of that hospital and having anything to go back to.

Would I be able to hold my babies in the afterlife? Would they be the chubby-cheeked, smiling angels I pictured them to be? Could I hold them close to me and breathe in their baby smell? Could I sing to them the same songs I remember my mother singing to me? Could I see my mother again? Would she be waiting for me, my two angel babies in her arms? Perhaps, we could all be together again. Maybe.

My thoughts were interrupted by Reeve's voice.

"Charlie, you need to come back to us."

The only thing that kept me tethered to this world was the fear that death would only bring nothingness. The pain I felt made everything real. The babies were real. The agony of remembering them would be better than not having anything at all to cling to.

"Charlie, please, look at me."

I finally rolled back over to look at Reeve who was also crying. The doctor still stood next to the exam table, a concerned yet professional look on her face.

"Why..." I choked on the words. "Why would this happen?" I asked the doctor.

"Healthy women miscarry babies more often than you'd think. It's a sad yet true fact. Sometimes the pregnancies just don't take or there is something wrong with the babies that we just can't see at this early stage. There is no indication that women who experience a miscarriage can't go on to have full-term, healthy pregnancies later in life. I'm sorry."

"But what was wrong with this pregnancy?" I asked again, desperate for answers, desperate for a reason. "Why my babies?"

"There's no real way to know, Charlie. Miscarriages, especially in the first trimester, are common, unfortunately. But listen to me when I say this. There is *nothing* you could have done to prevent this from happening. This was not because you did something wrong. This just happens and I can't give you a reason, medically."

No reason. No explanation. Nothing. Emptiness.

"What happens now?" I whispered. One question, so many meanings.

"Your body will continue to bleed," the doctor paused for a moment. "Eventually, the embryos will pass, along with the blood and clots. You will experience cramps, just like you would during your period, although they may be intense and more painful. You might bleed for up to two weeks. Most women feel fine within a week or so."

I hated my body in that moment. My body couldn't hold onto my babies. My body would soon eject them. Toss them away.

"I can prescribe you some stronger pain relief than you would get over-the-counter if you would like." I nodded. I would welcome any medicine that would take me away for a little while. "You should go home and take it easy. Rest. Perhaps not be alone," she said, looking at Reeve.

"I'll stay with her," Reeve answered. The doctor continued to talk and Reeve continued to listen, but I tuned everything out. I couldn't be bothered with any more thoughts, or facts, or apologies. The doctor brought in a pair of mesh underwear that looked like fishing net and a large pad. The whole thing looked ridiculous but I put it on and decided to leave my pants behind. Reeve and I walked out to her car, her helping me keep my hospital gown closed. We drove through a pharmacy, got my pain meds, and then went home.

After a week of crying, staying in bed except to shower and eat, not hearing from Asher, and not answering any of Reeve's questions about him, I made the decision to leave. To leave it all behind. There was nothing left for me there. Nothing outweighed the pain of being there. Reeve went out to the store and I took the opportunity to pack a small bag. I left most of my things behind because they simply didn't matter. I left Reeve a small note, apologizing for leaving without saying goodbye, but explaining that I would call her when I could.

And then I left.

Part III

Chapter One
Asher

The knocking on the door dragged me away from my computer screen and forced me to blink, something I wasn't sure I'd done in the last hour. At least, I hadn't done it enough. My eyes felt like they might be filled with saw dust for all the scratchy-stickiness that came with the blinks I gave at the sight of Phil at the door to my office.

"Hey man," Phil said. His voice sounded worried. "We just got a call from Willow Falls Memorial." My heart plummeted at those words because I already knew what they meant. I'd been waiting for this call every day for the last month. Waiting for the news that I knew would change my world forever. I'd been dreading this phone call, but knew there was nothing I could do to avoid it.

"Yeah?" I said, even though I could feel the words before he said them.

"The nurse on Charles McBride's floor says it's time."

"Damn it." I rubbed my hands up and down my face. "Ok, thanks. I'll leave right now and head down there."

"You gonna be ok?" Phil asked sincerely.

"Yeah, thanks man." Was I going to be ok? Probably not. But that didn't matter. I hadn't been ok in a long time. I hadn't been ok in over thirteen years. That's how long ago it was I made the biggest mistake of my life, and I was still paying for it. But that was ok; I would gladly pay my debt forever. Pay for my mistakes. Nothing that happened to me would make up for what I had done thirteen years ago, so this was just a drop in the bucket of pain I would endure because I knew I deserved it.

I closed my laptop and grabbed my suit jacket off the coat rack by the door. I rode the elevator all the way down to the bottom floor and walked through the lobby and out the doors of Libman & Carmichael Law Offices.

The drive to the hospital was one I was familiar with. I drove to the hospital to visit Charles once or twice a week since he was admitted. The fact that I pulled into the parking structure with no real recollection of how I had actually arrived there wasn't surprising. I had a million things running through my mind, and driving to that particular hospital became second nature to me recently. I walked through the main doors to the hospital and wound my way through the corridors, took the elevator up to the fifth floor, and found the room that was home to Charles for the last three months.

I'm not sure what I expected once I arrived at his room, but I wasn't expecting it to be so quiet. In the past when I had walked into this room, Charles greeted me with a smile, a wave, and a quiet hello. As the weeks passed, his strength waned, and in the last week I was lucky if he'd been able to speak. But the silence in the room now was filling the empty space like water, pouring in, making me nervous. Drowning in this silence was inevitable. The only noise to be heard was the heart monitor beeping at regular intervals, keeping time to the emptiness.

After a few minutes of sitting in the uncomfortable chair next to his hospital bed, Rachel, a nurse I was familiar with, entered the room.

"Hello Asher," she said sweetly with a sad look on her face.

"Hi, Rachel," I responded, rubbing my hands over my face. She walked to the other side of his bed, checking his IV and looking at the paper printing out of the machine monitoring his heart.

"You seem comfortable, Charlie," she said to him. My heart lurched at the name. His name was Charles. Charlie was someone else entirely. Charles always understood how it affected me whenever someone called him Charlie and tried to correct them for my sake. But he was unconscious now and probably would never be awake again. These were his final hours and I'd let Rachel call him whatever she wanted. I'd deal with the pain of hearing her name; it was the least I could do. Today wasn't about me or the guilt and pain I carried around. Today was about Charles. "Do you need anything?" She asked me. I smiled at her thoughtful question. She was more than likely accustomed to helping families dealing with the loss of their loved one. But I wasn't family.

"I'm fine, thank you."

"Let me know."

"Rachel?"

"Yes?"

I looked over at Charles and then back to her. "How much longer?"

"Not long. Hours, maybe."

"Has anyone called his daughter?"

She shook her head. "He said he didn't want anyone to be called but you." I nodded, understanding. She left, quietly shutting the door behind her. I turned back to look at Charles McBride. The man who I had grown so close to over the last thirteen years. The man who became a friend, but more like a second father to me. The man who I selfishly and admittedly used as a lifeline to the one person I knew I had to live without.

"Charles," I said, moving closer to the bed, seeking out his hand. I never held a man's hand before, but I figured that if I was trying to cross over, if I was on my death bed, I would want someone to hold my hand. "I'm here, Charles. I'm here. I came." I paused, looking down at our hands, mine clasped around his. His hand was limp in mine, not responding to me. "I don't know if you can hear me, but I want you to know that I'll take care of everything, Charles. You've done a great job planning for this, making sure everything is laid out right, and I will make sure it gets done."

Over the last thirteen years Charles and I developed a friendship. At first, I needed him in order to feel close to her. I went around to try and breathe in a piece of her, to soak up any part of her I could. But, eventually, after it become obvious that any relationship between him and I wouldn't involve any piece of her, our own friendship developed. As the years passed, we only spoke about her in theory and only recently. He never told me any detail about her life now. He never discussed where she was, what she was doing, how she was. If I was going to be his friend, it wouldn't include her in any way.

Then Charles became ill. The illness, the cancer, didn't go away as we originally hoped. And once we accepted that the cancer would, in the end, take him from this life, we started planning. I'd never planned for anyone's death before, but Charles was adamant that she wouldn't be burdened with another parent's death due to cancer. He made decisions, and even though I didn't agree with all of them, I honored them. Who was I to argue with a dying man? His choice, to not tell her he was dying, was something I struggled with. I tried, over and over, to convince him that she would want to know. That she would want to spend as much time with him as she could.

"To do what? To watch me die? She did that with her mother and I watched it ruin her. I watched her sit next to her mother as she withered away. I saw what it did to my Charlie and I won't have her go through that again. She doesn't need to know."

Charles was a hard man to persuade. I'd done it a few times in my life, when I was younger, trying to convince him to let me date his daughter, to take her away for a weekend, to sleep in her bed when we were home for breaks from college. But I couldn't convince him to tell his daughter he was dying. He knew what I knew. That she would be at his bedside, crying and remembering her mother, crying and mourning her father, and breaking on the inside. He didn't want that for her. I understood.

"I love her, Mr. McBride." I hadn't called him that in years, but it felt right at that moment. I felt like I was fifteen again, asking him in his living room if I could please be his daughter's boyfriend. That was the first time I admitted, out loud, that I loved her. And it remained true since then. "I love her and I always will. I will do everything to make sure she is taken care of. You don't have to worry and you don't have to hang on."

I felt the slightest pressure on my hand as his fingers gripped mine in the faintest way, the way you would imagine a man on death's door would squeeze your hand.

"I promise. I will take care of her."

I saw his chest rise, then fall, and then rest. The beeping of the machine slowed, his heart rate dropped, crawled, stilled. Rachel came in to make the machine stop its slowing, dragging beeping, and I watched as the monitors went blank.

I found myself, an hour later, sitting in my car outside of a house I never thought I'd visit again, not until a couple months ago anyway. This was one place I avoided, one person I avoided. I knew, from the beginning, when I stood by Charles as his only ally in death, that this was the next step. I knew it was coming, but it didn't make it any easier. I walked slowly to the red wooden door of the house. I gathered my courage and finally knocked. I heard footsteps from inside the house quickening, like my heart rate, as they neared. It pulled open and I was face to face with a piece of my past.

Chapter Two

Asher

"Hello, Reeve." I watched as her face moved from the pleasant look you plaster on your face when you answer your door, to the anger and annoyance that came naturally to Reeve when she encountered me. It had been quite a long time since we'd seen each other, since she told me frankly to "Fuck off" back in college. She was a loyal friend and that was what I was counting on when I showed up on her doorstep.

"What are you doing here, Asher? How did you find out where I live?"

"It's a matter of public record. And it's a small town, Reeve."

"What do you want?" She was just as icy as she was before and with good reason.

"Can I come in?" I asked, hopefully, not wanting to have this conversation on the porch.

"I don't think that's a good idea."

"Mom, who is that man?" A little girl had poked her head between the door and Reeve's hip. She had short blonde hair and bright blue eyes. Reeve bent down and put herself at eye level with her daughter.

"He's just someone trying to sell something, Baby. Go back in the living room and keep an eye on your brother, ok?" The little girl skipped away and I felt the clenching in my chest that I was accustomed to feeling when put face-to-face with children. Reeve stood and turned back to me. "I think you should leave. I have nothing to say to you." She moved to close the door and I put my foot in the way.

"It's about Charlie," I said, knowing that will catch her attention. I saw her face, clearly contemplating what to do next, and as I expected, her loyalty won out. She creaked the door open and stood back, silently and regretfully inviting me in.

"You have five minutes." I nodded, knowing I'd need more than that, but I'd take the five to begin with. She led me into her kitchen and motioned for me to take a seat at the table. She didn't offer me something to eat. She didn't ask me if I wanted some water. She just sat and stared at me expectantly.

"Mr. McBride passed away about an hour ago." Immediately her frosty demeanor melted away as her hand came to cover her mouth.

"What?" She whispered.

"Yes. He died at Willow Falls Memorial Hospital about an hour ago due to complications of bone cancer." I watched as a tear fell from her left eye as I coldly told her about the death of a man we all regarded as one of the best on the planet. Inside, I was just as upset about his passing as she was, but I couldn't show it. Right now, I wasn't Asher, childhood friend of Reeve. I was Mr. Carmichael, lawyer and representative of Charles McBride.

"Does Charlie know?" She asked through a broken sob.

I nodded. "Someone from my office should be calling her shortly.

"Calling her? She wasn't there?"

"She didn't know. Mr. McBride had very specific wishes and Ms. McBride wasn't informed of his condition."

"Ms. McBride? What the hell is wrong with you Asher? Her name is Charlie."

I ignored her comment. I knew it seemed like I was being an ass, but I didn't know how else to act in the moment. I didn't know how to be all the people I was at the same time. I couldn't be friend, enemy, ex-boyfriend, lawyer and man completely torn apart all at once. I had to pick one and stick with it, so I chose lawyer.

"Mr. McBride wanted to make sure that Ms. McBride wasn't alone, so I am here to make sure that you will make yourself available to her at his service, but most importantly at the reading of his will. Mr. McBride was afraid that she wouldn't contact you, so I am here to make sure that if you don't receive a call from her that you are aware of the times of the service and the reading." I paused and looked down at my hands. "He thought she might not reach out to anyone. That she might close up again and he wanted me to make sure you were there for her, that someone was there for her."

"Close up *again?* Damn it, Asher, she hasn't opened up from the last time."

That tiny piece of information was like salt in a wound, but also like a sip of water in a desert. I was thirsty for information about her, desperate to know any tiny bit of information I could gather and I had been since the last time I saw her that day. But hearing that she was closed up, like a flower refusing to bloom, burned going down – stung like guilt.

"Someone from my office will contact you with the exact date and times of the service and the reading. Can you agree to be at both?"

"Yes. Of course I will be there. Will you be there too?" I looked her in the eyes for a moment, willing myself to be honest with her, to tell her that I would be there in an instant if I thought it was what Charlie wanted, but I knew better.

"It was nice seeing you again, Reeve. You have a beautiful daughter." I stood and walked through her door and out to my car without looking back. I started my car and drove to my place, purposefully avoiding the neighborhood that held all the memories burned into my mind. I prepared myself for an agonizing evening, and thought I might as well get some bourbon to ease the ache growing in my heart. My throat already burned from hearing her name on someone else's lips, from hearing about how still, after all these years, she was still not the same person she had been before I had ruined everything. If I was going to burn from the inside out, I might as well get drunk while it happened.

Chapter Three
Charlie

I routinely tried not to study myself in the mirror. I never liked what I saw. Unfortunately, I found myself to be less in control than I would wish. So, here I sat, at my expensive vanity, in my expensive bedroom, of my expensive New York City apartment that overlooked Central Park, and all I could see was emptiness. But I didn't want to see anything else anyway. I didn't want to feel anything. Because, when I felt something, it was usually pain.

I'm sure to everyone else I looked normal, maybe even happy. But I knew better.

I picked up the big brush from the table top and used it to paint color on my cheeks, to fool everyone around me into thinking that my heart worked well enough to pump blood throughout my body, to make my cheeks this color. It didn't though. My heart hadn't worked in a long time. It was a miracle I was even here, breathing this air, existing in this world.

"You ready to go, Bit?"

My lungs stopped working, the air in them froze like blocks of ice. My throat closed up, the lights in the room dimmed. The brush in my hand fell with a loud bang onto the vanity again.

He must have noticed my distress, because he came running into the room, his hands cupping my face.

"Charlie, what's happening? Are you ok?"

I grabbed his hands and looked into his eyes, trying to remind my lungs how to work properly. "Why did you call me that?" I managed to gasp at him, holding tears back.

"Call you what? Charlie?" He said, looking fully and truly confused.

"No. Bit," I cried, shocked by the pain it caused to even say the word. He continued to look confused, his brows crinkled together at the center of his face. Then they relaxed and I saw realization come over him.

"I asked if you were going to be ready to go in a little bit." He said softly. I finally realized what he had actually said and then I let the hurt wash over me. I allowed myself, as I had time and time again, to lean into David and use him as a receptacle for my sadness. He held me close to him, my face buried in his stomach, my tears staining his dress shirt which he would now have to change. But that wasn't unlike him, he always changed for me – changed his plans, changed his mind, changed his life.

When we met, he'd had so many plans for life. He was a successful doctor, moving up in the medical society of New York City, making a name for himself. He'd seen me and I knew he wanted me. I recognized when men wanted me. He wanted a wife, a mother for his future children, and he saw that it me, like many had. I was aware of how I looked on the outside and what I really was on the inside. It was more difficult for others to see what I wouldn't show them. David, however, was the only one who got this close to me. Selfishly, I haven't been able to let him loose.

I couldn't give him what he wanted, but didn't push him away either. He thought that eventually I would "come around", that I would marry him, give him children. I knew better and I told him so, but if I were a good person, I'd leave him. He was so good, so hopeful, so wonderful. And I couldn't let him go.

So like many times before, I let him comfort me and lied to him about the source of my sadness.

"What happened just then?" He asked softly, after I had calmed down. I pulled back from him, wiping my face with my hands. I couldn't look in his eyes as I lied to him. I never could.

"That was the nickname Asher use to call me," I said quietly, still trying to keep calm.

"Bit?" He asked, curiously. It pained me to hear it, physically hurt me. All my muscles cramped up, my throat constricted. I nodded, trying to catch my breath. "That's a weird nickname." I let his comment float between us because I had no need or want to explain it to him. "How long ago did he die again?" I closed my eyes and turned from him.

"Thirteen years ago."

I stood with my hands on the vanity, my head hanging between my shoulders, exhausted from everything that happened in the last five minutes. I felt David come up behind me and place his hands on my arms, brushing his palms up and down, trying to comfort me. Then his hand came down to the bare skin of my rib cage, just above my waist. He ran his hand along the tattoo I had done years before I met him. He softly caressed the letters that were forever scarred on me.

"Are you still thinking of having this removed?" That was another lie I told him, that I was thinking of having it removed. I would never get rid of it. I didn't want to. I wanted to see his name on me. I wanted to be reminded of everything. I wanted some part of him on my naked skin at all times, regardless of how sick and twisted it was. I needed it. But that's not what David saw.

"Does it bother you?" It should. It should bother him to see another man's name tattooed on his girlfriend. It wasn't small either. It ran along my entire side. It was beautiful.

"I know he was your childhood friend and that you were traumatized by his death, but if you feel like you need the tattoo removed, I would understand and support you." This was his niceness coming through again. He would never tell me how much it bothered him to see it on me. He would always say the right thing.

"I'm still thinking about it." Lies.

Most of what I had with David was founded on lies, but they were necessary to make it work. According to the lies I told David, Asher was simply a childhood friend who died tragically in a car accident my sophomore year of college. According to my lies, Asher was my best friend and then was taken from me suddenly and unexpectedly. According to my lies, I never really recovered. So, the lies weren't all lies. He was taken from me suddenly and unexpectedly, and I hadn't ever recovered from it, but he wasn't my friend. He was my everything, and I was fully aware the way I held on to him, even all these years later, was unhealthy and mostly sick. I didn't care enough about myself though to fix anything.

David gently kissed my temple, trying to sooth me. I saw his eyes meet mine in the mirror of the vanity and I watched as his mouth kissed down the side of my face, over my cheek, behind my ear. I watched as his lips moved to leave wet, open-mouthed kisses along my neck. I closed my eyes and leaned back into him, and I knew what it looked like to him. I knew he thought I was giving myself over to him, letting him make love to me to make me feel better, to feel close to him. He thought I was closing my eyes from pleasure. Lies. I closed my eyes so I didn't have to see him anymore. I didn't want to see him, I didn't want him to see me and I definitely didn't want to feel anything. No pleasure. No joy. No love. Nothing.

His hands moved my bra straps off my shoulders and pushed them down to my elbows. I felt him pull the fabric down, releasing my breasts. His hands cupped me, squeezed me, and I pushed out the obligatory sigh that was expected of me. Lies. His hands moved over me, feeling my arms, my back, my ass, but as his hands floated over my belly I grabbed them and pushed them back to my breasts. I never let him touch my stomach. I never let anyone touch my stomach. I could never tell him why though; I didn't have a good excuse. The truth was not something I wanted to share with him or anyone.

He spun me around and his hands grazed down my back, his fingers sliding between the material of my panties and my skin, pushing them over the roundness of my ass.

"What about the fundraiser?" I asked between his kisses, not really in the mood to pretend to enjoy myself.

"We can be fashionably late," he mumbled between my breasts. I gave in, because I always gave in. It was easier to give in than to answer questions or make up excuses.

He pulled one of my nipples into his mouth and I knew I should feel something, but I didn't. I heard my phone ringing across the room and moved to answer it. His fingers tightened their grasp on my hips. "Let it ring," he said around my nipple in his mouth. I conceded and ran my fingers through his hair, going through the motions, hoping he'd buy it. When my phone started ringing again, I heard him sigh against my skin. He stepped away from me and I hurried to my phone, pretending to be affronted.

I didn't recognize the number, but it's local to Willow Falls so my heart rate peaked and I answered with a little break in my voice, wondering who it could be. "Hello?"

"May I please speak with Ms. Charlie McBride?"

"This is she," I said as I pulled my bathrobe over my body.

"Hello Ms. McBride. I am calling on behalf of the estate of Mr. Charles McBride. My name is Phillip Libman. Do you have a moment?"

I was confused by the things he said, words that made me nervous. Why would he represent my father's "estate"? "Um, I'm free to talk now, yes."

"Ms. McBride I am sorry to be the one to tell you that your father passed away this afternoon."

My first instinct was to laugh, so that's what I did. I chuckled a little. Obviously, he called the wrong number. "No, there's been a mistake. You must have the wrong person. My father is fine."

"Ms. McBride, I know this comes as a shock and I feel terrible to tell you over the phone, but your father, Charles McBride, passed away this afternoon from complications of bone cancer."

"My father didn't have cancer. You're mistaken." Now I was angry. How dare this person call me and tell me my father died. David came to stand beside me, his hand on my shoulder, his eyes worried.

"Charlie, did your father live at 5280 Pine Grove Drive in Willow Falls?"

My heart faltered a little, skipped a beat or two. "Yes."

"Are you Charlie McBride, born to Charles and Anna McBride?"

"Yes."

"I'm so sorry. There's no mistake."

"He wasn't even sick," I whispered as I fell back onto the bench of the vanity.

"Can you come to Willow Falls as soon as possible? We have a lot to discuss with you."

I handed the phone to David and let him take down all the important information. He walked around, collecting pen and paper, writing things down, saying things to the man on the phone who told me my dad had died today.

If my father had cancer, he would have told me. I spoke to him every Sunday. Why wouldn't he tell me that he had cancer? I would have dropped everything and gone to Willow Falls. I would have been there for him, taken care of him. A tear fell from my cheek and landed on my hand on my lap. I didn't even realize I was crying. I looked into the mirror and saw my face, red and wet with tears.

"Baby, are you ok?" David was in front of me, kneeling on the ground.

"Did that man tell you what he told me?" I asked him, trying still to fit all the pieces together.

"He said that your father passed away today," he answered gently. "He said he had cancer."

I shook my head in disbelief. "Why wouldn't he tell me he had cancer?" I kept asking the question, but in the back of my mind I knew why he didn't tell me. I leaned into David and let him comfort me, let him hold me, let him bring me to bed and wrap his arms around me. The entire time I was wishing it were someone else.

"What about your fundraiser?" I was all cries and sniffles and tears.

"Charlie, I'm exactly where I'm supposed to be," he whispered against my hair.

There was a long silence between us. He stroked my hair and I continued to cry and wail. Eventually I felt like I cried all the tears I had in me. I was wrong, of course, but I was stable for the moment at least.

"I need to go to Willow Falls." It was difficult to call it home. For the last thirteen years I hadn't felt like I had a home, really.

"We can book flights tomorrow. I have some vacation time saved up." My insides froze up at his words. I didn't know before he'd mentioned coming along, but the last place I wanted David was in Willow Falls. In the five years we'd been together, I never found a reason to bring him there and now wasn't the time to figure out why.

"You don't have to take time off from work to come with me. I can go by myself." He rolled so that he was on top of me, using his hands to brush my hair away from my face.

"I will go anywhere to be with you right now. You can't tell me to stay home. Your father died. I love you. Of course I'm going with you."

I didn't anticipate this was going to be the moment where David realized I was a coward and a fraud. I didn't anticipate my father dying suddenly and me having to explain to my long-term boyfriend why he couldn't come home with me. And like the coward I was I smiled at him and nodded my head, let him kiss me on the cheek, and allow him to spoon me as we fell asleep. Well, he fell asleep and I did a good job of pretending to be asleep. Then I crept out of his arms and paced the living room, trying to figure out which lie I'd tell him next to make him stay out of my past.

Chapter Four
Asher

I made sure I was the last one to show up and that the service already started. I made sure I wouldn't run into her. I opened the door slowly and heard the pastor at the front of the church talking about how important it was to live each day like it were a gift. I found a seat in the very back pew for which I was grateful. I sat and tried to keep my eyes on the man speaking at the front of the room, tried to force myself to grieve, to see the casket and recognize that a man I loved and respected was being laid to rest. But nothing was sinking in because I knew she was in the room.

It has been so long. The last time I saw her I broke her heart. I betrayed her in the worst way. I remembered standing in her room, saying all the wrong things, but not knowing what else to do. I was so afraid, so unbelievably caught off guard, but also so incredibly stupid. I don't blame her for leaving; I would have left too. She didn't need to wait around for me to swallow my pride, to tell her that everything I said about our baby was a mistake, that in the end, all I'll ever think about is how I took the best thing in my world and ruined it.

I saw her sitting in the front pew right next to Reeve. I could only see her from the shoulders up, but I cherished every inch of her available. She looked thin, her neck slimmer than I remembered it, the pointy corners of her shoulders concerning. Her hair was pulled up into a bun but I could tell it was still long and I felt my breathing speed up as I remembered how I use to thread my fingers through her long tresses. I used her hair for comfort, for boredom playing with it while she did homework, and I used it to hold her where I wanted her. I closed my eyes tight, trying to fight back the images of her naked back, her hair wrapped tightly around my fist. I felt like the worst human possible, fantasizing about her at her father's funeral.

Luckily, to the random funeral attendee, it probably looked like I was emotional over the death of the outstanding man we were all here to remember. But the overriding emotion I was feeling was regret, mixed with a good amount of lust. This would probably be the last time I ever saw her and that weighed heavily on me. I wanted to be the one sitting next to her, holding her hand, comforting her. I looked back to where she was sitting and didn't see a man next to her, just Reeve. How could it be that she was here without someone? I couldn't imagine she was alone in life. There's no way she's out in the world and no one was trying to snatch her up. So why was she here all by herself?

I was brought back to attention when the pastor stopped talking and a hush fell over the room. I saw Charlie stand and begin walking towards the pulpit. My breath caught in my chest as I saw more of her. She was so small and fragile, so tiny. At least, that's how I saw her. I wanted to rush to the front of the church and hold her, protect her from everything she must be going through. The black dress she wore was conservative but still hugged her tightly. I remembered the way her waist curved into her hips, how her belly was toned and flat leading to the full roundness of her small breasts. She was far away, but I could see the dark circles under her eyes.

As she faced the congregation of people, she looked down at the paper she was unfolding in her hands. She took a deep breath in and we all heard it shudder as she exhaled. My chest clenched, wanting to be near her, to help her.

"When my mother died twenty years ago," she began, her voice shaking, "my father and I were with her until the end, from her diagnosis, to her doctor appointments, to her treatment. Finally, when there was nothing left to do but keep her comfortable and wait, we waited with her. We sat next to her, spoke to her, reassured her as best we could that we would be ok and that we loved her." She brought a tissue to her nose, pausing to collect herself. "I'm not sure if my father ever fully recovered from her death, from the absence of the one person he was meant to be with, but I know I didn't. And in this moment," she gave a quiet and soft laugh, "I'm a little jealous that he gets to be with the love of his life again, while some of us are still here, alone."

"I understand my father's choice to not tell me he was sick. I don't agree with it, but I understand. It's not surprising that even on his deathbed he was thinking of me, trying to protect me, to keep me from getting hurt. He was the best dad in that way. I think back to all the phone conversations we had while he must have been sick. He never let on that anything was wrong, never complained, never confided in me his fears of possibly dying." She paused again and a small cry left her, a hand coming up to cover her mouth. I nearly shot out of my seat, rushing to her to stand with her, to be with her. "In his effort to protect me," she continued, still upset and speaking through tears, "he robbed me of my right to say goodbye. I've had enough instances of goodbye in my life and I don't want any more, but I'll never get over the fact that I never got to tell him to his face, one last time, how much I loved him."

I could tell she tried very hard to hold herself together and the tension in the room was thick. Everyone's heart broke watching this young woman, just barely thirty, saying goodbye to her last parent. I wanted to take away all her pain, but more so, felt guilty that some of her pain, even if it was in the past, was caused by me. I hated myself a little bit more in that moment.

"I hope he can hear me and that Mom is with him." She took a deep breath and closed her eyes. I knew tears had started flowing down her face. "I hope they all know how much I love them and how much I miss them. I will try to make them proud."

The rest of the service was predictable, yet sad. I took deep breaths hoping to steady myself as I stood to sneak out of the church before the service concluded. I couldn't risk Charlie seeing me. I came to the service to say goodbye to Charles, but also to satisfy some sick need to be near her, to see her one last time. But I wouldn't bring her any more pain today by letting her see me. I left the church and tried hard to reconcile myself to the idea that I would never see her again. The last glimpse I might ever have of her was much like the one I had thirteen years ago.

Sad.

Crying.

Broken.

There was nothing I could do but go home and try to drown every piece of pain I was feeling, hoping to wake up feeling just as terrible because it was what I deserved.

Chapter Five
Charlie

I shut the door to my motel room and walked towards my car. I couldn't bring myself to stay at my father's house. I hadn't even been inside it since I'd been back in Willow Falls. I didn't know what to do about it and I figured I would have to go there at some point, but I was going to avoid it as long as possible. I wasn't ready to see all of my father's things waiting for him to return. Not ready to try and sift through the life he'd left behind. No. I'd let that wait for a little while.

I wasn't in any rush to get back to New York. I wasn't even really sure there was anything to go back to. Explaining to David that I didn't want him to come to my father's funeral hadn't left our relationship in a very stable place. He told me that if I went without him, if I chose to go through such an emotional and tumultuous time without him, then I didn't need him the way he needed me. I couldn't disagree with him. I didn't need him. I used him for five years - used him to feel a little normal, a little less crazy, and a little less lonely. But I didn't need him, didn't love him. So I was back in Willow Falls alone, only this time I was a little more alone than I had been in a while and it sucked.

I was on my way to pick up Reeve who insisted that she come with me to the reading of my father's will. There was no way to avoid driving past the elementary school we all attended. I told myself I wasn't going to look, wasn't going to force myself to think about the past, but my eyes couldn't be controlled and wandered over the school grounds as I drove by. I saw the swing set I'd spent countless evenings on with him, spotted the alleyway we would walk through together. Seeing all of these places, imagining ourselves young and carefree, reminiscing about our childhood, wasn't what I needed this morning.

When I pulled up in front of Reeve's house I saw her door open and she stepped out. Her husband was right behind her and she turned to give him a quick kiss on the lips. I had met her husband once when I attended their wedding. It was a destination wedding in the Bahamas which was the only reason I agreed to go. I would not come back to Willow Falls for her wedding, there was too high of a risk coming back here.

He seemed like a nice man and it was obvious he loved Reeve very much. Their kids were adorable. There were times I felt guilty that her kids didn't know me and I wasn't a bigger part of their lives, but being around kids was just too difficult for me. I hated being so broken. I hated that I couldn't let go of everything that happened, or move on, but I couldn't find a way to be ok.

"Hey Charlie," she said with a smile as she got in the car. I found it comforting that as we drove to the lawyer's office she still talked non-stop. She was going on and on about some disaster that happened that morning, something involving her youngest child and a toilet. I tried to listen but found myself focusing on the cadence of her words, the rhythm of her voice. Luckily Reeve rambled the entire way to the office never asking me for any interaction. When we arrived she continued her chatting until we were well inside the building standing at the receptionist's desk.

"Hi, my name is Charlie McBride and I have an appointment with Mr. Libman." The woman looked at her computer screen and then back up to me.

"Of course. Let me walk you back to the conference room. Mr. Libman is out of the building but should be here very soon." I smiled at her as she stood and led us to a room with a long conference table. I smiled politely at her as I took a seat while Reeve sat down next to me. "Can I get the two of you anything to drink? Water? Tea? Coffee?" The receptionist asked. I shook my head.

"No, thank you. I think we're fine," Reeve answered with a smile. She left the room and Reeve and I exchanged glances. "Thanks for moving the meeting up to this morning. I really appreciate it. We've had this birthday party planned for months now. Are you sure you don't want to come? We'd love to have you."

This was probably the fifth time Reeve tried to get me to come to her daughter's birthday party. I shook my head at her again. "I'm just not up for it. You can understand, right? I'm sorry."

Reeve placed her hand on my shoulder and I tried not to pull away from her touch. "I totally get it. I just hope we get to see each other a little before you leave town." I nodded and tried to smile, but didn't want to give her false hope. The only reason she was here with me was because she pretty much insisted and I didn't want to argue with her. I wouldn't be going to her daughter's birthday party, I wouldn't be going to their house for dinner, and I wouldn't be resuming my life like nothing had happened. I didn't know what I was going to do, but I didn't plan on telling her that.

A few minutes later a man opened the door and walked in. Reeve and I both stood and he eyed us. I stuck my hand out towards him. "Good morning, I am Charlie McBride." I tried to sound confident and strong, not like the scared young girl I was beginning to feel like. "This is my friend Reeve. She's here for emotional support." He nodded at Reeve and smiled.

"Hello Ms. McBride, my name is Phillip Libman. I am sorry for your recent loss," he said as he gently shook my hand, sounding sincere but still rehearsed. He was probably very used to saying that to people. I tried not to let it bother me. "Let us take a seat and get started." He motioned towards the seat I just vacated. I sat and took a deep breath, not ready to go through this. Reeve reached over and placed her hand over mine that rested on top of the table.

"Ms. McBride, I'm going to be honest with you, I don't usually handle wills. My law firm isn't typically involved in probate law. We did this as a favor to your father as we all respected him very much. So, if it's ok with you, I'd like to skip over the legal jargon and get to the real meat of the document." I nodded, agreeing, but confused as to how my father knew this man and how they'd come to respect him so much. "Your father was very well organized and did a very good job planning for his passing. He made it abundantly clear from the very beginning that you were his main concern and he simply wanted you to be comfortably situated after he was gone." He looked at me and I felt his sincerity in those words. The stinging I felt in the back of my throat was familiar by this point and I struggled to hold back tears at the mention of my father's thoughts towards me. If there was one thing I was sure of, it would always be that my father loved me. So, I wasn't surprised to hear that his will was a representation of that. Reeve pulled out a small packet of tissues from her purse and handed them to me. I took them from her, grateful for them, grateful for her, too, in that moment.

"Thank you," I mouthed at her, not trusting my voice to work. She squeezed my hand and it was the most comforting thing I'd felt in years.

"Your mother had a very good life insurance policy, Ms. McBride. When your father received the money, he never touched it. He put it into an account that had very generous interest rates and it's been growing for the last twenty years. Your father also had a large life insurance policy. After his diagnosis he wasn't able to add to it, understandably, but I am sure you will have enough to be comfortable for the rest of your life." Mr. Libman moved some papers around, looking for something in particular. He found it and pinpointed it with his finger, reading the words to me. "The total estate left by Mr. Charles Anthony McBride to his only heir, a Ms. Charlie Anna McBride totals six million, five hundred and fifty-five thousand, four hundred and twelve dollars."

"What?" I couldn't believe what he'd said. There was no way my father had that much money. He was a single father, a widower. He worked hard his whole life, never spent money on anything frivolous. He didn't *have* money. "That can't be right," I added, completely astounded. "Six *million* dollars?"

"There are about five million dollars in liquid assets; money in bank accounts or invested in stocks that can be liquefied at any moment. Your father met with our personal accountant before he passed and I can assure you that the money invested is protected and smartly distributed. You are welcome and encouraged to meet with him. In fact, your father prepared for that too and any meetings you have with him have been prepaid. We are hoping you avail yourself to that privilege your father put in place for you." He paused, again looking down at his paper. "The other one point five million dollars is in the house in Willow Falls, the 2004 Ford Focus that is currently on the property, and other smaller items that all add up to the figure I mentioned earlier."

I sat in that chair, silent and stunned, listening to this man talk. Money wasn't important to me, it never was. I was taught that by my father. So finding out that my father had five million dollars just sitting around was baffling. "How is all of this possible?" I whispered, more to myself than anyone else.

"Your father was a planner, Charlie. He wanted to make sure you were taken care of. That you had everything you needed to be ok."

That part I understood. New tears sprung to my eyes imagining my father putting everything in place before the cancer took him, preparing to die, making sure I would be set for life. All the while, he never told me he was sick. I would have done anything to be by his side during his last moments, to tell him that I loved him, to comfort him as he passed. As difficult as it would have been for me, I wished he hadn't denied me that.

"Were you close with my father? Is that why you agreed to handle his affairs?"

Mr. Libman shifted in his chair and I saw his brain ticking away, obviously searching for an answer. "I met your father on a number of occasions. I have nothing but respect for him and know he was an upstanding man. But no, I didn't handle his case myself." He paused for a moment, then continued. "Your father made it clear that you were to do whatever you wanted with the house in Willow Falls. Sell it or keep it, the choice is yours as it now belongs to you. Everything in the house now belongs to you as well. There is one last item." He reached into his briefcase on the floor and pulled out an envelope. "This is a letter your father wrote about a month ago. He was very insistent that you receive it at the reading of the will and that you were not to open it until later." He handed me the envelope over the table and my fingers reached for it, trembling. "I think he wanted you to wait a bit to read it," he said softly. "He didn't say when exactly. All he said was that you would know."

That answer made me angry. *This* my father expected me to know. He wouldn't tell me anything, kept me in the dark for months about his illness, his *terminal* illness, but he expected me to be able to read his posthumous mind and inherently know when to open a letter from him. I looked at the letter, with my father's very clear penmanship across the front that read "Charlie Bear", and tried to take deep breaths. I ran my finger over the words, trying not to think too hard about the fact that this was the last thing from my father I would ever receive; no more birthday cards, no more Christmas presents, no more silly Saturday comic strips cut out and mailed to me randomly. This would be it. The very last part of himself he gave to me. How could I possibly know when to open it? When would it feel right to use up this last little bit? I didn't want to think about what the letter meant or how I would know when to open it. I put it in my purse and tried my best to seem like I was ok with everything. I'm sure the tear that ran down my face didn't help my cause. I wiped it away and then coughed through a small cry. I needed this to be over.

"Is there anything else?"

"I just want to make sure you understand that if you need anything, anything at all, to come to us. We can help you with the sale of the house, if you choose to sell it. We can help answer any questions you have, legal or otherwise, please know that."

I nodded, unable and unwilling to answer.

"The only piece left is your signature. Feel free to read the document and then just sign at the bottom of the last page." He slid a packet of paper over to me, along with a pen. It looked huge and daunting. I would be kidding myself if I thought I was going to read through it all. I trusted my father and decided to just sign. I took the packet and my eyes were drawn to the top letterhead.

Libman and Carmichael

Attorneys at Law

Carmichael? I dropped the pen and looked up at Mr. Libman. I'm sure I looked panicked, because he looked like a deer in headlights. My gaze drifted to Reeve and she looked nothing but guilty.

"Carmichael?" I asked her.

"Charlie, just sign the papers and we can go," she said softly. That was all I needed to confirm what my gut had already told me was the truth. My eyes went wide and wild, desperately looking around, trying to ground myself in a room that now held a whole new meaning and feeling. I grabbed the pen and frantically scrawled my name along the line that begged for my signature.

I picked up my purse and nearly sprinted for the door to the conference room. 'Stay calm. He's not here. You won't see him. Everything's fine'. Those were the things I was repeating to myself to try and not freak out. I was tricked, tricked into coming here, tricked into thinking about someone I had tried not to think about for so long. I swung the door open and rushed towards the exit. I saw the receptionist stand as I ran past her, frantically trying to get to someplace with more air, someplace not closing up on me. I made it outside, anxious for a wide open space. What I found, instead, was Asher.

My eyes found every tall, dark haired man in a crowd for thirteen years. I searched him out, praying I'd find him but afraid of what would happen when I did. My mind hated him, with good reason, but I'd never fully convinced my heart. With every miniscule and tiny part of myself, I was afraid of what would happen if I ever saw him again. And now, here I was, looking right at him. I saw shock on his face. I saw remorse. I saw panic.

"Shit," I heard Reeve mutter from behind me.

"Charlie," he said quietly. I hated that he used my real name. I hated that I hated it. "You're not supposed to be here." He said it like it hurt him. Like being *near* me hurt him.

"We had to reschedule," Reeve supplied. I turned to her, anger surging through my veins.

"You knew about this? About him?"

"We were just trying to make this as easy on you as possible, Charlie. We didn't want to hurt you anymore than you're already hurting," she answered. Instantly I felt alone, but I was used to it by now. I closed my eyes, trying to control my feelings, trying not to feel, to block it all out. Even with my eyes closed I could still see Asher standing before me: his hair a little longer than I remember it being, his freckles still dark and distinct, his shoulders and arms filling out the three-piece suit I'd never seen him in. For just a fraction of a moment I was proud of him for becoming what he'd always dreamt of, what he'd always wanted. In spite of everything, he was able to achieve his ultimate goal. I guess I was glad one of us achieved something. I opened my eyes again, feigning resolve, masking my complete and utter brokenness, and turned, walking towards the parking lot.

The headlights of my rental car blinked as I pressed the unlock button on the key fob.

"Charlie, wait." His voice cut through me. I hadn't heard his voice in years and it still sliced right down into me, cutting me open. I didn't stop walking. "Charlie, please, let's talk. I didn't mean for this to happen. Please let me explain." He sounded desperate, but not as desperate as I was to get away. Reeve ran up beside me and placed her hand on my arm.

"Maybe you should talk to him," she said, a little out of breath.

"You need to find another way home." I got into the car and drove away, fully aware of the fact that I was leaving everyone behind. Again.

Chapter Six
Asher

"Fuck!" I screamed as loud as my lungs would allow. I watched her car drive away and my mind raced with things I could possibly do to fix the situation. "Where is she staying?" I asked Reeve.

"I don't know. She picked me up."

I sprinted back to my car and peeled out of the driveway, hoping she'd been caught at a light and I could still find her. I wove in between cars hoping to catch up with her, hoping that I was observant enough and correct when I thought her car was black. I stopped at a red light and my open fist slammed into my steering wheel. "Ahhhh!" My frustration was no match for the wheel firmly attached to the dash and the palm of my hand stung from the impact. But that was ok. I welcomed that. I didn't see any black cars around, but I did see one soccer mom staring at me from the lane over. That's ok. Let her witness my breakdown. How could this have happened? Why didn't Phil call to tell me the meeting had been rescheduled? I ran a hand through my hair and gave it a slight tug, wishing I had stayed home for the entire day instead of trying to dodge her. That was a lie. I wouldn't take back seeing her again for anything. I just wished she hadn't seen me. To see her, up close, to see the color of her eyes, the way her long hair fell around her shoulders; it was a sight I would likely take with me to the grave and cherish just as long. This had to be the longest red light in the history of traffic. The light finally changed and I continued to pass slow-moving cars to try and find the one that might hold her.

An hour later and I still hadn't found her. I thought about stopping at every hotel and motel in town, but the only thing that stopped me was the knowledge she didn't want to be found. She didn't want to see me. She wanted to run from me, to hide from me. Didn't I owe her at least that? To be left alone? The idea of letting her go again, of letting her live more of her life without telling her everything I'd kept bottled up inside, well, it would surely eat me alive. But if there was one thing I was convinced I didn't deserve, it was her or anything she had to give me, including forgiveness. I pointed my car back towards the office and began to feel the gnawing of regret eating away at me.

I stormed into Phil's office, the door swinging open so fast it bounced off the wall behind it. "Why the hell didn't you tell me the appointment had been moved? You knew how important this was to me."

"Asher, calm down. You're right. I should have told you. The Anderson case got moved around and I was swamped. I was rushing from one meeting to the next when I got word of the time change. I just forgot. I apologize."

Well shit. I couldn't be angry at that. I just sat down in one of his arm chairs and rested my head in my hands, contemplating what to do next. "Did you see her face? Did you see how much she hates me?"

"I saw a lot of things between the two of you, but I don't think I saw hate. I saw a woman who just lost her dad and then she saw a ghost. She looked terrified. I'm not sure what happened between you two, but she's definitely not a fan of yours."

Hate or terror, I wasn't ok with either emotion, not when it was Bit. I desperately wanted her to love me again, to forget the words I spoke, the way I acted, how I'd walked away from her that day. Hell, I wanted to forget. I looked up at Phil.

"How was she during the reading?" How much I wished I had been there to comfort her while she learned of her father's last wishes. I already knew what they were. I helped Charles prepare everything. I was the one to sit with him and decide how to invest his money, how he could leave Charlie with the most, how she could be best provided for. I did it just as much for him as I did for me and I would admit that to anyone. I don't think I had to tell Charles though. He knew. He knew every time I went to see him over the last thirteen years it was to feel close to her. I will always have a deep respect for Charles McBride. He was a great man, but I used him. It was a two-way street though. I think he liked having me around to remind him of Charlie when she was younger. My love for her was comforting to him. That's how it seemed anyway.

"She was quiet. A little shocked when she heard the number, understandably." I nodded. It was a big number. "I'm glad her friend was here; she seemed to help, even had tissues ready. I suck at reading wills. I should have thought to have tissues ready." He sighed. "Oh well." He walked back to his desk and sat down in his high-back chair. "What are you going to do now?"

"What do you mean?"

"I mean, how are you going to handle the situation? It's obvious there's a history there. She wouldn't have run from here so quickly if she didn't still have some sort of feelings towards you."

"It's complicated."

"It's always complicated. If it weren't, we'd be dead. That's all life is, one complication after another. If you hide from one, the rest just pile up behind it."

"When did you become a philosopher?"

"I'm a lawyer. Same difference."

"So, you think I should try to talk to her."

"I think you should try to fix whatever it is that's made you act like a crazy person for the last week."

I nodded. That would be her. She's the one who's made me act like a crazy person. "Did Reeve get home?"

"Yes. Her husband came to pick her up."

"I think I'm going to take a personal day and head out. You all right with that?"

"Do what you have to do." His words sounded cold, but I knew Phil was simply trying to stay impartial. He wouldn't begrudge me the time off.

"Thanks. I'll see you tomorrow." I headed towards the door of his office.

"Asher," he called out. I turned around, resting against the frame of the door. "If you need anything, or anyone to talk to, give me a call." I gave him a small smile.

"Thanks. For everything. I know you didn't have to handle the will this morning. I really appreciate it."

"Ok, get out of here."

I got back in my car and headed to Reeve's house. She wasn't thrilled to see me and I wasn't surprised. She glared at me from behind her partially closed door.

"Reeve, please talk to me."

"What is it that you want, Asher?" That was a damn good question. In this moment all I knew was I wanted Charlie to know how sorry I was – for being at the office, for her dad dying, and for a list of things that happened years before.

"I just want to make sure she's ok." Reeve puffed out a big sigh and took a step out of the door on to her porch. I stepped back, allowing her some room to breathe.

"What makes you think that you deserve to know anything about her? You made the biggest mistake of your life all those years ago and this is the price you have to pay for it, Asher. You don't get to know anything about her."

"Reeve, I know I messed up. I get that. And I totally understand why she doesn't want to see me. But please, tell me she's ok." She was silent for a few moments, tapping her foot on the concrete, avoiding eye contact. Finally, her shoulders relaxed a little and she let her arms fall to her sides.

"Charlie hasn't been ok for thirteen years, Asher. She's not the same girl you were in love with. What happened between you two, what happened to her, what *you* did to her, it changed her. She was never ok after what you did."

"I know what I said to her about the baby was wrong, Reeve. I know that, truly, I do. I regret that every day of my life."

"It's not just what you said, Asher. Although, what you said was bad enough. It's what you *did*. What you did to her is pretty unforgiveable."

"I know. *I know*. I should never have walked out on her. Please. You have to help me find her so I can talk to her. The silence has gone on long enough."

"Walked out on her? That's all you've got? All you're sorry for? You're a real piece of work, Asher. I knew you were an asshole, but this is a new low. There is no way I am going to help you find her. I have no idea where she is, but even if I did, you are the last person on this planet I would tell. You can go to hell." She turned and headed back towards the house. Desperately, I reached out and grabbed her arm. She snapped around and eyed my hand wrapped around her bicep. "Get your hand off of me, Asher."

"Reeve, please, I'm so confused. I feel like I'm missing a piece of the puzzle. What are you talking about?" She looked like she was about to slap me. I would have definitely let her if it meant she would keep talking. I'd take any abuse she wanted to give me, as long as it was accompanied by information. Finally, she looked like she was going to give in.

"Tell me what you know about Charlie's pregnancy." My mouth gaped open, then closed, like a fish. I wasn't expecting Reeve to ask me that and I wasn't, at all, prepared to answer.

"What kind of question is that?"

"A valid one. You want to know about her, so you're going to have to talk to me first. Answer the question. Tell me what you know about her pregnancy." I ran my hand though my hair, trying to formulate an answer. What kind of information was she looking for? What was it that she wanted me to say?

"I guess there isn't much to tell. I don't know that much about it." I realized my first sentence wasn't so good. I wasn't painting a good picture of myself. I understood that I wasn't going to be able to redeem myself here, but I didn't want to dig myself any deeper either. It felt like Reeve was my last shot. Perhaps, even, my only shot at getting in touch with

Charlie. "I remember that Charlie kept getting sick. I came to the house to check on her one morning and one of the girls at your house said you'd both gone out." I tried to bring back the memories that I'd managed to not think about for so long.

"When you guys came back Charlie was a mess. She was crying and looked really upset. I took her upstairs and we took a small nap. When we woke up she told me she was pregnant." I swallowed hard, knowing that the rest of the story was an ugly part of my past that I hated. I hated who I was in that moment and I wished I could take it back. I'd do anything to take it back.

"I, admittedly, didn't take the news very well. I asked her what she was planning on doing about the baby. I was upset that she wouldn't consider getting an abortion. I got angry and I went back to my house." It was so much more than that, so much more. But I couldn't bring myself to tell Reeve anymore. Those were words I saved for Charlie, if I ever got to see her.

"A few weeks later her dad called me and told me she had a miscarriage. He told me that she wouldn't be returning to school and that she needed some time to heal." I looked away from her, down at the ground, remembering the time I spent trying to give Charlie what she wanted, what her father had told me she needed. "When I finally thought enough time had passed, when I tried to reach out to her, she was already gone." I looked back up at Reeve and her expression hadn't changed. Her eyes were still cold and empty, unforgiving, and that was fine. I didn't need her forgiveness, I just needed information.

"And how many girls did you sleep with between finding out she was pregnant and finding out she'd lost the baby?" Her tone was icy and she was stone cold. If her question was a physical act, it would have knocked me over. I was so caught off guard by it, by what she was insinuating, that I had to force myself to speak.

"I didn't sleep with anyone." Panic slowly started making its way through my body. Those few weeks, for me, were miserable. And I did things I wasn't proud of, found myself in situations I wasn't used to, but I was hurting. It had never occurred to me that Charlie thought I was anything but faithful to her.

"You're a liar, Asher. You're the worst kind of asshole and you don't deserve to know anything about her. You took her away from all of us. I don't believe one word out of your mouth." She turned and made it all the way inside of her door before I managed to put myself in between the door and the frame.

"I'm not lying, Reeve. I didn't sleep with anyone. Am I an asshole? Definitely. Do I deserve anything from you or Charlie? Absolutely not. But what does Charlie deserve? I think she deserves to hear an apology, at the very least. She deserves to be able to tell me how she feels about me and what she went through. You say she's been lost all this time? Let me try and help her find a way back. I can't do that without your help." She still looked like she wanted to kill me. She pointed a finger at me and her eyes narrowed.

"I don't believe one single word you've said. Let me make that clear. Whatever happened between you and her, is between you and her. If you find her, if you convince her to listen to you and you hurt her again, I will find you. I will find you and I will hurt you like I wanted to thirteen years ago." She paused, contemplating. "If you're telling the truth right now, you need to find Charlie and tell her."

"That's all I want to do. I want to tell her the truth. I want to tell her everything. Please. Help me find her."

"Much like the last thirteen years of my life, I have no idea where she is. Good luck finding her. You're the reason she's hiding." Her words pushed me backward, out of her doorway, and she slammed the door in my face.

Well, fuck. I was no closer to finding Charlie as I was before I spilled my guts to Reeve. I groaned in frustration and walked back to my car. I slammed my fist into the steering wheel a few more times, trying simply to calm down. It had been a long time since I purposefully remembered everything that happened between Charlie and me. After a few deep breaths I was feeling less antsy, but I was still at a loss as to what I was going to do next. There really was only one more place to go and I hadn't been there in weeks.

A half hour later I was parked outside of Mr. McBride's house. That house was bittersweet for me. It held some of my favorite memories. Some of the best times we had together were in that house. But the best memories were also the worst. I can recall sitting on her couch watching movies on Saturday night, wanting so badly to put my arm around her, not being able to pay any attention to the movie on the screen. I was consumed with the thought of just reaching behind her and gently wrapping my arm around her shoulder, pulling her into me and holding her. I wanted to inhale her perfume, run my fingers through her long hair, to feel the warmth of her pressed up against me. But I never could muster enough courage to just do it. I missed the plot of many movies that way.

I was so afraid to lose her friendship, so worried that if I told her how I felt that I would scare her away or ruin things somehow. I put our friendship ahead of all of my feelings for years. She was so pure and inexperienced that I was convinced she didn't feel the same way for me, or that there was no way she would want me. There was no way I was lucky enough that the one girl I had feelings for shared them for me. It was truly the summers apart that solidified the real us. Everyone always talked about distance making the heart grow fonder. No one ever told you that royally fucking up and pressuring the one person you love more than anything in the world to get an abortion makes her heart break into thousands of pieces. I guess that reality was implied.

Even though the McBride house was filled with memories of Charlie, there were an equal amount of memories of her father there too. He was a good man and some part of me would miss him. He'd been kind to me when he really had no reason to, when he probably shouldn't have been. But that was the kind of man he was.

I stared at the house for a good ten minutes and I hadn't seen any indication that anyone was inside. There was no car in the driveway and no car parked on the street nearby. No lights were on. I wouldn't have been surprised if Charlie had decided not to stay there. Not only was it the house that held all the memories of her father, it was also just down the street from my childhood home. If Charlie wanted to avoid me and any thoughts or memories of me, this house was not the place to be. But it was my last hope. I figured, as difficult as it might be, she would have to come back at some point to handle the business of the house. I hoped I could be here when and if she decided to make an appearance.

Chapter Seven
Charlie

I stood in front of the fogged up mirror of my cheap motel room. My hair was wrapped up in a towel, twisted up on top of my head, another towel wrapped around my body. I reached out and used my hand to wipe away the condensation from the mirror and saw someone staring back who I didn't entirely recognize. I was thinner than I had ever been, my cheeks hollowed and gaunt. My collarbone protruded and my ribs could be counted. I didn't like the way my body was rebelling against me.

I hadn't been able to eat for a week. My appetite was non-existent and if I tried to force something in my stomach, it was rejected. I was surviving on coffee and oxygen. I knew I wasn't going to be able to continue this way; something had to give.

After the reading of the will, after my eyes had seen him, I fell into a darkness that I wasn't sure I was fully out of yet. I was caught completely off guard seeing standing just a few feet in front of me. I'd imagined that moment a million times in my mind, but when it came down to it, I froze. I panicked. My heart betrayed my mind by wishing that he came there to comfort me, hoping that he rose above the silence we'd condemned ourselves to so long ago, thrown all the rules of heartache out the window, and just came to *be* with me. My mind berated my heart, reminding me of what he'd done, what he hadn't done, what he'd wanted me to do. I was in the worst kind of purgatory because I was battling with myself. I felt guilty for still wanting the old Asher to comfort me and I felt weak that I couldn't grasp on to the anger and move on. I had grown weak in more ways than one, it appeared.

Perhaps the worst part was that when he saw me, when it became apparent that he had wrapped his mind around the fact that I was, indeed, standing in front of him, all he could say was that I wasn't supposed to be there. I didn't really belong anywhere any more. I made the decision to sell my father's house; I didn't belong there. I would sell it and take all the money I had been given in exchange for both my parents, and find some way to fit in somewhere. The first step to disappearing was forcing myself to go to my father's house.

I turned away from the woman in the mirror and forced myself to prepare to see the house that held memories of my father, and also of Asher.

An hour later, I checked out of my motel, had my one suitcase in my hand, and I was staring at the front door of my father's house. It was still early in the day, not yet noon, but I knew I had to go in because there was a lot to do. I put the key in the door, a key I hadn't used in years, and pushed the door open. I stood on the porch looking in, trying to decide if I was going to freak out or not.

The house was quiet and empty, the only light flooding in from the windows. My father never bothered with blinds or curtains, claiming that if the neighbors could see into his house at all times it forced him to keep it clean. And it always was. He had been one of those 'A place for everything and everything in its place' kind of people, very organized. *He was even organized in death apparently.* I chastised myself for thinking something so insensitive and crass about my own father's death. I was still trying to deal with the fact that my father planned his death, planned everything about it, right down to having pre-ordered the flowers that he wanted at his memorial service. And yet, he couldn't call and tell me about it - wouldn't allow me to be there for him. Angrily, I walked into the house. When had I let other people start making decisions for me? When had I given up that control over myself?

I closed the door behind me and headed towards the laundry room. Everything I'd brought with me to Willow Falls was dirty and if I was going to go through with my plan to go it alone, I would at least need some clean clothes. Just as I plopped my suitcase up on the dryer, I heard that damned doorbell ring. I froze, knowing exactly who was ringing it, but hoping I was wrong - kind of. It went on and on forever, just like I remembered. I stood incredibly still, trying not to make a sound. I wanted to disappear. I wanted to melt away. I wanted to hide. It rang again and I rolled my eyes at his persistence. In reality I knew that Asher wouldn't stop until he got what he wanted, I was just afraid to find out what that was exactly. I waited for a minute or two after the doorbell ended its chiming, and I relaxed a little, feeling like I could breathe a little easier. I unzipped my suitcase and started sorting clothes into the washer when I heard the front door open.

"Charlie?" His voice floated through the house. "Charlie, I know you're here. I saw you go in."

My hand came up to cover my mouth. I didn't know if I was planning on screaming or crying, but the sound of his voice hurt and soothed me at the same time. I craved it; his voice was like a salve. But it was impossible for him to heal the wound he inflicted himself. Wasn't it? I heard footsteps and the door latching closed. He was coming to find me. I had a choice. I could confront him and be strong, or hide and let my lack of strength make another decision for me. I took a deep breath and swept my hair from behind my neck to the side, cascading down the front of my chest. I had been pretending for thirteen years that everything was fine; I could do that for another five minutes, surely. I took one last moment to make sure that my necklace was hidden beneath my shirt and then stepped into the kitchen.

We stood, for one eternal moment, in a darkened kitchen, and stared at each other.

He wasn't wearing the three-piece suit from the other day, but he still looked good – jeans and a sweater. The blue sweater made his gray eyes shine. His hands were in his pockets and he seemed to be waiting for me to say something.

"Hello, Asher," I managed. The words stung my throat. My body wanted to cry at the mention of his name. For so long I tried not to say his name, tried not to think of him, or picture his perfect face. In that moment, standing in my father's kitchen, everything I had been avoiding all those years was being thrust at me and I was drowning in the need to push it all away. I couldn't see his face without imagining how my baby might have looked with his freckles. Had either of my babies been a boy? Would he have looked like Asher? What would we have named him? Them? It was taking everything in me not to run out the door, get in my car, and drive away forever. There were days I was sure that in some other dimension Asher and I were happy with our 12-year-old twins. Perhaps a boy and a girl, they were happy and healthy. Asher and I were happily married. Everything worked out perfectly for us. It was a tough road at first, but our love got us through. I, however, was stuck in this reality where everything I had ever loved was taken from me.

"Charlie." He paused, looking like he wasn't entirely sure what he came here to say to me. "How are you?"

His question struck me as funny so I laughed, not a real laugh but an 'I can't believe you just asked me that' laugh. "I'm great. You?" He ran his hand through his hair.

"I'm so sorry about your father, Charlie."

"What part are you sorry about? The part where he got sick? The part where he didn't tell me? The part where he died? Or the part where you knew all along and still kept it to yourself?"

"I understand why you're upset. But, Charlie, he didn't want me to tell anyone. As his lawyer, I couldn't."

"Did you want to?"

"Did I want to what?"

"Did you want to tell me? Did you try to convince him to call me and tell me?" I don't know why all of a sudden I had so much to say, but part of me wanted to figure out what happened that brought us both to this point.

"Until the very end, until it was clear he wasn't going to make it, we never discussed you. I never brought you up and neither did he."

"What do you mean by 'until the end'? How long had you been in contact with him?" He looked down at the floor and my heart dropped. "Asher, answer the question."

"I've always been in contact with him, ever since you disappeared."

Well, fuck. That stung.

"I think you need to leave," I said as I turned from him, trying to go anywhere else in the house besides where he was.

"I think we need to talk about this," he said calmly. There was nothing calm about me, but I tried so hard to pull it off. I didn't want his pity or his sympathy. I continued to walk down the hall, headed for what once was my bedroom. I planned on avoiding this room, planned on staying away from a room that would bring back the worst and most vivid memories of being with Asher, but at this point I had nowhere else to go. "Don't you think you've hidden long enough?" His words were like ice down my spine. I froze. Indeed, I felt like hiding, but for the first time in years, all of a sudden, I felt more like fighting.

"How *dare* you come into my father's house and talk to me about hiding. I am not the one who ran the very second we hit a road block. I am not the one who left my girlfriend for weeks after finding out she was pregnant." I marched over to him with every word I spoke and I felt my face reddening with rage, a flush spreading up from my chest. When we were chest to chest, I pointed a finger right in his face. "You, of all people, do not get to judge me. I left because it was time to move on. My absence didn't hurt anyone." I turned again, set on disappearing, leaving him with those last words, hoping they hurt him even one tiny fraction of the amount of hurt I had acquired due to him.

"It hurt me," he said quietly, stopping me mid-stride. I knew, deep down in my soul, in the depth of my being, that I didn't owe him one damn thing. I should have kept walking, and I should have written him off years ago as the stupid boy in college who broke my heart, but the majority of my self, of the person I was, wouldn't deny him.

"I never got the chance to apologize to you," he continued. I heard him walking towards me and I knew he was getting closer. I just wasn't sure how close I'd allow him. "Please," he said, not two feet away from me. "Please let me talk to you. We can talk about what happened, talk about your father, talk about anything you want. I just want the opportunity to spend a little time with you."

There were so many things running through my head at that moment. Could I spend a little time with him? I wasn't short on time. In a few weeks I had to be back in NYC for an art show – my art show – but until then I was free as a bird. Did he deserve to spend any time with me? Did I want to see him? What could we possibly do besides talk about painful memories? Or talk about memories that were so sweet and special that it made them painful?

"Why?" I whispered. I heard him move again, and I felt him inch closer to me. I couldn't tell if he wanted to touch me, but I knew I'd crumble if I felt his hand on me anywhere.

"Don't you think we owe it to ourselves?" He paused and I could tell he'd inched even closer. I could smell his aftershave he was so close and I began to tremble. "At the very least, we owe it to our child."

In the one conversation we'd ever had about our baby, he'd only used the term "it". To hear him say "our child" broke something in me I'd been trying to hold together for so long. My hands came up to cover my face and I tried to cry quietly as emotions I'd tried to bury were brought to the surface by his words. Something inside of me needed to hear him acknowledge that there had been a baby, and once I heard it, I couldn't contain the rush of relief. But even as I cried, even as my heart tried to put itself back together again, I was nagged by a new guilt. He still didn't know there were two. Two babies. Two lives that I lost – that we lost that day.

My father was the only one who knew about the miscarriage – besides Reeve. Reeve knew because she was in the room with me, but my father knew because he could see the pain I was in and knew something was wrong. When I came home after the miscarriage, after one week of realizing that my life was no longer at college, I told my dad what happened. I told him I'd gotten pregnant, that Asher was the father, and that I'd lost the pregnancy. I cried and sobbed as I explained there were two babies, that I'd lost his twin grandbabies, and he held me through my cries. That one tiny piece of information was something I treasured, something I knew that Asher didn't, something I felt like, at the time, he didn't deserve to know. Immature? Perhaps. Warranted? Absofuckinlutely.

I was certain that Asher didn't know there'd been two babies. One thing I wasn't sure about though, was whether he knew that I'd seen him with that girl. I played that scene over and over in my mind a million times. In my head, I opened the door and saw that girl on top of him, his arm wrapped around her waist, my name staring back at me as his arm held her to him. But I didn't make a sound and she never turned to look at me. And even though that was the worst day of my life, even though I saw him with another woman and hated him entirely too much, I always thought that if Asher had known I was there he would have come after me. Maybe now was the time for honest conversations and answers - for both of us.

I wiped the wetness from my face, appreciating the fact that he let me cry without trying to comfort me physically. It seemed that he at least understood my need for space. I don't know if I was in denial or just lying to myself, but I should have known that if I came to this house he'd find me here. Maybe even my subconscious wanted me to talk to him. I turned back to him, trying not to look him in the eye.

"Not tonight, Asher. I just got here and it's the first time I've been home in a really long time. I miss my dad and I think I just want to go to sleep. Can we meet tomorrow sometime? Maybe get some coffee?"

He hesitated and I could see that he wanted to argue with me. "You'll be fine here by yourself? Are you sure you don't want me to take you to a hotel or something?"

I laughed a little pathetic laugh. "I just came from a hotel. I just want to go to bed, really."

He nodded, finally accepting my decision.

"So, can we meet tomorrow afternoon then?" I asked, trying to get him to leave so I might finish my breakdown, or my laundry - whichever.

"Sure, how does three sound? There's a little coffee shop downtown called Java Jive."

"Perfect. I'll see you there."

He hesitated again. "Are you really going to meet me or are you just trying to get rid of me?" He kind of smiled, like he's partly joking asking the question, but can tell it's laced with the fear of the truth.

"I'll be there."

"Ok. I'll see you then." He turned and left, walked right out of my father's house and left me wondering why I'd agreed to meet him, why I'd even come back to this house. But I shook my head at myself. I knew why. Part of me still wanted to see him, still wanted to feel the rush of my blood thrumming through my veins at the sight of him. Part of me still loved him.

Now I just had to figure out how to keep that part of me silent.

Chapter Eight
Asher

It was finally here. The day I hoped for. The day Charlie and I would get to say everything we'd never gotten to. I imagined this conversation a million times before. Sometimes, in my mind, after I would tell her everything, she would nod and understand why I made all the decisions I did. She would be open. She would listen. She would forgive. In other scenarios she would cry and tell me all the ways I destroyed her and then she would disappear again. Sometimes she would joke around with me, telling me that I'm taking it all too seriously and that she moved on years ago and I should too. Sometimes she would just walk up to me and slap me across the face and then walk away. All would be valid responses. I would take any of them. I would take whatever she gave me. I deserved whatever came my way. All I hoped for is that by telling her everything that happened, telling her how much I regret what occurred between us, would ease some of the pressure in my chest that I've dealt with for years. It's a selfish endeavor, I know, but my expectations could be much higher. I could be asking the world of Charlie, expecting her to come back to me, to let me prove to her that there was nothing I wouldn't do for her. But no, my need was simple – just to explain. And then to take whatever reaction she had and deal with it.

Finally, Charlie walked into the coffee shop. I sat in a far corner so she didn't see me right away. I should have stood and greeted her. I should have waved her over. But I just couldn't. As selfishness was the theme of the day, I took a minute to drink her in, to commit her to memory as this could very well be the last time I would get to wash my eyes over her in earnest.

She still seemed so small to me. In reality, she was small. She never grew after she turned thirteen, at least not in height. Her hips became fuller in her teen years, as did her breasts and ass, but her head never really got much higher than my shoulders. Her smallness was no surprise to me, but it did trigger the possessive feelings I always had over her. She needed to be protected, shielded, and treasured. I'd done a fantastic job of fucking all of that up. If I didn't know her, if she were a stranger walking into the coffee shop that day I might take a look at her and think she was attractive, that she looked confident and determined. But I knew better.

She was rail thin and although she'd always been small, she'd never been this frail. I understood she was dealing with the death of her father, but something told me that this wasn't due to her recent loss. Her eyes were empty and her skin was ashen. She didn't look healthy. She didn't look happy. She looked like she needed help or someone to offer her a burger. Beyond all that, she was still beautiful. She was still my Charlie. Her eyes met mine and I gave her a weak smile, not sure if she'd picked up on the fact that I'd been watching her. She walked over to the table and I stood, wanting to take her and pull her against me, but lamely standing still and waving instead. I motioned with my hand for her to sit in the vacant chair across from me.

"Thanks for meeting me," I said, trying to sound serious, trying to convey the fact that I knew this wasn't a social call. She tilted her head at me and smiled. I felt a little bit of my stiffness ease with the upturn of her lips.

"Honestly, I'm glad to be getting out of my dad's house. It's harder being there than I anticipated." I nodded, not wanting to bring up that I'd been there many times in her absence. "I guess I just wish he'd told me what was going on. It's like he was preparing to die. He nearly cleaned out the entire house, only leaving things that he thought I might want. There's not one piece of junk mail, not one old newspaper, not even anything in the refrigerator to clean out." She shook her head to herself and grew quiet.

"He didn't want you to have to deal with everything," I said quietly. I wasn't sure if this was where she wanted our conversation to start, but we might as well discuss it while we were here. She brought it up, after all.

"Why?"

"He said that he knew what it was like to watch someone die and then have to deal with their life after they passed. He didn't want that for you. He didn't want you to clean out his refrigerator. He didn't want you to see him that way; sick, weak, dying." A waitress walked up to our table and interrupted. It wasn't her fault, but it was hard not to glare at her. Charlie and I both ordered coffee and the waitress left again.

"Did he suffer for long?" She looked down into her coffee mug as she asked the question, swirling a spoon around, mixing the creamer into her coffee that blended in thirty or so swirls ago. I wanted to reach over and calm her, place my hand over hers and comfort her.

"The chemo was hard on him. For about six months he went through treatments and was never given good news. Eventually the doctors came to the conclusion that he wasn't responding and had a conversation with him about quality of life." Her hands came up and covered her eyes and I chastised myself for revealing too much. Charles wanted to spare his daughter from the hurt, to prevent her from seeing him in pain, and here I was giving away the information he wanted to take to the grave. Before I could think enough to stop myself I reached over and took her hand away from her face and held it; I gripped her fingers gently in my palm.

"He lived about six months after he went off chemo and the first two months I think he tried to live a little bit more. He went to visit you," I nodded towards her, trying to engage her, to make sure she wasn't just emotionally crushed. "He went to see a few places he'd always wanted to. Eventually, though, he came back here and got very serious about making plans.

"You were always his main concern, in everything. We had countless conversations about how to best provide for you, how we could take what he had and make the most of it, how he could spare you the most amount of pain and hassle. That's all he ever wanted, Charlie, to take away your pain."

She pulled away from me at that and I thought maybe I went too far.

"Is that why he never told me that you two were close?"

I shrugged and then smiled because, typically, that was her move. "I'm not sure. We never spoke about you, really. I was there a few times while you two had phone conversations, but we never talked about you. Not until he was trying to prepare for his death."

She scoffed. "For thirteen years you hung around my dad and the two of you *never* talked about me, or about *us*?" She didn't believe me and I didn't blame her.

"I think the first time I showed up at his house, looking for you, looking for answers, was the only time." Her eyes were big and round with surprise.

"You came looking for me?" I had become numb to the term 'broken heart'. My heart wasn't broken. The word broken implied that it could be fixed or repaired. My heart wasn't fixable, my heart shriveled up like a flower in the fall when the summer sun had beaten it to death, when the heat evaporated the life from it. My heart cracked and shattered and crumbled until it wasn't even recognizable anymore and then I tried to piece it back together by searching for her, but every day I gave a shard of it away to keep breathing. There was no fixing my heart, but I'll be damned if it didn't break a little more to hear her question whether or not I looked for her.

"Of course I came looking for you. I loved you." It tore me up to use the past tense, but she didn't want to hear me telling her I loved her now, that would just make this even more awkward. I saw something flash over her face as she took in my words and it looked a lot like anger. She was mad at me. Hearing me tell her that I loved her and made her angry.

"What did he say to you about me then?"

I swallowed hard. This was it, the moment I longed to have with her - to apologize.

"He told me that you lost the baby. And that you left." She sniffled again and I wished to God she'd look at me. I didn't want to apologize to the top of her head. Honestly, I didn't want to apologize to her in a coffee shop. To my amazement she did look up at me, tears gleaming in her eyes.

"Can we go someplace more private?"

I exhaled loudly.

"Definitely. Where should we go? To your dad's house?"

She shook her head. "No, can we go to the park? The one we always used to go to?"

Something gripped my lungs, squeezed the breath right out of me. She wanted to go to back to *our* park? The place that held most of the sacred memories I had of her and I together?

"Are you sure?"

She nodded and a tear slid down her cheek.

"Of course. Come on, let's get out of here." I threw some money down on the table and walked her out of the shop, my hand naturally going to the small of her back. Once I realized I'd placed it there, I knew I should pull it away. But I'm a selfish bastard today so I left it there.

Chapter Nine
Charlie

I stopped my car down the street from the park entrance. I haven't been here in years. Even if I had come back here often to visit my father, I know I would have avoided this place. It's almost worse than my bedroom. This is the place where we came to be alone, where we shared secrets, plans, words. This was hallowed earth.

I took a deep breath and got out of my car to see Asher walking towards me from his. His car was sleek, a two-seater, nothing a man with kids would drive. I kind of resented that car. He didn't have a ring on his finger; I noticed while we were having coffee. No wife. No kids. He had the life he wanted, I supposed. I tried not to let my thoughts run away with my feelings. I tried not to be resentful of what he became since it had nothing to do with me. It was, in fact, the complete opposite. He became what he was due to the absence of me.

We silently fell in to step with one another, walking along the path of the park that wound around the perimeter. Neither one of us spoke. We just kept walking. Eventually we came to the gazebo and I closed my eyes for just an instant to push back the memory of a young girl and a young boy standing in that gazebo sharing a kiss, breaking boundaries, giving in to something that had been building between them. I opened my eyes to see Asher, grown and even more handsome, staring back at me from inside, the pond his background.

I walked towards him, without even thinking about it, and we stood next to each other against the railing, like we had a thousand times before. Only now, his arms weren't around me and I wasn't lost in his scent. I was, however, ridiculously aware of the space between us. Just inches separated us, and if I leaned my head over, it would rest against his arm. I had done that in the past, in this very spot. This was getting a little surreal, even for me.

"I'm so sorry, Charlie." He spoke suddenly and it caught me off guard. His tone was serious and I looked over at him, only to see so much sadness in his eyes. Instinctually I moved towards him, closing the distance between us and placed a hand on his forearm that rested against the railing. "I wish I could take back everything I said to you that day. I wish I could just go back and start over, you know?" He looked to me and I couldn't help but nod. I kind of wished he could have a do-over too. I wished everything was different.

"I was supposed to be the one person you could count on, the one person who was supposed to stand next to you through everything, and I managed to fuck up the very first time we were faced with anything of importance." He sniffled and rubbed his hands together, his head bent down, trying to compose himself. "I was a stupid nineteen-year-old boy. The very last thing I ever expected you to tell me was that you were pregnant, Charlie. And when I heard those words: pregnant, baby, adoption. Fuck, I shut down. I wish to God I hadn't. I wish everything was different. But it's not. What happened, happened. All I can say is that I'm sorry." He looked up at me and I was stunned by how much grief I saw reflected back at me.

"It's ok," I said. Those were words I never thought I'd say to him. I never thought it would *be ok*. Ever. "We were both young and inexperienced. It was a less than ideal situation and we handled it the way young people ought to, with fear and panic."

"Please don't make excuses for me, Charlie. I should have been there for you. I should have swallowed my fear and stayed by your side. I should have been there when you lost the baby." His words were lost in quiet sobs and I tried hard to hold my own back, but there was something so entirely damaged about him in this moment. He was vulnerable and cracked, and for a moment I saw my best friend and wanted to comfort him. I pulled him into me and he came, willingly. I wrapped my arms around his neck and his arms came around my waist and we stood there, comforting each other for a while.

Every once in a while he mumbled an "I'm sorry," and I hushed him and responded with a soft, "It's ok." Eventually he pulled away from me, wiping his eyes and taking deep breaths.

"Wow," he said through his hands that were covering his face. "I feel like that was a long time coming."

I didn't know what to say. I honestly felt like I could forgive the nineteen-year-old who had made a mistake in a moment of high stress. He didn't react to a pregnancy any differently than many boys his age would have. Was it shitty? Yes. Could I forgive him, years later, for it? I knew I could. I could let that one piece of heaviness off of my chest. But I knew I needed to give my own apology.

"Asher, there's something I need to tell you." My eyes were on the pond, but I knew he turned to me, his cheeks still wet from tears, eyes red from crying. "I haven't told anyone this, so you'll have to forgive me if it's difficult." I looked down and my hands clasped together, holding me up against the railing. "When I was losing the pregnancy," my voice shuddered. I shook my head, trying to shake off all the guilt and shame I felt for so long. I raised my head and looked Asher right in his beautiful gray eyes. "When I was having the miscarriage," I began again, "in the hospital, they gave me an ultrasound. They were trying to figure out what was wrong." I took in a deep breath, readying myself to say the words I avoided for so long. "I could see them, Asher, both of them." His eyebrows scrunched in confusion, not understanding me. "I was pregnant with two babies. Twins. I lost them both." My last words were lost in my cries, unable to hold them back as I had hoped, but also I was muffled by Asher pulling me into him. He held me, comforted me. And in that moment I allowed myself to feel it. I allowed myself to get lost in the feeling of his arms wrapped around me.

This was all I ever wished for. All I ever wanted was for Asher to be there for me, to share the pain with me. Now that he knew and he was here, I was equally upset by reliving the loss of my children as I was by the feeling of his arms encasing me. He put a piece of my soul back together and he didn't even know it. There was no way for him to realize what this moment meant to me. I let myself feel all of it, wanted to ache from all the emotions running through me, wanted to be exhausted, for once, from feeling instead of hiding.

I hugged him harder and let myself cry into his chest. It was his turn to comfort me, running his hand through my hair, whispering apologies into my ear. I heard him and I felt him. With my eyes closed it was almost as if we were young again – two kids, in the throes of a passionate and all-consuming love. I wanted to go back to that time when we were young and in love and nothing could hold us down, before life's tragedies took our sunshine, took our innocent love and made it dark and twisted.

"I'm so sorry," he whispered into my hair. That's all it took to remind me. He was sorry because he wasn't there. And the one reason he wasn't there was because I shut him out. I shut him out because I found him with another girl wrapped around him. I could forgive him for his response to the pregnancy, but I could not forgive him for burying himself in someone else.

I stepped back, pushing my hair back behind my ears, trying to put a few feet between him and me. I needed some distance; his arms felt too good and I didn't fully trust myself.

"I think it's good that we had this conversation," I said coolly. I made sure I turned from him, wiping my eyes. "I think closure is something I've been lacking from our whole situation. So, thanks for making me meet with you and allowing me to get this off of my chest."

"Closure?" He asked. I could hear the strain in his voice.

"Yes. Closure. I think it's important to have a little closure in order to move on. Lord knows I could use a little moving on in my life." I laughed a little, trying to make it seem like I wasn't being shredded on the inside.

"Hey," he said as he gently gripped my arm and turned me towards him. I shied away from his hand but turned to face him. He dropped his hand and I saw the hurt on his face that came when I pulled away. "Are you going to run away again? Hide from all of us?"

"Hide from who, exactly? I've got no one to hide from." I swiped my empty hands through the air, motioning to the emptiness around me, emphasizing my point, that I was all alone.

"From Reeve. From me."

"Reeve has moved on, Asher. She's got a family now, a husband and children. Her life is full and complete without me interfering."

"I don't think you're giving her enough credit here. She cares about you. She worries about you. She wants to be your friend." He paused, his eyes searching mine. It took all my strength not to look away from him. I held his gaze, not allowing myself to shrink away. "And what about me? You're going to run away and hide from me too?"

"We're not friends, Asher."

"We could be."

"No. We couldn't."

"Charlie, don't push me away. We were friends for so long before. Best friends."

Before. I couldn't go back to before. Before what? Before I lost my two babies? Before he cheated on me? Before my father died? There was no going back. There would only be moving forward.

"I can't go back, Asher. I can't pretend like nothing ever happened. It's not possible for me. I appreciate your apology, and I hope you can appreciate and accept mine. Our history is too painful to allow us to have anything between us in the future. I think it's best if we just move on. Separately." I started to walk towards the entrance of the park where my car was parked, but I knew he was following me.

"Wait a damn minute. Why do you get to decide everything? What if I'm not ok with this?"

"It's not up to you, Asher. I can't be around you."

"Why?" He nearly yelled. "I've already apologized and I meant it too. I meant every word. I just want to be a part of your life again. We don't have to be anything but people who don't hate each other. Charlie, please."

To hear the pain in his voice felt like tiny knives were taking stabs at my heart - a sharp pain, a slow burn. Everything about being around him was painful, except when he was holding me. That seemed to heal more than anything. In that moment I wished I could let go of everything and just live in his arms. I shook my head at the thought. He didn't want me like that; he wanted my friendship. And I couldn't give him that. I couldn't give him anything.

"I hope you have a good life, Asher." My quiet words sliced as they left my mouth. I turned from him, once again, and walked to my car. This time he didn't follow me.

I drove to my father's house, angry that I had to go back to perhaps the only other place on the planet that held more memories of my friendship with Asher. Every room of the house had a piece of him in it, a memory of who we use to be together. With the renewed and fresh memory of his arms around me, I wasn't sure it was the smartest place for me to be. I knew, though, that I had to take care of my father's house. I owed it to him, and to myself, to face the process of moving on, of letting go.

I decided, however, to let today end and start fresh the next day. There was only so much emotional turmoil I could handle. When I entered the house I went straight to the bathroom, intending on taking the hottest shower I could stand, hoping the water would ease some of my tension. I stripped off my clothes and turned on the shower. When I saw myself in the mirror, I stared intently at the script emblazoned on my ribcage. *Asher.* My eyes fell to the necklace that was around my neck. A simple silver chain with the ring he gave me nestled between my breasts. Since the day

I put it on, I never took it off. Every once in a while I thought about it. I question whether or not it was healthy to have this physical reminder of him hanging on me. In the end, every time, regardless of how harmful I thought my actions to be, I wasn't giving them up. The tattoo, the ring, they both brought me a sense of peace.

The shower helped alleviate some of the anxiety from the conversation with Asher and I found it surprisingly easy to slip into my old bed and fall into a restful sleep.

When I woke the next morning it was past noon. I rubbed my face with my hands and tried to remember the last time I slept for more than four or five hours at a time. I still felt a little groggy, but it was a good feeling, a feeling like my body was finally relaxing. I felt loose.

As if the universe knew exactly how I was feeling and how to ruin it, I heard the doorbell ring again. My instincts told me it wasn't Asher, not after the fight we had yesterday. I couldn't imagine he was in a hurry to talk to me. I pulled on my bathrobe and walked to the front door and opened it, not really caring that my hair was most likely doing its best impression of Medusa.

A man stood on my porch holding a very large and beautiful arrangement of roses.

"Charlie McBride?"

"That's me," I said, a little baffled at the beautiful sight.

"These are for you. Have a nice day." He handed the flowers off to me and I carried them into the kitchen, kicking the door closed.

The roses were all different shades of yellow – light yellow like you might find in a baby's nursery, buttery yellow, darker shades that remind me of sunlight; they were all beautiful. I spotted a card mixed in with the flowers and pulled it out.

Dear Charlie,

Despite everything that's happened between us, I cannot forget that at first, in the very beginning, we were friends. Best friends. Yellow roses signify friendship and I very much still want to be friends with you. Please don't push me away.

My mom and dad are having a dinner tonight and I would like for you to come. Reeve and her family will be there. My mom would love to see you, as would I. Please consider coming. Six pm. You know the place.

~Asher

Perhaps it was the full night's sleep or the fact that, in the end, I could always use a true friend, but I found myself softening to his invitation. I could be friends with him, couldn't I? Besides the appeal of having him back in my life, in any capacity, the idea of seeing his parents, especially his mother, made my heart clench a little. I could use a little Mrs. Carmichael love at the moment.

I grabbed my cell phone and called Reeve.

"Hey, how are you?" She answered. I could hear her children in the background, her house filled with sounds of happy and loud kids.

"Better, thanks." I paused, wondering how to best broach the topic. "So you spoke with Asher?"

"Yeah. A few times. He is worried about you. We all are."

"Are you going to dinner at the Carmichael's tonight?"

"Are you?" She retorted.

"I want to. But I don't think I can go alone."

"Well, you won't have to. Riley, the kids, and I will be there."

I smiled hearing that, glad that I hadn't pushed Reeve so far away that she was completely out of reach.

"What are you going to wear? I didn't bring anything that doesn't scream "I'm in mourning"."

"Sounds like you need to go shopping. I'll be there in an hour!" I heard the line go dead and I knew that in sixty minutes or less Reeve would be here to help me. I smiled, my mood lightened by how even though things were so drastically different than they were in college, some things were still the same. It was remarkably comforting.

Chapter Ten
Charlie

Reeve and I sifted through a few racks at a boutique downtown. Turns out that Reeve's husband, Riley, was home on vacation and Reeve was looking for the perfect reason to get out of her house. Who'd have thought that being home with your husband and children could be stressful? She showed up to my dad's house with two coffee drinks, a smile, and an excitement she attributed to being "child-free" and given a valid reason to shop. I was more than happy to supply her a reason to escape her house.

"So what's it like living the exciting life in New York City?" Reeve asked with sparkling eyes.

I shrugged my shoulders. "It's different. Exciting. Fast. But it's also normal and boring. I don't know; you get used to it I suppose."

"Do you see many famous people?"

"I spend a lot of time in my studio, drawing. But a few smaller celebrities have come to my shows before. No one huge though." I found it funny that she was so enraptured by my life. To me, my life back in NYC was a bandage. Something I used to cover up my painful past. I didn't really enjoy being there, but it was better than being here. Well, it used to be, anyway.

"That's really great that you've been able to do your art in New York. You are so talented. Once I graduated from college I just took the first job I was offered." She shrugged her shoulders, like it was something she'd thought about before but decided it wasn't worth the effort to worry about it.

"Where do you work?" I asked, casually flipping through some dresses, trying to hide my shame that I didn't even know what Reeve did for a living, let alone what she'd ended up getting her degree in. I was a terrible friend.

"Well, I started working for a PR firm. You know, started at the bottom and was trying to work my way up when I met

Riley. We dated for three years before we got married and when I had Chey, I decided to be a stay-at-home mom."

"Chey? That's an interesting name."

"It's short for Cheyanne," she said with a smile, thinking fondly of her oldest. It was a dreamy look that obviously alluded to the deep and immeasurable love Reeve had for her. "Cheyanne is three and Ryder, my son, is just one."

"Well, I'll be really glad to meet them tonight," I said. My thoughts drifted to the children I would have had by now. My twins would be almost old enough to babysit Reeve's children. If I had a daughter she would be here, shopping with us, looking through these racks with an eagerness only a preteen could muster. Would the twins have been it? Would there have been more? If Asher and I had stayed together, would there be more children?

"Hey, Charlie, we don't have to talk about kids," Reeve said with concern lacing her voice.

I exhaled loudly, both glad and sorry that Reeve could read my thoughts. There was no reason she needed to worry about me and she definitely shouldn't feel bad for talking about her children.

"I'm sorry. Honestly, I try really hard not to think about kids. But being here, in Willow Falls, it sometimes sneaks up on me."

"That's understandable. Being around Asher probably makes you think about a lot of things you've tried hard to forget." I looked up at her, meeting her eyes, and tried to remember a time when she had been this insightful. Reeve was a great friend all through school, and had always been able to see things that I couldn't or didn't want to. I don't know why I was so surprised now.

I nodded, not sure what words would be suitable at that moment.

"You don't have to pretend to be ok with me, Charlie. I feel like you've spent a lot of time in the last decade trying to act like everything was fine. And if you continue to do that, I'll let you. But you don't have to with me. I understand." I looked up at her again and she was wearing a sad smile. Not full of pity or sorrow, but like she wanted so badly for me to reach out to her. "Don't forget, Charlie, there was a time in my life where I felt so very alone and if you hadn't been there for me I don't know if I would have gotten through it. Please don't push me away anymore."

I took in her words, knowing they were true and heartfelt. I pushed everyone away and in that process I lost my father long before he died. If I hadn't been so distant, if I had let other people in on my sadness, let other people help me, I might have been able to really have a relationship with him before he passed. That was the truth of the matter. I wasn't a nineteen-year-old girl anymore. It was time to stop shutting people out, because soon enough, I would be more alone than I could imagine.

"My kids would have called you Auntie Reeve," I said as I looked back down at a dress on the rack. "Sometimes, like now, I wonder if I would have had a girl if she would have liked shopping. I wonder if she would have been here with us, right now, looking at dresses and jewelry, asking me if she could get every cute thing she encountered."

"She probably would be more like you," Reeve replied. "A healthy and balanced girl who likes art, boys, playing in creeks and her parents." The smile on Reeve's face was warm and sincere.

"Perhaps," was all I said in response. I felt like there was nothing left to say. I liked the picture we had painted of my angel baby.

"Oh, Charlie, this dress is perfect. Not too dressy, cute, but totally sexy." She held up a cotton maxi dress, a coral color with an empire waist with a turquoise belt. She turned the hanger around and I caught the 'sexy' part. The back of the dress from the waist up was a sheer and delicate lace. I could easily cover it with a jacket if I wanted to, but it was very feminine and pretty. "Let's try it on," she said and walked back towards the dressing rooms.

I came out of the dressing room and Reeve's eyes lit up.

"Yes, Charlie. You have to buy this. It's gorgeous. The coral color is really pretty against your tan skin and dark hair. It's beautiful."

I turned to show her the back which was my favorite part. "I'll need a strapless bra," I said. Reeve flipped her hand in the air as if to say, 'No problem'. "It is really pretty though."

"Asher will love it," Reeve said, not looking me in the eye anymore.

"I'm not trying to impress Asher."

"Of course not, but it never hurts to look good around your ex-boyfriend." I shot her a glare. I wasn't sure how I liked the idea of Asher being my ex-boyfriend. I didn't like that title for him. He was so much more than just a boyfriend back then. He was the love of my life, the person I was supposed to spend forever with. And even so, now he wasn't just an ex, now he wanted to be my friend. That trumped the ex-boyfriend status anyway. "Are you ever planning on telling him what you saw that day?"

Her question caught me off-guard, it made my heart pump furiously in my chest.

"No."

"Why not?"

"What difference would it make? What happened, happened. There isn't anything we can do to change things, Reeve. Bringing up the past, throwing that in his face, it wouldn't help anyone."

"Talking to him about it might make *you* feel better. I'm not worried about him. I think talking about it would help you."

"No. It's not worth it. It would just cause problems."

"I asked him about it," Reeve stated. She calmly just dropped a bomb, like she'd confessed to eating the last piece of pizza or something.

"Please tell me you didn't," I begged. I knew she had though. She always prodded and poked and made people uncomfortable, even if she was just trying to help and do what she thought was right.

"I didn't tell him you'd seen him. He doesn't know anything about it. I just asked him if he was with anyone while you were pregnant, if he'd cheated on you."

I froze. I couldn't understand why she would have asked him that, especially since all of us knew the answer to the question. I turned quickly and went back into the dressing room, peeling the dress off my body, trying to get it off of me so I could get dressed and leave. I wasn't comfortable talking about this. I hadn't anticipated this conversation and I wasn't prepared to have it here, with her.

"Charlie, I'm sorry," she said from the other side of the thin drape separating us. "I was so mad at him for what he did to you back then. I've been angry at him for years. For abandoning you, for screwing that other girl, for not being there for you through everything, for taking my best friend from me." She went silent and I stood there, staring at my feet, contemplating her words.

She'd lost a lot that day too. I had to take that into consideration. I put on my clothes and opened the drape. I wrapped my arms around her and pulled her to me.

"I'm sorry I've been gone for so long," I whispered into her hair. "I'm sorry I've been absent, that I've been a terrible friend. I can't apologize enough."

"You're forgiven, as long as you promise not to leave me again." She pulled away and wiped a tear from her cheek, laughing a little as she exhaled. "There's something else, Charlie."

Of course there was.

"What is it?" I asked hesitantly.

"He said he didn't do it."

"What do you mean?"

"I mean, I asked him if he'd slept with anyone and he said no. He was actually a little offended that I even asked him. He seemed really sincere."

"Reeve, I *saw* him with her." Instantly my mind flashed the image of that girl on top of him. I closed my eyes, trying to block it out, but it's impossible to escape your own mind. "It doesn't matter what he said, I saw him with her. You can't argue with that."

"Why would he lie to me about it?"

"Why not! He probably feels like shit for what he did, knowing what happened. Anyone would lie about that. He doesn't know I saw him, Reeve. He doesn't know about any of it. Please, promise me you won't say anything else to him about it."

"I won't. I promise. But I still think you should say something to him. Talk to him about it. It might help you."

My lungs started to constrict, my chest squeezing me too tight. I couldn't have that conversation with him. I didn't want to listen to him justify sleeping with her, telling me why I wasn't enough. I couldn't. There was no need. I could imagine everything he would say and that was torture enough for me.

"Can we just buy this dress and then look for a bra?" I pleaded with her silently to let the topic drop. She looked right into my eyes for a few moments, seemingly trying to figure out how much she wanted to push me. Eventually, the corners of her mouth turned up slightly and I could tell she was letting it drop.

"Sure. I know the perfect place."

Chapter Eleven
Charlie

Even though I felt silly about it, I had to take a few deep breaths before I could walk up to the Carmichaels' door. How long had it been since I was in this house? It was winter break my sophomore year of college. Like a habit, I reached for the ring hanging around my neck and made sure it was hidden beneath the fabric of my dress. Once I was sure it was secure, I reached up to knock on the door. After a few moments, it opened and I looked at a woman who I loved like a mother for so many years.

"Charlie," she sighed, as if saying my name brought her some sort of relief. I smiled because I was so happy to see her. She opened her arms and I floated right into them, not even trying to pretend like I didn't need to feel her comfort. "I'm so glad to see you," she said after she'd held me for a few moments. I pulled away and smiled at her, genuinely, which was something I was still getting used to.

"It's really good to see you too, Roberta" I said.

"I am so sorry about your father, Charlie. He was a good man and he loved you so much."

"Thank you. I appreciate that."

"Well, come on in. Everyone is in the family room," she said, leading me towards the room where I spent much of my adolescent years.

I entered the large room and felt a warm sense of familiarity wash over me. The room had newer furniture, but the walls were the same sage green color they were so many years ago. A large flat-screen television hung on one of the walls, an obvious update from the box TV Asher and I used to watch scary movies on late into Saturday nights.

Reeve and her husband were sitting on a couch, her two children at her feet. Asher's dad talked to Riley about something. It sounded like sports talk, so I understood why Reeve had tuned out and was making faces at Ryder.

Asher leaned against one of the walls, but stood up straight when I entered. Our eyes met and I saw a smile come across his face. Before I could stop myself I returned it. He walked over to me and I noticed his mother moved away, heading into the kitchen.

"Charlie," he said as he came to stop a foot or two in front of me. "I'm so glad you decided to come."

I shrugged my shoulders.

"I decided it would be stupid of me to turn down a friendship. It seems I could use a friend or two," I said, my eyes flitting over to Reeve, who gave me a smile in return.

"Well, I'm glad you could make it."

"Thank you for the flowers too. They are beautiful." I saw his eyes sparkle and I tried to keep the blushing warmth from reaching my face.

"Anytime," he said calmly.

"I think I'll go see if your mom needs help with anything," I said quietly. I turned and let my memory carry me to the kitchen. I walked in and saw Mrs. Carmichael standing at an island in the middle of the kitchen.

"Wow. You remodeled your kitchen. It looks amazing." Dark granite matched well with the black cabinets. The darkness of the counters and cabinets were contrasted against the beige walls.

"It only took me ten years to convince Adam to let me do it," she said with a laugh. "It was a pain in the butt. It took two months longer than it was supposed to and I'll never do it again, but I do love this kitchen," she said wistfully as she looked around the room.

"Can I help you with anything?" I smiled at her, wanting her to give me something to do to keep me occupied.

"Sure. If you'd like to prepare the salad, everything is out on the counter already. I would just need you to chop and toss."

"I think I can handle that." I started chopping up vegetables and placing them in the large bowl placed out on the countertop. We worked in companionable silence for a few minutes before she spoke up.

"Charlie," I heard the pity in her voice and it made me cringe the way she said my name, saturated with sorrow. "I feel so terrible for everything you've been through." I could tell she stopped what she was doing and turned towards me. I stopped chopping vegetables, but didn't turn to look at her in return. I didn't want to see the pity in her eyes. It would only make it hurt more. "I understand why you kept your distance after you and Asher broke up, but I just want you to know that you can still, always, come to me for anything. Adam and I have always thought of you as a daughter. Even though Asher never shared the details involved in your break-up, I understand you wanted your space."

I heard her voice tremble and my heart clenched in my chest at her distress. I turned to see her frowning, obviously trying very hard not to cry and not doing a very good job. I walked over to her and felt her embrace me. It had been so long since I'd had a mom hug. I relaxed into her chest and felt her running her hand over my hair, trying to soothe me, her maternal instinct kicking in I suppose. After I felt like I had soaked up all of her motherliness, I stepped back and gave her a weak smile.

"I never meant to hurt your feelings by staying away, Roberta. I just couldn't be around Asher. I hope you understand that."

"Oh, I do, Sweetie. I do. Adam and I both understand it was a rough situation." She paused and I could see her debating with herself over something in her mind. "Do you mind if I ask what happened? Asher would never tell us."

I was at a loss for words for a moment. I didn't really know how to respond. I hadn't told anyone besides my own father about the miscarriage and had only just told Asher about losing twins. I wasn't prepared to tell this woman who I loved for a good majority of my life that I couldn't hold on to her grandbabies. I don't think those were words I would ever want to say to her. However, a small part of me believed she deserved to know.

"Roberta, if it's all the same to you, I think I will let Asher tell you. I'll make sure he knows I'm ok with it." Her eyes went from curious to gentle understanding and I knew she would let me off the hook. I hoped she could tell that I wouldn't be able to make it through the story without a breakdown.

"Of course, Sweetie. I'm just so glad you're here tonight." She squeezed my arm like she didn't want to let go, didn't want me to slip away. I wanted to exist here just as much as she wanted me to.

Dinner was pleasant and comfortable. I felt at ease with Asher's family and with Reeve's as well. I loved watching Reeve parent. It wasn't something I had ever really witnessed. Growing up together she'd been so impulsive and irrational, and to see her have what seemed to be an untapped reservoir of patience boggled my mind. Her husband was a winner, taking on his share of the parental duties that came with dining with two small children. They worked as a team and seemed to anticipate what the other needed. Together they seemed unstoppable.

I found myself sneaking glances at Asher, wondering what he was thinking when he saw the children being difficult or adorable. Did he wish he had his own? Was he glad he was still childless? His eyes met mine and my mind was put at ease when I saw regret staring back at me. I looked back to his mother and smiled, pretending that I had been paying attention to the conversation.

When dinner was over, I helped Roberta clear the table and I felt a warm hand grip my elbow.

"Charlie," his smooth and familiar voice was so close to my ear. I could feel the heat from his chest radiating off him. "Will you come outside with me for a little while? I haven't gotten a chance to talk to you alone yet. I'd like to."

I turned to look up at him and nodded, words not cooperating with me at that moment. His hand never left my elbow as he led me towards the sliding glass door and out onto the back porch. When his hand finally released me, I felt the sharp sting of cold where he'd touched me and rubbed my hand over it. His touch still caused my heart to speed up, still caused my words to abandon me, still made the swallow-sized butterflies twirl around in my stomach. The fact that he still affected me wasn't lost on me, but I tried to ignore it, push past it. I didn't want to think about him, and his hands, or his touch.

He motioned for me to take a seat in one of the patio chairs. After I was seated and comfortable he took the chair right next to me.

"It meant a lot to my mom that you came tonight." He stated.

"It was really good to see her." I paused, wondering the best way to broach the sensitive subject. "Can I ask you something?"

"Anything." The sincerity in his voice made my heart ache a little.

"Why didn't you tell your mom what happened? About the pregnancy? The miscarriage?" I turned to look at him, even though common sense told me I should refrain from it.

He thought about my question for a moment and then took a deep breath before he answered. "Honestly, I was ashamed of the way I treated you. Even before you left, even before you lost the babies, I felt terrible about what had happened."

Then why did you sleep with that girl? That was all I could think. The deep emotion I could feel in his voice, his true remorse and regret, it didn't fit with what I saw with my own eyes. He couldn't have felt badly about everything that had happened and then jumped into bed with someone else. It just didn't make sense. But I wasn't about to bring it up. I didn't need an explanation from him. It didn't matter. I tried to redirect my thoughts.

"Don't you think she deserves to know? They would have been her grandchildren. She has a right to mourn them too."

"I hadn't thought about it that way." His voice went quiet with contemplation. "At first I didn't want to have to explain how poorly I'd treated you. Then, after a while, it seemed like telling her would cause her unnecessary pain."

"She asked me what had happened between us when I was helping with dinner. I told her she should hear it from you." I stared at him for a moment, trying to really grasp the forgiveness I had given him, the forgiveness I had allowed and welcomed. I looked away from him, hoping my voice didn't waiver. "You don't have to tell her what happened between us. Not the details. But she should know about the babies."

"You're right. Of course you're right."

I looked over at him and tried to give him a reassuring smile. It probably came across as something more like confusion. I *was* confused.

"So what will you do now?" Asher asked.

"You mean right now?" I asked, confused.

He laughed a little, his always familiar chuckle sounded older and deeper. "No, I mean, what's next for you, like, in life?"

I shrugged, not sure how to answer. I wasn't even sure I knew the answer.

"No shrugging, Bit. Words." My breath came to a stop in my lungs like a freight train colliding with a tanker. My heart exploded in my chest, or might as well have with the pain I felt shooting through all of my limbs. I hadn't heard him call me that in thirteen years. He caressed my nickname with his voice and the sharp pains of longing took my breath away. "Shit, I'm sorry, Charlie. I didn't mean to call you that. I'm sorry."

I swallowed the pain along with all the memories coming back to me. I pushed them down, pushed them back. I wanted to seem unaffected. I wanted nothing more than *to be* unaffected. I was a good pretender.

"It's ok, Asher. No big deal." I took a breath, plowing onwards. "I think I'm gonna stick around for a few more days and get my father's house all sorted out and then head back to New York."

"You have a life waiting for you back in New York?" He didn't look me in the eye as he asked the question, but I gathered he was asking a deeper question than he led on.

"You could say that." I didn't want him to think I was some loser woman who hid behind her art and made a man believe she loved him just to keep the perpetual loneliness at bay. Even though that's exactly what I was. He was silent in response. Perhaps my cold answer had pushed him even farther away. "I think I should head home Asher. Please make sure you tell your parents what they deserve to know. Thank you for inviting me to dinner. I had a lovely time." I stood up and all but ran into the house. I hastily said goodbye to his parents and to Reeve and her husband, making false promises to call and meet up before I left.

I had no intention of seeing these people again.

Chapter Twelve

Asher

Going to see her was taking a big risk. She made it pretty clear to me the night before that she didn't have any desire to continue seeing me while she was still in town. There was a part of me that understood her hesitation, a part of me that respected it. I didn't want to make her uncomfortable and I didn't want to push her. But I did want to hold her and be near her. She seemed to only be pieces of herself and I wanted to put her back together. I wanted to fix her. Although, it was difficult knowing that I was the reason she was broken in the first place.

At the park, in the gazebo, we'd shared our demons. I'd admitted how sorry I was for the way I reacted to the pregnancy and she'd admitted keeping from me that there were two babies. Forgiving her of that was simple. It wasn't even necessary. She didn't need my forgiveness because she did nothing wrong. I pushed her away and gave her no reason to seek me out to tell me anything.

She also forgave me and that was more than I deserved. And even though she said the words and I felt she meant them, something was still off. Going to her, I was risking her finally telling me to leave her alone. But I had no other choice. Until she looked me in the eye and told me to go, I was going to try to be near her.

I rang the doorbell of her father's house and tried not to smile knowing how much it irritated her. I heard her voice from beyond the door, yelling loudly.

"Asher Carmichael, if I open this door and see you standing there I'm going to kill you." Her voice got louder as she came closer to the door. She swung the door open and I just shrugged my shoulders at her and pushed the flowers I had brought towards her. She eyed the flowers, but didn't reach for them. "Why must you ring my doorbell?" She asked, cocking her head to the side and narrowing her eyes at me.

"Because I know it irritates you," I said simply, hoping she would remember how many times in the past I had rang that same doorbell. It was my signature move. She always knew it was me when it rang and I was hoping the nostalgia would soften her towards my unannounced visit. She eyed me for a moment and I could tell she was trying to hide a small smile. I motioned towards the flowers again. "These are for you." Again, she looked at them, but didn't take them from me.

"Asher, you don't need to buy me flowers."

"I know I don't *need* to, but I wanted to. I felt bad about the way our evening ended last night."

"I'm fine. I was just tired."

"I know you have a lot going on, but do you think I could at least come in for a little while?" She took a step backwards and opened the door wide, allowing me to come in. I handed her the flowers as I walked past her. "They're purple hyacinths, meant to represent remorse and apology."

"You don't have to apologize anymore, Asher. We've been through this already."

"Yes, but I don't think you've really forgiven me." I put my hand up in front of her when she opened her mouth to argue. "You're forgetting that I know you, Charlie. I know you better than anyone probably. I know you're still having a hard time letting everything go - understandably. I just want to be here and try to help you. That's all."

She looked a little nervous and that made me feel better. I didn't want her to be comfortable around me. I wanted her on edge. I wanted her unsure. Some part of me wanted her to be just as confused as I was. I wanted her to be conflicted with herself because in the end that meant I still had some chance to win her back.

"What can I help you with?"

"Don't you have to work?"

I walked past her into the living room that was looking bare. "I have some vacation time saved up. Also, I'm a partner. What's Phil gonna do? Fire me?"

"You shouldn't be spending your vacation time packing up your ex-girlfriend's father's house." She closed the door and moved around me to start working on some boxes, her back to me.

"You've never been just a girlfriend, Charlie." She stilled at my words and I saw shoulders sag a little as she exhaled, taking in my words.

"You can help me pack up the living room," she said quietly. Good. I grabbed a box and silently started putting Charles' things away, carefully packing them so nothing broke. We worked quietly but every once in a while I looked over at her, trying not to get caught sneaking glances. Since that first image of her at my office all those days ago, I was still surprised by my attraction to her. It never wavered. She was thin. She was sad. She was frail. But she was beautiful. Today she was simply wearing a pair of jeans and tee shirt, but she looked comfortable and that was alluring. She looked normal. She looked like she could be someone's wife, someone's everything, packing up their own house.

It was also hard to ignore her hair.

I would never, ever, deny my attraction to her hair. From day one it was my kryptonite. I was so glad to see it was still long, still fell around her, still caught in the wind when she turned her head. Today it was in a braid. It was practical. She packed boxes, moving around, bending and lifting, she didn't need hair in her way. But I wanted to pull the tie from her hair and run my hands through its silky lengths. The braid was not my favorite.

Charlie

After an hour of working in mostly silence and moving into the den, Asher ventured to ask me about my life outside of Willow Falls.

"So, tell me. What's waiting for you in New York?"

"Life," I answered quickly.

"Want to be a little more specific?" He probed.

"I have to be back soon for an art show," I supplied.

"You still do your art?"

"It's all I do." He nodded at me and I moved on to another box. This is exactly what I didn't want. I didn't want to spend time with him and I didn't want to act normal around him. I was holding on to the one piece of information that made me remember why I shouldn't want him. *He was with someone else, Charlie. While you lost your babies, he was with someone else.* I had to keep reminding myself. I had to find a way to make him leave. It was difficult to be near him, to feel him in the same room, and not gravitate towards him.

The night before, at his parents' house, I was sure I made the right decision. I left and I left with the intention of never seeing them again. Asher would tell his parents what happened, I got an apology from him, and I saw Reeve's beautiful family; it was time to move on, to let it all go.

But I should have known Asher wouldn't be that easy to get rid of. As soon as I heard to doorbell, I knew it was him. I had to fight the part of me, the sadistic part, that was glad he came.

"Is it still drawing? Or have you branched out and tried new things?"

"Mostly still just drawing. At least, that's where I spend most of my time."

"And you can make a good living in the big city? That's really impressive, Charlie. I'm proud of you."

I didn't dare tell him that even though I made decent money selling my drawings, my lifestyle was supported by David, or had been anyway. It was clear that when I got back to New York I was on my own.

"Yeah, I guess I'll have to look at buying my own place now that I have the money."

"You don't like the place you've got now?" He asked, innocently, just trying to make conversation. I stilled at his question, trying to find a sufficient answer.

"It's just not an option any longer," I stated coolly.

"Well," he said as he huffed out a breath and stood up from hunching over a box on the floor. I could see his shoulder muscles flexing underneath his tee shirt. "Let me know if you need a hand looking for a place, looking over contracts or whatever. Reeve would probably love to help you look too." His hands rested on his hips and he looked concerned. "We're here for you, Charlie."

And there they were, every day that week. Asher made his daily appearance, each time showing up with a flower that held a particular meaning. After a few days passed the kitchen island was a forest of flowers, all fragrant, all meant to convey something different, a message from Asher to me.

Forget Me Nots because he said he wanted me to always remember him.

Geraniums which were a symbol of true friendship.

Tall reeds of blue salvia tied together with twine, because "I'm always thinking of you," he said. The next day a bundle of red salvia because "You'll always be mine."

"Asher, you have to stop bringing these flowers." At first it was nice - comforting. The flowers representing friendship, flowers that let me know he thought about me. I could handle that. I couldn't, however, handle the flowers that held deeper meanings, flowers that were meant to make me feel things again. I stood at the island in the kitchen, breathing in the fragrance of all the different flowers, urging him to stop.

"Why?" He said. I could feel him come up behind me, close enough to feel the heat from his chest cradle my back. I felt a tingle on my scalp and knew he was running his fingers through the ends of my hair hanging at my waist. I closed my eyes, guiltily allowing myself to feel my heartbeat race, my pulse quicken at his touch. Over the last few days, I found it more and more difficult to keep my distance, to not let my eyes wander over him, to long for him. I was in dangerous territory and I knew I could just turn around and he'd welcome me into his arms, welcome me home. But I couldn't. *Don't forget, Charlie. Don't let yourself forget that girl on top of him, his arm around her.*

"What do you want from me?" I whispered. I gasped when I felt one of his hands graze my waist and land on my hip, his whole body shifting closer to me, his breath floating past my ear.

"I just want you to be happy."

It took all my willpower, but I stepped to the side, out of his grasp and moved to the sink. I washed my hands simply to give myself something to do, something to focus on while I gathered together all the pieces of my soul I felt crumbling around me. Happiness? I gave up on happiness a long time ago. I'd settle for content. In fact, I aimed for content. I didn't need to be fulfilled. I didn't need to find joy. I simply needed to exist, to make it from one day to the next, with as little pain as possible. And when Asher touched me it hurt.

"I am happy, Asher." Lies. "And as soon as we can all get back to our normal lives, the better off we'll both be." I tried to sound convincing, I hoped he was taking my words in and listening to me. A few moments passed and then he spoke as if the words he'd just spoken to me never occurred. It was exactly what I wanted, but it killed me a little inside.

"So, you're planning on leaving the day after tomorrow then? Saturday?"

"Yeah," I said, staring out the kitchen window, still not ready to turn around and face him. "I think I should be done with the house by tomorrow and I have to get back to New York."

"Reeve and I were talking and thought it would be fun for all three of us to go out tomorrow night. You know, like a farewell celebration. Who knows when the three of us will be together again?"

Never. We'd never be together again because I never planned on coming back here. I thought about spending an evening with Reeve and Asher. A night out. A distraction. I knew that if I didn't go, one or both of them would just be at my house anyway.

"Sounds good," I said as I turned and gave him a smile.

He smiled back, the dimple in his left cheek winking at me, tugging at something buried deep inside. "Great. I can pick you up around seven. Is that ok?"

I shrugged. "Sure."

Asher left an hour or so later, pulling me in for a hug on his way out. Again, I felt him gently finger through my hair, wrapping it around his palm, gliding his hand down to the ends. I didn't stop him. I let him do it, wanted him to, really. The more times he reached out to touch me the more comfortable it became, the more I longed for it. He stepped away and left, and I breathed a little easier.

Later in the evening Reeve called.

"I'm so excited to go out tomorrow. You have no idea how long it's been since I was anywhere that didn't allow children along. Adult time sounds fantastic."

"Is Riley coming?"

"No, he's going to stay home with the kids," she said, sounding a little forlorn.

"You can't find another sitter? It would be nice if the two of you could go out together."

"I wish we could both come, but his parents are out of town and both my parents have some sort of flu bug. We've never left the kids with anyone else. It's ok," she said, sounding firm all of a sudden. "I will come over early and get us all pretty and ready for a night out."

"I think we're just going out for drinks," I stated with a small laugh. "I don't think we need to put too much effort into this."

"Charlie, I will not allow you to put a damper on my one night out in months. I want to look pretty, even if it's just for a couple of hours and you will humor me."

"You're the boss," I replied.

"And don't you forget it," she said with a laugh.

Chapter Thirteen
Charlie

Reeve showed up with an arsenal of beauty supplies.

"Are we having a fashion show in my living room?" There were at least fifteen dresses, and three suitcase-looking contraptions that I was told held her make-up.

"I know you've managed to hold on to your youthful face," she said as she playfully patted my cheek. "But I've been through two pregnancies, three years of sleepless nights, and more gallons of ice cream than I can count. I need all the help I can get."

I had to laugh at her. And even though she didn't look like the nineteen-year-old Reeve I left behind at college, she looked grown-up and happy. Perhaps she didn't realize how much I'd trade wrinkles and dark circles under my eyes for the kind of happiness she exuded.

"I'm ready to be covered up, dressed up, and shown off," I said as I put my arms out to the sides. I would give her complete control, only because I knew it would make her happy.

"Perfect," she said slowly as she pressed her palms together in front of her face and tapped her fingertips together, reminding me of an evil mastermind.

Two hours later, we looked good. Reeve was in a sexy black dress that accentuated her new cleavage that I was informed came from breastfeeding her son who "loves boobs more than his father," which made me laugh uncontrollably.

Reeve put me in a flirty purple dress that flowed around my thighs with every step I took. It has a sweetheart neckline, empire waist and black straps that crisscrossed below my breasts and then came up over my shoulders as spaghetti straps. It was shorter than the dresses I normally wore, but it wasn't indecent. Reeve curled my hair into large ringlets, but it was a lost cause because the curls wouldn't hold and had transformed into very loose waves instead. It was still very pretty and I liked it because it was different than the way I usually styled it.

"I really miss this," Reeve said, a touch of sadness in her voice. She was behind me spraying something in my hair to make sure it behaved throughout the evening.

"Miss what?" I asked as I looked into her eyes in the mirror.

"I miss having you around. I miss having my best friend."

My gut churned at her words. Part of me missed her too. Part of me wished I could move back and work towards a normal life. The idea of being healed enough to live in Willow Falls and not be tortured every day by memories and thoughts of what could have been was too good to be true. Being here was nothing but a reminder of everything I lost. So the other part of me, the part that sided with self-preservation, wasn't about to put myself through that.

"I miss you too, Reeve. You should come to New York and visit sometime." That was an empty notion. I knew Reeve wasn't in a position with two small children to just jump on a plane for a frivolous weekend, no matter how desperately I wished she could. She just gave me a slight smile and moved on.

"We definitely look awesome," she said. "Will you take a picture of me so I can send it to Riley? He hasn't seen me in a dress in ages." She walked to her purse and pulled out her phone. Her face became tense when she unlocked her screen and just before I could ask what was wrong the doorbell rang. Asher.

"I'll go grab that."

When I opened the door, I could not ignore the fact that Asher's eyes immediately began to roam up and down my body. His gaze heated my skin and I felt an arousal spread through me I hadn't experienced in a very long time. He looked amazing and I let my eyes wander just as his were.

He wore dark jeans with a gray button-up shirt. His sleeve were unbuttoned and rolled up to his elbows. He reached up and swiped his hand through his hair and I saw my name branded on his arm. I hadn't seen that tattoo since I walked in on him and seeing it again instantly cooled the burning that had, just moments ago, flamed through me.

"Charlie," he said softly, his voice catching in his throat. "You're beautiful."

My heart ached a little hearing him utter those words. His voice was full of sorrow, and I understood the feeling. Seeing something you wanted so badly but couldn't have. What were we doing? Why had we insisted on torturing ourselves like this? I shook my head, trying to push the unwanted feelings away.

"Guys, I've got bad news." Asher and I both turned our heads to see Reeve coming down the hall. "Apparently, the flu bug wasn't contained to my parents. Riley's got it and he thinks Chey's about to become a victim as well. So I'm going to have to bail."

"Oh no. That's terrible," I said, thinking that her evening is about to get all kinds of gross. "Is there anything I can do to help?"

"No, just have a drink for me," she said. I started to panic a little. If she wasn't going, I wasn't going. I couldn't get drinks with Asher - alone. That would definitely not be a good idea for either of us. Reeve came to hug me goodbye and I heard her whisper in my ear. "Go with him, Charlie. Talk to him. Tell him. You both need it." She pulled away and smiled at me and I gave her a tiny nod. I didn't know if I was going to tell him everything, but she was right about talking to him. I avoided this conversation since I arrived.

Reeve gave Asher a brief hug and then she's gone. She left Asher and me staring uncomfortably at each other.

"Are you ready to go?"

"Listen Asher, it's ok if you don't want to go out anymore. Tonight's kind of a bust anyway now that Reeve's gone."

He took a few steps towards me and cocked his head a little.

"What's the matter? Are you afraid to have a few drinks with me?" He wore a sexy smirk and I found it hard not to grin back.

"I'm not afraid."

"Great. I'm driving. Let's go."

Asher

My hand naturally found its way to the small of her back as we walked through the bar. The fabric of her dress was so light and sheer, I could feel the firmness of her back through it and it was enticing. Everything about her was enticing. She opened the door at her house and something gripped my heart and my cock at the same time. It squeezed hard and hadn't let go yet. Every part of me was aching and with my hand on her, I was silently praising the flu bug that took Reeve back home. I wanted Charlie to myself and I wouldn't let this opportunity go to waste.

The bar was dark inside with mellow jazz music playing; the perfect atmosphere for a first date or getting to know someone. I wanted the opportunity to get Charlie to open up to me, not to spend the evening trying to hear each other over loud music and drunk people. I led her to a table along the far edge of a mostly empty dance floor. I motioned for her to sit down on one of the high barstools and then leaned in closer to her.

"I'm going to go get us some drinks. You still drink vodka and cranberry?" I felt her nod as her hair moved along my lips. "Good." I pulled away and headed to the bar, trying to remain calm. It wasn't very busy yet, although I expected it became busier as it was a Friday night. It took a few minutes for the bartender to get to me and as I waited for our drinks, I noticed a man walk up to Charlie, smiling, striking up conversation. She obliged him and looked like she was politely answering whatever questions he had for her. My shackles raised and I felt my blood begin to pulse rapidly through my veins.

Just as I was about to go back to our table to interrupt their friendly conversation, our drinks were placed in front of me. I tried to give the bartender a smile but was so distracted it probably looked more frightening than friendly. I tipped her and then headed back. I saw the man walking away and I was half-relieved to see him go but also half-disappointed that I wouldn't be able to tell him she was with me.

"Who was that?" My words sounded harsh and I chastised myself for it. She shrugged her shoulders.

"Just some guy. I don't remember his name."

Well, that was good news I suppose. She must have picked up on my irritation.

"He came over here to ask me if he could buy me a drink and I told him I was already here with someone." I relaxed a little at her words. Obviously, it went without saying that this wasn't a date. But I'd be damned if some other guy was going to move in on my territory right in front of me.

Her eyes finally looked at the tray I set down on the table.

"Uh, Asher, what is all of this?"

"This," I said dramatically as I waved my hand over the tray, "is a drinking game." The tray had her cranberry vodka and a rum and coke for me, but it also has six shots on it.

"A drinking game? Asher, come on. I haven't played a drinking game since college." She looked nervous which excited me.

"Well then, it's time for a refresher. Here's how it's going to go." I sat down on the barstool across from her. "We are going to ask each other questions, you know, things we're curious about. Things we want to know about each other. You can either answer the question or take a drink. Every time you take a drink you alternate between a shot and your mixed drink." She raised an eyebrow at me which was incredibly sexy.

"Are there any topics that are off limits?" Her question caught me off guard and I felt my eyebrows coming together and my forehead tensing as I think about what she asked me.

"I don't have anything to hide."

She nodded slowly, contemplating. "Me either," she stated.

"Ok, you get to go first."

She sat for a moment trying to think of a question and I just grinned at her. For once in the last two weeks we weren't packing up boxes, or at a funeral, or cloaked in sadness. We were out, in a new setting, making a new memory. This fact brought me hope. This is exactly what I wanted for us – to move forward.

"All right, here's a question." She wriggled in her seat as she sat up straight, obviously pleased with her first round question. "When we were in tenth grade, Robbie Wallis called me a tease because I wouldn't go out on a date with him. The next day his tires were slashed. Did you do it?"

"Of course I did it," I laughed. "You knew I did that."

"No! You would never tell me! You said ignorance was the best bet."

"I thought the answer was obvious." She shrugged her shoulders. "Ok, my turn." I looked her in the eyes, grateful that she wasn't turning away from me, wasn't shying away from the contact as she had so many times since she'd been back. "Do you have a boyfriend back in New York?"

"No." She answered very quickly. My eyebrows shot up before I had the chance to stop them. I couldn't imagine her living in a city like New York and not being snatched up. Her answer didn't sit right with me.

"Why not?" I asked, wanting more information.

"No, no, no. That's not how this works. It's my turn to ask a question." She took another moment to formulate her question and then asked, "Why did you go to see my father so often?" My answer came without hesitation.

"He was my only link to you. He was the only way I could feel close to you. He never spoke about you and I gathered that was because you didn't want him to, but he never turned me away either. We spent a lot of time together and eventually he became more than your father to me, more than the man who lived down the street from me during my childhood." I paused, thinking about Charles and some of the conversations we had, how he gave me priceless advice and help all through college and law school. "It started out as a relationship I needed to feel like you were still a part of my life, but at some point he became my friend." I looked down at my glass and decided to drink even though I'd answered the question. I welcomed the slight sting as the rum coated my throat, and gloried in the warmth that spread through my stomach. "I think," I continued carefully. "I think he needed me too. I know you spoke on the phone with him often, but I think he used me to feel close to you as well."

Charlie reached over and squeezed my hand. "I'm sorry Asher. It never occurred to me that you were hurting over his death. I've been really selfish lately. I'm so sorry." I flipped my hand over and linked my fingers with her and gave her a smile. She smiled back but pulled her hand away. That hurt.

"My turn," I said right before I took another drink. "Who was the last person you dated?"

"His name was David." She said his name coldly. I couldn't pick up on any emotion attached to his name. "Who was the last person you dated?" She asked.

"Define dated." I quipped.

"Someone you would consider your girlfriend."

"So you're asking who my last girlfriend was?"

"Exactly."

"You." I said the word without taking my eyes off hers, and took a shot of tequila while I held her gaze. Her eyes grew wide when she took in what I'd said.

"Me?"

"That's what I said."

"It's been thirteen years, Asher. Surely you've been with someone between then and now."

"That's not what you asked me. You asked who my last girlfriend was. It was you." She was quiet as she considered what I'd said. Then she shook her head and looked down at her hands.

"Why didn't you tell me about the miscarriage?" Her eyes snapped back to me. She reached for a shot glass and my hand shot out, stopping her, my eyes pleading with her. I needed to hear why she kept that from me. "Bit," I whispered. "Please." She shook off my hand and took the shot. I watched as she put the empty shot glass back on the table, her eyes finding mine. The sorrow in her eyes matched the disappointment I felt. I wanted her to let me in so desperately, but I didn't know if I would ever be able to break her open. "Your turn."

"Did you tell your parents about the babies?" Her question caught me off guard, but I answered her.

"Yes. That same night we all had dinner."

"How did they take it?" She asked with sadness in her eyes.

I took in a deep breath, trying to figure out how to answer her without hurting her. "At first my mom was upset that I didn't tell her when it happened. It didn't feel right to lie to her anymore, so I told her everything. I told her what I had said to you, and that you had pretty much left, and I thought it was over. My dad didn't say much, just that he understood where I was coming from. Both he and my mom told me that they would have supported me and that everyone makes mistakes." I paused and watched her take in my words. She unconsciously took her hand and brought her hair forward so it rested over her shoulder. A black, shiny waterfall of silky hair fell down to her waist. The contrast of the dark hair against her olive skin was stunning. I cleared my throat, catching myself staring at her.

"In the end I think my mother was more upset that *you* hadn't told her. She didn't understand why you left so suddenly. None of us do. Why'd you run away?"

"Asher, I don't want to talk about it. Trust me, it will do neither of us any good to re-hash our past."

"Then take a shot." She paused but then picked up a shot glass and swallowed the tequila quickly.

"Tell me about your most favorite case," she said as she winced through the burn of the liquor. So, this was it. I could tell she was pulling away from me. So I answered her questions.

For the next hour or so we sat at that table and had a normal conversation. No more shots were taken, but she finished her drink. I found out all about her art, where she sells it, what she found in New York that inspires her, what books she's read recently. All of it was informative, but none of it was important, not important enough. Nothing I could learn about her life now would mean anything unless I could put it into context with why she had run away, why she continued to run.

She took in a deep breath and exhaled loudly. "Asher, I'm getting really tired. I think I'm ready to go home." She stood up and stumbled as soon as her foot hit the floor.

"Whoa, Charlie." I jumped off my stool and caught her before she tumbled to the floor. "You all right?" I asked.

"Yes, I'm just a little drunk," she said with a smile. I shook my head. She was so small, so tiny, the alcohol plowed right through her.

"Ok, let's get out of here." I wrapped my arm around her waist and she leaned her head against my shoulder.

"I can walk on my own, Asher."

I smirked. "I know. I'm just helping."

"Ok," she sighed.

We made it to my car and I helped her in, then got into the driver's seat, turning the key in the ignition.

"Asher," she whispered. I turned towards her. Her voice sounded sad.

"Yeah?"

"Can I ask you something without you reading too much into it?"

My pulse raced at her question. "Ok," I replied, just as apprehensive as she was. I'd just made a promise I couldn't possibly keep.

"Can I go home with you? I don't want to spend another night alone in my dead father's house." My heart ached at her words. She was broken, no matter how hard she tried to come across as put together and strong.

"Of course." I smiled weakly at her. Then my smiled faded as I realized I would be sleeping in the same house as her and I wasn't allowed to touch her.

"I'll sleep on the couch," she said, almost reading my thoughts.

"No, you'll sleep in my bed."

"Asher, I can't sleep with you," she said panicked. That made me smile. Sickly, it made me glad she got just as much anxiety about it as I did. She was afraid to be in a bed with me, afraid of what would happen.

"Don't worry. I'll take the couch."

"Ok," she said as she breathed out a sigh of relief. "Thank you." I pulled out of the parking lot and saw her head lean over onto the window. She spent the entire drive watching the street lights pass as I drove us to my house.

Chapter Fourteen

Asher

When we got to my house it seemed as if she'd sobered up a little bit. She didn't need my help to walk to the door, but her speech was a still a little off. I opened the door and led her into the living room, flipping on the lights as I walked through the house.

"This is a really nice place," she said quietly.

"Thanks. It's not much, but it's just me so I don't need a lot." I looked around the living room, noticing how it must look to her: bare, empty and cold. I didn't spend a lot of time here. I was usually at the office or sleeping. There wasn't a need to make this place comfortable. Right now, however, I wished I had something more than stark walls and uncomfortable chairs. "You can follow me back to the bedroom." I pointed down the hall, then led the way.

I walked in, flipped on the light, and went straight for my dresser, not wanting to take any time to see her in my bedroom. I wanted her here, in my house and with me. I wanted as much time as I could steal with her. But I knew it would be torture to see her in my bedroom and not be free to touch her, free to feel her skin under my hands, free to breathe in her scent and bring her body as close to mine as I could manage. I gripped the clothes in the drawer, my fists clenching around shirts, trying to ease the frustration that came with the situation.

I took a moment to calm down and then grabbed a shirt and a pair of basketball shorts, both of which would be comically huge on her, but I figured it would be better than trying to sleep in the dress she wore. I turned around and was accosted by the image I was so desperately trying to avoid: Charlie standing in my bedroom, sleepy eyes and nervous smile. There was no way for her to understand how much I struggled with keeping my hands to myself in that moment. I shoved the clothes towards her and my voice sounded harsher than I intended.

"You can change into these. The master bathroom is just through there," I motioned with a nod of my head towards the door on the other side of the room. She walked towards me and gingerly took the clothes from my hand. She walked past me to the door and my eyes closed, ignoring the ache in my chest that wanted me to stop her. An overwhelming part of me that wanted to hold her, slide her dress off her body, and *feel* her. I would give anything to be given the privilege. I heard the door to the bathroom click shut and I ran my hands over my face, trying to rub away the tension.

I turned back to my dresser to get some sleeping clothes for myself when I heard a loud crash come from the bathroom followed by Charlie's voice.

"Ouch! Son of a bitch," she yelled. I reacted immediately and pounced on the door, flinging it open.

There was no blood, or even any real indication that anything terrible happened. Charlie sat on the edge of the tub, gripping her ankle, examining it closely.

"Are you ok?" I asked eagerly.

Charlie's head snapped to look at me and instantly I saw the panic come across her face. She scrambled on the floor trying to grab her dress to cover herself. And in that very moment, that one tiny and miniscule moment in time, my entire world tilted.

It halted.

It screeched to a stop.

It nearly exploded.

My eyes took her in. She was frail looking, thinner than I had imagined her to be. She was in just panties and a strapless bra. On her side, covering every single rib bone that was clearly defined, was a large, black and intricate tattoo. I saw it and it took just a second for me to recognize my own name. My eyes went wide and locked on hers.

She looked guilty, scared, and sad.

"Why is my name tattooed on your body?" I asked, confused.

"No, Asher." She whispered. I recognized the look of a woman on the verge of tears, but I wasn't going to back down. I took another step into the bathroom and she took another step away from me, backing herself up against the counter.

"You can't ignore me, Charlie. You can't run away from what's happening right now. Tell me. Why do you have that tattoo?" She scrambled reaching for her dress, trying to cover up what I'd already seen. I rushed further into the bathroom, grabbed her wrists, and tried to get her to answer me. "Please, Charlie, tell me." My eyes finally found hers as she stopped struggling against me. Her mouth didn't open and she didn't move to answer my question. Something around her neck caught my eye and I followed the silver chain down over her collarbone and my eyes came to rest on the ring that hung between her breasts.

The promise ring I gave her thirteen years before.

I was shocked and my mouth opened slightly as my mind tried to form words that never came. I was brought back by the sounds of the sobs coming from Charlie and I looked up to see her face wet with tears. Without thinking I pulled her into me, wrapping my arms around her waist.

"No!" She shouted and pushed me away.

"You're wearing my ring around your neck. My name is tattooed on your ribs. You can't hide from me anymore. I see you. I *see* you, Charlie. It's time to let me in." I stepped towards her again, hoping this time she'd let me touch her, let me ground her here with me.

"Don't," she whispered, almost choking on the word. Wisps of her hair became wild, framing her sad face, sticking to the tears that tracked along her cheeks. I moved my hand slowly up to her and trailed my finger down her temple, catching the hair, and pushing it behind her ear. Her eyes closed at my touch and her head tilted into my palm. "You can't do this to me, Asher." Her voice, still whisper soft, shot through me. "I won't survive you again."

"Bit, you have to tell me what you're talking about." She began to worry me.

"That!" She wailed, gripping both of my hands that were now framing her face. She wasn't pushing me away, or even pulling me in, she was just holding on. "You're getting too close. This," she reached down and grabbed the ring. "And this," her hand ran over the tattoo. "These are mine. They're all I have left. You were never supposed to see them."

"But I have. I've seen them and now you have to tell me what it all means." She turned away from me at my words, but still had no place to go as she was still up against the counter. I could still see her face in the mirror, her chest heaving up and down as she tried to control her breaths. "When did you get that tattoo?"

"About a year after I left."

A whole year later? She's had that for twelve years? For twelve years now, every time she undressed she saw my name? I moved closer to her, eliminating the space between us, pressing up against her, hoping my presence would convince her to open up and tell me everything.

"Why did you get it?"

"Because I still loved you and I wanted to remember it forever."

"If you still loved me, why did you leave? Why didn't you come back to me?"

"I TRIED!" She screamed. Her body shook with rage and I met her eyes in the mirror. "I came to find you. I was in pain, my babies bleeding out of me, and all I wanted was you, Asher. I only ever wanted you. I nearly had to crawl up the stairs of the frat house; that's how much pain I was in. Gripping my stomach, praying I wasn't losing the pregnancy, but needing you. I *needed* you, Asher. Needed you to be there, to help me, to comfort me, to tell me you still loved me."

"I do still love you," I said softly, reaching for her.

"DON'T! Don't touch me. I saw you. I saw you with her. I opened your door and saw her on top of you and I saw your arm wrapped around her, the arm with *my name* tattooed on it. You wrapped my name around some other woman."

"No," I said automatically. "No." I repeated, as much for her as for me. I shook my head. "I never slept with anyone else." Charlie spun around in my arms and her hand came up to land a cracking slap across my face. It stung and it caught me off guard, but I was more shattered by the look on her face. I never wanted to see her broken, never wanted to be the cause of her pain.

"You can't lie to me about this. You can't make me forget what I saw. I SAW YOU."

"I don't know what you saw, but I didn't sleep with anyone. I couldn't have. I wasn't even coherent for weeks after we broke up." My eyes frantically searched hers, looking for something that resembled forgiveness or her realization that this was a mistake. "Please..." I begged her. She froze up, realizing how close we were and she tried to back up, caught between me and the counter, she didn't go far. "Please, tell me what you saw. There has to be some mistake."

"I opened your door and saw a blonde girl sitting on top of you. Naked, you were both naked. And I saw my name tattooed on your arm. It was you, Asher, and some girl. Don't try to deny it."

I grabbed at the hair on my head in frustration and backed away from her. I had no idea what she was talking about. Ever since I walked out on her, the day she told me she was pregnant, every single day since, I thought of no one but her. Sure, years later I ended up sleeping with other people, but in the months and even years following that terrible day there was no one.

"I don't understand," my mind reeled. What had she seen? How could she have seen anything?

"Don't try and lie, Asher. It doesn't matter what you say. I know what I saw."

I tried to rewind my mind, thinking back to the weeks I spent in a drunken stupor over our break-up. There were girls around. There were always girls. It was a frat house. A blonde? I remember a few blondes. Damn it. Why did I have to drink so much? A fuzzy memory started to surface. Shit.

"Wait," I said as much for her as for me. Images were coming to me and I finally realized what she was talking about. "Charlie, wait," I said as I rushed towards her again, my hands going to her shoulders.

"No, I've waited forever," she said, trying to shrug my hands away. "I can't be here anymore. I've been stuck here, Asher. Stuck in this place where I hate and love you at the same time, and it's exhausting. I'm exhausted." She nearly crumpled in my hands, her admission exhausting her even further.

"I never slept with her. Let me explain. Please, don't let everything end like this – with a lie or a misunderstanding." I stared into her eyes, pleading with her to let me make it all right, praying she would allow me to fix everything. To fix her. To fix me.

She didn't say anything, but she didn't struggle away from me either. I took that as a green light.

"That day, when I left you, when I said those miserable things to you, it was the worst day of my life. I was so shocked by the pregnancy, so upset by everything and the way I'd treated you, I literally went back to the house and drank. I drank for weeks, Bit. It's a surprise I managed to pass any of my classes that term. If I was awake, I was a mess." I moved closer to her, wanting to feel her a little more. If this was the last time I was allowed to touch her, I would take advantage. My hands slid up her arms and I felt goose bumps flood her skin.

"There were a few girls, here and there, who noticed I was alone and realized we'd broken up. They flirted with me.

They came on to me, and they tried to sleep with me." She stiffened at my words and I could feel her try to pull away. "But I didn't care," I said quickly, trying not to lose her. "I didn't want any of them; I just wanted you. There was one girl who seemed more eager than the rest, but I told her every time that I wasn't interested." I swallowed hard, knowing the next part would be the hardest to say out loud, the hardest part to watch her hear.

"One afternoon, I was smashed. So drunk I couldn't even stand up on my own. It was the middle of the afternoon and I was nearly passed out drunk. There was a girl there and she was blonde. Do you remember Tracy?" I watched as Charlie's eyes iced over at the mention of her name. "That day, the day you must have seen me, I was drunk, Bit. I couldn't get to my room alone. She walked me up the stairs and I was too drunk to stop her when she tried to take my clothes off." I shook my head at the memory, as fuzzy as it was. I remembered that night and nothing had happened.

"Eventually, she realized nothing was going to happen because nothing *could* happen, and what you saw was me *removing* her from me. I was saying your name, telling her I loved you. I never slept with her. Ever."

Charlie was shaking her head.

"The next morning Tracy apologized to me for what happened and told me that she felt badly about it. We decided to let it go and never really talked about it again. It was a non-issue, a nothing. If I had known what you thought I would have told you immediately, but I never saw you again. Not for years."

"You're a liar," she spat at me.

"Why would I lie? Why? And if I'm lying now, why wouldn't I lie then? Why wouldn't I tell you then that I hadn't slept with anyone? Think about it; I've had no reason to lie. You never gave me any reason to think that I had a chance at being with you. I didn't know you lost the babies at that moment. I DIDN'T KNOW! Because you pushed me away. But I had no reason to lie to you about it. I've never lied to you – not once, ever. You never gave me a chance to tell you what really happened. Why did you leave? Why didn't you say something then? Why would you just run away from everything?"

"Because I loved you! I loved you regardless of what had happened! I stood there, watching you with her, with blood running down my legs, and thought that seeing you with her, that was my punishment. This life? The life I lead where I think of you every day, where I am reminded every single day of the lives I wasn't strong enough to hold on to, that is my punishment."

"Charlie," I say as I run my thumb over her cheek, as I search her eyes for the girl I have loved for most of my life. "It isn't your fault. It wasn't your fault. You did nothing wrong." I press my lips on to hers, just making contact, a kiss meant to soothe.

"I lost our babies," she said against my lips, through tears, breaking the very last piece of my heart.

"Oh, Bit, you didn't lose our babies. They weren't ready yet." I moved my mouth along her face, kissing away tears that were still flowing down her face. "They're waiting for us. I promise we'll meet them someday. But it wasn't your fault. It wasn't anybody's fault." I leaned back and pushed her hair back from her face again, wanting to see her eyes. She didn't shy away from me; she stared right back at me.

"I've spent so many years wondering how you could have been with someone else. How, if you felt even one fraction of the love I felt for you, you could give that part of you to someone so quickly. I didn't know how to deal with it, deal with you being with her, deal with the miscarriage. I still don't know how. I just ran. I left. I borrowed money from my dad and I went somewhere new." She closed her eyes and swallowed, gulping down emotion.

"Don't run away from me anymore, please. I'm here. I've been here all along. I've got nothing without you. Please..." I pressed my lips to hers again, but this time I meant to convince her, to end the separation, to crush the space between us. My lips crashed into hers and she didn't fight me, didn't push me away, but didn't kiss me either. "Let me in, Bit. Let me back in." I kissed her again, softer, making silent promises, invisible vows that I wouldn't break again. I'd never let her hurt again – not for a misunderstanding. I kissed her as if I was trying to save her or myself. I kissed her to bring her back.

My entire world exploded when I felt her hands slide up my back and her lips kiss me back.

Charlie

Was this really happening?

Were Asher's hands really running freely through my hair? And were my hands running along his back? How had we gotten to this place? My heart began to race as my mind tried to take over, fears leaking through this wonderful moment.

"Asher," I said against his mouth. He didn't answer me. He just kissed me harder, with more passion. I gave in to it, allowing my body to enjoy his for a little while. It was hard not to; he was all I had wanted since forever. Our mouths fused and our tongues slid across each other, and I was reminded of how our bodies seemed to be made for each other. His hands stretched all over me: my waist, my hips, my arms, my stomach, my neck. It was as if he couldn't feel enough of me, as if I was going to slip away.

"Asher," I repeated as his lips pulled away from mine, only to travel down my neck. "Please, let's slow down. I need a breather." Even saying the words hurt. He slowed, but he didn't stop.

"If I let you go," he said between kisses that were slipping between my breasts, making me gasp, "I'm afraid I'll never get you back." He grabbed my waist and lifted me to sit on the edge of the counter. I was eye level with him and he wormed his way in between my legs, pushing his hips into mine. I became instantly aware of the fact that I was just in my underwear and I lost all control of the situation. I raised my hand up and placed it on his chest, pushing him away. I had to add my other hand and push hard, but I finally got him to step backwards so I could look him in the eyes.

"I don't think this is a good idea." I tried to wiggle down from the counter but was just met by the brick wall that was his body. He wasn't moving for anything.

"Give me three reasons why this is a bad idea." He crossed his arms in front of him, unwilling to budge.

"Well, for one, we haven't even really solved any problems. I am just supposed to take your word for it that you didn't sleep with her?"

"Yes. You are. I've got no reason to lie to you. I was a nineteen-year-old boy, Bit. I was dumb and stupid and I never should have walked out on you the way I did, but I did not sleep with her. I'm not sitting here trying to rationalize anything. I did not sleep with anyone. Not until you'd been gone a long time."

"And your words are just supposed to be enough? I've been grappling with this for years and I'm just supposed to move on? Forget it? Assume you're not lying?"

"Yes. Now give me the second reason."

"We're two completely different people than we were back in college. We might not even be compatible anymore." At those words Asher gave me the biggest and brightest smile I had ever seen. I didn't smile back, but seeing his dimple definitely made my wall crumble a little more.

"That's the dumbest thing you've ever said," he said with his sexy smile. "We'll always be compatible. You're an extension of me. A piece I've been missing for so long, Bit." His voice softened and his smile disappeared, replaced by a sad look in his eyes that tugged at a part of my heart that had been dormant for a very long time. His hand rested on my bare knee and then slowly slid down my calf. His other hand did the same thing and when his hands reached my ankles, he grabbed them and wrapped them around his waist, once again pulling me into him. His eyes never left mine as his hands left my ankles and moved to my waist. One hand wrapped around my middle, pulling me even closer into him. His other hand moved up to the clasp of my bra.

"You're going to have to give me one more reason, Bit." As the words fell from his mouth, the clasp of my bra popped open and it fell to the floor, next to my dress. His hands obviously felt like they had more room to roam and he didn't waste any time. My eyes rolled back into my head as his hand found my breast. And if I thought the feeling of his fingers brushing against my nipple was the most wonderful feeling in the world, I wasn't prepared for his hot mouth to close over the other one.

"Give me one good reason," he said around my flesh, the vibrations of his words mixed with the heat of his mouth making both breasts ache with need. I hadn't felt need like this in years – over a decade. I didn't want him to stop, not really. I wanted everything he was offering. The problem was, I wanted so much more.

"If we do this, Asher, if we have sex tonight, there's no going back for me. I won't be able to walk away. I'll fall right back in love with you. Do you understand that? The more you touch me, the more you make me feel *alive* again, the worse it's going to be for me when this is over. So, as much as I want this, as much as I want you, or us, I can't put myself through another thirteen years of trying to get over you."

As I made my declaration, as I spoke the truest words I'd spoken since the day I told him I was pregnant, his hands moved to cup my face and my chest came to rest against his. Our noses were nearly touching, our breaths intermingling. I was waiting for him to pull away, realizing what I had, that this was a mistake.

"Bit," he whispered right before he placed a gentle kiss against my mouth. The kiss was sweet and soft, and my eyes began to water when I thought it was a goodbye kiss. If this was the last time, then last kiss, I wanted to remember it. I threaded my fingers through his hair and brought my body against his. I felt the sobs coming and I knew I wasn't going to be able to hold it together much longer. I felt his hands move from my face and my heart started pounding at his absence. His lips moved off me and a cry escaped me.

Then I felt his hand float through my hair and wrap around it, tugging it down, pulling my face up to look at him once more. Then he pulled it to the side, causing my neck to bend, exposing the delicate skin. He ran his nose up and down the curve created for him, smelling and tasting me, before he landed his lips right in the juncture of my neck and shoulder, the sensitive spot that made my toes curl.

"We aren't going to have sex tonight," he said against my neck making me shiver. "I'm going to take you into the bedroom, lay you down, and show you how much I love you. How much I've always loved you. And tomorrow, when we wake up, it will be something new. A beginning. You'll never have to get over me again, because I'm not going anywhere."

I made the decision at that moment, with his mouth against my skin and his hands in my hair, to trust him and to trust myself to make the best decision.

"Show me," was all I said and he had me lifted into his arms instantly. As he carried me out of the bathroom and into the bedroom, his mouth found mine again and his previously sweet and soft kisses had a more urgent feeling now. Thirteen years of built-up tension and longing made everything intensify. He laid me down on the bed and climbed over me. His nearness was overwhelming. I reached up to unbutton his shirt and the feeling of his warm skin beneath the fabric nearly burned me. When his mouth found the spot beneath my ear that he used to be so familiar with, it sent shockwaves through my system.

I reached up and slid his shirt over his shoulders and down his arms, feeling the tight muscles along the way. In college he was always in such good shape from basketball and summers on his grandfather's farm, and although his frame was still sturdy and strong, he was more masculine than I ever remembered him being. He'd grown up and I realized I laid with a man. This would be different and for that I was glad. I didn't want a reminder of what we used to be, I wanted to move forward.

His mouth moved down from my neck and over my collarbone. He splayed light kisses everywhere his mouth went while his hands roamed over my heated skin.

"You feel so good, Bit."

I smiled at his words, at his nickname for me. It was the first time I'd heard it and not felt my heart clench in pain.

"I agree. I feel pretty damn good." I felt him chuckle against the soft tissue of my breast, but then gasped as his mouth closed around my nipple, sucking fiercely, his tongue alternatively flicking and licking. His other hand moved to my empty breast and gave the other nipple a gentle yet firm tug. My hands found their way to his hair and threaded through his locks, gripping slightly. Each tug and suck of my breasts ignited a fury of flames between my legs and I found myself grinding my hips up towards him, looking for contact.

His mouth moved down, skimming over the skin of my stomach, stopping to tease my navel. I felt his hands lightly trail down my sides, stopping at my waist and holding on. He lifted his head and I saw him move over to my ribcage that bared his name.

"I like seeing my name on you," he said as he placed one small kiss over it.

"I liked having it. In a small way it was like you were always with me." I continued to push my fingers through his dark hair, the feeling of it almost hypnotizing.

"I never left you, Bit. I promise. I never moved on and I never wanted anyone else. It's always just been you."

"I know," I replied softly. His hands moved down to my panties, the only article of clothing I had left. His fingers eased themselves inside the top and he looked at me with raised eyebrows, asking for permission. I gave him a nod and a smile – all the go-ahead he needed. I lifted my hips as he pulled them down. Once I was bare, I watched his eyes glide over me, stopping to focus on my core. His hands ran up and down my thighs and I inhaled sharply as he gently pushed my knees apart, spreading me open for him. He must have sensed my nervousness because he leaned forward and pressed a small kiss just above my mound, his hands wrapping around my hips to grip my ass, pulling me closer to him.

"It's just me. Just you and me here. I've missed you and I want to love all of you. Relax for me."

I sighed and willed myself to breath in and out, hoping my nerves would calm. I wanted this and I wanted him, but I was afraid of feeling so much after so long being numb. I felt his fingers gingerly glide over my wetness, teasing me, letting me acclimate to being touched by him again.

"Every part of you is so beautiful," his whispered into the curls above my core. His words distracted me from the fact that his thumbs were gently spreading me open. I gasped when I felt his mouth near me, blowing warm air over my sensitive flesh. When his tongue dipped inside I stifled a groan and my back arched off the bed. "You're gonna have to hold still for me, Baby." I felt his hands grip my hips and press down, his attempt at restraining me, as he continued his assault. His tongue lapped at my opening, dove in, and swirled around. I felt every movement deep inside of me, rocking me back and forth.

My hands came up to my forehead out of glory and frustration. Everything felt so amazing, but I needed more.

"Oh God, Asher. Please..." I begged. For what? I wasn't sure.

"Trust me," Asher replied. Wasn't that clever? The last thirteen years of my life had been torturous because I had been afraid to trust him, afraid to believe that perhaps, in the end, I should give him the benefit of the doubt. And now, here we were, in the most intimate situation I could imagine, and he asked for my trust. He asked me let go and let him lead me, to abandon the thoughts and life I had gripped on to so tightly for all these years, and to give him the control. It might have been a pinnacle moment in my life and it might have been a bigger deal to some others, but in this particular fragment of time, it was clear and simple.

"I trust you," I whispered, not even sure he heard me. Whether or not he heard me wasn't important. The important part was that I decided to let myself forgive. I forgave him for making a mistake when he was younger and I forgave myself for accepting the blame for something that wasn't my fault. I felt myself relax at my realization. The tension I always carried with me, the constant tightness in my shoulders, as if I was a rubber band waiting to snap, moved away and was replaced by a new, delicious tension in between my legs.

Asher felt the difference and took advantage. His mouth moved up as he found my clit, sucking and gently nibbling on it, while he pushed two fingers into me, causing me to cry out.

"Fuck, yes," I moaned.

His tongue moved against my clit quicker and his fingers found their rhythm against the bundle of nerves hiding inside me. I breathed hard, in and out, trying to relax and let myself feel the release I missed for so long.

"Bit," he moaned against me.

"Asher, don't you fucking stop," I wailed.

"Come for me."

I heard his words and it felt like someone had pushed me off of a bridge. My stomach dropped, my heart stopped, and my entire body convulsed around him. Tiny volts of electricity shot through my limbs. My legs tingled and my toes curled. My back arched off the bed, trying to milk every last piece of feeling from the most cosmically awesome orgasm I ever had. And Asher, bless him, had continued to kiss my core throughout the entire experience.

After I came all the way down from the highest of highs, he moved up my body again. I instantly grabbed his face and pulled him towards mine. He was a breath away from me, breathing hard, and I leaned forward the last inch to connect our mouths. I tasted myself on him and I loved it. I loved what he did to me, how he made me feel, and this kiss was an extension of that. I rolled us over and straddled his lap, still kissing his lips while I worked on unbuttoning his jeans.

His hands ran up my back, hooking over my shoulders, then running back down to cup my ass.

"Is it possible that you're smaller than before?" He asked, then kissed my neck.

"Mmm... I haven't eaten much in the last thirteen years." I felt him push my hair over my shoulder and then cup my cheek, bringing my face back to look at him.

"That stops now, Bit. You've got to take care of your body. No more punishing yourself."

I nodded at his words, then pressed a kiss against his lips. Next, I moved down his body and pulled at his jeans, working hard to get them over his massive body. He had to help push them over his hips and we both laughed at how clumsy we suddenly became. Once he was naked, I took just a moment to admire him. He looked exactly as I remembered him, but somehow manlier. He was older – more powerful. I climbed back up to him, straddling his waist, bringing my face level with his, my long dark hair falling on either side of my face creating a curtain around us. His hands came up and tried pushing it behind my ears, but eventually gave up, as it proved to be a pointless task, the hair just falling back to cocoon us in a veil of darkness. He smiled dreamily up at me, his thumbs lovingly floating across the skin of my cheeks, his large fingers threaded in the hair at the nape of my neck.

"I love you, Charlie, more than anything." His words burrowed into my heart and put some of the broken pieces back together. He leaned up and captured my lips in a kiss. I let him kiss me and when he pulled away, I pressed my forehead against his.

"I couldn't love you more, Asher." He kissed me again, but this time as he kissed me he pulled me against him and he moved to a sitting position, leaning against his headboard. With my knees on the bedspread, I raised up and angled him at my opening.

"I've been on birth control for a while, Asher, and I trust you. Do we need a condom?"

"No." he whispered and that was all I needed to hear before I sank down over him.

My head fell back as he entered me. He filled me entirely, completed me in a way no one had before. I stretched and pulsed around him, my hands gripping his shoulders.

"Damn, you feel good," he muttered through clenched teeth.

"Mmmm. The feeling's mutual," I said with a smile. I took just a few moments to appreciate how full I felt. Asher was the only one who gave me this sensation, the only one who fit me this way. Once I was satisfied and ready to move, I slowly brought my body up and down his shaft, letting him feel all of me. He watched me as I slowly rode him, speeding up fractionally with every slide. I tried hard to make him feel good, but got lost in the sensation myself, and felt my eyes closing.

Suddenly, I felt Asher's hand clasp around my loose hair, gathering it behind my back, tugging, and urging my head back. His other hand gripped my hip, holding me to him firmly. He quickly maneuvered so that his feet were under him, his knees resting on the bed, and me still firmly impaled by him, my legs wrapped around his waist. His grip on my hair hardened and I yelped as he thrust into me. One hard thrust and my mind scattered. His mouth came to rest between my breasts and he grunted as he gave another powerful thrust.

"Just so we're clear," he said between thrusts. "You're mine now. Forever." Thrust. "No one but me will ever touch you like this again. Understood?"

"Yes. I understand. Just please, don't stop."

"Not on your life," he said with a smirk. He picked up speed and tapped into some endless supply of energy as his thrusts became steady and stronger. Every time he pounded into me, I lost a little bit more control, my cries became louder, the sound of our flesh slapping together brought me closer.

Suddenly he stopped and I must have looked like a child who just had their candy stolen because he laughed and soothingly ran his hand down the length of my hair.

"Don't worry, Babe. I'm not nearly finished with you yet." He kissed me quickly and then laid my back down on the bed. He stretched my legs so that my heels rested against his shoulders. I let out a soft moan, the stretching of my muscles felt so delectable after being in that position for so long. He rubbed my calves, seeming to know what I needed.

Slowly, as he kneaded my muscles, he began to move in and out of me. Our position allowed such a deep penetration that every time he entered me, he nudged against a wall and it felt divine. The tip of his cock rubbed gloriously along the inside of me, causing all kinds of synapses to fire simultaneously and after a few minutes I wasn't sure I could take much more of his particular torture.

"I'm almost there, Asher. Please...don't stop."

"Do you love me?" He questioned. It caught me off guard and my eyes opened to him staring at me, siding slowly and purposefully in and out of me. His eyes were full of lust, but something else was hiding in them as well. "Will you leave me when this is over?" His vulnerability showed, and my heart broke a little.

"I never left you. I was with you all along. Of course I love you." He collapsed onto me, closing his fingers around my hair, his face buried in my neck, and he brought us both to the edge. He came first and I followed quickly after, spurred on by the sound of him whispering "Bit" sweetly into my ear as he emptied himself into me.

Chapter Fifteen

Charlie

The next morning as we woke I was greeted by the brilliant smile of the man I never thought I'd get to love again – the man who held my heart for so many years, but that I was too afraid to give myself over to, or allow myself to have. We spent the night exploring each other, laughing, talking, napping, and cuddling. When the sun broke through his curtains, I knew it was time to leave, the light from the day making everything a little more real.

"What time is your flight?" He asked, as he brought the back of my hand to his lips to kiss.

"Noon."

He groaned and I shared his misery. It was too soon for us to be apart; we'd just found each other again. On the other hand, the responsible and rational part of my brain was trying to convince me that jumping into a fully-committed relationship with Asher wasn't a great idea. Obviously, I loved him and wanted to be with him, but for the longest time I hadn't really been in control of my life and now was the time for me to take the reins. I wanted him to be there for me, to support me the way someone who loves you should, but I wanted to prove to myself that I could stand on my own two feet.

"Can I drive you to the airport?"

I gave him a smile that I hoped showed how happy I was to be with him in that moment. "I'd love that."

It was a few hours later and we walked from the parking garage at the airport up to the departure terminal. My hand was clasped in Asher's and every time I thought about holding his hand it made my heart race a little faster. So much happened in just the last twenty-four hours that my head was still a little off kilter from it all. I checked my bags, got my boarding pass, and we headed towards security.

"Will you keep an eye on my dad's house for me? Make sure no squatters get in there and set up camp?"

"Of course. Do you think you're going to sell it?"

I sighed heavily. "Yeah, probably. But I'm just not ready yet. Maybe in a couple months. Plus," I said as I turned to him and ran my hands up his chest. "I was thinking I needed a place to stay if I was going to be coming back to visit Willow Falls." I felt him wrap his arms around me, his hands coming to rest on my backside, giving a gentle squeeze as a smile spread across his face.

"So you'll be back then? I don't have to worry about you running away and leaving me here, angry and confused?"

I reached up on my tip-toes and pressed a kiss against his lips. "I want to be with you, Asher, only you. But I've got to figure out my life right now. I'm going to go back to New York, get my art show behind me, and see what feels right after that."

"This feels right," he said, pushing his fingers through my hair, cupping his hand behind my head, pressing our foreheads together.

"It always has," I responded softly.

"So we're just going to trust each other and trust that everything will be ok in the end?"

"That and work at being better for each other than we have in the past." I paused, closing my eyes. I opened them again to see his slate gray eyes staring back at me. "We've both made mistakes and I still need to work on letting go of some things. I want to be whole for you, if that makes sense."

"So, this isn't a goodbye then?"

I shook my head and smiled shyly.

"Good," he said, returning the smile. "I hate goodbye kisses." His arms snaked around my waist and picked me up off the ground, bringing my lips up to meet his, and he kissed me as if he missed me for years. And I kissed him right back.

A few hours had passed, the plane ride boring and a little bumpy. After landing, I made my way to a hotel near the gallery where my show would be taking place the next weekend. The city looked different to me. The buildings taller, the crowds on the street louder, the pace of life seemed to be in fast forward. I'd always felt a little out of place in the city, but I chalked it up to just being out of place in life. I hadn't felt like I fit in anywhere, so it made sense that the city was a stranger to me.

But now, I didn't feel out of place so much as I felt like a visitor, an imposter. Any minute someone would look at me hauling my suitcase behind me and tell me to go back to where I came from. The feeling was unnerving, but also a relief. It was the first time I had any strong feelings about where I belonged – or didn't belong. It was a small step in the right direction. For the next week, I had a job to do. I had to make it through the art show and then I'd be free to make the decisions that were best for me.

I tried to unpack my clothes into the dresser of the hotel room I would be staying in for a while when my phone buzzed on the bedside table.

Just wondering if your flight went well and if you've made it to wherever you were going ok.

I smiled at the text from Asher. He was worried that I didn't have a concrete plan on where I'd be staying. I'd tried to tell him that the possibilities were endless and that I'd be fine to just find a hotel when I arrived, but that made him nervous.

The flight was predictable and I am settling in my four-star hotel as we text.

Four stars, huh? Don't let the money change you, Bit.

I wasn't about to tell him that I was accustomed to staying in nice hotels with David. I wasn't a snob and I wasn't with David for his money, but no one could deny the comforts of a nice hotel if you could afford it.

*I'm sorry, from now on you'll have to send all communication through my personal assistant. She'll be

handling my personal affairs while I roll around on hundred dollar bills. *

* *Will you be clothed while you roll around in your money? And can your personal assistant take pictures?* *

I laughed out loud at his text, didn't take him long to get inappropriate. I shook my head. I laughed more in the last twenty-four hours than I had in years. It made me feel light and nearly carefree.

* *Wouldn't you like to know?* *

* *Seriously, which hotel are you staying in?* *

* *It's just down the street from the gallery, The Franklin.* *

I went back to unpacking and my phone buzzed a few minutes later.

* *Ok. I checked out your hotel and it looks pretty safe. You don't take the subway, do you? Take a cab if you go anywhere, or a town car would be even better.* *

* *You're forgetting I have lived in this city for years now. I'll be fine.* *

* *I just realized that if I had known where you were this whole time we've been apart, I probably would have gone crazy worrying about you.* *

* *No need to worry. I can take care of myself.* *

* *Don't deny me the privileges that come along with loving you. Worrying is one of the perks.* *

That made me smile. I'd never tire of hearing Asher say he loved me.

The days passed and I worked hard in my studio preparing for the show. I already picked most of the pieces weeks before the show, so most of the work this week was framing pieces, transporting them, and coordinating with the gallery to get them hung and lit accordingly. My mind often wandered to Asher, wondering what he was doing, where he was, if he was thinking of me as much as I was thinking of him. Of course, he never let me forget about him, and every day a different kind of flower was delivered to the hotel for me with a sweet note.

On Sunday a vibrant bunch of honeysuckle was waiting for me at the front desk. – *Dear Charlie, honeysuckle represents the bonds of love. I am forever bound to you. All my love, Asher*

Monday, when I opened my door for the breakfast I'd ordered through room service, the cart outside my door also had a bundle of lavender sitting in a vase. The note read – *Bit, lavender is for devotion. My heart has been devoted to you since I was eleven. There's never been anyone else. Xoxo, Asher*

The lavender is beautiful. And it makes my hotel room smell divine.

I'm glad. I hope the flowers are making it hard for you to forget about me.

I think the fact that I can't stop thinking about you in general is making it hard to forget about you.

When can I see you again?

I sighed at his text, my face bright with a smile. It had only been two days since I saw him, but I already missed him.

I'm not sure yet. Maybe this evening we can talk? Call me when you're home?

Count on it, Babe.

My day brightened considerably knowing that I'd get to speak with Asher that night. I found myself sketching in the afternoon and when I stepped back from the pad to examine what I drew I recognized the creek running underneath the bridge we used to spend so much time at during our childhood. Under that bridge Asher told me he loved me for the first time. In that park we shared our first kiss. For everything that had happened between us, I would never deny how much Asher loved me. He always found ways to show me how much he cared for me, and he was always there when I needed him.

Suddenly, my happiness faded away and stinging sadness moved in. For all the years that Asher had protected me, and knew when I needed him, showing me unwavering support, love and friendship, I had abandoned him the instant the waters became rough. If I hadn't pushed him away, or at least given him time to acclimate to the pregnancy before keeping him at arms-length, perhaps we'd be in a different situation now.

I cocked my head at the drawing. The creek was a reminder of how things used to be between Asher and me: steady, continuous, stable. When real life hit us, we both ran from each other. We were young and scared.

"God, it's good to hear your voice," Asher said that evening when I answered his phone call. "You don't know how difficult this has been for me. I've spent so many years knowing you were out there but having no idea where you were. Now that I know, and now that I feel like you could be mine again, I'm fighting every urge to jump on a plane and find you."

He sounded happy to talk to me, but I could also hear weariness in his voice. The separation was doing different things for both of us. I was using the time apart to repair things inside of me that I had been fighting for so long, and he was focusing on the anxious part of himself that wanted to be near me.

"It's good to hear from you too, Asher. We'll see each other soon enough. I promise." I paused and heard him exhale loudly. I knew he was trying to be respectful and give me my space, but I didn't like hearing him upset. "How was work this week?" I asked, trying to change the subject.

"Busy, as usual. I'm working on a few cases and one of them is going to be a real struggle."

"Why is that?" I asked, interested. I didn't know lawyer Asher very well.

"Because my client is somewhat of an idiot and signed a contract when he shouldn't have. On the other hand though, the other party was being shady throughout the negotiations and I think we can get them on negligence. I just wish people would take some time to think through their decisions before they made them."

"But then you might be out of a job," I joked.

"Well, as true as that might be, there will always be people who need lawyers."

"And there will always be people who act before they think," I said, solemnly, my thoughts moving in a depressing direction. "Can I ask you something?"

"Always," he said firmly.

"If I had come to you a week after our big fight, you know, after I told you I was pregnant, do you think we would have been able to work it out?"

He was quiet for a few moments and I laid down on the bed, pulling a pillow under my head, trying to give him the time he needed to formulate his answer.

"By the time a week had passed, I was so miserable without you, I'm pretty sure I would have done anything to get you back. I was just so ashamed of myself. I couldn't forget what I'd said to you and the look on your face. I'm still ashamed. It's the worst moment of my life."

"One thing I'm realizing while I'm here is that I can forgive you all I want, Asher. I can wash everything away, give us a clean slate, a free pass into our future, but unless I truly forgive myself, there's probably no hope for us." He was silent, taking in my words. "Do you think you've forgiven yourself?"

"I don't know, really," he answered honestly. "I've never thought about it. I know it means a lot that *you* forgive me, and that goes a long way in making me feel better about the situation, but I can't say if I truly forgive myself."

"What would you say to another nineteen year old guy who was in your situation? Would you hold what he said against him? What he said moments after learning something that would change his life forever?" He was quiet again.

"No, I suppose not. I'd tell him it was really shitty, but I wouldn't hold it against him."

"We were so young, Asher." I said sadly. "We were supposed to make mistakes. I'm sorry I walked away and never went back for you. That was *my* mistake."

"Is that what you're forgiving yourself for?" He asked softly.

"I'm working on forgiving myself for a lot of things, but yes, running from you is one of them. You have never been anything but supportive of me, and the one time you messed up I pushed you so far away you were never able to find me again. I'm sorry."

"Can you tell me what else you're sorry for? You don't have to, I understand if it's private."

I smiled at that, at his acknowledgment of my privacy, but still wanting to know that part of me.

"No, it's ok." I sighed, trying to put into words everything my mind had been sifting through for the last couple of days. "I'm forgiving myself for getting pregnant in the first place. I'm forgiving myself for *blaming* myself for the miscarriage. That wasn't my fault." I felt a wave of emotions wash over me when I heard the words come out of my mouth, and I stifled back a small cry.

"Oh, Bit. I wish I was there with you right now," he said painfully. I could hear the ache in his voice, the discomfort that came with wanting to be near me. Again, I was denying him the ability to be with me.

"I need to forgive myself for not being with my dad when he died. For putting that distance between us, for building the kind of relationship with him that he didn't think he could tell me he was dying." The cries came for real then and I couldn't control them. Tears streaked my face and all I heard from the other end of the phone was Asher's voice whispering comforting words and hushing me. When I'd calmed down a little, Asher's voice was there to bring me back.

"Babe, he didn't keep his illness from you because he felt like he couldn't tell you. He kept it from you because he didn't want you to suffer through another parent's death. Trust me, I tried to convince him many times to call you and tell you, but he was trying to protect you."

I took his words in and tried to process them. I knew my dad would have done anything to keep me safe and to protect me from harm, but now I'd never know what might have happened if I'd been more present, if I'd been less distant.

"I know you're right, Asher. It's just something that's going to take some time to get over."

"It's another one of those things that you can't blame yourself for, Bit. Your father was a grown man and he knew what decisions he was making. Don't turn his actions around and make them into something you have to feel sorry about. That's not what he'd want."

"I know," I whispered. After a few moments Asher let out a frustrated growl.

"This is killing me. I need to see you. I can't be so far away from you when I know you're hurting." I smiled and wiped residual tears from my face.

"I'm ok, Asher. This is all part of the process. We both need this. If we're going to be together after this, we both need to move on from everything, start over."

"I know you're right. I just want to hold you. I want to smell you and touch you." I shivered at his words. His voice was deeper and I knew his intentions weren't just to comfort me, but to make me feel him.

"I want that too," I whispered.

"Can I ask you a question now?" I blinked in surprised, thrown off by the quick directional change of our conversation.

"Of course," I replied.

"Have you seen David since you've been back?"

I nearly laughed at his question, but had enough sense not to. But I did grin stupidly. He'd always been so territorial over me. Thinking about him worrying over whether or not some other man was near me or talking to me made my heart rate spike. I wanted him to assert himself over me, to be possessive.

"No."

"Does he know you're back?"

"I don't know what he knows. I didn't tell him. But he knows I have a show coming up, and he probably figures I'm in town preparing."

"Will you see him?"

"Not on purpose."

"Do better than that, Bit."

"I have no desire, whatsoever, to see David while I am here, or ever. He's a part of my past, Asher. I never loved him. I used him and I am ashamed of that. He deserved way better than I gave him and I wish him all the happiness in the world, but I don't want him." Asher was quiet and I let him digest my words.

"How long were you with him?"

"Five years."

"Shit... that's a long time."

"It was."

"Well, I can tell you one thing. I know how men work, and if he had you for five years there's no way he's going to just let you go – no one could just give you up. If he knows you're in town, he's going to try to contact you."

"And if he does, I'll tell him I've moved on and that we can't see each other anymore."

"Your show is Saturday, right?"

"Yes."

"Do you miss me?" Again I was startled by the turn in the conversation.

"Desperately," I answered honestly.

"Oh, you're desperate, are you?" His voice took on a flirty tone.

"Mm hmm." I moaned a little, trying to bait him.

"Shit, Bit. Your voice is really sexy on the phone. I remember all those times we talked on the phone while I was away over the summers. I always had a hard-on talking to you."

Hook, line, and sinker.

"Do you enjoy phone sex?" I rasped at him.

"No," he said quickly.

"No?" I said, surprised and in my normal voice, all sexy raspiness gone. "What do you mean no? What kind of red-blooded, American man are you?"

"Don't go getting all offended on me, Babe. I just like the real thing better. Phone sex is like teasing my cock. He gets all worked up expecting something soft and warm and all he gets is my hand. It's mean."

"Oh my God." I laughed at his words – big, loud fits of laughter. I rolled on the bed until I was on my back, the laughter taking over my body. I cried from all the laughing. "You might be the only man on the planet to ever say that," I cried as I wiped the tears from my face.

"Think about it. You're sitting there, all alone in your hotel right now. I could use my voice to turn you on," he said, his voice going soft and slow, dropping to a gravelly timbre. "I could tell you how much I wanted you, how badly I need to be inside of you. I could talk about my tongue flicking over your nipples, about my hands gripping your ass as I rubbed myself against you."

I gulped at his words, swallowed any laughter that remained and replaced with panting breaths.

"I could talk about grabbing your hair, holding you in place, while I sank into you from behind, rocking you back and forth, hitting every spot you love that I remember."

"Fuuuck..." I groaned, rolling to my side and squeezing my thighs together, trying to relieve some of the pressure that was pounding between my legs.

"Now tell me, Bit. Which sounds better right now?"

"Mmmm..." I mumbled in response.

"Your tiny fingers? Or my cock?"

"Shit."

"That's right. You want my cock. But I'm so far away."

"You're an ass."

"Perhaps," he said with a laugh. "But you love me."

"Perhaps," I said with a smile.

Chapter Sixteen
Charlie

After Asher and I hung up that night, I couldn't keep my thoughts from my father and of what Asher tried to convince me. My mind fluttered to the letter my dad left for me, the letter he wrote to me before he died. I kept it in the top drawer of my dresser in my hotel room. I peeled myself off the bed and walked to the dresser, slowly pulling open the drawer. I moved aside the undergarments that I used to cover it, although, covering it was useless as I always knew it was there. It might as well have been smoking and red hot for how it seemed to burn in my mind. It pulsed. I was aware of it always. I reached for it, hand trembling, not sure if I was ready to read the last words my father had for me.

Slowly, I peeled back the lip of the envelope and saw a piece of paper with indentions all over it from the pen marks my father made. A small cry escaped me as I came to terms with the fact my father held this paper in his hands, wrote this for me. I was suddenly angry I didn't read it sooner.

I pulled the paper out, opened it, and sat down in the big arm chair in the corner of the suite, curling my legs up under me, trying to get comfortable.

My Dear Charlie Bear,

Just the salutation reduced me to tears. I smiled through the sobs, remembering and loving the nickname my father had for me my entire life, no matter how old I was or how mad I made him.

The first thing I want to say to you is that I'm sorry. I know it will be hard for you to understand my decision to keep my illness from you and part of me is very sorry to put you in this situation. But there's a bigger part of me, the Daddy part of me, that knows this was the least painful way to leave you. I watched you hold your mother's hand while she was sick and I know what that did to both of you. I couldn't put you through that again. Know that you were with me the entire time, and that I thought of you until the end. I never loved anyone the way I loved you, Charlie Bear, and I am so lucky that I got to be your father.

In time you will heal and the sadness will fade away. Trust me. I want you to move on from this and live a good life. I am not afraid to die, Charlie. I know that when I go I will get to see your momma and the two beautiful babies that neither of us got to meet. I will hug them and tell them how much their mother loves them, Charlie. Your mother and I will take care of them for you.

My hands came up to cover my face, the sobs ripping through me, a hurricane of sadness brewing inside my chest, the pressure threatening to tear me in two. The image in my head of my mother and father, each holding a baby, was enough to stop my breath. For just a moment, I didn't want to breathe anymore. I wasn't ready to die, but I wanted to hold my children. I wanted to hug my mother again, kiss my father's cheek. I wasn't envious of their deaths, just a little jealous that they didn't have to feel the hurt anymore. I used my shirt to wipe away the tears and picked up the letter to continue reading.

Now I must move on to more important matters. One benefit of knowing you're about to die is that you get to make one last request. This request holds far more weight than any request you made when you were healthy for some reason. I'm not going to question the logic, but I am going to take advantage of my situation and make one last dying request, a request on my deathbed, if you will.

Forgive him. Tell him. Let him love you. Let yourself be happy.

There have been two times in my life when Asher Carmichael impressed the shit out of me. The first time, you were fourteen and just started high school. I pulled Asher into my office and we talked about what had happened to you at school, and what he did to protect your honor and reputation. He told me then he loved you and I believed him. I knew at that moment that boy would spend his whole life protecting you, fighting for you, and loving you.

Then, a year later, Asher came to me asking if I would let you date him. Only, he didn't actually use the word date. I believe his exact words were, "Sir, I'd like permission to start spending the rest of my life with her." What fifteen-year-old boy says something like to that to a girls' dad? A brave one.

When you left and he started coming around here, I knew he was hurting and wanted some tangible thing to hold to. He wanted to be near you, to feel you, without hurting you. So I let him be here, but I thought it better to not get involved. Well, that's the funny thing about death, it makes you reconsider a lot of decisions you've made throughout your life. Now, I've decided, is the perfect time to get involved.

Promise me you won't push him away anymore. Reach out to him. Let him help heal you. I know, if you let him in, he'll spend his whole life making everything right again. He needs healing just as much as you do and you are the only one who can help him with that.

I love you Charlie. I will always love you and you will always have your mother and me watching over you. Don't grieve my death for too long and please try to find your happiness again. I think it lies in the one person you've been trying to push away - yourself.

A lifetime of love will never be enough, but it's all I have to offer,

Your Father

Papa Bear

I folded the letter back up, making sure the creases were all lined up correctly, not wanting to damage the letter at all. I placed it back in its envelope and moved back over to the bed. I laid down, placing the letter under my pillow, and quietly cried myself to sleep.

Tuesday started with a bouquet of beautiful, pink roses. *Bit, Pink roses symbolize grace, joy, and sweetness. All three are synonymous with you, but I picked pink because it reminds me of your lips. Kisses, Asher*

Wednesday's dinner was served with the most perfect violets I'd ever seen. *My flower, violets represent loyalty. You will always be confident my loyalty lies with you. Xoxo, Asher*

"You've got to stop sending me flowers," I said to him over the phone Wednesday evening.

"You don't like flowers? What kind of red-blooded, American woman are you?"

"Ha ha. I think the hotel staff thinks I'm some kept woman. The lady at the concierge desk rolls her eyes at me when I walk by. She probably thinks I am some mistress here to see my boyfriend who is cheating on his wife with me."

"You've got quite the imagination," he said with a chuckle.

"Well, you haven't seen the looks she gives me."

"They can't be that bad. How's the show coming along? Everything working out the way you want it to?"

"Yes," I sighed. "The show is pretty much put together. I've spent more time drawing than anything else, which is good. But my work is different now. If you put the piece I was working on today next to any of the pieces from the show, you'd think two different people drew them."

"Do you like the new direction you're going in?"

"Yeah, I mean, I'm really inspired and the drawings are turning out beautiful. They're just different."

"Different can be good." His tone was wistful, as if he meant more than he was saying.

"Yes, it can." My smile could be heard through my voice and I felt it all over.

Thursday, when I came back to the hotel from the studio, there was a ridiculously large display of long-stem, red roses on the concierge desk. My mouth dropped open and then I rolled my eyes, figuring out exactly what was going on.

"Ma'am," the woman behind the desk called out to me. "These were delivered with *explicit* instructions to leave them here for you."

I scrambled over to the counter and peeked around the roses at her.

"Your *admirer* is getting bolder," she said with a sneer.

"Listen, he's not my admirer. I mean, he admires me, but it's not like that."

"It's none of my business," she said sharply as she handed me a card.

Red roses symbolize passion and lust. The meaning behind these should be self-explanatory, but if you need clarification, turn the card over.

I cringed, but turned the card over anyway.

You're naughty, turning the card over and everything. I miss you and I want to be inside of you – desperately. XXX, Asher

Before I could stop myself, I started fanning myself with the card and the bitchy concierge woman narrowed her eyes.

"Do you need help getting your flowers to your room?"

"No. I've got it," I said, grabbing the vase awkwardly and trying to navigate my way through the lobby. I turned around and shouted to the woman, "He's an old boyfriend. Well, a new boyfriend. He's not married and I'm not a hussy!" The woman held her hands up as if to indicate she didn't have anything to say about it. For added flair, I spun around quickly knowing my hair would fan out dramatically. That'll show her.

You're ridiculous.

I trust you got my flowers.

Shut. Up. I got your flowers. You're an ass.

We've covered that already. Let's talk about your ass and when I'll get to see it next.

You'll get no sexy talk from me after that stunt you pulled.

I don't respond well to threats, Bit.

Not a threat.

We'll see.

His last text was confusing and I was wiped out from making some final arrangements for the show. All I had left to do tomorrow was pick up my dress and try to relax.

I'm headed to bed all alone. Too bad you're not here to keep me warm. I texted him, hoping to tease him and get him riled up.

Now who's the ass?

Sweet dreams.

Friday came and I admitted I was a little disappointed when there were no flowers on my breakfast tray. I even frowned a little when there were none waiting at the concierge desk. I shook it off and continued on to my appointment with a stylist my agent insisted I hire for the event. The meeting we had six weeks prior proved to be exhausting and an experience I never wished to have again, but here I was, at her mercy, and dreading it.

"Elena," I said as I gave the petite blonde woman a kiss on each cheek. She was European and insisted double-cheek kissing was the polite way to greet someone. I didn't have to balls to argue with her about it. She'd been in the states for over twenty years, but her accent was still thick and her scary attitude even thicker.

"Charlie, your dress is here. You try on." I nodded at her and followed her back to the dressing rooms of her boutique. She showed me to a room and, sure enough, my dress was hanging on a hook. I delicately took it off the hanger and slid it over my body. I had to admit; I loved the dress. It was beautiful. Black satin gathered at the waist with a twist and a tasteful bow, one shoulder, and it flowed out at the bottom to create the most gorgeous, yet manageable, train. I loved it. My olive skin and dark hair looked good against the shimmering black of the fabric and it looked classy, yet sexy.

"I think it looks pretty good," I said as Elena's eyes bulldoze over me. I was waiting for her opinion because, honestly, it was the only one that mattered.

"Dress is perfect," she said with a dramatically rolled 'r' as she says dress. "I do an excellent job."

"So... that's it then?" I asked, confused. I was prepared for a three-hour ordeal.

"Do *you* think there is something wrong with dress?" She asked, perching her hand on her hip, cocking a perfectly tweezed and drawn-in eyebrow at me.

"No, God, no! I love it. I was just checking."

"You take off dress. I have it delivered to your hotel tomorrow after pressing."

"Ok, then." I had obviously offended Elena. I took the dress of, delicately hanging it back up and leaving it on the hook I removed it from. I went to leave the boutique, but Elena stopped me, making sure to kiss both my cheeks. Alright then.

With an extra few hours I hadn't planned on, I decided to walk back to the hotel instead of taking a cab. It was a beautiful afternoon in the city and I felt much more at ease being here than I had even a few days ago. Something about being here solely for my art, and talking with Asher about the things that were bothering me, had made the city not so excruciatingly lonely for me. I still felt like a visitor, but more like a visitor who was happy to be there. I could enjoy the city, not feel overwhelmed by it.

After a few hours of strolling through the streets, admiring the buildings, wandering through parks, I finally made it back to the hotel. Again, I was disappointed with the lack of over-the-top flowers waiting for me on the counter. It was nearly dinner time and I still hadn't gotten any flowers. Maybe he took me seriously and stopped sending them.

"Ma'am!" I turned back to the concierge desk with a wide grin and the woman rolled her eyes at me. She waved me back over and when I got to the desk she leaned forward. "This display is far less impressive. You might want to hold out on him." I quickly leaned back, moving away from her with a confused look on my face.

"Excuse me? That's rather rude." She shrugged her shoulders at me and placed a small clear container on the counter. When my eyes fell upon it and registered what it was, my hand came up to cover my mouth and my eyes immediately began to water.

On the counter sat a clear plastic container that held a single, coral colored, rose corsage, on a bed of baby's breath.

"Oh my god," I whispered, my hand still covering my mouth.

"Here's the card," she said with irritation as she slid it across the counter. I took it with trembling hands.

Bit, coral roses symbolize desire. I desire you, in every sense of the word: physically, emotionally, intellectually - did I mention physically? When I first gave you this corsage when we were fourteen, I hoped that one day you would be mine in every way. I desired you. Today, I give you this corsage with the same hope. I want you for myself. I'm afraid I can't wait any longer to spend forever with you. Hoping to be all you desire, Asher. P.s. Don't forget to tip the delivery guy.

I looked up at the woman with tears in my eyes, confused by the last part of the note.

"Is the person who delivered this still here?"

"Yes," she said as she pointed to a chair in the lobby.

Sitting in the chair was Asher.

As soon as I laid eyes on him, he stood and he looked delicious. He wore dark jeans with a black tee shirt and a gray blazer. He looked better than anyone should have after riding an airplane and then sitting in a hotel lobby for who knows how long. My stomach jumped at the sight of him, my throat closing a little, not letting enough air in. He walked towards me purposefully, as if he was supposed to be here all along.

"Hello, Bit," he said, stopping just inches from me, his hand coming to rest on my waist.

I looked up at him, a smile appearing on my face, giving away my extreme happiness to see him.

"What are you doing here?"

"You," he said as his hand slid from my waist and traveled dangerously close to my ass, "refused to give me a date as to when I could see you again. So I decided to take things into my own hands." He gave my ass a firm squeeze with the last words and I gasped a little at his forward gesture. He moved forward and I felt his mouth at me ear. "Don't make me have to ask to go upstairs with you," he whispered. I swallowed hard, instantly set ablaze by his words.

"Would you like to go upstairs?" I said softly, feeling his hand move gently back up to my waist, definitely a more appropriate touch for a hotel lobby, but still doing inappropriate things to my heart rate. His face moved so that his mouth was just barely touching mine.

"I'd love to," he said against my lips before kissing me senseless - so much for appropriate displays of affection.

We didn't say a word on our way up to my room. I still swam in a pool of disbelief, not really comprehending that he was here, with me, in New York. At my door, I took out my keycard and smiled a little when he took it from me, amused by his incessant need to be in control. He unlocked the door and led me inside. He set his suitcase on the floor next to the king-sized bed and I tried to keep my eyes completely open when they threatened to flutter closed as he slid his suit jacket off and laid it over a chair, the sight of his body straining through the fabric of his shirt affected me immediately.

"Come here, Bit," he said in a gravelly voice, using his fingers to motion me towards him. I took a few steps towards him, my hands instinctually went to his chest and they slid over the firmness of his muscles. "I missed you," he said before leaning down to kiss me.

"Is that why you came all the way to New York?" I asked shyly after pulling away.

"Yes and no. I came because I missed you, but also because I wanted to see your show." He pushed back a wisp of hair from my forehead, his fingers continuing down to the ends. "I'm proud of you and your work, and I'd like to see you in your element." He smiled at me with something that looked like pride in his eyes.

"Ok," was all I could say in response. Hearing him say he was proud of me, seeing him show up here, it affected me in a way I couldn't have anticipated. It had been a long time since I felt like someone was in my corner. I knew it was because I spent a good portion of my life pushing people away and keeping them at an arm's length. I never expected anything from anyone because I knew that meant that they would have expectations of me. Allowing Asher in brought me a startling and wonderful rush of warm elation and contentment. I pressed my cheek into his chest and snuggled in, embracing the happiness that washed over me. "I love you."

"Mmm. I love you too, Bit."

Chapter Seventeen
Asher

Nothing compared to waking with her in my arms. Her soft skin humming against mine was the best feeling in the world. Her hair, wrapped around every single part of me, well, that was awesome too. I pulled her in closer, her back pressing up against my chest, naked and warm. We used each other last night too many times to keep clothing on. I needed to be buried inside of her and she needed to be consumed by me. I could see her when I closed my eyes: atop me, underneath me, on her side gazing into my eyes, and bent over in front of me, crying out my name. It was the reunion I imagined on the plane ride over and it didn't disappoint. The only disappointment would come from leaving New York and not knowing when I'd see her again.

"It's too early," she mumbled sleepily. I kissed her temple.

"Agreed."

"Then why are you waking me up?"

"Did I?" She nudged her round ass up against me and felt my cock harden even more. "I'm sorry. He has a mind of his own. I can't control him."

"Mmm. You did a pretty good job of controlling him last night." She rolled over to face me and wore a sleepy grin. The golden sunlight coming through the windows illuminated the soft colors in her dark hair and brightened her face. The dark circles she worn under her eyes since the day she returned to Willow Falls were nearly gone and I could have sworn she'd began to eat during the week we'd been away from each other.

"You're beautiful," I said, sweeping my thumb over her cheek. Her smile grew and the sight of it anchored something in me. Resolution? Possession? Need? All of these feelings flowed through me and in that very moment, with my hand cupping her face, her hair flawlessly flailed around our bed, and her beautiful amber eyes smiling up at me, I knew we'd been brought together for a reason. I could only hope she felt the same way. I kissed her chastely and pulled away, content to just hold her.

"What time is it?" She asked a few minutes later.

"It's just after eleven."

"What?" She cried as she shot out of the bed like a rocket. "How in the hell is it eleven in the morning? I've never slept this late."

I smirked to myself, knowing exactly why she slept so late; I'd worn her out.

"Don't look so pleased with yourself, Asher. It's not cute." She pulled clothing out of the dresser drawers so quickly I wasn't sure how she'd managed to stuff so many articles of clothing in there.

"Is there something I can do to help you?" I couldn't help but smile. She was frazzled and running around like a mad woman.

"Please please *please*, call room service and get me a bagel and a latte while I take a shower?"

"You got it."

"Thank you," she said, leaning down to kiss me, a bundle of clothing in her hands. She attempted a small kiss of gratitude, but I snagged her around the waist and pulled her back down on the bed. "I don't have time for this right now," she said through a laugh that made every muscle in my stomach clench.

"You don't have time for a kiss?" I asked with mock innocence.

"I don't have time for what comes after the kiss."

"Who said anything about coming?" I rolled her under me and threw her bundle of clothes on the floor, pinning her wrists above her head. My mouth moved to her neck and I did my best to make her regret getting out of bed.

"The coming was implied," she groaned.

"You inferred an orgasm?" Teasing her quickly topped my list of favorite things to do.

"I *expect* an orgasm, every time. You never disappoint. But like I said, I don't have time for an orgasm right now." She writhed against me, trying to free herself from my grasp. I moved from her neck back up to her mouth, kissing her deep before pulling away.

"If I let you go right now, can you promise to make it up to me later?"

"I'll make it worth your while," she said, blasting me with the sexiest smile I'd ever seen, shamelessly grinding her hips up against my cock which was so not on board with the waiting plan.

"You better run before I change my mind." I rolled off of her, groaning quietly, angry with my self-control.

"Don't forget to order my breakfast," she sang as she danced into the bathroom.

I was left to be a tourist for the afternoon as Charlie had "important artist things" to do in preparation for her show. I offered to help but she insisted I would be more of a distraction than helpful and even though I wanted to help, that made me damn happy. I didn't have an enormous amount of time, so all the iconic tourist sites were out of the question. Perhaps tomorrow we could visit the Statue of Liberty or the Empire State Building. For now, I settled for Rockefeller Center and Fifth Avenue. I strolled down the busy street, glancing at the busy window displays, watching all the people who passed, and thinking about all that had happened in the last month.

All the years I remained friends with Charles, the thought that someday I would come face-to-face with Charlie again had crossed my mind. I tried hard, for thirteen years, not to think about it, but now that we were together, I couldn't help but think about the future. Before our separation it had been somewhat of a known conclusion; we would be together forever. Forever, in our minds, was such a naïve conception. We pictured a wedding, perhaps children, and everything that a young adult can comprehend.

Now, well, now I wanted something different. I still wanted forever, but I wanted a deeper kind. I wanted Charlie to listen to me when I had something to complain about. I wanted her to hold my hand without even thinking about it. I wanted to bring her flowers and have her be surprised by it, even though I bring her flowers all the time. I wanted her to call me on my bullshit. Did I want a wedding, children? Hell yes, I did. But I wanted to experience life with her by my side more than I wanted to check life experiences off of a preconceived list of accomplishments. More than anything though, I wanted her to want me the same way.

When I passed by Tiffany & Co., it was tempting to go in, to look around and try to imagine one of the rings on her fingers, but something told me she wouldn't want something new. I imagined something intricate and antique. The idea made me smile. I pushed the thought away and decided to make my way back to the hotel to get ready for her show.

I pulled down on the cuffs of my tuxedo, adjusting the length, making sure everything looked decent. I didn't have a whole lot of uses for a tuxedo, but at the moment I was glad I purchased one a few years ago. I wiggled my bowtie as I looked at myself in the mirror, not because it looked crooked, but because that's what one does when they wear a bowtie. They wiggled it. I just finished running my fingers through my hair when the bathroom door opened. I turned around to see Charlie walking towards me. My mouth fell open and I'm sure I looked like an idiot as I ogled her with little discretion. She did a twirl and my hand absently reached down to adjust myself.

"You look stunning," I said softly. I meant to sound much manlier, but all that came out was a whisper.

"Yes. Dress fit perfectly," she said with an exaggerated Russian accent. I cocked my head and gave her a questioning look. She laughed. "Sorry, long story. Thank you. You look pretty too." She gave me a peck on the cheek and I was gifted with the scent of her perfume mixed with her shampoo. I controlled the urge to lick her neck, to tear that gorgeous dress right from her body and show her how much a Russian accent turned me on.

"Do we have to go to your art show?" I had better plans in mind.

She lifted an eyebrow at me and a lesser man would have shriveled at the glare she shot my direction.

"I love it when you're stern," I said, purposefully making my voice low and dark.

"You're ridiculous," she said, laughing. "We have to go. If you don't behave I'll renege on the promise I made earlier." And that was enough to get my ass in gear. I could spend the evening thinking of every way I could peel the dress off her after the show. "The limo should be waiting downstairs."

"Ooh, a limo, huh? You're pretty fancy."

"This isn't me, it's the gallery. I'd love to walk in with some overalls and a braid, but apparently they frown upon ordinary." We entered the hallway and walked towards the elevator.

"Bit, I can assure you, you'd look anything but ordinary in overalls and a braid."

"Well, all I'm saying is I feel ridiculous in this dress. But," she said as she looked down at herself. "I look smokin' hot."

"Yes, my love, you do."

It was amazing to watch her work a room. She was a little flustered when people offered her compliments on her work, but for the most part she was graceful, humble, and entirely captivating. My chest pushed out and my shoulders were pulled back, filled with pride. My Charlie, even when fighting through a life that she colored as less-than-happy, was pursuing her dream and making waves in the art world. I could not have been more proud of her in that moment.

She was in the middle of a conversation with a representative from some art magazine in the city, offering insights to her process and her technique. I leaned over and whispered in her ear, "I'm going to get a drink. Can I bring you something?"

"I'll take champagne," she said softly. Our hands linked and I brought her fingers to my lips, kissing them lightly before I turned away in search of the bar. Waiting for our drinks, I smiled as I overheard the couple next to me talking about Charlie's work.

"Such depth. I don't think I've ever seen a charcoal drawing that evoked so much emotion from me before." I glanced over to see a woman, probably in her mid-sixties, sipping a drink, complimenting my Bit.

"Well, it goes to show you that truly talented artists don't need color or even texture to convey meaning. She's nailed every single piece. We'll be in a bidding war by the end of the evening, I'm sure." This came from the man standing next to her who I assumed was her husband.

"Oh, there she is," the woman said excitedly. "Let's go talk to her, shall we? Before someone else monopolizes her."

I was ready to monopolize her. I thanked the bartender for our drinks and turned to make my way back when I spotted a different man standing with Charlie. When I made it close enough to hear their conversation, my concern immediately spiked. She looked uncomfortable and nervous. She shook her head, looking around the room frantically. When her eyes landed on me, I thought I saw sadness wash over them. Ignoring my instincts I sidled up to her, handing her the champagne, wrapping my arm around her waist. Possession was something I always reverted back to. I didn't know who this man was, but one thing I was sure of was who Charlie belonged to.

I sipped my scotch, slowly, my eyes never leaving the man who was currently watching my arm pull Charlie to my side. He looked like he wanted to rip my arm from my body, which gave me an indication as to who he was.

"Good evening," he said coolly. He stuck his hand out in my direction. "I'm David, a friend of Charlie's."

I looked at his hand but made no move to shake it. I had Charlie in one hand which was too important to let go of, and scotch in the other, also ranking as more important at the moment.

"Nice to meet you," I replied. I felt Charlie trembling and thought I heard a small cry leave her. "I'm Asher, also a friend of Charlie's. A close friend."

David's face slowly fell from its stuffy polite expression. His eyes widened, his mouth opened slowly, and his eyes wandered back over the Charlie.

"Asher?" He asked her. "The Asher? *Asher* Asher?" His voice went from pleasant to an angry whisper and he took a step towards her. I quickly moved to stand in between them, my free hand splayed behind me to keep her away. He would not be getting any closer to her.

"David, why are you here? Please leave," she begged. I could tell she was trying to maintain a level voice, but I could hear the pain seeping through.

"This is the Asher whose name is tattooed on your body?" My fist clenched at what he had implied. He'd seen her naked. The idea of another man seeing her body, seeing what was mine, enraged me. In the back of my mind, I knew it was rational that her boyfriend of five years had seen her naked, but she never belonged to him. She had always been mine.

"She asked you to leave. I suggest you listen to her." I took one small step towards him again, closing the distance. I was taller than he was although not by much. But I was much broader than him. I had no doubt I could take him if I had to remove him myself.

"David, please." She begged him and later I would remember to ask her why she sounded so afraid, but at that moment I was only worried about getting him away from her.

"What's wrong, Charlie? You look pretty upset for someone who just found out her best friend from childhood isn't dead after all. Shouldn't this be a happy occasion?" He took a drink from his glass and grimaced as he swallowed the alcohol down. His eyes never left Charlie and when I looked back at her I saw her face streaked with tears. I began to realize that I had no idea what they seemed to be communicating silently between them. David's eyes came back to me. "Did you know the entire time we were together, for five years, she told me that you had died in a car accident?"

I looked back at Charlie and her face was pointed towards the floor.

"How does it feel? You meant enough to her that she branded your name along her ribs, but not enough that she could admit you were alive. What a strange lie to tell the man you were sleeping with."

I watched as she lifted her face to look at me, not denying anything, not telling me that he was lying. She looked guilty. Tears streamed down her face, her mascara created black streaks along her cheeks, and her eyes drowned in sadness. But she wasn't denying it.

"You told him I was dead?"

"Asher, please, let me explain," she begged. Still not a denial.

"Explain? I'm not sure that needs an explanation." I sounded calm. Even to me, my voice came across as smooth and even. Inside, however, inside my body it felt like my organs were being compressed. There wasn't enough room within me to contain the pain that was blossoming inside. Before I even realized what was happening, I was turning from her, heading towards the exit. I never wanted to imagine a scenario when I was turning away from her, but at that moment, I couldn't be next to her anymore.

"Asher, wait." I heard her heels clicking against the floor and knew she followed me. "Asher!" She followed me all the way onto the street and I kept marching, not really knowing where I was headed. "Please, listen to me." Finally, the pain had made way for anger and I turned around to confront her.

"There is nothing, *nothing*, in this world that could compel me to tell one single person that you were dead. Is that how you thought of me? Of us? For the last thirteen years you wished I was dead?" My hand came up to my forehead, rubbing, trying to ease the headache that had built there, the throbbing causing my eyes to strain in discomfort.

"No, Asher, no." She took a step closer to me and I countered with another step backwards. I could see the hurt in her eyes. "I told him my childhood friend had died because, at the time, I thought that was the easiest explanation."

"So you never told him about us?"

She shook her head. I felt a cracking in my chest as if I was being torn open by her words.

"What would have been so difficult to explain about having an ex-boyfriend?"

"It's not that simple," she pleaded. "You wouldn't understand."

"Make me understand!" I screamed. I turned away from her as she flinched. I was going to lose my temper and I didn't want to be near her when it happened. My head was in my hands and I knelt down, bending my knees and resting my elbows upon them. "Tell me, please."

"There was no way to explain to David that I could never love him, that I could never fully be with him, because I was still in love with the man whose name was permanently drawn on my skin." She sniffled, and under all the pain and heartache, it tore at me that she was crying. A part of me still wanted to keep her from pain. "I couldn't let you go, but I couldn't move on either. The only way was to pretend, to make up a reality where my sadness, my inability to give him everything, made sense."

"So I was dead. Did anyone in your new life know about me? Did you tell him about the babies?"

She shook her head, crying.

I started walking away. I couldn't get away fast enough. I was angry, and hurt, and so very close to a nervous breakdown. I felt her hands grip my shoulders; her tiny, undernourished arms, trying to pull me back to her.

"Don't," was all I said as I continued to walk, while she tried desperately to hold on to me.

"You can't leave like this, Asher. You can't," she wailed. I spun around on her and my hands came to grasp her face. I wasn't violent, but I was forceful.

"You don't get to keep me, Charlie. You can't kill me one day and love me the next. It isn't possible."

"I never stopped loving you!" Her tears ran into and over my hand.

"You're mistaken. *I* never stopped loving *you*. I never told anyone you were dead. I never lied about something so sacred and special to me in order to make myself feel better. I loved you, God damn it! I can't fault you for not telling anyone about the miscarriage. That's personal, private. But I can't just move past this. I can't *pretend* you didn't wish me dead for thirteen years." I still held her face in my hands, my eyes roaming over her features. She was so beautiful and for the last few weeks I had imagined that my life, my future, laid with her. I was angry. I was hurt. But more than any of that, more than those emotions that can come and go at the drop of a hat, I was shocked. I didn't recognize her anymore. She wasn't the same person I had been in love with all of my life. "I have to go." I dropped my hands and took a step away from her. I turned my back on her and I walked away – from everything.

I heard her cry out, and then I heard what I thought was her falling to the ground. But I didn't look back. I couldn't. There was no way to guarantee myself that I wouldn't go running back to her if I saw her in pain. I would want to fix her. I always had. This time, she would need to fix herself.

Chapter Eighteen
Asher

A few weeks passed. When I left New York, I left in a tuxedo. I went straight from my fight with Charlie to the airport. I made it home and did my best to try and move on with my life. It was like starting over without her all over again, only this time, I didn't have this looming feeling of guilt keeping me from remembering the good memories. All I had was the dark pressure expanding within me, reminding me that for all those years, she wished me away. She regretted what we had so much, she didn't even want me breathing.

Perhaps the hardest part was thinking about the night before I left. Those few hours we had together where I allowed myself to imagine what would come next. When I imagined everything I had within me and how much I wanted to give it to her, how much I wanted to share it with her.

My phone rang and I grumbled. I didn't like the interruptions. I had thrown myself into my work in an effort at distraction. I saw that Reeve was calling and grumbled even more.

"What do you want?" I answered, trying to sound just as annoyed as I actually was.

"That was a very rude way to answer your phone," she said snidely.

"Good, my intended tone came across just as I'd hoped it would."

"You're an asshole when you're heartbroken."

"What is it that you want, Reeve? Don't you have a husband to annoy?"

"I was driving past Mr. McBride's house a few minutes ago and I saw some strange men looking in the windows. I would have stopped, but I've got the kids with me and I didn't feel safe. Do you think you could go over there and see if anything looks strange?"

"Yeah, of course," I felt like an ass for being rude to her. Of course I didn't want her confronting homeless squatters with her kids. "Sorry, Reeve. I'm not always trying to be an asshole."

"I know. You're sad. I get it." All I could do was sigh in response because she was right. I was sad.

"What did the men look like?"

"The homeless squatters?" She sounded confused.

"Yeah, them."

"They looked like homeless squatters, you jackass." At least she was laughing when she swore at me this time.

"Ok. I'll go and take a look in a little bit. I still have a few things to finish up here."

"Asher, I don't think it's a good idea to go after dark. What if they're dangerous?"

"The homeless squatters?" I spat her words back at her with a smirk on my face.

"I'm not talking to you anymore."

"Promise?"

"Watch yourself. I might be your only friend."

"You might have a point."

"Don't wait too long, Asher. You might miss it." These last words sounded important, wise almost.

"Ok... I'll leave soon."

"Good. You work too much anyway." And she was back.

I found myself turning onto the street I avoided for weeks. My mom tried to get me to come over for dinner multiple times but I couldn't bring myself to go there. I didn't want to see the house where we shared so many things together. But there I was, pulling around the corner, straining to see the house she'd moved into so long ago. The girl with the dark hair who stole my heart.

As I drove closer, I didn't see any homeless men milling around. Nothing looked out of place except for the paper that was on the door. Until Charlie made arrangements to sell the house, all communication regarding it was supposed to come to my office, handled by Phil. I rolled my eyes wondering what Phil had fucked up. I pulled in to the driveway and parked my car. I made it to the door and pulled the paper down, flipped it over, and began to read.

Dear Asher,

Don't crumple the paper up and throw it away, at least, not until you've read it. I know you're angry at me and I know you have every right to be. All I am asking is for the opportunity to explain myself. I need to explain better than I did that night. Please. Meet me at the swing set.

Love,

Charlie

My heart pumped rapidly and my hands sweated. I hadn't expected to hear from her, and I definitely didn't expect her to be here. I thought she would become a ghost again, a figment of my desires. Despite everything that had happened between us, I couldn't change the one thing about me that would always be true; I couldn't stay away from her if she needed me.

I turned and began jogging through the neighborhood, weaving through cars and mailboxes, taking the shortest route that we carved out some twenty years previous. The paper became crumpled in my hand, but I never let it go; I carried it with me. I came up to the alley, the cut-through that led from the neighborhood to the school yard.

The sun began to set so the alley was veiled by shadows. I could almost see our pre-teen selves walking under the tree canopy, talking about school, or a movie we wanted to see, or our plans for the weekend. Then I pictured us at sixteen, walking hand-in-hand to the school to steal moments alone, to escape the fatherly watch of Charles, to explore each other. I ran out the other side of the alley, thinking maybe I'd catch a glimpse of her on the swings, but I saw no one.

Disappointment shot through me and I cursed myself for the emotion. I should be disappointed she wasn't there. I shouldn't *want* to see her. But I did and it was useless to deny it. I stopped jogging and walked the rest of the way to the swings. My heartbeat sped up again when I saw the note taped to one of the swings. I picked it up and eagerly opened it.

My Asher,

I'm so glad you're here. I'm still waiting for you, but you'll have to travel a little farther to get to me. I promise though – it will be worth it.

Meet me where you first told me you loved me.

Xoxo,

Charlie

The bridge. The stream. I ran there, jogging wouldn't get me there fast enough. Halfway through the parking lot of the school, I ditched my suit jacket, throwing it down on the ground, thinking I would come back for it later. It took me less than five minutes to run to the park and I didn't stop until I made it to the bridge. It was getting darker, the sun set, and I squinted into the dusk and tried to find her. She wasn't waiting on the bridge, but she wouldn't be. I told her I loved her under the bridge, pressing her up against the support beam, holding her face in my hands. I walked down the bank to the small creek and followed it under the bridge. There sat another note for me.

Dear Love,

Forgive me, I'm not waiting here for you. But this is where it all started. Those fall days spent here with you, catching fish, building a friendship that saved me. I remember us here. All the time, Asher. I think about you all the time.

Being with David was hard for me. I never loved him. I stayed with him to make myself feel a little bit normal. Normal women didn't cry every day for their babies. They didn't wear a ring their ex-boyfriend gave them only to remind them of a love they'd never get over.

I didn't lie to David because I wished you were dead. I told him that lie because I couldn't live with the truth. I would have taken our love to the grave, Asher. It was sacred to me and no one needed to know about it. If I spoke about it, the loss felt more real. I guess I don't expect you to understand why I lied. I just want you to understand it was a lie, not how I truly felt, not how I truly feel. Was it the right decision? Probably not. But it was the best choice I could make at the time. I'm not the same girl I was five years ago, not even the same person I was five months ago.

You changed me Asher. You gave me the opportunity to forgive myself, to love myself, to accept that things happen for no reason at all, and it's no one's fault. I don't have to hide behind my sadness anymore, because it isn't shameful. I lost a pregnancy, our babies, but it wasn't my fault. I ran from you in college because I couldn't handle everything all at once. But I'm not running anymore, Asher. I'm here – waiting for you.

All of a sudden this seems silly. There's a very good chance that you read my letter at the house and drove away. I wouldn't blame you if that was your choice. But I hope, so much, that you're reading this letter. And I hope you'll come and find me in the very spot where you asked me to be with you. The first time.

I looked around frantically, hoping to see her. I breathed quickly, my heart beating out of my chest. I climbed back up the bank and followed the path around the park. When I saw the gazebo the first thing I noticed was that it was lit up. There were string lights hanging from the top, but as I got closer I noticed the entire interior was filled with candles. The flickering light of the flames made an orange haze float out from the gazebo and reflect off the water.

The candlelight also illuminated the hundreds of yellow roses that filled the space surrounding Charlie.

She wore a white dress and I was reminded of the day when I was fifteen when I first kissed her. The candles sent light flickering over her, making her dress dance in the light, her hair shining and flowing down to her waist.

She smiled when she saw me and her hands came to cover her mouth. Tears came from her eyes and I knew she was happy. Happy to see me. Happy that I'd followed the trail, read the letters, and came to her.

I had never been happier. She came back to me and in the end that was all I ever really wanted from her. For her to accept us both, for all our flaws, and love us anyway. Nothing would have ever worked between us until she could do that. And her standing here, waiting for me, was the best apology I ever received.

I didn't stop running until I was close enough to hold her in my arms. I picked her up and brought my lips to hers, kissing her like I wanted to for thirteen years - with absolutely nothing between us - no lies, no misunderstandings, no blame and no guilt. From now on, the space between us would be filled with love.

"Are you really here?" She asked against my mouth. I pulled away and brushed her hair away from her face.

"I've always been here, Bit. I was just waiting for you."

She brought her hands to my face and pressed her lips to mine.

This was a hello kiss. This hello kiss was perfect. A greeting. A beginning. Something new.

The End

Acknowledgements

There are so many people who deserve a thank you from me it's a little ridiculous.

First, always, is my husband. Thank you for supporting me emotionally when I decided to quit my job! You were the right amount of hesitant, understanding, supportive and awesome when everything started happening for me. Thank you for trusting me enough and believing in me enough to say, "Sure! Quit your job and become a full-time writer. Surely, nothing can go wrong with this plan." I don't know how long this will last but thirty years from now I can look back at 2014 as the year that changed my life. Changed *our* lives. Thank you.

To Team Anie! Brook and Krysta, what the hell are we doing? Krysta, your continual drive and interest in all my stories motivates me. You want to make me better and I want to be better because you make me feel like I can be. I feel like we have both grown so much in the last year, learning the ins and outs of this profession, and there's no one I would have rather been on this journey with than you. Brook, you inspire me. Truly. Your vision impacts me, motivates me, and does not compromise. You are gifted and I am so lucky that you lend your gifts to my stories. Thank you both for making me better.

To my street team, the original members and the new, I love you all so much! You make me laugh, smile, and sometimes cry – but in a good way. I appreciate every one of you and hope you understand that I know the work you do for me. I see it and I feel it and I am thankful for it.

To Lesley, I'm not sure if you'll read this, but if you are I know you're probably shaking your head and thinking how unnecessary it is. But I wanted you to know how many times I've been thankful for you while writing this book. Every time you sent me an encouraging message, or just chatted with me about nothing relating to the book, it's helped me. I value your friendship.

To all the blogs, I have no way to name all the blogs that have promoted me, or helped me, or mentioned me. There are too many and I am too blessed. So, here are some that I feel like I can lean on, blogs I feel *have my back*: Prisoners of Print, Two Book Pushers, Once Upon a Crush Book Blog, A Literary Perusal, 50 Shades of Gabriel's Crossfire Unscripted Destiny – Book Club, Book Boyfriend Hangover, Randy Raunchy Romantic Book Blog, Reading Amore, Author Stalkers, Romance Obsessed Book Blog... and I'm sure I've missed a few. Know that I appreciate all the blogs and am so thankful for all of you!

Carrie, thank you for using your talent to bring my words to life! You are awesome!

Rhiannon, again, thank you for reading this book in pieces as I wrote it. Thank you for being trustworthy and for loving Charlie and Asher as much as me.

To my mom who will always be a source of comfort and who I will always go back to when I'm feeling insecure or unsure. Thanks for always reflecting back to me my best self, for ignoring my weaknesses, and highlighting my strengths. You're awesome. Thank you.

Lastly, and most importantly, to my readers. You have all *changed my life*. You have no idea. I am the luckiest person I know and I appreciate every single one of you. Every time you send me a message, or talk to me on Facebook it makes my day. I wouldn't be doing any of this if it weren't for you. Thank you. Thank you. Thank you. I hope you keep reading my books and keep giving me a reason to write.

Other books by Anie Michaels

The Never Series

Never Close Enough

Never Far Away

Never Giving Up

The Never Duet

Never Standing Still

Never Tied Down

The Private Serials

Private Affairs

Private Encounters

Private Getaway

Private Property

Stand Alone Novels

The Space Between Us

The Absence of Olivia

Instead of You

The Presence of Grace – *coming in 2016*

Please feel free to follow me on any and all media platforms!

http://www.facebook.com/AuthorAnieMichaels

https://twitter.com/Anie_Michaels

http://www.instagram.com/aniemichaels

Shoot me an email!

anie.michaels@gmail.com

www.ingramcontent.com/pod-product-compliance
Lightning Source LLC
Chambersburg PA
CBHW030014180626
46810CB00001B/30